THE DANGEROUS
MR. WOLF

BRIAN DRAKE

WOLFPACK
PUBLISHING
— EST 2013 —

The Dangerous Mr. Wolf
Brian Drake

Paperback Edition
Copyright © 2022 (as revised) Brian Drake

Wolfpack Publishing
5130 S. Fort Apache Rd. 215-380
Las Vegas, NV 89148

www.wolfpackpublishing.com

Paperback ISBN: 978-1-63977-611-5
eBook ISBN: 978-1-64119-649-9

THE DANGEROUS
MR. WOLF

THE KILL FEVER

There are only three rules in this city:
Never cheat your partner,
Never take more than your share,
And never cross

– WOLF

Five bodies littered the dry street. Blood smeared the pavement, mixing into the asphalt grime to produce a red/black gunk.

The police had blocked off the street at either end; patrolmen directed traffic around the crime scene while detectives and the forensics team examined the casualties. The two a.m. chill made the work a chore. A large utility truck with a spotlight lit up the scene but cast odd shadows about. Everybody held up an arm or a hand to block the blast of light.

When Inspector John Callaway arrived and exited his car, he didn't know where to begin. Or even if he should. His men had the place covered. He wandered around. The guys were dead, all right. The ambulances had only been summoned as a formality; the medics hung about doing nothing. Callaway stopped. He put most of his weight on his left foot. His right was sore, for some reason. It had been aching lately. Maybe it was finally time to shed some of the extra pounds he carried around. Maybe then his feet would stop aching. He waved down one of the detectives.

"What do we have?"

The detective was young, maybe late 20s; his hands shook as he flipped back the pages of his notebook.

"Take it easy," Callaway said.

The detective nodded. "Five victims. Shot with an automatic weapon. Jesus, skipper, their guts are everywhere."

"Stay focused."

A deep breath. The detective said, "From what the witnesses say, the guys exited the club over there, and when they crossed the street to that Cadillac at the curb, the shooter got out of a car and opened up on them."

"One shooter?"

"With an automatic weapon."

"One guy?"

"Yes, sir."

"Then he got in the car and drove away?"

"Like he'd stepped on a spider, skipper," the young detective said. "We're checking the red-light cameras and we think the jewelry store on the corner may have had a security camera looking this way, but other than that–" he shrugged.

"Good. Let's go see one of the stiffs."

The detective led the way. They stepped under crime scene tape and the young man stopped at a body lying face down on the asphalt, a hefty fellow with a toupee now askew and matted with blood.

"I didn't know guys even bothered with toupees anymore," the detective said.

"You'd be surprised what guys bother with," said Callaway. He knelt beside the body and examined the man's face. His eyes were still open. He wore a large gold ring on his left hand. Callaway stood.

"Know him?" the detective said.

"Ben Belasis. He's one of Gulino's boys."

"*These are mob guys?*"

"Take it easy."

"But, skipper–"

"Just do your job. Let me worry about what it means."

It didn't make sense. Carlo Gulino and the other capo in town, Pedro Sanchez, had coexisted peacefully for over twenty years. The battles of the old days were long settled. Had something happened to change the situation? The rumor mill, usually the most reliable source of such goings on, had offered nothing in the weeks prior to tonight.

Callaway stood and scanned the crime scene, holding a hand up against the glare of the spotlight. There was indeed nothing he could do here. He needed to be elsewhere, and fast.

Almost as if on cue, his phone beeped. A text. Callaway gave the screen a quick glance, said, "Stay loose, kid," and returned to his car. The young detective watched him drive away.

Presently Callaway turned into another neighborhood, parked the car and stepped out. He checked the text again and turned into an alley. He climbed the fire escape to the roof. Why did his friend always want to meet on rooftops? Grunting, he swung his legs over the edge of the roof and stopped, winded. Bloody hell, he had to go on a diet.

Another man stood a few feet away looking out at the sleeping city. The glow of the city lights highlighted the man, tall, head-to-toe in black, standing with the steadiness of an eternal sentry.

"Why do you always make me climb something?" Callaway said as he approached the other man.

"It's good for you," the man said. Callaway knew him only as Wolf. Nobody knew his first name. He had arrived in Las Palmas four years ago, taking a leave of absence from military service to find out why his sister Shelly had stopped writing letters, only to find that she'd been murdered. He tore the city apart to find the man responsible. Callaway provided a helping hand, and the two formed an unlikely bond between lawman, and outlaw. With his sister's killer vanquished, Wolf made his exit from the military permanent and stayed in the city, operating on the fringes between the cops and the crooks. Callaway didn't think he was a bad guy; wasn't entirely sure he was a good guy; what he did know was that sometimes Wolf came in handy. Because justice, the ever-present underdog, often needed a little help, and, for some reason, Wolf didn't mind lending that help. Callaway wasn't sure what to do about him, so he did nothing. Sometimes it was best to just see how things shook out.

"My guys tell me there was only one shooter. I got half a mind to think it was you, Wolf."

"What's my motive?"

"That's the only reason I'm positive it wasn't you."

The city's glow hit Wolf's face just right. It was a rough face. There was a small scar on his lower lip. Dark eyes, darker hair, a silver chain around his neck which disappeared down the front of his shirt.

Wolf said, "Whatever started tonight, we don't have long before it gets out of control. You know Gulino will blame Sanchez and he *will* retaliate. Innocent people are in danger."

"Neither of them is that stupid. They'll want answers first. Have you heard anything about problems between them?"

"Nothing." Wolf frowned. "You're right, we would have heard something."

"Especially you."

Wolf let out a grunt. "Nobody's perfect."

"Do you have any action going?"

"I've already started working my end, but so far I have nothing for you."

Callaway sighed. "I probably won't get any sleep this week."

"Try to." Wolf patted him on the shoulder. "In your condition you need your rest." He laughed. He started for the fire escape.

"You're a real smart ass, you know that?"

Wolf made his way back to the street.

Callaway stood on the roof for a little longer watching the city. Most of the city slept and had no knowledge of the violent event. Other parts were awake and active and hiding in the cover of darkness.

His phone rang. He answered it. "Inspector Callaway."

"Skipper," another of his detectives said. "We got another body. This one belongs to Sanchez's crew. He was shot on the front step of his home."

"Terrific," Callaway said.

———

WOLF STOOD beside the steps of his apartment building smoking a cigar near the ABSOLUTELY NO SMOKING sign the landlady had nailed into the outer brick wall. The lady knew better than to tell Wolf no.

His watch read 5:30 a.m. The dawn of a new day. People went by on the sidewalk and cars passed on the street and the morning's chill made its presence felt. The smell in the air announced itself with every gentle gust of wind. The closer one lived to the bay, as Wolf did, the stronger the sewer-like stench wafted from the slotted gutters. Home sweet home. He could afford a better place, but he needed to be close to the action.

Wolf wrinkled his nose at a particularly strong whiff when a white Chevy Cruze paralleled into the last open spot on the curb. The woman who climbed out locked the car and walked toward the steps. She walked with the tired movements of somebody coming off the grave-yard shift.

She wasn't what anybody would call striking but she had that girl-next-door cuteness that everybody noticed. Long dark hair that was never quite done right and eyes that were big and brown and always focused on the ground. Victim eyes, Wolf called them, and had first thought so when she and her husband moved into the building two months ago. She had said her name was Melody Chapman. Wolf knew her husband, Cain, who was fresh out of prison. Her eyes scanned the cracks in the sidewalk as she neared the steps. She wore a T-shirt and faded blue jeans that showed off more of the muffin top above her waist than Wolf figured she liked but the blessings on her chest more than likely deflected atten-tion from her middle.

"Good morning," Wolf said as she started up the steps.

She hid her face from him. "Hi." She pushed through the lobby door.

Wolf shook his head. He had heard Melody and her husband arguing the night before. They lived across the hall from him. The argument had ended so abruptly that he knew the punk had hit her. It made Wolf mad. He wanted to throw Cain Chapman off the roof.

He finished the cigar and went up to his apartment. He was too keyed up for sleep. He picked up a book about Churchill's adventure with Lawrence of Arabia and sat under a lamp and read for a while.

A little after seven the shouting started. Melody's husband had a loud voice. He yelled a little. She yelled back. Then she screamed.

Wolf closed the book and stared at the spots on the ceiling above his chair and let a countdown tick in his head. He didn't need anybody to draw him a picture. The woman screamed again. Wolf rose from the chair, dog-eared his book and set it down. With clenched fists, he left the apartment. His shoes thumped on the carpeted floor and he pounded on the door across from his.

The door flew open and a bony man with a dark goatee glared at him. Melody sobbed out of sight. The bony man raised a pointed finger; Wolf saw the blood on the man's knuckles. He grabbed the wrist and twisted, pulled. The bony man let out a cry of his own as Wolf hauled him out into the hallway, kicked the man's legs out from under him. No snide remarks escaped Wolf's lips. He delivered a hard punch to the bony man's face; once, twice. Skin under the man's left eye broke open. Wolf lifted the man to his feet, twisted the arm back, forcing the man to face the wall, and shoved. The bony man left a smear of blood on the wallpaper. Wolf hammered two blows into the man's back. The man's breath rushed out and he crumpled onto the carpet.

Melody stepped into the doorway. Tears streaked her face. A bloody welt grew on her cheek. She put her hands to her mouth.

"Need a doctor?" Wolf said.

"Ohmygodohmygod," she said. She dropped her hands. "He's going to kill you!"

"Melody, do you really think he could?"

Other doors along the hall opened, tenants poking out their heads to see the commotion. Somebody offered to call the cops. Wolf didn't answer.

WOLF WOKE up late in the afternoon, showered and shaved and walked around the corner for a late lunch at a corner deli. He ate a large turkey sandwich with only pickles, mustard, and tomatoes and sipped black coffee. Dressed in his prerequisite black, he had another piece of his wardrobe under the long leather jacket, a custom-built five-inch Colt Series 70 .45 automatic.

Taking another cup of coffee to go, Wolf dropped behind the wheel of his Cadillac CTS and started making the rounds. He stopped and spoke with his usual informants in their usual hangouts to see if they had any answers to his previous queries. Nobody could provide anything useful. The street was abuzz about the shootings, and as news of the follow-up killing of one of Pedro Sanchez's men spread, everybody expected an even bigger battle. Cops beat the turf looking for information; some of the guys Wolf talked to were packing up and taking a vacation. They didn't need the heat.

The street reps of each crime family were incredulous, blaming the other side, but when Wolf pressed them further, they could not provide even a speculative reason why the killings had taken place.

Wolf steered the Cadillac into the parking lot of a fish market and went through the door. The clerks were busy with customers and didn't notice him. He ignored the chill of the place, caused by the open freezers which displayed various kinds of seafood, and made his way to a back door. Moving on through, he shut the door carefully behind him. The back room was warm. Jimmy "Count Em" Koontz sat at a desk, talking on the phone, typing notes on a laptop. He said goodbye and put the phone down.

"Placing any bets?" Short and stocky with long hair, Jimmy folded his stubby fingers together and smiled.

"Not today. Hear about the action last night?"

"Did I? I heard from the boss himself. He's stunned. Not pissed. I mean he's in a panic, Wolf. Gulino didn't order the hit. He got no reason to order a hit."

"*Somebody* shot those guys."

"And right now, Carlo would give his left nut to know who. He's gotta get ready for a fight, you know. He can't help it. The guys need to be ready."

"I don't blame him."

Jimmy gestured behind Wolf. "Now *there's* a guy you should talk to."

Wolf turned to look at the man entering the room. He didn't smile.

Cain Chapman stood almost as tall as Wolf, but had lost most of his hair, still prison-skinny and his cheekbones jutted, and his arms were taught and sinewy. He had a black eye.

"Wolf," he said. "When do you want a rematch?"

"Hurt your wife again and I'll kill you."

"Guys," Jimmy said, putting up his hands. "Not here, okay?"

Wolf nodded. Chapman fumed.

Jimmy said, "Placing a bet, Cain?"

"Yeah," and Chapman went to the desk with a sheet of paper and wad of cash. He did his business with Jimmy, said good-bye, and left. He did not look at Wolf, but Wolf watched him leave.

Jimmy said, "Sure I can't tempt you, Wolf?"

"No, thanks."

"What's the problem?" Jimmy said.

"Where's Chapman working now?"

"His old spot was taken, so Gulino put him downtown with Jake Rossi's outfit."

"Really?"

"I think his old temper has mellowed a bit. He lost about $1500 last week and didn't bat an eye."

"I don't buy that for a second."

Wolf said goodbye and went out.

———

CARLO GULINO LIVED in a white mansion on the western side of the city. It was the largest home in the western hills and surrounded by a wrought-iron fence. Cameras, armed security guards, warning signs–the works. If you ventured anywhere near the estate, you knew very well that something bad would happen if you tried to get over the fence.

Wolf steered the Cadillac onto the short driveway approaching the main entrance. A guard sat in a shack. He stepped out. His shirt strained against a pot belly, and a revolver hung below his left arm. He held out a hand. Wolf stopped the car.

"Tell Carlo that Wolf is here."

"He's not seeing anybody."

"He'll see me."

"I got my orders. Beat it."

Wolf said, "Don't make me get out of this car."

The guard stepped back and yanked his radio and took out the revolver. Wolf bolted from the car. The guard started talking into the radio and swung the gun up at the same time. Wolf grabbed the gun, twisted, forcing the guard's body to turn with the twist, and socked him in the mouth with his free hand. The guard dropped onto his rear. The radio clattered beside him. Wolf was ejecting the shells from the revolver as more guards ran over.

Each of the guards held a weapon on Wolf from the other side of the fence. The man in charge, a trim fellow this time, stepped forward and said, "What's the idea, Wolf? Carlo ain't seeing anybody."

"Will you ask him, already? Maybe I got a clue about last night."

"You can tell me."

"I don't even know your name, bub. Get your boss down here or we're going to piss off the neighbors with a lot of shooting." Wolf opened his coat and took out the Colt. He kept it beside his leg as he scanned each face of the men before him. One or two started looking nervous and tightened the grips on their own weapons.

The shack guard moaned a little.

"Everybody take it easy," the trim guard said. He took out his radio and spoke to somebody about Wolf. After a short wait and a positive response, he told his guys to scoot and opened the gate and told Wolf to drive up to the front of the house.

Wolf put his gun away and followed directions.

An escort met him at the front and took him to a terrace on the side of the house where Gulino waited.

The capo was going gray at the temples but the rest of him was in good shape. He still looked like he could go a few rounds in the ring. He had started as a boxer, got in with the so-called bad crowd, and worked his way up through the organization. Now he ran his own section of the west coast. He shook Wolf's hand and said, "I would have liked watching you try to gun down my men."

"Maybe next time," Wolf said.

They sat at a table and Gulino told Wolf's escort to bring them a couple of beers. They burned through small talk while they waited. When the beers arrived and the escort departed, Gulino took a long drink and said,

"I don't know how to explain last night."

"Are you and Sanchez arguing?"

"Over what? We settled our territory disputes decades ago. It's been live and let live ever since. Heaven knows New York won't let us clash, and when they hear about this, if they haven't already, we're both in the wringer. No, it has to be somebody else. What have you learned?"

"Only that there was one shooter. One guy with a machine gun. He probably capped Sanchez's man, too."

"No names?"

Wolf shook his head.

"Well I've stopped everything," the capo said. "Told all my guys to lay low. Don't tangle with nobody. Of course, the cops are knockin' on doors looking for answers and I told them to cooperate."

"Bet that wasn't easy."

"You're telling me."

"But you've also told them to be ready to fight."

Gulino nodded. "That's true."

"Who do you have on the street trying to get the answers?"

"Vince Manning. I'll tell him you're on the job, too, in case y'all want to share notes. So why are you here?"

"I wanted to hear you say you weren't responsible, number one. Though you could be lying."

"I wouldn't lie, Wolf. Not something like this."

"Fair enough. Number two, I need ideas. Who in the organization might want to get rid of you?"

Gulino laughed. "Sixty-four thousand-dollar question. It could be anybody."

"Who have you made unhappy recently? Cain Chapman, for instance."

"Him? He gets out of jail and expects me to have kept his old job open. I couldn't do it. He was a good earner but I gotta fill holes when a guy's going to be gone for eight years. He should have understood that. I gave him a job and he's back on the street so he shouldn't be upset for long. I don't think he'd have the connections to pull off a hit, either. Or the money, for that matter. He's starting over entirely."

"Anybody else?"

"Not that I can think of."

"What about the independents? The guys who kick back to you."

"You think one of them weasels has the balls to move up in the world? Independent means small fry. There's a reason they're small fry."

"Gotta be somebody, Carlo."

Gulino drank some beer and thought it over. "There's one. Maybe. He's crossed into our block once and I had to smack his wrists."

"Name?"

"Victor Marcus. Runs the–"

"Bay Meadow Poker Room, I know."

"Play there?"

"Victor's number two and I had a nice match up recently. I cleaned him out."

"You beat *Nitro Randall* at a poker game? That hasn't happened in–"

"I know. He was shocked. Threatened to kill me and everything."

"You want some extra guys to go with you?"

"Carlo. It's *me* you're talking to."

Gulino laughed and finished his beer. Wolf drank down the rest of his and stood up. They shook hands again.

Wolf said, "You think of anybody else, get word to me."

"You giving me an order, Wolf?"

"Pretty much."

"And only you can get away with that. Come on, I'll walk you out."

————

THE BAY MEADOW Poker Room sat on prime real estate just off the 80 freeway. Situated right on the edge of the bay, the private card room on the backside of the club had an amazing view of the blue water and the double-deck bridge connecting one side of the bay to the other. Wolf parked in front. He entered through the front, stood in the main lobby. White walls, red carpet, no clocks. It was cool inside, the temperature always consistent. Not too hot or too cold, just right. Most of the play happened in the main room off the lobby. Players bought chips from a guy behind a counter, which wasn't covered by bars or a bullet-proof screen. Off to the right sat the tables offering the various versions of poker. Almost all of the tables were full.

It was through a pair of double doors, always closed, that allowed one to access the private room in back. You had to have special connections to get back there.

Wolf went up to the counter.

"Victor in?"

The clerk wore glasses perched on his nose and set aside a calculus book. "I haven't seen him."

"Can you call him?"

"Do you have an appointment? He's only seeing appointments today."

"Tell him it's Wolf."

The clerk nodded and picked up a phone, spoke briefly, hung up.

"If you don't have an appointment–"

"Call him again."

Another voice, "Leave the phone alone, Billy."

Wolf looked to his right. From around the counter came another man, about as tall as Wolf, dressed in a dark suit, white shirt, thin black tie. He chewed on a toothpick.

"You're not welcome here, Wolf," the man said.

"Hello, Nitro." Wolf turned so he could face the new arrival. "Have you lost weight?"

"Get out of here," said Nitro Randall.

"I need to see Victor."

"He's not talking to you or anybody else."

"Nitro–"

"I'm not telling you again." Randall stepped closer. He let his coat open a little. The butt of a revolver stuck out under his left arm.

"And I'm done asking nicely," Wolf said. "You're the second guy today who thinks he can make me go away."

"Yeah, you're the big bad Wolf. You're like herpes. Every time you do go away, you always come back again."

Wolf threw back his own jacket to show the butt of the Colt. "Are we really going to do this, Nitro?"

"Maybe I'll let you see him if you give back my money."

"I took it from you fair and square. It's not my fault you didn't have the ace."

"You son of a bitch."

Nitro spat the toothpick while clawing for his gun and Wolf stepped in at the same time, grabbing the barrel, forcing it to one side. The clerk yelled and dived under the desk. Nitro punched Wolf in the gut. Wolf recoiled, bending at the waist, letting go of the gun. Wolf straightened and Nitro smiled as he cocked the revolver.

"Put it down, Nitro!"

On the upper level, standing at the rail, stood Victor Marcus in his usual tan suit.

Nitro saw for the first time that all play at the tables had stopped. All eyes were on him and Wolf. He lowered the hammer and put the gun away. Wolf straightened his coat.

"What do you want, Wolf?" Marcus called.

"We need to talk."

"I'll give you five minutes."

Wolf passed Nitro on the way to the steps and joined Marcus in his private office. A window behind his desk overlooked the private room. It was also packed. Marcus poured a glass of whiskey from a small bar but did not offer Wolf any. He sat behind his desk. Wolf remained standing.

"So, talk," Marcus said.

"You heard about the killings."

"Yeah."

"Did you do it?"

"Are you kidding me?"

"Don't answer a question with a question, Victor."

"Why would I want to upset Carlo and Pedro? I have a nice set up here and they leave me alone."

"Carlo says you tried crossing into his business once. Is that true?"

Marcus swallowed some of his drink. "Yeah, it's true. I overstepped. Carlo put the hurt on me. Said if it ever happened again, he'd tear me apart. You think I want to cross him again?"

Wolf shrugged. "Maybe. Nitro was ready to kill me. That poker game was months ago. With me out of the way your scheme might have a chance."

"You have a big ego. And Nitro has a temper, you know that. I keep telling him to take a vacation and cool off."

"Any back room gossip?"

"Hey, anything that gets said back there, stays back there."

"It goes onto your recorders, Victor. How would you like it if everybody found out that what they think is private you're keeping a record of?"

"How do you know about that?"

Wolf smiled.

Marcus took a deep breath and finished the whiskey. He set the glass down on the desk beside some papers. He moved his hands to his lap.

"Keep those hands on the desk, Victor."

"Don't insult me."

"Victor?"

"Fine. *Fine!*" He placed both hands on the desk. "Okay so maybe I heard something."

"So, talk."

"Why should I?"

"You'll get to keep living."

"Oh, you're *funny.*"

"I'm all ears, too."

"You need to spend less time with me and more with Carlo."

"Meaning what?"

"He's the next target, dummy. They're gonna cap him when he leaves the Lexington Club today. After lunch. That's one hour from now."

Wolf stepped toward the desk. "You little punk."

Victor held up his hands like a shield. "Hey! Who knows if it's true? You know how guys make stuff up."

"Who talked about it?"

"I don't know. I swear!"

Wolf took out his gun.

"Okay. *Okay!*" He sucked in some air. "So maybe I do got a beef with him, all right?"

"But not the stones to do anything yourself."

"It was Sean Masters, know him?"

"He runs the gambling ship off the coast. What else?"

"That's all I heard. You'd have to talk to him. He's out on the boat."

Wolf put away his gun. "See how easy that was, Victor?"

"Someday, Wolf, somebody's going to erase your sorry ass."

Wolf grinned as he opened the door. "It won't be you, Victor. You'd probably piss yourself before you could pull the trigger."

Wolf went back downstairs. Play at the tables had returned to normal but he felt everybody's eyes on him as he descended. The clerk at the counter looked nervous. Nitro Randall stood at the door. He stepped aside as Wolf neared and said, "See you soon, Wolf."

"Not if I see you first." Wolf went out.

———

INSPECTOR CALLAWAY HAD a direct order from his boss to find out who burned the Gulino and Sanchez people before anybody else did. He couldn't believe the police department was trying to solve the murders of gangsters who would otherwise be low priority. They usually only shot each other, so who cared? The city did not want a war between the capos because they didn't want innocent people caught in the crossfire ending up on television.

They had managed to get halfway through the day without another shooting. Callaway considered that a good thing.

While the rest of the department scoured the street for information, Callaway parked his car in a No PARKING spot in front of the Lexington Club and stepped out. He flashed his badge at the greeter inside the restaurant before the mousy little man could tell him members only and asked where Gulino's table was.

The capo sat alone eating a plate of spaghetti with

meat sauce in a back booth. A stack of garlic bread sat on an adjoining plate. Callaway approached the table with his hands exposed.

"Eating alone, Carlo?" The spaghetti smelled good. Callaway's stomach rumbled.

Gulino swallowed some food. "Good afternoon, Inspector. I've already spoken with our mutual friend."

"Then you can repeat everything to me."

Callaway caught movement at two other tables, men shifting in their seats. So, Carlo wasn't *really* alone after all. The capo waved the men off and kept eating.

He gave the inspector a rundown of his conversation with Wolf.

"How about this," Callaway said. "What if Sanchez has been killed? Who would take his place?"

"His daughter?"

"Sure. But then why would she want you dead?"

Gulino paused to think for a minute.

"Don't be a smart ass," Callaway said.

Gulino laughed.

"I'm glad you think it's funny, Carlo."

"Look, it's not funny. I'm just as concerned as you. Eventually me and Sanchez will talk but it sure as hell isn't going to be *me* who makes the first move."

"Pride cometh before the fall."

"You're a philosopher, too?"

"No, just a tired cop trying to do his job."

"Your job is out there on the street."

"What have your people reported to you?"

"Nobody knows nothing."

"Where's Vince Manning?"

"He's on the street looking for answers. If he can't find them, nobody can."

Gulino went back to his food. Callaway watched him eat.

"Tell Vince to keep his nose clean," the inspector said. "I really don't want any trouble with you guys, Carlo. I just want whoever pulled that trigger."

"Can I finish my lunch now?"

"You might want a Tums after all that. Just looking at it is giving me heart burn." Callaway went out. Back in his car, he rolled down the windows and watched the front of the club.

A half hour ticked by. The street stayed packed with cars; pedestrians on the sidewalk. Normal life. Callaway fidgeted in the seat.

A black Cadillac limousine double-parked at the curb in front of the club. The doors opened. Gulino and his men exited, went down the steps. The driver stepped out of the limo and held open the back door.

A gunshot cracked.

Callaway saw Gulino fall, but not because he was hit. One of his men tackled him. The others drew guns and formed a circle around the boss and stuffed him into the limo. Another gunshot. People on the sidewalk screamed. Some cars sped up while others screeched to a halt. Horns blared. Another shot. The limo lurched into traffic, trying to weave around stopped cars.

Callaway jumped out and ran across the street, gun in hand. The shots had come from the top of the parking structure facing the Lexington Club. Great. More running and climbing. Callaway hustled all the way to the roof. He stopped short as another man carrying a long tote bag with something of equal length stuffed inside met him at the top of the steps. The man was thin and wiry and wore dark glasses.

Callaway aimed at the man's neck. "Police!"

The man started to raise a pistol of his own. Callaway fired, missing, and the man returned fire as he ran the other way. The shot struck the cement at Callaway's feet; bits of shrapnel nicked his left ankle. Callaway took off in pursuit. He chased the other man through the parked cars toward the other side of the structure. Callaway knew the roof of the neighboring building lay beyond. It would not be a hard jump for somebody in shape. For him? Forget it!

He huffed after the shooter. The man turned around again, lined up a proper shot–

When the gun fired, Callaway expected to feel the bullet puncture his body. Somewhere. *Anywhere*. He indeed heard the bullet whistle over his head, but when the gunman fell face first onto the ground with a pool of blood forming below him, it made no sense.

Callaway, stunned, panting, kept his gun aimed at the gunman.

"You really need to be more careful, John."

Callaway looked over his shoulder.

Wolf, holding his Colt, casually approached. "It's okay. I think I killed him," he said.

Callaway put away his gun and went to the body. He felt for a pulse in the man's neck. None. He kicked away the tote bag and the pistol in the man's hand.

"I suppose I should say thank you?"

"The thought had occurred to me." Wolf holstered his gun.

"What's the deal?"

Wolf recounted his conversation with Victor Marcus.

"That good for nothing snake," Callaway said. "I'd like to burn his place down."

"I'll see Sean Masters tonight."

"Say hello for me. The department doesn't have jurisdiction off the coast."

"Has anybody heard from Sanchez?"

"Not a word. I asked Gulino if he thought maybe somebody killed Sanchez and took over, but he doesn't think so. I think it makes a lot of sense. Why wouldn't he have called Gulino by now? You still chummy with his daughter?"

"Of course."

"While I'm cleaning up the stiff, maybe you can go ask *her*. You might as well have *all* the fun, right?"

"Didn't you say last night's witnesses mentioned only one shooter?"

"Yeah."

"Was this him?"

"Awfully skinny. I pictured somebody bigger. If it is, what do you think will happen next?"

"You mean was this guy their only play?"

"Something like that."

"No. Somebody's got the kill fever. They won't stop because of this. Maybe they have others on stand-by. Or maybe they'll have to bring more in."

"Any other suggestions? I know I'm just a dumb cop, Wolf. I don't know so much. Please tell me more."

Wolf grinned. "Don't step in the guy's blood." He patted Callaway on the shoulder and walked away.

———

WOLF SAT in a corner booth at Gordy's Restaurant, a popular bar and grill that offered live music every night and, for those who were properly connected or who knew the password, a game room in the back with everything except slots. On the stage, the piano player, a short blond man in a white shirt and dark slacks, played through an arrangement. The female singer, a tall brunette in loose jeans and a t-shirt, did the vocal work. Their starts and stops didn't annoy Wolf.

The restaurant wasn't officially open for business, but Wolf was welcome any time. He liked being the only one in the dining room. The lights were low; the strips of light lining the walkways provided a quiet glow.

He used a fork to cut his chicken fried steak, mixing it with mashed potatoes. He'd eaten the vegetables first, steamed broccoli and carrots. Presently he finished the meal, downed what remained of his Fireball whiskey and Coke, pushed the plate away, and lit a cigar.

Gordy, the rotund owner of the restaurant, eased his bulk into the other side of the booth. What remained of his hair was slicked against his skull. Parts of his skull showed through the black strands.

"Good dinner?"

Wolf, puffing smoke, nodded. He placed the match on the table. A waitress walked by. She had her dirty-blonde hair tied back in a ponytail and a neck that looked too thin to support her head. She waved away smoke from her face. "Since when can we smoke inside?" she said.

Gordy said, "Hey, Melissa."

The waitress turned. She slumped her shoulders and looked bored.

"This is Mister Wolf. He's a preferred customer. What he says come from me, got it?"

"OK," she said, and went away again.

"New kid," Gordy said. "Got a mouth on her."

Wolf grinned and sat back. He had known Gordy as far back as his teens. They had run in the white gangs together in the inner city. Wolf had gone away for a long time while Gordy remained to build his business and cement his relationship with the local Outfit. He wasn't a major player but that was okay with him.

"Been keeping busy?" Gordy said.

"You haven't heard? I'm a regular terror."

"What else is new? So, tell me the scoop. What am I not reading in the papers?"

"Sanchez may or may not be dead," Wolf said. "Nobody's been able to reach him."

"Have you?"

"Not yet. I'm going out to Sean Masters' boat tonight to ask him a few questions."

"Masters isn't a pushover," Gordy said. "You want some of my guys to go with you?"

Wolf puffed on his cigar. "I think I can handle it, Gordy." He smiled.

"Come on. Just one guy to watch your back."

Wolf figured Gordy wanted to volunteer for the duty, but Wolf had lost enough pals in battle. If the night went south, he wanted to die alone. "I got angels looking out for me, Gordy. I don't need anything more."

"You're full of shit."

Wolf laughed.

Ferries sailed out to the gambling ships every thirty minutes. Wolf boarded the 8:30 ferry and sat in a quiet corner, reading a racing magazine. He ignored the chatter around him. Everybody had a strategy; a set amount of cash and no more; the usual social-gambling talk. Wasted words. Some people wore fancy clothes, others not-so-fancy threads. Ever since the coastal ships had started running again, they had faced an avalanche of business which piled extra tax revenue into the state coffers. Not that ship owners complained. Most of them were tied up with the mob anyway; those who weren't also reaped the benefits.

Wolf left the magazine behind when he disembarked with the rest of the crowd, blending in. He wore his usual dark clothes; under the jacket he wore his pistol.

The *Princess Z* spent its past life as a cruise ship before Sean Masters retrofitted it for his needs. It carried a crew of nearly 400, which included wait staff, gourmet chefs, a full orchestra, and various other performing acts. It also housed Masters' crew of security officers, a rotating group which some gunmen joined when they needed to disappear from the street for a while. Able to host 2000 passengers, there were overnight accommodations for those who could afford it; everybody else had to take the ferries back at the close of the night.

The passengers climbed a staircase mounted to the side of the boat. Halfway up, the wind made the staircase sway a little; the crowd of people didn't help with stability. Wolf moved up a step at a time while listening to the couple in front of him. The female half had the jitters, holding tight to the railing; her boyfriend kept easing her along. She glanced back with a nervous smile.

Once aboard worries about the wind faded fast.

Wolf followed the people into the large playroom. Table games filled the room to the brim. If you wanted slots, you had to go to another section. The ship had dozens along with restaurants and bars.

The A/C tried to keep it comfortable but too much body heat overwhelmed the cooling system. Crowded tables, bodies pressing together; clicking roulette wheels, the tapping of chips; cheers, jeers; calls of encouragement and caution. Wolf dodged and stepped between people who were too focused on gambling to notice him. He made it to the other side of the room, found the bar, leaned against the rail and waved over the bartender.

"Bulleit and Coke," he said.

Drink in hand, Wolf turned back to watch the play.

Now he was able to see beyond the faces of the customers. The suckers. The security team wore black slacks and blue blazers and the blazers weren't cut to hide artillery. They stood at strategic positions around the playroom, a scene that would be repeated in every other game room on the ship, more of them than Wolf thought was needed.

Wolf caught one eye in particular, and raised his glass, smiling. The man came over. He wasn't wearing a blue blazer but a light windbreaker instead. He had thick, gray hair and a stocky build. He leaned against the bar next to Wolf.

"Are we here for the same reason?" the man said.

"Hello, Vince."

Vince Manning, Gulino's top enforcer, ordered a beer.

"Carlo told me you were on the job," Wolf said. "How did you find your way here?"

"Been up top yet?"

Wolf sipped his drink. Manning wasn't known for paying attention to others. But if he was on your side he was as loyal as a dog. Wolf said, "Just got here."

"Follow me after we finish."

"Got even more up top?"

"Uh-huh."

"For what?"

Manning shrugged. "I didn't come all the way out here to go home empty handed. I get seasick."

"You?" Wolf grinned. "I didn't think anything could touch your cast-iron stomach."

"Uh-huh," Manning said.

———

WOLF LOOKED OVER THE SIDE. He didn't know how fast the ship was going, but the wake generated proved that they were indeed moving further away from shore than the three-mile limit the boat usually anchored at.

"What business does this ship have outside the limit?" Wolf said.

"Dunno," Manning said, brushing past Wolf to continue forward.

Wolf followed. He took out the .45 and clicked off the safety and held the gun beside his leg. The narrow walkway allowed them to walk side-by-side should they want, but Wolf stayed a few feet back. A warm rush filled his body. There would be action soon.

They passed the darkened portholes of the state rooms and had to stop when yellow tape blocked their way. NO PASSENGERS BEYOND THIS POINT. But the winking flashlights up ahead showed that somebody couldn't read.

Manning hunkered down in a space between the staterooms and the tape. Wolf joined him. He tried to see into the darkness ahead but had trouble making out any shapes. Part of the bridge superstructure blocked the view.

"We need to get closer," Wolf said. He didn't whisper. There was no reason to. The rush of the wind nearly drowned out his words.

Manning said nothing. But he had taken his gun out, too, a revolver Wolf knew to be a Colt Python .357 Magnum. Just ahead, light spilled onto the deck from a stairway leading up from below, and shadows grew along the splash of light. Two men, their voices lost in the wind, stepped onto the deck and moved forward into the dark. The splash of light highlighted only one of them, very briefly. The man had broad shoulders and a bald head.

Sean Masters.

Wolf left Manning in his spot, bent under the tape and stopped at a rail that overlooked the stairway. He could drop over the rail and onto the steps but if there was somebody else coming up, he'd have a spotlight on him brighter than any stage light.

Manning joined him, put away the revolver, and swung his legs over. Apparently, he had no such hesitation. He grabbed the rung of the rail and dangled a moment, dropped. He landed on the steps, moved quickly into the darkness. Wolf shook his head. Would it kill the guy to talk? He put the .45 away and duplicated the move. Nobody came up the steps. He found the other man once again crouched beside a wall, gun out. They both advanced, staying close to the wall. The winking flashlights looked like busy fireflies. They stopped at the corner. Light shined above them from the windows of the bridge but none of it touched them. The light did, however, help them see who was out there with the flashlights.

Wolf stopped counting when he reached ten. There could have been more, out of sight, but the ten men clustered around the bow were all armed with automatic weapons. Masters and his companion watched the ocean. So did some of the troops. Their gaze lay further ahead, in the water itself.

Waiting for something.

Manning took out his phone, typed a quick text message, put the phone away. "I got another boat following us," he said. "Off the port side."

"Nice of you to tell me in advance," Wolf said.

They were on the starboard side of the boat, the one facing away from shore. Broken words from Masters and his companion drifted their way but neither could make them out.

Presently the ship slowed to a full stop but the anchor did not drop. The wind died down. The chill of the night crept along the walkway and Wolf shivered a little. The swells of the sea rocked the ship.

Something flashed in the dark water. A light. It flashed again at repeated intervals and the troopers responded by flashing their own lights. Not long now.

After a while, another boat approached the *Princess Z*. It moved slowly, stopping short, and a lifeboat dropped from the side. A small motor started chugging and the lifeboat closed the distance. The troopers sprang into action, lowering a net over the side. Four men climbed up the net and stepped onto the deck. Masters greeted each one and the lifeboat returned to the other craft.

Masters, his companion, and the four new arrivals moved out of sight. Probably for the entryway located just under the bridge, Wolf thought. The troops stayed put for a little while after the others had gone and they, too, eventually went below deck.

Each of the new arrivals had carried loaded canvas sacks.

When the *Princess Z* started to move again, it turned slowly around. Soon the lights of the shore were on the starboard side and the boat started back for its usual place of anchor.

Manning's phone flashed. He read the message and stowed the phone and his gun. "Move," he said. Wolf followed him back to the stairway and they went below deck, following a labyrinth of corridors that eventually took them back to the top deck and the game rooms. They entered a lightly-crowded dining room and made for the bar.

"New shooters to replace the one you killed," Manning said as he swallowed some beer.

"What about your people in the other boat?"

"Never mind them."

"I guess this was a good way to get them in without using the airports," Wolf said.

"Uh-huh."

"Which means I need to go have a talk with Mister Masters. You in?"

"Nope." Manning drank some more beer. He did not look at Wolf. His thoughts were elsewhere.

"It's always nice to talk to you."

Wolf left the bar.

———

WOLF WENT BACK outside the superstructure, climbed more steps, and followed a path to an entryway which he stepped through. Ahead of a short hallway was another door with a guard in front. The guard said, "Who are you?"

"Wolf. I'm here to see Mister Masters."

"Get out of here."

"Not this again."

The guard didn't reach for a gun. He instead pulled a walkie-talkie from his belt. Wolf closed in and bashed him over the head with the .45. He dragged the unconscious man into a corner, propped him up, and twisted the knob on the door. It did not open. He found a key in the guard's pocket, unlocked the door.

Masters had left the lights on. The carpet felt soft beneath his feet; the white and wood paneled motif, with pictures of other sea ships on the walls, provided a nice touch. A wooden desk sat in a corner, cluttered with paperwork. A panoramic window covered the right side of the office but there was nothing to see now. Wolf checked the private bathroom; no sign of Masters.

Wolf moved to the desk and sank into the chair behind it. The papers were all business, so he didn't waste time looking for a clue among them. He reclined back, held the .45 in his lap, and waited. The wind beat against the windows. After a few minutes, the door swung open and Sean Masters stared at Wolf for a few moments. Or, rather, he stared at the snout of the Colt automatic in Wolf's hand.

"Shut it."

Masters closed the door and shook his head. "You think I'm stupid enough to keep anything in this room?"

"Why do you think I'd be looking for anything?"

"I'm not an idiot. I know you've been stomping all over trying to find out who killed those guys."

"Sit down."

"I don't take orders from you."

"Sit down or I'll shoot your left kneecap."

Masters sighed and dropped into a chair on the other side of the room. "You're supposed to search me, aren't you?"

"I'm not an idiot, either. Two-finger your roscoe and drop it on the carpet."

Masters used the thumb and index finger of his right land to pluck the .38-caliber short-nosed Smith & Wesson Model 60 revolver from under his left arm. He tossed it. The gun plopped on the carpet.

"Now keep your hands on your lap."

Masters placed both hands on either leg, sat straight up.

"Who were the guys who came aboard?"

"Part of the future," Masters said. "Things are changing in this city. I'm changing it."

"So, the killings were your idea?"

"Hardly. But I helped facilitate."

"Who are you working with?"

Masters cracked a smile. "You'd be surprised who I'm working with."

"Has Sanchez been killed?"

"I have no idea."

"Tell me who the mastermind is."

"What's in it for me?"

"You get to live."

"Wolf, you're on a boat in the middle of the bay. That's why I just walked in here without calling my guys. Go ahead and shoot me. What's your escape plan?"

"You let me worry about an escape plan."

"Right. Wolf never fails. Big bad Wolf."

"That's the second time somebody's said that to me. Have I become a joke?"

"Once the shift in power is complete, I'll be the one giving the orders. You'll just be part of the scenery."

"You know me," Wolf said. "I just don't sit around looking pretty."

"With a face like yours?" Masters laughed.

"You can't be working with anybody in the city," Wolf said. "You can't keep this sort of thing quiet. Who on the outside would want the territory?"

Masters shrugged.

"I'll get the answers the easy way or the hard way, Sean. Make it easy."

"What have you ever done for me?"

"Okay, I'm done being nice."

Masters grinned. "Come and get it."

Wolf started to move and then part of the panoramic window shattered inward. Wolf bolted from the chair, swinging the .45 around. Somebody outside stuck a weapon through the hole and fired a full-auto blast. The slugs ripped into the chair and desk. Wolf fired several shots in quick succession, blowing out the rest of the window and wasting the man behind the gun.

Masters dived for the .38, scooping it into his hand, lining up on Wolf just as Wolf pivoted and fired again. A neat hole appeared between Masters' eyes. Masters dropped flat on the carpet.

Cold wind filled the office. Wolf put his gun away and stepped over the body.

"We'll do it the hard way," he said.

He rejoined the fuss in the game rooms. None of the security team seemed alarmed. Perhaps Masters had only called the one gunman. When the next ferry arrived with a new load of players, he got on for the ride back to the coast and drove home.

He was smoking a cigar by the porch when Melody Chapman came down the steps. Almost midnight. Time to go to work. She still kept her head down. Wolf said, "Good evening."

Melody Chapman stopped, looked at him.

"Are you okay?"

She stared.

"Are you?" he said.

"Why did you hit him?"

"He was hurting you. Didn't you want him to stop?"

"He'll never stop."

"So why do you stay?"

"Sometimes it's not bad. It's only because he's frustrated. Gulino should have given him his old job back."

"That's no way to live, Melody."

"I have to go." She started toward her car.

"I may not be around next time," he said.

She stopped and turned. "You're the only one who cares. Tell me why."

"See this?" Wolf pulled up the silver chain from his shirt. A locket dangled at the end of the chain. "This belonged to somebody I used to know who was just like you. There was a time when I was just like your husband. I made her a promise that I would change that."

"Where is she?"

Wolf dropped the chain back down his shirt. "She's gone."

"You don't know how hard it is."

"Yes, I do."

She stared at him some more. "I'm going to be late," she said, and turned for the car again. Wolf smoked and watched her drive away.

———

CALLAWAY HUFFED and puffed as he stepped onto the roof. Wolf was already there, hands in pockets, grinning.

"One of these days, Wolf," Callaway said. He took a deep breath. "Tell me about the boat."

Wolf gave him the rundown.

Callaway said, "They must be hushing it up. We've had no word."

Wolf added, "Don't forget that Masters' main office is downtown. Go talk to his second-in-command."

"Harry something, right?"

"Harry Rudd."

"What are your plans?"

"I need to find out what's going on with Sanchez. I'm meeting his daughter in twenty minutes."

Callaway's phone rang. He answered, spoke a few words, hung up. He stared into space a moment.

"What's wrong?" Wolf said.

"Your four shooters just hit their first target."

Wolf's expression froze. "Uh-huh."

"Couple of Gulino's guys. Two of them. In a car. They got the guys in the car and a couple of bystanders."

"Uh-huh."

"One dead, two wounded. Gulino's guys are dead, too. The killers used full-auto weapons."

"We need to work faster."

"You're telling me?"

Wolf patted Callaway on the shoulder and headed for the fire escape. Callaway remained.

———

THE DOOR OPENED. Petra Sanchez, daughter of missing capo Pedro, looked out at him. She looked stressed.

"OhmyGod, Wolf," she said, throwing her arms around him. She was about his height, slim with wide hips and long black hair. He squeezed back but as usual she felt very fragile and was afraid if he squeezed too hard, he'd break one of her ribs. She stepped away.

"Come in, we gotta talk."

She grabbed a couple of beers from the fridge and they sat in the living room. The TV was on. The talking heads were outraged at the continuing bursts of violence throughout the city and they wanted it stopped. She turned off the TV.

"Is your father alive?" he said.

"I don't know!" she said. "I can't reach him! Nobody can. And it's almost been three days."

"What does that mean?"

"Daddy always said that if he's ever out of touch for three days or more it means something's wrong."

"Have you been by the house?"

She shook her head. "I've been afraid to go."

"We'll go now." He set his beer down and stood up.

"Should I bring a gun?" she said.

"Bring a tank."

He brought her up to date as they drove. When he finished, Petra sank in the seat a little. Wolf stopped talking. He steered the car up into the interior valley, up a winding road to the top of a hill. He parked off the road. Trees more than covered the car. Grabbing a tote bag from the back seat, Wolf and Petra started walking through the woods. They hiked up a rise and Wolf dropped onto the ground. Petra hesitated a moment and stretched out beside him.

The rise overlooked her father's estate. It sat on top of another hill, surrounded by a fence. A turret-like structure topped the mansion, extending the height of the place. Wolf took a pair of binoculars from the tote bag. The butt of a double-barrel shotgun also stuck out of the bag, along with a box of shells.

Wolf looked through the binoculars. The spread of the estate consisted mostly of well-manicured grass. A pool. Sanchez wasn't much for gardening or fancy land-scaping. Wolf scanned the troopers roaming the grounds. Each carried an automatic rifle. Wolf lowered the binoculars.

He said, "Your father picked this spot for the isola-tion, right?"

"Yeah."

"Are those guards normal?"

"Let me look."

He gave her the binoculars and she scanned the mansion.

"Too many," she said. "And the guys are usually in the house. There's always one man at the main gate but these roaming patrols aren't part of the routine."

"He could be beefing things up because of the situation in town," he said.

"And not talking to Gulino? Or answering the goddamn phone?"

Wolf did not respond.

"Do you think he's still alive?" she said.

"If he wasn't, they wouldn't have guards there."

"Who's *they*?"

"Good question."

Wolf stood and brushed dirt off his clothes. He took the shotgun from the tote bag and Petra followed him back to the car.

"Are we just going to blast our way in?" she said.

"Not we. *Me*. You stay with the car. If your father's in there, I'll bring him out."

"And if you don't?"

"Then you get to Inspector Callaway as fast as you can."

He started the motor and pulled back onto the road, following the winding asphalt back into the valley and up the hill leading to the Sanchez mansion. He parked again, got out with the shotgun, and took off into the forest. He did not say good-bye. Petra watched until she could see him no more, then scooted behind the wheel and tapped nervous fingers on her lap.

Wolf stomped through the forest, dodging trees and fallen logs and branches. When he figured he was 100 yards from the fence, he dropped behind one of the fallen logs to listen and wait. As his breathing returned to normal, he heard other footsteps. His ran his thumb over the safety catch on the shotgun. It was off, but he only wanted to fire if he had to.

Birds chirped and other animals moved about in the trees above; Wolf ignored them. The animals with two legs and guns were on his mind. They entered his field of vision off to the left. Both held their guns low. They weren't expecting trouble. Wolf moved from the log, started moving parallel to the patrol but in the opposite direction. He hooked a right turn, dropped onto the trail the pair followed, and worked his way up behind them. One turned and shouted an alarm. In the time it took for him to get his rifle up, Wolf bashed him with the butt stock of the shotgun. He dropped flat. Wolf pivoted, swinging the stock again, and conked the second trooper on the side of the face. Both hit the ground, unconscious.

Wolf started running again, following the trail, which eventually led to the main gate. Wolf left that area and went back the way he'd come. The main gate wasn't the spot he wanted. He followed the fence a little more, finally found a spot to climb. He faced the rear of the property where the patrols had passed through already. He vaulted over the fence and landed on the grass. Shotgun in hand, he started for the house.

It was a long walk. At least it felt that way. Wolf scanned left and right and behind him as he moved. When a figure appeared in a window on the second floor of the house, saw him, and shouted an alarm, Wolf knew the time for stealth had ended. Time now to blast away. He lined up both barrels on the gunner in the window and fired. The window shattered; the man fell back. Wolf snapped open the barrel. Both spent shells ejected. He loaded two more as guards rounded the corner. He fired once, running for a back door. He fired again to keep the troopers back as he crashed through the door, rolling onto the floor. He reloaded again. The troops came through the door firing, stitching the walls with slugs. There was nothing else in the room except lawn care items. Wolf fired both barrels again, blasting the pair back through the door they'd entered.

Wolf slapped fresh rounds into the shotgun and moved through another door behind him. Down a short hallway to a living room. Off to the left, the entryway of the house and a staircase. He ran for the staircase. The front doors slammed open. Troops came in. Wolf fired at them as he reached the steps. He ran. Rounds punched the walls behind him, split the banister. Wolf drew the .45 and emptied the clip, spraying rounds, driving the troops to cover. He reached the second floor and stopped against a wall. A fresh clip went into the .45 and two new rounds into the shotgun. Both weapons in hand, he advanced down the hall, kicking open doors and checking each room. He'd looked in three of the bedrooms, each one empty, by the time the troops regrouped and came up the steps. Wolf, in a doorway, met them with the shotgun, two blasts followed by potshots from the .45. Some of the men fell, others retreated. Wolf moved on. He found a door in the hallway with a set of steps leading up. He followed the steps as they spiraled to the next level, keeping the shotgun ahead of him. The stairs led to the turret on the roof. He didn't know if Sanchez would be there, but it was a good guess. It's where the man kept his office. He reached the landing, kicked open the door, and moved in. A trooper raised a pistol; Wolf cut him down with one blast from the shotgun. He swung left to face another threat but held his fire. It wasn't a threat at all, but Pedro Sanchez tied up on his own couch, gagged. Wolf went over and yanked the gag from his mouth.

Sanchez sucked in a load of air. He said, "I knew you'd get here eventually."

"Sorry I'm late. What the hell is going on?"

"Some turkey named Lazzo has been holding me here. He's gone now. Just the troops. Cut me loose."

Wolf set the shotgun down and used a knife to cut the ropes holding Sanchez's wrists and ankles together. While Sanchez sat up and rubbed his wrists, Wolf went to the windows and examined the battleground.

"They have orders not to kill me," Sanchez said. "They won't attack us in here."

"But they can seal us off."

"Was it such a good idea to come blasting in here?"

"I have Petra with me."

"Here?"

"She's with the car. I told her to get help from Callaway if I take too long."

"What's happening on the street?"

Wolf told him and gave him the progress of his own investigation so far, adding that Gulino had Vince Manning on the job as well but Wolf had no idea what Manning had done since the previous night on the *Princess Z.*

Sanchez said, "I hope Carlo isn't going off half-cocked."

"He's restrained himself. He knows there's something more to it. And if this Lazzo guy is connected to Sean Masters, we might have something."

"All I know is that he's from New York."

Wolf kept looking out each window. The guards had not moved to cover the yard; they were probably all clustered inside, waiting for Wolf to come down with Sanchez. He looked around. The office had the basic equipment. Desk, bookcases, a wall safe, small bar, couches and chairs.

"What are you looking for?" Sanchez said.

Wolf held up a hand and went to the door. Footsteps in the stairwell. Wolf fired the shotgun, peppering the wall in the stairway with holes. Whoever was down there scrambled away.

"They may have reconsidered their orders not to hurt you," Wolf said. "Got any rope?"

"In here? Why would I? This is my office. There's nothing useful in here."

Wolf laughed. He took out the spent shell and put in a new one. "Good news, I found you," he said. "Bad news, we're stuck up here."

"Until Petra brings the cops."

"When is Lazzo due back?"

"No idea."

More movement in the stairwell. Wolf fired the shotgun once, heard yelling; he saw part of a man's body come around the corner and fired again. The man screamed, tumbled down the steps. Wolf broke open the shotgun and patted his pockets for shells. None. "No more howitzer," he said, dropping the shotgun on the carpet. He took out the .45. "We need an escape route *fast*."

Wolf ran around the windows of the turret once again and saw the pool below. "Well this isn't a good idea, but we can jump to the pool from here and get to the garage, right?"

"I'm not exactly dressed for swimming."

"You're not the one carrying all the guns." Wolf smashed out the window. He stepped out onto the roof and Sanchez followed. Both inched along the rooftop to the edge, looking down at the blue pool below.

"Which side is the deep end?" Wolf said.

"I can't believe we're doing this."

Wolf leaped. The air rushed around him and his stomach lurched into his throat. The pool grew larger very quickly and then the splash. He dropped through the water, his descent slowing, crashing into the bottom. He kicked with his legs and reached the top, rolled up onto the patio.

Sanchez still stood on the roof. As Wolf shook water out of the Colt, he scanned the back doors, gesturing for the other man to follow. Sanchez hesitated.

"Come on!" Wolf shouted as armed troops headed for the patio doors. He fired twice.

Sanchez jumped. The splash of water hit Wolf and spread along the patio. Sanchez quickly climbed out, Wolf covering him with another pair of shots. The troops hadn't left the house yet, but he could still see them gathering near the patio doors.

Sanchez ran for the garage attached to the house. Wolf followed. By the time he entered through the side door, Sanchez had the motor of his Mercedes going. Wolf climbed in. Sanchez didn't bother with the garage door. He pressed the gas pedal and the car crashed through the garage door and out onto the driveway. The driveway wound toward the main gate. Troopers fired at the car, bullets *thunking* into the body work. Wolf fired back. As they neared the main gate, the guard from the shack fired a pistol, popping holes in the windshield. Wolf leaned out the window and gave him the last shots in the Colt. He missed, but the guard had no choice but to dive for cover as the Mercedes crashed through the gate.

Sanchez started driving along the access road. Wolf told him where to find Petra.

————

INSPECTOR CALLAWAY ENTERED the interrogation room and shut the door. He held a cup of coffee in his left land.

"Is that for me?" the man at the table said. His hands were free. He was stocky with thick black hair and a jowly face. Harry Rudd, Sean Masters' second-in-command.

"No, it's mine," Callaway said. He sat at the table with the coffee in front of him. "You only get coffee if you talk."

"I don't know what happened to Sean. Other than he was shot on the boat."

"That's not what I'm concerned about," Callaway said. "Somebody is trying to start a gang war in this town. We have information that Masters has something to do with it. The killings have to stop. Innocent people have already been hurt."

"You're making me cry."

"Rudd. Come on. You're a businessman. This isn't good business."

Rudd sighed. "It wasn't my idea."

"I didn't say it was. Tell me your side of the story."

"Masters has always wanted more than his share. He wasn't happy with just the boat and the protection. A couple of months ago, two guys came to him and had an idea to force Gulino and Sanchez into a fight to get them out of the way."

"Who?"

"There are two. Andy Lazzo is one of them. I never met the other guy. He's been more of a silent partner."

"Who's Andy Lazzo?"

"Big shot on the East Coast but he's on the outs with his gang because of some stuff I never quite understood. He's been roaming around looking for opportunities. His cell mate offered him one."

"Where does Andy Lazzo hide?"

"He's been at Sanchez's place, keeping him tied up and out of contact. He wanted Gulino to think Sanchez was the one doing the killing. He hangs around the Cherry Hill bars."

Callaway pushed the coffee across the table. "It's still hot." The inspector left the room and returned to his desk to make a phone call.

He reached Wolf on the first try. "Where are you?"

"On the road. I have Sanchez and his daughter with me." Wolf gave him the update.

"That's a load off my mind," Callaway said, and described his interview with Harry Rudd. "All we need to do now is find Lazzo and the silent partner. I'm going to dig into his prison record and find out who his cell mate might have been."

"Okay," Wolf said. The line went dead in Callaway's ear. The inspector hung up the phone.

WOLF DROPPED Sanchez and his daughter at her place.

"I'm going to call Gulino right away," Sanchez said, "and get our sides organized. If we all work together, we can find Lazzo and whoever he's working with."

Wolf returned home to change clothes and eat. He was sitting at the kitchen table, staring out the window, when his cell rang.

"Yes?"

"It's me," Manning said. "I hear we're looking for a guy named Andy Lazzo."

"Sure. Found him?"

"I know where his gunmen are staying."

"I like this tune."

Manning rattled off an address. "Midnight." He hung up.

When Wolf arrived at the address, he found Manning parked across the street. He pulled in behind and went to Manning's car, sliding into the passenger seat.

"What's the plan?"

"Let's tell them we're the Avon lady."

"We're both pretty ugly for the–" Wolf was about to say "the Avon lady" but Manning was already getting out. He shut the door. Wolf joined him on the street. He left his coat open for easy access to the Colt; Manning held his revolver against his leg. Manning started across the street. A Honda sat in the driveway. To the left of the garage door was a gate that had no padlock. Wolf watched the gate as he walked across the street.

Not a soul stirred on the street. Most of the homes had lights on behind curtained windows; somewhere a dog was barking. Wolf didn't want a fight here, but he had a feeling there was no choice in the matter. He clicked off the safety on the .45.

Manning stepped up to the door and pressed the bell. Nobody answered. He rang again and then pounded on the door.

"What is it?" said somebody through the door.

Wolf watched the gate beside the garage with occasional glances elsewhere. Average police response time was eleven minutes from the time the emergency call went through dispatch; once the shooting started, they would need to be gone in half that time. Wolf's pulse quickened.

Manning pounded on the door. "Open up."

The front door opened a bit. A pair of eyes attached to a small face looked out. "Who sent you?"

As Manning raised a foot to kick in the door, the side gate opened and another man with a scatter gun swung around the corner.

Wolf yelled, "Shotgun!"

Wolf dropped and rolled as the shotgun roared. He returned fire. The shotgunner crashed back against the open gate. Manning kicked in the door, entered the house, firing twice. Wolf scrambled up and ran inside. He stepped over the small-faced man who had two slugs in his chest. More shots from Manning's .357. Another gunner came through the connecting door from the kitchen. Wolf triggered a round into his shoulder. The man went down but still raised his gun to fire. Wolf shot him again.

A girl screamed from somewhere in the house. Wolf advanced down the hallway, turning a corner into a sitting room, the kitchen off to the right. Manning was down a hall, kicking open a door; pounding footsteps above sent Wolf scrambling up the stairway off the kitchen. He reached the first landing and from a bedroom doorway came a fusillade of automatic gunfire. He hit the carpet. The bullets chewed up the railing behind him. He raised his gun and fired a string of shots, moving the muzzle back and forth. He charged up the second flight of steps, still blasting, diving for the open door of the master bedroom. Another burst of fire followed him.

Wolf stayed flat on the carpet, reloading the Colt, easing along until he was almost near the door. More gunfire shattered the doorframe. He fired back. The shooter appeared to be in the smaller bedroom directly across the landing. Wolf fired through the opposing wall, but the gunman made no sound. Another burst. Wolf rolled away. Bullets chewed more of the doorframe and tore into the carpet. Wolf rolled back to return fire but held as the gunman exited the bedroom and tossed a black spherical object toward him. Wolf rolled again. The object exploded and spewed thick, white smoke. The smoke flooded the bedroom and the landing. Wolf charged through the smoke, catching a glimpse of the gunman as he raced down the stairs. Wolf misjudged his footing and missed the first step, tumbling end-over-end onto the middle landing. His head banged against the railing. He managed to hold onto the Colt.

Scrambling to his feet, his head spinning, Wolf rushed down the remaining steps as the shooter shoved open the patio door and ran outside. Wolf followed, swinging around the corner of the house, catching the gunman as he ran for the still-open gate. The gunman turned and fired; the slugs tore a chunk out of the corner of the house, pelting Wolf with sharp bits. Wolf fired twice and the gunman screamed, pitching forward to slam face-first into the fence.

Wolf went back inside as Manning came out of the hall just off the kitchen. He dragged a woman with him. A redhead. She screamed, fighting his grip, but he held on. He tossed her on the carpet.

"Did we get everybody?" Manning said.

Wolf nodded.

"Don't hurt me!"

"I'm not going to hurt you," Manning said. "Who else is here?"

"Nobody! Just me and the four guys." Her eyes focused on Wolf. "What the hell is going on, Wolf?"

"You got mixed up with the wrong people, Stacy," Wolf said. He knew her. She was a working girl that normally made the rounds of the bars in the Mission District. "Did they pay you?"

"The guy who answered the door did," she said, getting up. She straightened her clothes.

"Did they talk about anybody else?"

"All I know is they had a fight about me being here. They had to hide a bunch of guns."

"We got lucky," Manning said, putting away his revolver. "We gotta go."

"Take me with you!"

Manning said, "Get a cab," as he moved to the door.

"Wolf!"

"Come on," Wolf said. He held out a hand and led the woman out of the house. Sirens in the distance. He put her in the back of his car. Manning was already driving away. Wolf started the car and followed him. He drove with his hands tight on the wheel. They had cleaned up the shooters. News of the fight would spread fast once the cops showed up. Now they had to find Andy Lazzo and his silent partner before they skipped town.

He looked in the rearview mirror at Stacy. "Where to?"

"Just take me home," she said.

―――――――

WOLF STOOD beside the ABSOLUTELY NO SMOKING sign puffing on a cigar. He had cleared his mind of the night's activities.

When Melody Chapman pulled up in her Chevy, she carefully parallel parked and exited the car. She approached the building with her head down. Wolf said hello and she stopped.

"Your husband's not home," he said.

"Uh-huh."

"Melody, if there was one thing I could do for you, what would it be?"

She moved her mouth a little but did not reply.

"Follow me," he said. He placed the cigar on a step and went inside. They went up to his apartment. She stood by the door while he went into the bedroom. He came back with a small revolver which he offered to her.

"I can't take that," she said.

"The next time he tries to hurt you, shoot him."

"Wolf–"

"Some people need others to tell them that they can do things they don't think they can," Wolf said. "Take the weapon."

"I don't want it."

"Melody. Please. I may not be here next time."

"You said that already."

Wolf lowered his arm. He watched her. Melody kept her eyes on the floor but did not make a move to leave.

"Okay," she said.

Wolf handed her the gun.

He saw her into her own apartment and then went back outside. He had to relight the cigar. After he finished it, he climbed into the Cadillac and started driving.

It was a short drive. He parked in an alley and climbed the fire escape to the roof. He waited.

Presently the fire escape squeaked, and a man grunted with effort. Wolf watched Inspector Callaway reach the top. The cop dusted off his jacket and went over to Wolf.

"Can't we just meet at Starbucks?" he said.

"Their coffee is too bitter," Wolf said.

"Do you know anything about a house in the 'burbs with four dead men in it?"

"Nope."

"They were all shot with either a .45 or a .357."

"Common calibers, Inspector."

"Sure, they are. They're also from Chicago. Known gunmen. Wanted for all kinds of things. We have no record of them arriving in town."

"Must have come by boat."

"Sure. Maybe they landed in Oregon or upstate and found a boat. Whatever. But I think that's the end of the mass shootings."

"One hopes," Wolf said. "Gulino and Sanchez want to see me tomorrow. Pow wow and all that."

"Be sure and give them my regards."

"I know they'll appreciate it," Wolf said.

Callaway pulled an envelope from his coat pocket. "You might want this."

Wolf took it, opened the envelope, looked at the picture inside. "Lazzo?"

"Uh-huh. Don't say I never help you."

————

Petra Sanchez met Wolf at the entrance to Gulino's place. She wore a red dress with her hair down. The dress accentuated her slender curves and round rear end. Wolf grinned at her.

"What?" she said. "Never seen a woman before?"

"I wasn't expecting a formal meeting."

"Like you'd dress up anyway. Come on."

Sanchez and Gulino waited on the back patio at a table with cold cuts and other munchies. Gulino told Wolf to help himself, and Wolf piled up a plate.

Gulino said, "Vince tells me you two had a good night."

"Callaway says the shooters were from Chicago," Wolf said, and relayed the rest of the conversation he had with the inspector.

Sanchez chimed in. "So, we need Lazzo and the other guy. Spare no expense, no resource."

"We need to leave them for the cops," Wolf said.

"No way," Gulino said. "This is our business."

"It's the public's business," Wolf said. "Innocent people have been killed. The public needs the reassurance. The cops need the victory. We find them, we turn them over."

"I can't order my people to do that," Gulino said.

"Or mine," Sanchez added.

"You need to put that attitude aside," Wolf said.

"Who the hell are you to tell me I need anything?" Gulino said.

Wolf just smiled.

"He's not kidding, Daddy," Petra Sanchez said.

Gulino swallowed some salami. He said, "If we let the cops handle this, the point isn't made that you don't mess with the organization."

"Of course, the point is made," Wolf said. "Once they're in police custody, maybe even in jail, you know how accidents happen."

Sanchez nodded. "Good point."

Gulino let out a sigh and looked away for a few moments. The rest of the table watched him without comment. Eventually he said, "Okay, Wolf. We'll do it your way."

"Don't sound too excited."

"I want those two found, and fast," Gulino said. "This has gone on too long already. You got a lead?"

"Yup."

"Then I don't want you at my table anymore. Get out of here."

Wolf stayed in his seat.

"Don't argue with me, Wolf. Not right now."

Wolf grinned and stood up. Petra showed him out.

———

WOLF PUT the photo on the seat and left the car. The Cherry Hill neighborhood sat atop a hill overlooking the city. From the very top you could have a nice 360-degree view, but from where Wolf stood now only the eastern side of the city showed itself. The bright city lights shimmered with the post-day haze. Wolf started making the rounds of the bars, scanning faces, and quickly felt like he was pushing a boulder up a mountain. He worked up and down the block with no success and then stopped in an alley to light a cigar and think about it.

If Andy Lazzo stayed in the Cherry Hill neighborhood it was a small area to search, but also a crowded one. If he wasn't in any of the bars, where would he be?

Considering he had just gotten out of prison and had been used to a flashy lifestyle before his conviction, he'd hang out at the fanciest hotel in the area.

Wolf stubbed the cigar and returned to his car. He drove up the hill and parked on a steep incline, but he was directly across the street from the Excelsior Hotel. The hotel had four exits leading to the street but only one garage. Wolf left the Cadillac, went into the hotel and bought a news magazine. He sat in the lobby and watched for Lazzo. He scanned as many faces as he could, but nobody matched the photo.

He was halfway through a story on a retiring Israeli colonel who was pregnant when he saw Lazzo and two other goons exit the elevator and mix with the lobby traffic. They left via the main door the one Wolf had entered through. He tossed aside the magazine and went back out to the street. By the time he reached the sidewalk, he saw Lazzo, alone, getting into a car. He didn't see the two goons. Were they following in another car? He ran across the street, dodging the slow-moving traffic, and reached the Cadillac. He merged onto the street and stayed a few car lengths back from Lazzo's four-door Infinity. He kept flashing eyes to the rearview mirror watching for the two goons.

They started going downhill, approaching an intersection. Lazzo's car breezed through. Wolf cleared half of the intersection when two cars on either side ran the red, and smashed into the Cadillac. The impact jolted Wolf in the seat, his head smacking the side window. His body strained against the seatbelt. All other traffic stopped. The goons had been in their own cars, he realized, as he unbuckled the belt. Then the gunfire started.

The Cadillac rocked with bullet hits. Wolf dived for the floor, clawing out the Colt. He pushed open the passenger door and shoved out onto the street. The goon on that side was still behind his own car, his automatic weapon smoking. Wolf rolled up and shot him in the head. He rose, pivoting, but only had his gun halfway up when the other goon started to squeeze the trigger.

Two shots. The goon rocked with hits and fell. Wolf turned to the new arrival that had stepped out of yet another car but quickly lowered the gun.

"You need to be more careful," Vince Manning said, a trail of smoke drifting from his revolver. "Come on."

Wolf jumped into Manning's car and the enforcer flipped a U-Turn, ignoring horns, speeding away from the intersection.

"I got people following Lazzo," Manning said. "They'll get him to the cops as agreed."

"I take it you don't like the idea."

Manning grunted. "We're going to your place."

"What for?"

"Because the silent partner is there."

WOLF'S STOMACH tightened as they went down the hall. They stopped at the Chapman apartment.

Manning took out his gun and tapped the barrel on the door.

It opened slowly. Melody Chapman seemed very small as she stuck her head out.

"What is it?"

"Let us in, Melody," Wolf said. She stepped back. Wolf and Manning entered. Her leg bumped an end table beside a couch, and she stopped.

Wolf closed the door.

Manning said, "Where's your husband?"

"What?"

"Your husband," Manning said. "Where?"

"I'm right here, dummy."

Cain Chapman came out of the bedroom with an automatic in his hand. "Both of you freeze," he said.

"Cain—"

"Stand by the kitchen, Mel. Now."

"But—"

"Do it, stupid. *Now.*"

Melody hustled over to the kitchen but still had a clear view of the front room where the three men were. Her husband had his back to her.

"You got sloppy, Cain," Manning said. "Know how easy it was to find out who Lazzo did time with?"

"Not gonna matter in another few hours," Chapman said. He held the gun steady.

Wolf breathed deeply, waiting for a chance to draw. Chapman's gun and attention did not waver.

"You got *more* people coming in?" Wolf said.

"Lazzo does. He's the money man."

"Of course, he is," Wolf said. "You don't have any."

"But I got ideas, Wolf. Plenty of them. Gulino should have given me what I earned, not send me back to the minor leagues."

Melody dashed from the kitchen to the bedroom.

"I got ideas of my own," Manning said. "They include you on a slab."

"You first," Chapman said.

"Stop, Cain! Put it down!"

Melody stood in the bedroom doorway with the revolver Wolf had given her.

Chapman frowned, turned. He laughed. "Are you kidding me?"

Wolf moved out of the line of fire. He said, "It's over, Cain. Drop the gun and let's go."

Cain Chapman kept his eyes on his wife. "This is for grown-ups, stupid." He started to turn. Melody fired. She fired all six shots and each bullet punched through her husband's chest. She kept firing once the gun was empty–*click, click, click.* Her eyes stayed focused on him, wide, animal-like.

Chapman's body fell onto the couch, rolled to the floor between the couch and coffee table.

"That's self-defense if I ever saw it," Manning said.

Wolf went over and pried the gun from her hands.

THE DARK

There are only three rules in this town,
Never cheat your partner
Never take more than your share
And never cross

— WOLF

"YOU MISTER WOLF?" the black-haired man said as he extended a big hand that looked like somebody had modeled it from marble. His manicured fingernails completed the sculpted look.

Wolf said, "I'm not Paris Hilton."

"Thank the Cosmos for that!" The black-haired man laughed and shook hands with Wolf. "I'm Murray Fulton."

"Just call me Wolf."

Fulton invited Wolf to sit at a table with an umbrella extending from the middle. Wolf sat. Looking around, he was glad they were out on the patio rather than inside. The back yard featured a pool, a large section dedicated to roses, and a massive smog-free view of the entire city, clear out to the bay. The light breeze touched the back of Wolf's neck just right; a fly buzzed around in an erratic orbit.

The black-haired man poured two glasses of sparkling water, handed Wolf a glass. Wolf scanned Fulton's face, wondering how often he had a Botox shot. His skin was way too smooth for somebody over 50. He kept his real age a secret, as if it mattered, while fostering the image of a high-flying, risk-taking, grab-all-you-can businessman, emerging as a quasi-national celebrity. The public could find Fulton's cool gray eyes and youthful smile inside the pages of the gossip rags quite often. His Hollywood friends always invited him to their parties, and he flew out in his private jet to oblige them.

Wolf didn't buy the flash. Fulton's thick black hair looked dyed and sat on his head like a wet towel. The mustache and goatee combo around his mouth and chin, both oily black like his hair, made his face seem small. His eyebrows were black, too. All that black made his eyes stand out. Those eyes bored into Wolf, but Wolf didn't blink. Instead, he took a long drink of water. It was nice and chilled and bubbly with a hint of lime, and Wolf liked it.

Fulton said, "You're not an easy man to reach."

Wolf wasn't exactly in the yellow pages, either. The trail began at a bar called Lucky Tom's Orbit Room where any individual asking for him is told that he wasn't there and to leave a name and number. When they leave, a fellow to whom Wolf paid a monthly retainer follows the person to make sure they aren't a former enemy setting a trap–Wolf had plenty of former enemies. Whether or not they're a citizen honestly looking for help is pretty obvious after the first day or so, and that's when Wolf himself stepped in for a look. If the prospect looks good, he returns their call. Fulton was a good prospect.

When Wolf didn't respond, Fulton watched the bubbles in his glass a moment. "Somebody is stalking my daughter," he finally said, "and I want you to make it stop."

"You've managed to keep her out of the public eye so far," Wolf said. "What went wrong?"

For all his phony flash, Fulton never let any paparazzi near his 16-year-old daughter Suzi, which included punching a photographer who tried to crash her 15th birthday party. The photographer sued instead of pressing charges and Fulton paid him off. But the paparazzi heard the message and stayed away.

Fulton said, "All I know is that somebody is following her and scaring her, and I want him stopped. I was told you're good at making problems go away with no fuss. It's very important that I avoid any fuss in this matter."

"Would it mess with the CompuSoft takeover?"

"Yes." He paused a moment. "You do your homework."

Fulton's latest business acquisition concerned CompuSoft, the second biggest software developer in the country. Fulton planned to buy the company and close it down. His own software companies didn't want the competition any longer.

Wolf said, "Your own security people can't handle this?"

"I don't trust them to keep their mouths shut. I'm told that's the other service you provide–silence."

Wolf swallowed the rest of his water. It tingled down his throat. "I'll need to speak with Suzi," he said.

Fulton tried to frown but his face didn't move. "You know her name already?"

"I do my homework." Wolf smiled. "You're not hiring an amateur."

"She's upstairs," Fulton said, adding, "I'll get her," as he rose from the chair. He entered the house.

Wolf turned his seat to take in the view, the massive city about as quiet as it would ever be, the bay a shimmering oasis. The fly continued buzzing around like a memory that demanded attention, so he tried not to think. When that didn't work, he poured some more water and counted the bubbles.

———

FULTON RETURNED within a few minutes and saw Wolf sitting at the table, watching the bubbles in his refilled glass. Fulton examined the man again. He didn't say much but stood tall with his shoulders back, a confident stance; trim but muscular; hair shaved close to his skull; dark clothes; brown leather jacket. He approached Wolf with his lips pressed into a flat line. His eyes showed his anger, but his face couldn't communicate the emotion.

"She'll see you upstairs, Wolf," he said. "She can be impossible sometimes."

Fulton led Wolf up a flight of stairs, down a hallway. The walls of both levels were covered in light wood, with matching carpet; the quietness of the place seemed disturbing, like a museum at night. There were paintings and expensive furniture and expensive items on display, but everything was so clean and tidy it didn't look like anybody lived there. The hall narrowed, and Fulton finally stopped at a plain white door. He pulled it open, and another set of steps greeted them. There was only room for one of them to go up at a time. Fulton went first, stopping before he reached the top. The roof above him slanted downward, preventing him from rising to full height.

Fulton said, "Wolf is here, Suzi," and came back down. He let Wolf go up.

————

SUZI FULTON LAY on her bed, running the tip of an index finger over the display of her iPhone. Shelves up and down the walls contained stuffed animals of all types and sizes. Plastic eyes stared at everyone and no one. Wolf rested on the top step, back against the wall.

She said, "Hello."

"Hi, Suzi."

She had long, frizzy blonde hair. Loose T-shirt with the logo of the local football team in the center, baggy jeans, no shoes.

"Did my Dad tell you about the scary black man following me?" she said. She didn't put down the phone.

"Is that what the person looks like?"

"That's what Mom said when I told her about it." She increased the pitch of her voice, said, "'Was it a scary black man,'" and then shook her head back and forth. Her long hair moved with the shakes. "My mother is so retarded."

Wolf said, "So who is following you?"

"I don't know. But he isn't black." She put the phone down, sat up, and looked at Wolf with bright blue eyes. "Are you serious?"

"Your father wants the problem solved."

"How do I know you won't sell this to the tabloids?"

She reminded Wolf a little of his sister, had she lived as long. He said, "I don't like publicity any more than you. People like your father hire me because of that."

"Are you one of those private detectives, like on TV?"

"No."

She blinked a few times. "Lawyer?"

Wolf shook his head.

"So, what are you?"

"A problem solver."

Suzi Fulton's eyes dropped to Wolf's open jacket. He followed her gaze to the exposed grip of his .45-caliber Colt automatic.

She said, "Ever kill anybody?"

Wolf covered the gun. "I don't want to talk about me anymore, Suzi."

She stretched out again and picked up her phone.

"When did you realize somebody was following you?"

"I don't want to talk to the hired help anymore," she said.

Wolf remained for another two minutes but the girl cycled through iPhone apps and acted as if he wasn't there. Should he have given her a body count? How many would it have been okay to kill before she called him names?

And then he realized he didn't know how many people he'd sent into the dark; or any idea how many had gone because he'd failed to save them.

Wolf scooted back down the steps, out the door. Suzi's father stood in the hallway. He turned. Wolf shook his head, walked past the black-haired man, who followed.

Kids either learned from their parents, Wolf thought, or they did not.

———

"So?" Fulton said. They'd moved to his study where he broke out the good scotch. Ice crackled as he filled the glasses. Wolf ignored the paintings and looked out a window that showed the rolling hillside behind the house. Tan grass swayed; trees remained unmoved. Fulton handed Wolf a glass; they sat across from each other on a soft leather sofa. The cushions sighed under their weight.

Wolf explained Suzi's behavior, added, "I don't know if she's scared, lying, or frustrated that you and your wife aren't taking it seriously."

"If I wasn't serious, you wouldn't be here. As for my

wife"–and he let out a breath–"she has a questionable sense of humor."

"Where is your wife?" Wolf said.

"Out."

Wolf looked over at a painting that showed the front of a large white building surrounded by palm trees. Fulton sat still long enough for Wolf to count the palm trees and make up his mind. He downed the scotch and said, "What's on your agenda the next few days?"

"I have a meeting tomorrow with the CompuSoft people. We're making the final arrangements for the buy-out. If it goes well my lawyers will put the papers together."

"What about Suzi?"

"She has school, but we've been keeping her home."

"Tomorrow I want you to let her follow her normal routine. I'll keep an eye on her for three days. You will pay me ten thousand dollars now with more expected if this turns into something and I need more than three days."

Fulton put his glass on the center table, went to a large desk in a corner. He lifted a black metal box from a drawer, unlocked it with a key, and began counting out American greenbacks.

"Here's twelve thousand," he said, holding out the thick stack for Wolf. "Whatever it takes, Wolf. Suzi is the only thing I have that's worth a damn."

————

WOLF BEGAN THE NEXT DAY. He followed Suzi as her mother drove the girl to school but spotted no suspicious vehicles or other individuals watching the girl.

After school Suzi's mother picked up the girl and a few of her friends and dropped them off at the mall. Wolf stayed with the girls as they shopped, hanging back. Nobody but him, as far as he could tell, was watching her.

Suzi and the girls prowled around, shopped, ate some food, shopped, and shopped some more. Only an expert could vanish into the crowd, and Wolf knew all the tricks from too many years living in the shadows. Nobody had melted into the waves of people. Suzi bought another stuffed animal that her friends appeared to approve of. When Suzi's mother picked them up, Wolf continued following, and still saw no sign of any extra attention being paid to the girl.

Wolf parked a ways away from the Fulton home when Mrs. Fulton turned up the drive. Another vehicle, a black Lincoln, departed at the same time. Wolf counted four people inside the Lincoln. Fulton's negotiations were over for the day. Wolf remained in his car and watched the house. It looked as if Suzi's story wasn't holding together.

———

WOLF BOUGHT a Coke from a sidewalk hot dog vendor, entered the park, and found a bench, the wood of which was partially wet from a recent sprinkler blast. Wolf sat anyway. He popped open the Coke and tore open a fresh bag of broken bread pieces. He tossed a few pieces on the ground. Within seconds, pigeons emerged from hiding, swarming the bread. Wolf tossed more. While the pigeons bopped and cooed and gobbled the bread, Wolf replayed the events of the day.

Feeding pigeons was good, cheap therapy. He told them about Murray Fulton, both verbally (but quiet) and in his head, bouncing around ideas. The birds could be trusted not to repeat anything; their cooing sometimes punctuated a thought in just the right way. But Wolf knew that as soon as the bread ran out, even if he hadn't finished talking, the pigeons would find another benefactor. Fickle beasts. But they served his purpose.

By the time he'd gone through half the bag, he knew he needed more input. Two heads were always better than one.

Wolf tossed the remaining bread pieces at the sea of pigeons, grabbed his Coke and left the bench.

——————

SUZI'S AFTER-SCHOOL mall routine duplicated itself the next day.

Wolf sat at a small table in the crowded food court. He ate a slice of pepperoni pizza that had been glazed with grease. He didn't really swallow the bites as let them slide down his throat. Suzi Fulton sat laughing with her trio of girlfriends. They'd stored the day's packages underneath the table.

Nobody, as in the day before, appeared to have any interest in Suzi Fulton.

Later, a pair of teenage boys joined the girls. Wolf used the crowd for cover when Suzi gathered up her packages and departed with one of the boys, a stocky, shaggy-haired kid in a long black coat, blue jeans.

Wolf tailed the pair to the parking lot where the shaggy-haired boy held open the passenger door of an old Chevy Nova. Suzi stowed her packages in the back and jumped in. The car's body sported several dents and chipped paint. Wolf wanted to lecture the boy on the proper care of fine automobiles but ran for his Camaro instead.

Wolf almost lost the Nova on the busy expressway. The old car looked like a wreck, but the young man could make it move. Wolf kept up once the traffic cleared. The Nova led to a quiet suburban neighborhood where the young man stopped in the driveway of a two-story home with an immaculate lawn, blooming rosebushes.

Suzi left her packages in the Nova, followed her companion inside.

Wolf remained parked a few houses away. He didn't shut off the engine. It made sense for Suzi to make up her story. Her parents were so caught up with being rich celebs that she needed this sort of thing to get their attention. She didn't behave like somebody who was frightened by a stalker.

WOLF SHOWED up at Fulton's home a few hours later. Fulton ran out the door, holding a cell phone above his head, shouting Wolf's name. Wolf shut the Camaro's door and Fulton shoved the phone at Wolf. A red flush covered his face. "They called! They have Suzi!"

Wolf stared at the man, his heart dropping into his stomach. He'd followed the Nova from the suburban home after Suzi and her boyfriend departed, but lost the car on the freeway, and headed for the Fulton residence to intercept. Wolf grabbed the black-haired man's arm and led him back into the house. They entered the study. Fulton's wife, Kimberly, sat on the sofa in a trim white pantsuit, black hair down to her shoulders. Her smooth, pretty face showed that she required no Botox. She looked Wolf up and down as her husband made introductions and did not say hello, but instead turned her eyes to the floor.

Fulton dialed his cell phone's voice mail and handed Wolf the device.

Suzi's voice was obvious enough. "Daddy!" she screamed. Another voice, male, "Fulton. No cops. We'll call again. You mess around and the kid dies." Click.

Suzi's mother turned to Wolf; Fulton, mouth open, took back the phone.

Wolf wandered over to the window and looked out at the pink evening sky. He couldn't see the rolling hills or the trees. He wished the peace outside was something he could have inside.

Fulton started talking. The cops had already visited and said Suzi's boyfriend had been run off the road. The boyfriend, Daniel Stark, suffered a concussion and several broken bones and now lay in a hospital room. Stark, at the scene, told the cops that two men grabbed Suzi before he lost consciousness. Fulton added, "I've called in a few favors to keep this quiet, but it won't stay that way for long."

Wolf wanted to speak but could not. He clenched his right fist as tight as he could until his fingers hurt. His pulse pounded in his head.

Wolf parked in the back of the Lexington Club. He spotted Gulino's black Lincoln SUV right away and parked next to it. Gulino's driver noticed him as he exited the Cadillac. Wolf ignored the man. He entered through the rear door and walked through the kitchen. The head chef, wearing a stained white apron, told him he couldn't be in there; Wolf ignored the man and passed through another door to the quiet dining room.

Carlo Gulino, one of the two mob capos in the city, sat at his usual booth slurping spaghetti. He sat alone, but he had guards at nearby tables who spotted Wolf and were poised to pounce. Wolf slid into the booth.

Gulino looked up with a full mouth but showed no surprise on his face. He swallowed and wiped his mouth, set his fork down and said, "You should have called first."

"No time for that." Wolf explained the situation, adding, "We may be dealing with amateurs but the whole thing seems very organized and that means either the outfit is involved, or you know who is."

"Would I kidnap a child?"

"Your people might."

"Why I tolerate your smart mouth I don't know. Kidnappings bring Feds. I got enough attention from the Feds without giving them something like this to try and pin on me."

"I'm blitzing," Wolf said. "I'm going to tear this town apart until I find that girl."

"Do what you gotta do. If you find out some of my people are involved, take care of them however you see fit."

"You don't know of any new players in town?"

"Not a thing."

"Somebody does."

"Go find that somebody. It's what you do best. I'm going to finish my lunch now. This chat is over."

Wolf slid out of the booth without a good-bye. The guards watched him. He ignored the guards. The maître d' stood by the kitchen door with a grim look on his face so Wolf left by the front door.

———

WOLF DROVE from the Lexington Club to an apartment building across town. He drove with his hands tight on the wheel and his jaw clenched so tight that his teeth hurt.

He knocked on the apartment door and the raven-haired woman who answered smiled and leaned against the door. She wore a black spaghetti-strap dress that muted her curves, but she was still stunning.

"I'd say I'm surprised," said Petra Sanchez, the daughter of the city's other mob capo, "but you never come by unless there's a problem."

"I'll only take a few minutes."

"I've heard that before." She grinned and let him in. They sat out on the deck. Wolf refused a drink. Petra sipped iced tea. On any other visit Wolf would have taken in the city view; today it did not interest him. A pigeon landed on the deck rail, but Wolf paid no attention.

He told her the problem same as he told Gulino; when he was finished, Petra said, "Why not go see my father directly?"

"I don't have time for a four-hour round trip," Wolf

said. "If not Gulino and not your pop, who is behind this?"

"My best guess would be one of the independents."

"That's a long list."

"I'm sure you'll figure out how to narrow it down."

Wolf stared off into space a moment. The pigeon flapped his wings and flew away.

"Is this one personal for you, Wolf?"

"Maybe."

"Tell me."

Wolf stood up. "Later," he said. "I'll let myself out."

"You weren't kidding," Petra said. "Less than ten minutes total." She raised her voice as he continued for the door. "I think that's a new record for you, Wolf!"

WOLF RETURNED to his home to rest; he had a big night ahead. He slept on his bed, clothed, and dozed off while staring at the spots on his ceiling.

My best guess would be one of the independents.

At 10,15 p.m., dressed head-to-toe in black, Wolf raided the basement poker game run by Nate Mason, a small-time operator whose game catered to pros who wanted to play off the grid. At the point of a shotgun Wolf robbed the game, stuffing the cash into a tote bag, keeping the players and the two guards covered with the double-barrel howitzer. He told them that somebody knew who had kidnapped the Suzi Fulton. He wanted to know who. Everybody would hurt until somebody told him who.

Around midnight, at a large mansion in the heart of the suburbs, Wolf kicked in the front door. Men and women in the front room screamed as he fired the double-barrel into a grandfather clock. The ancient block fell in a thousand splintered pieces. The women were dressed for work–that is, not wearing much–while the gents were there to pay for services for sale. A gunman who tried to show Wolf out got a butt stock in the face for his effort, and Wolf told Jenny Samson, the madam who ran the place and arrived after the gunner, that if she knew who had kidnapped Suzi Fulton she had better cough up and there would be pain until she did. To motivate her, he took out an incendiary stick, pulled the pin, and tossed it under the drapes. The fire rapidly spread; Wolf slipped out as the ceiling sprinklers blasted a shower of water and the bulk of the house began evacuating.

Two a.m. The semi turned off the freeway and followed the ramp to Fremont Street, passing a construction site which was currently dormant. It made the perfect place for a sniper to hide.

From behind a concrete barrier, Wolf fired single shots from a high-powered rifle. The front tires of the cabin exploded, and the cab sank into the ground, stopping the rig. As the two-man crew jumped out to inspect the damage, Wolf approached cradling the rifle.

The contents of the semi didn't interest him, but he knew it contained smuggled and stolen goods meant for fencing by small-fry hood Tommy Dugan. The crewmen dug for their own hardware, but Wolf shouldered the weapon and one look at the big hole in the barrel made the pair freeze and put up their hands.

"You tell your boss," Wolf said, "that I want to know where Suzi Fulton is. Everybody is going to hurt until I find out."

It was the same message, delivered over and over throughout the city; Wolf hoped the seeds would produce fruit. And quickly. Otherwise it was a waste of time and the people who got angry with him weren't the kind of people one wanted to have a beef with. But he didn't mind making enemies. He didn't exist to make friends. He existed for himself and what little good he might accomplish—because long ago he had made a promise that he wouldn't waste what remained of his life. Anybody who thought otherwise would see the difference after the night finally ended.

————

"You've been busy," Inspector Callaway said.

Wolf stood on the roof of a downtown building, watching as Callaway caught his breath and straightened his topcoat after climbing the fire escape.

It was the next day, a cloudy and muggy day. Rain threatened but it was still warm.

"A lot of people are saying your name," the inspector said, "and they're not happy."

"I'm on a case."

"On a rampage is more like it. What's going on?"

"I told you."

Callaway held back his frustration, but it showed on his face. Nobody knew Wolf's first name, not even Callaway, and they'd shared many private moments such as this. Nobody knew where Wolf had come from, but, for some reason, he'd made the city his home, making connections with cops and crooks alive. He operated on the fringes in between. Callaway didn't think he was dangerous, though plenty did; wasn't entirely sure he was a good guy, either. Callaway did know that some-times Wolf came in handy. But he also, sometimes, was a real pain in the neck.

"When you start robbing poker games and burning down brothels, you're doing more than working a case."

"I have a client to protect."

"Murray Fulton, by chance?"

Wolf frowned.

"Witnesses say you're asking where his daughter is," Callaway said. "Something like this you need to leave to the cops."

Wolf laughed. "You don't have any more on her whereabouts than I do."

"So, your stunt didn't work?"

"Let's just say we haven't seen results yet."

"There's a contract out on you. Came across it a couple of hours ago."

Wolf frowned. He hadn't been followed to the meet; had seen no evidence that anybody was giving him more of a look than normal. He also hadn't been tipped off.

"Ten grand. Dead. Nobody wants you alive. I'm not even sure I do."

"All I'm worth is ten grand?" Wolf grinned.

"You've declared some sort of war on the independents. They don't have much cash to begin with. If you were taking on Sanchez or Gulino–"

"This has nothing to do with them."

"Are you sure?"

"I asked," Wolf said.

Callaway shook his head. "You're going to get some-body killed. Maybe even yourself."

"If what I did last night has resulted in me being

marked for a hit, then that part of the job is done. This will be over soon."

"You figure whoever comes after you will have the answers you're looking for?"

"Uh-huh."

"You're playing with the girl's life. One of these days you're going to pay for all of this. Nobody's luck lasts forever. Nobody runs forever, either."

"Are you done?"

Callaway let out a breath but never took his eyes off Wolf. "I suppose."

"Then I'll see you in church."

———

WOLF STOPPED five feet from his door. Whoever had broken the lock did a lousy job. The wood near the deadbolt had split.

Wolf took out .45, kicked the door, somersaulted through the doorway and came up tracking movement on his left. The gunner who stood there fired twice but Wolf's forward momentum carried him away from the path of the shots. He fired twice in return. The gunner fell back and crashed against a bookcase.

Wolf dropped, pivoting, as the second shooter emerged from the kitchen. The shooter raised a shotgun. The hot blast of buckshot seared Wolf's face. Shot parted his hair. The automatic in his hand spoke once. The shooter spun around, colliding with the kitchen doorway, stumbling to the carpet. As he tried to get the shotgun up again, Wolf closed the distance and kicked the shooter in the mouth. He plucked the shotgun from the man's hands and tossed it. As the shooter held a hand to his bloody mouth, Wolf dragged him from the doorway to the middle of the carpet. Kneeling, Wolf jammed one knee into the man's groin, hauled his bloody hand away, and stuck the hot muzzle of the pistol into the man's cheek.

"Who sent you? Tell me!"

The shooter mumbled through his bloody mouth. He spat blood but missed. Some of the spray landed on Wolf's jacket. Wolf shoved his knee further and the shooter's eyes widened. He cried out. Wolf repeated his question.

"You'll kill me anyway!"

"I love how you tough killers always turn into little bitches when the gun is pointed at you," Wolf said. "You get a fifty-fifty chance because I may kill you if you talk or not."

"It was Marcus!"

"Victor Marcus? Why? Tell me!"

"Why do you *think*, dummy?"

Wolf stepped back and kicked the killer again and when he was sure the man was unconscious he left the apartment.

As he drove away, the Cadillac's motor humming, he stared through the windshield, his face an unemotional stone, jaw locked tight. He relaxed his grip on the wheel, took a deep breath, and slowed down. He would have answers soon.

———

WOLF DROVE to one of his back-up apartments and slept the rest of the day. The coming night promised to be as busy as the night before.

Victor Marcus ran the Bay Meadow Poker Room, which sat on prime real estate just off the 80 freeway. He was a small fish in a big pond but stayed clear of Outfit activity despite leanings to the contrary which once got him in trouble. He always followed the same routine once he closed up the card room for the night. A round of night clubs, bars, an expensive dinner. Wolf patrolled his favorite haunts for over an hour and finally found him at a jazz club called the Hedley Club. Wolf took a stool at the bar and ordered a beer. Patrons crowded the place; the band played an up-tempo number; from where Wolf sat, he could watch Marcus and his lady friend in the mirror behind the bar.

The bartender handed Wolf the glass and Wolf took a long sip. Anchor Steam. Good stuff. He took another sip and set the mug on the counter.

He wasn't expecting a major engagement tonight, but it helped to be prepared. Along with the Colt .45 under his left arm, he had a .32 Derringer clipped to his right wrist.

Marcus and his girlfriend laughed, talked, ate, drank. Marcus appeared to have no muscle nearby, but he only had one fellow who provided that, Nitro Randall, who had it in for Wolf over losing a poker game.

Wolf sipped his beer and watched the woman. She was a little thick, with long black hair, and she filled out her blue cocktail dress so that every curve could be taken in. Gina Abato. Certainly not a civilian. She didn't run a racket of her own, but she liked the lifestyle and was never far from the arm of somebody connected to graft one way or another.

A waiter delivered food to Marcus' table. Wolf

finished his beer and left. They were going to be a while. He wanted to make sure he could follow them when they departed. Back in the Cadillac, which he had parked on the street, Wolf left the driver's window cracked. The meter he had fed still flashed a green light. Plenty of time left. He called Fowler but there was no news, no contact from the kidnappers. Wolf explained he might have a lead and to hold tight. Fowler's voice shook a little when he said okay. After he ended the call, somebody tapped on the window.

"Get out of the car, Wolf."

Wolf looked at the man outside. The man held a matte-black automatic pistol. His name was Nitro Randall, second-in-command to Victor Marcus, and a man Wolf constantly had trouble with. Wolf once cleaned him out in a poker game, and Randall had yet to put it behind him.

Wolf opened the door. Nitro stepped back. Wolf got out of the car. He kept the door between him and Nitro. Nitro held the gun low and close to his body.

"Let's see those hands."

Wolf placed his hands on top of the doorframe. He said, "This is a public street, Nitro."

They were on the side of the street not heavily traveled. Two darkened warehouses fronted the street, with a dark alley between them, smelly Dumpsters near padlocked doors. Not the most inviting place for pedestrians, who preferred the opposite side. So, while they were relatively free from people observing them, a gunfight would attract attention no matter what.

"Get in the alley," Nitro said.

"You could have shot me in the car and collected the

money, Nitro. Once again you prove you have an educated mind."

"That would have been too easy. Get in the alley."

"Why don't you just shoot me right here?"

"Don't tempt me."

"But you won't."

"Really?"

"Your boss wants to know why I'm following him. Saw me, did he?"

"You can't hide for shit."

"Funny. I wasn't trying. Why would Victor offer ten grand for my head when you'd do it for free?"

"He didn't put up the contract."

"I got a couple guys in my apartment that say otherwise. Or at least they said they were sent by him."

Nitro laughed. "You really want me to explain? Get in the alley."

"No."

"You're gonna make me blast you right here?"

"I didn't hit any of Victor's operation the other night, Nitro."

"He wants to collect the money. Same as I will. And I get to get even with you at the same time."

"Ten grand is chump change to you. I took more than that from you at the poker game."

"Don't remind me."

"So, pull the trigger."

Nitro darted his eyes around but still hesitated.

"He took the girl, didn't he?" Wolf said. "Why?"

"Like I'm gonna talk."

"Is he working for somebody? With somebody?"

"Get in the alley, Wolf."

"You won't shoot because you don't know if I'm

working alone or not. Nobody believes it was just me the other night, do they?" Wolf grinned, but the grin faded fast. He said, "Were those guys at my place ordered to kill me or take me prisoner?"

Nitro opened his mouth but never spoke the words. Wolf snapped his right arm down and forward, the .32 Derringer released from the spring clip and slipping into his hand. He fired both barrels. The two pops echoed up and down the street and Nitro Randall grunted, stumbling back. He struck the warehouse wall and collapsed to the ground. He wasn't dead. He still had enough energy to point his gun at Wolf but by then Wolf had the .45 out and planted a third slug between Nitro's eyes.

The big automatic sounded like a cannon and the noise battered up and down the street. Wolf dropped back into the Cadillac and drove off. People saw him. He saw them watch him. The car was just another tool; once he disposed of it, he'd get another.

Now he had a solid lead. Knowing this, he drove with a loose grip and relaxed shoulders. He was close. Suzi would be home soon.

———

THE KEY TURNED in the lock. Wolf gave the silencer at the end of the Colt's barrel a reassuring twist but made no move to turn on the light. The door opened. Gina Abato entered alone.

She switched on the light, shut the door, turned and screamed. Wolf bolted from the couch as Gina dug into her purse and pulled out a pistol. Wolf batted it from her hand and shoved her onto the couch. She glared at him with hot eyes, her face flushed red.

"What do you want, Wolf?"

"Your boyfriend needs to answer some questions. He was supposed to come home with you."

"Well he didn't. He's got stuff to do."

"Like what?"

"Like what the hell do I know?"

"A kidnapped girl, by chance?"

"I told you–"

"Right, you're deaf and dumb. Call him."

"What?"

"I said, call him. Tell him to come back. Tell him you need him."

"No."

"Gina, there's a sixteen-year old girl who's being used as a pawn and Victor is up to his eyeballs in it. He has some sort of beef with her father, I'm not sure what it's all about. She's an innocent girl and shouldn't be involved. You may hang out with punks, but you aren't one of them."

"Gee, thanks."

"Call Victor."

"You'll kill him!"

"He's just a middle- man. I want to know about the one pulling the strings."

"It's probably that bimbo I saw at his place the other night."

"Get a name?"

"No, but I almost ripped Victor's balls out. He told me it was just business and when the lady told me the same thing I cooled down. He's probably meeting her again tonight."

"Call him."

"All right, all right." She rolled off the couch and reached for the phone on the side table.

"I'll dial," Wolf said. He moved around her to pick up the phone, dialed Marcus's number, and handed the phone to her.

Marcus didn't answer right away, and Gina almost hung up, but Wolf gestured with the silenced Colt and she kept waiting. Finally, she started talking. She tried the vamp act, first–"Come back, I *need* you"–but when that didn't work she started to stutter.

Wolf grabbed the phone and said, "This is Wolf talking, Victor. Nitro's dead and Gina's next unless you get your ass over here and talk to me."

Marcus uttered a string of curses and hung up.

Wolf put the phone down.

Gina Abata scrambled off the couch. She tried to scream but the cry choked off when Wolf grabbed her hair, pulled her back onto the couch, and smacked her. This time she fell unconscious and lay on the couch with the skirt of her dress hiked up and one strap off a shoulder. Wolf unlocked the door, switched off the light, and sat in the dark once again. But not before he picked up Gina's gun and stuck it in a pocket.

———

VICTOR MARCUS DIDN'T BOTHER with a key. He tried the knob first. The door opened and he stopped short once he saw that no lights were on. The hallway light lit him up, though, and Wolf saw the gun in his hand. He also saw enough of his legs to take aim and shoot him just above the left knee. The Colt .45 made a sound like a heavy book falling onto a desk.

Marcus yelped, staggered forward and fell. The gun he held flew from his hand when he hit the floor. He reached for it, struggling to move closer. Wolf stood up, kicked the gun away, shut the door and turned on the light. He held his smoking gun on Victor Marcus who stared at him with a grimace.

"I'm gonna kill you, Wolf! If it's the last thing I do!" He lunged for his gun, trailing blood on the carpet. Wolf went over to the gun and put a foot on it. Marcus spat at him but stopped crawling. He lay on the carpet panting.

"Where's the girl?" Wolf said.

"I'm not telling you anything!"

"Nitro told me enough that I can hand you over to the cops and the Feds," Wolf said. "You'll be looking at hard time when they get done with you."

"Is there a second choice?"

"Sure. Tell me who organized this, and I'll give you a chance."

"To get away?"

"Why not?" Wolf took his foot off Victor's gun and stepped back. He put the .45 away and covered it with the flap of his jacket.

Marcus eyed the automatic hungrily. He said, "Trish Newman is the twist I'm working with. It was her idea. She came to me for muscle."

"Who is she?"

"She works for a company Fulton is trying to take over. Everybody knows that when he does that, he'll close the company and lay off every single employee. Trish is using the kid to make him back off."

"Doesn't make a lot of sense."

"Well you'll have to ask her about it."

"Okay."

Wolf kicked the gun toward Marcus. He grabbed it and fumbled getting his finger on the trigger. When he raised the gun, he was smiling but Wolf had Gina's gun out and already pointed at Marcus. Marcus's eyes widened and he hesitated. Why he did not fire Wolf didn't think about or really care about. He could never figure out what made Victor Marcus tick. Instead he pulled the trigger twice.

He stepped over Marcus's body as he wiped off Gina's gun. He dropped the gun near the couch and left the apartment.

————

WOLF WENT into his bedroom and donned jeans, black sweater, black boots. From a trunk in his bedroom closet, he gathered a selection of telephone equipment, and steered the Camaro across town. He stopped at the phone pole down the street from Trish Newman's condo complex. She lived in a small condominium with her husband and autistic 10-year-old nephew, of whom they were legal guardians. Wolf slung his pack of gizmos and climbed the pole to the junction box. The pack moved back and forth across his back, some of the gear digging through the sweater as he shifted his body for each step. His stomach quibbled at the height, so he didn't look down.

The quiet slanting rooftops scattered around, with their lit windows, were of no interest; he thought he heard a cat meowing from a nearby tree. A football game blared from an open window somewhere, with accompanying shouts and cheers. Popping open the junction box he examined the wires and connections and plugged in a portable handset. The CompuSoft files had provided Trish Newman's number, but the wires weren't labeled that way. He had to call each line in order to get the one he needed. He rang the lines, asking for Trish each time. After a string of wrong numbers, a woman with a rough smoker's voice said, "This is she."

"Missus Newman," Wolf said, "you're one of the lucky few who have been chosen—"

"Not interested." Click.

Wolf tugged her line free from the jumble of wires and exchanged the handset for a small remote transmitter which he connected to the box's power supply and spliced to Trish's line. A light on the transmitter flashed when he pressed a small button on the side.

A car with a clanking engine drove by, but did not stop.

Wolf closed the box, shimmied down, and climbed back into the Camaro. He screwed an earpiece into his left ear and drove to a new parking spot directly across from the condo complex. Easing back the seat, he took a cigar from his inside jacket pocket, snipped the end, and lit the tip with a gold Zippo. By the time half the cigar had turned to gray ash, the earpiece crackled to life. Trish answered the call. The voice on the other end said the girl was having a freak out—Wolf heard a female screaming in the background—and what should they do? Trish told them to handle it. The 24 hours were almost up so she wouldn't be a bother for long.

Wolf tossed the cigar out the window and the earpiece on the floor. He exited the Camaro and collected a black dart pistol from the bag of tricks in the rear compartment. He crossed the street.

The husband answered the door. He started to open his mouth and Wolf fired a dart into his chest. The husband's eyes rolled back, and he dropped. Wolf stepped over the unconscious man. Trish, on the couch, screamed over the sounds from the television; Wolf's next dart struck her above the heart, and she plopped against the cushions. The 10-year-old nephew, unsteady on his feet with a glass of milk in one hand, gaped at Wolf from the kitchen. Wolf fired a third time. The kid dropped, the milk spilling over his clothes, the floor. Wolf jammed the dart pistol in his belt, slung Trish Newman over his shoulder, grunting under her weight, and hustled out to the car.

————

THE JUICE WORE off within a half-hour. Wolf hadn't loaded the darts to full capacity. He watched the woman's eyes open, look around the cold room, and wince from the bright light which blasted up her nose. She was a stocky brunette with short hair. Leather straps confined her to a hard metal chair, a metal table between her and Wolf. The lamp sat on the table.

As the woman squinted, Wolf removed the Colt .45 auto from under his arm. He leaned into the light so she could see the muzzle. He said, "Tell me where Suzi Fulton is, or I'll blast your head in half."

A professional would have argued the logic of such a statement, Wolf knew. But Trish Newman was not a professional.

IT TOOK two hours to reach the cabin, the Newman's weekend home, where the hired goons held Suzi. Wolf stopped the Camaro at the end of the long driveway. Decked out head-to-toe in black, he stayed in the shadows as he advanced up the length of the drive. Pine needles crunched under his boots and crickets stopped chirping as he moved. In the old days, his enemies would have taken the sudden silence as a sign of impending attack; tonight, he need not worry. The chilly night cooled the sweat on his face and neck. His Colt .45 auto rode on his right hip; he carried a stubby Heckler & Koch MP-7 submachine gun in both hands. He squatted in the dry brush near the front, examined the porch and windows. The drapes were closed.

Wolf aimed the MP-7 at the door, fired three controlled bursts that destroyed the hinges. A kick sent the splintered door spinning inward. He moved into the house. Down the hallway in front of him, a man in baggy clothes dug behind his back and hauled out a pistol. Wolf stitched him stomach to chest and continued forward.

A girl screamed from somewhere in the house.

A gunman with long hair swung around a corner across the room and zeroed in as Wolf pivoted, triggering the HK. The slugs split open the gunman's head.

Wolf followed the wall down the hallway to the living room. The screaming continued, getting louder. As he cleared the corner, two more males in T-shirts and jeans let a few rounds go, Wolf dropping low, the wall spitting chunks of plaster and dust over his head. Some of the plaster landed on his neck and trickled down his back. Wolf hit the floor and fired. The MP-7 burst drilled one of the shooters; the sub gun clicked empty. The last shooter jumped from cover, firing with one shaky hand, the rounds going wide, as Wolf clawed the .45 from leather. The man in black fired twice. The slugs struck the last shooter in the chest; his mouth opened in a silent scream, and he landed atop his dead compatriot.

Wolf's eyes hit the screaming, wrecked figure on the floor near the television, covered in soiled blankets. Suzi. She wore only a T-shirt, no pants or underwear, hair in tangles, face cut and inner thighs bloody. When Wolf approached, she screamed, pulled knees to chest, tried to bury her head in the blankets. Wolf found clean blankets in a hall closet and returned to the girl. That's when she peeked at Wolf's face, stopped screaming, and started crying. Wolf wrapped her up and carried her out.

WOLF BROUGHT Suzi to the home of a doctor, Harry McNeil, whom he trusted to keep his mouth shut and not phone the police. He'd patched up Wolf on several occasions. The doctor and his wife treated Suzi in a back bedroom. Wolf went into the kitchen, flicked on the lights, and called the Fultons and told them how to get there.

Wolf sat at the kitchen table with elbows on knees, staring at a spot on the tiled floor, shoulders in a deflated slump. He wondered where he had gone wrong. Maybe he should have investigated the Compu-Soft people sooner. Maybe he should have brought in help to follow Suzi. He wouldn't have lost her in traffic that way. Maybe he should have–

He stopped. It didn't make a difference anymore.

———————

FULTON SHOWED up with wife Kimberly in tow. She didn't take the news well, and McNeil's wife led the crying Mrs. Fulton into another room while the doctor said to the father, "She suffered a lot of blunt trauma. No fractures or broken bones, though. The physical wounds will heal. The rest? Well, I know a good rape counselor if you'd like her name."

Fulton asked to talk to Wolf out in the car. They sat in the back seat. The doors seemed to block any air from getting in, and the two men sat silent within the silence. Fulton's body shook. Wolf sat still, breathing evenly, hands in his lap, unable to comfort the man. He knew all too well that there would never be any comfort after this night.

"Tell me everything that happened since I saw you last," Fulton said.

When Wolf finished the story, Fulton said, "Where is Trish now?"

"Where I can get to her."

"Options?"

"She can be found in an alley with a broken neck, or I can turn her over to you."

Murray Fulton said nothing for a long time. Just stared at his shaking hands.

"She'll say this wasn't supposed to happen," the black-haired man said. "She'll say she only wanted me to back out." He looked into Wolf's eyes. "Give her to me. My people will take it from here."

Fulton let out a breath, rubbed his face with both hands, but held together. Wolf sat with him until he was ready to go back inside.

———

THE NEWS and gossip rags picked up the story once Suzi checked in to the local hospital and cops arrested Trish Newman. After the CompuSoft president did the perp walk following her arraignment, Fulton spoke to reporters. "Whatever it takes, my family will get through this. My daughter will be okay." The Botox had worn off, and his face made lines here and there as he spoke.

A few nights after the arraignment, Inspector Callaway joined Wolf on yet another rooftop.

"The contract on you hasn't been canceled," Callaway said.

"I know."

"What are you going to do about it?"

"Later," Wolf said. "I'll deal with it later."

Callaway laughed. "I bet." He paused a moment. "I hope I never catch you with a gun, Wolf. I'd hate to...well, you know."

"I'm glad we have that understanding."

"How desperate can somebody be to organize a kidnapping?"

"This would have been the second time Trish lost a job because of Fulton," Wolf said. "She has a huge responsibility to her nephew. The way things are right now, that was all it took to push her over."

"I'll never figure people out," Callaway said.

Wolf found sleep difficult once the trial began. He'd dream about smashing into the cabin over and over, but he never reached Suzi in time.

A few months later a jury convicted Trish Newman and sentenced her to ten years in prison, and Wolf figured that was the end, until the following morning. He stood out on the deck watching the morning traffic in the streets below with the television news in the background. The anchorman began talking about a young woman who, the previous evening, had sped onto the Richardson Bay Bridge, reached the middle of the span, and tried to drive off the side. The concrete side-wall stopped her. The young woman blasted out of the car and leaped over the wall.

Three days later, Suzi Fulton's body washed ashore. She'd joined all the others in the dark.

When authorities escorted Trish Newman into prison on a bright sunny day, Wolf watched from the parking lot with his right fist clenched tight. He'd have to wait ten years, but he'd see her again. One last time.

THE RED RUBY KILL

There are only three rules in this city:
Never cheat your partner,
Never take more than your share,
And never cross

— WOLF

THE DEADBOLT NEEDED EXTRA FORCE, but it turned.

Wolf entered the apartment. The occupant was dead, presently lying in a downtown alley from which he had ambushed Wolf twenty minutes earlier. He didn't get off more than one shot before Wolf nailed him with a pair of .45 slugs in the chest.

The contract was still open.

Not that Wolf had heard otherwise. He hadn't heard much at all about the contract since learning that he was a marked man. Nobody on the street knew anything. Some would more than happily lie if it meant getting rid of him, but even the informants he trusted were stumped.

But somebody wanted him dead. After his last adventure, somebody had put out the contract. Worse, the dead killer wasn't local; that meant either imported talent, or every trigger-happy gun thug was on his way to try for the ten grand. It didn't even seem worth the effort.

Wolf searched the place. No furnishings except a futon for a bed and couch along with a small TV and scattered personal items. Nothing to indicate there was a second occupant. He found clothes in a suitcase. An x-ray proof bottom fell away once he found the lock and revealed two boxes of .45 ammo and a gun to shoot it with, a Government Model like the one Wolf carried. He put the ammo in his jacket pockets and the extra pistol in his belt. One could never have enough guns, especially ones that weren't traceable to him.

He sorted through the personal items. Usual electronic junk. Wolf found a cell phone, but it was of the use-it-and-lose-it variety with no stored numbers.

Wolf locked the apartment and left. There wasn't

anything worth stealing, but the cops would ID the body soon enough and he wanted the place secure so they could try their luck.

Back on the street he climbed into his car and drove off.

He had an appointment.

———

"YOU'RE NOT OUT OF BREATH," Wolf said.

Inspector John Callaway of the city police smiled as he crossed the rooftop to where Wolf stood.

Callaway said: "I've been hitting the treadmill."

"You're looking good."

"How can you tell?" Callaway wore his usual rumpled suit and overcoat combo over his overweight frame.

"Your face is brighter."

This was their routine. When Wolf needed to talk, they met on a rooftop. Climbing fire escapes was getting to be part of a regular routine for the inspector, but he still didn't know what to make of Wolf. The man had no past that anybody knew of, never spoke of one; the only thing that gave Callaway a clue that Wolf had even existed in the past was the silver locket he wore. Callaway saw the chain, as always, hanging from the other man's neck, but Wolf kept the locket hidden under his shirt. The inspector hadn't worked up the guts to ask what it meant yet.

Wolf might have been sketchy, but Callaway had to admit he came through for the cops a lot and offered services for-hire to anybody who needed a friend. Some guys got dead when Wolf went into action, but it was usually only the bad guys.

Callaway said: "What's up?"

"Find any stiffs today?"

"Who have you hypothetically killed?"

"You may recall that there's a contract out on me."

"Yeah."

"Somebody tried to cash in. Not a local. Either out-of-towners are arriving to give it a shot or the mastermind is bringing in his own people."

"Where might this alleged wanderer be?"

"Potentially in the alley near 16th and Bryant."

"What happened?"

Wolf told him.

"I'll ask about it," Callaway said. "That's not my territory."

Wolf handed Callaway the apartment key. "Found that on him along with a post-it in his wallet with the address. I stopped by but there wasn't anything good."

Callaway pocketed the key. He pressed his lips together.

"What's on your mind, John?"

"Rumors. You say this guy isn't local. I'm going to bet money he's from the east coast. We've heard that several free-lancers are coming here, but nobody knows who they are or anything else. Your guy may be the first positive ID we get."

"Ten grand is nothing to people like that," Wolf said. "They're coming in for something else."

"You stirred up a hornet's nest last time. Maybe they think you're a threat."

Wolf shrugged. "I probably am. It would be nice to

know what I'm threatening, though." He started for the fire escape. "Let me know what you find."

"Goes both ways," the inspector said to Wolf's back. "I'm not your secretary, Wolf."

————

SOMEBODY HAD to know something about Callaway's rumors.

After finishing his scrambled eggs and bacon the next morning, Wolf wrote a list of the independent operators not connected to the Gulino or Sanchez syndicates, but allowed to operate in the city as long as they kicked back a portion to the two capos. The contract had gone out after he hit the indies looking for Suzi Fulton's kidnappers. It didn't matter if he'd hit a gang not involved. *Somebody* knew where she was or who had her, and he made them hurt until one delivered the information.

But by then it had been too late.

Wolf examined his list and figured it was enough to start. Shaking cages had worked once; now it was time to shake some more.

————

THE ASSASSIN HAD FIRED his first and only shot through the windshield of Wolf's Cadillac. As he drove on the western expressway, wind whistled through the hole. Wolf figured he'd plug it with chewing gum until he properly replaced the windshield. He chewed the gum as he drove.

He exited the expressway and drove along city

streets to the Shipwreck Bar, owned and operated by the first name on his list: Nate Mason. Mason also ran an off-grid poker room which Wolf had raided while looking for Suzi Fulton, stealing twenty grand. Want somebody to talk? Hit 'em in the pocket-book.

Wolf parked at the curb. As he reached the sidewalk, he took the gum from his mouth and stuck it in the hole in the windshield.

He left his jacket open for easy access to his Colt .45 should the gun be required. Wolf entered the bar.

No customers this early. The neon beer signs were off; a morning chat show played on the muted TV on one wall. The bartender's welcome smile faded as soon as he recognized Wolf's map.

"No trouble here, Wolf," the bartender said.

"I want to talk with Mason. Tell him to come out and there won't be any trouble."

"He's not here."

"Where else would he be?" Wolf glanced at the back-office door, where a small camera hung above the door frame.

"He's out–hey, stop!"

Wolf moved briskly along the bar. The bartender shouted, "Stop!" again and pumped a shotgun. Wolf spun around with the .45 out and pointed at the bartender's left eye.

"You didn't get up this morning to go home in a box," Wolf said.

The bartender swallowed a lump, put down the shotgun and raised his hands.

Wolf winked and pushed through the office door. Nate Mason sat behind his cluttered desk with folded arms. He'd been watching the exchange on a black-and-white TV monitor.

"Thought he had you dead-bang," Mason said.

"You'd have liked that."

"You took twenty big ones from me the other night. How am I going to collect if you're dead?"

"You can have it back," Wolf said. "I don't need it. But I'm not giving it back unless you provide something in return."

Mason cocked his head to one side. "What?"

"Who wants me dead?"

"Maybe half a dozen guys."

"So, tell me."

"Can't tell you what I don't know, Wolf," Mason said, but his cocky grin said otherwise.

"You're lying."

"Yeah, maybe I am. Maybe I heard a story in the bar. I hear lots of things in the bar."

"Tell it."

"You're in the way. You and another guy."

"In the way of what and who's the other guy?"

"You got a pal named Harry Ames, right?"

Wolf frowned. He hadn't heard anybody say that name in a long time, not since Harry had gone to prison for stealing cars. Prior to that, Wolf had helped him out of another jam. And prior to *that*, Harry knew Wolf in his past life. They had grown up together.

"What about Harry?"

"He's getting out of the slammer today. He's on the kill list, too."

"I'm losing my patience," Wolf said, leaning across the desk. "Who?"

"I don't know who, okay? That's all I heard. Somebody wants you and Harry dead so they can pull off some caper, sounded like something Harry was into before he went to jail, okay?"

Wolf went around the desk and punched Mason once. Mason's face slammed into the desk. He grabbed his head, spitting curses between painful moans.

"That's all I know!"

"It better be. Or I'm coming back here."

"When you come back you better have my money."

Wolf laughed and headed for the door. "I'll put a bow on it."

———

WOLF CONSIDERED the story as he drove. The chewing gum kept the wind from whistling so only the engine noise mingled with his thoughts.

Neither Harry nor his girlfriend, Maggie, had sent word about needing more help. If Harry didn't know he was a marked man, he couldn't very well sound the alarm just yet. Wolf needed to get to him first. On the freeway, his cell rang. It was a disposable cell that he used only to communicate with Callaway, and the inspector's number showed up on the caller ID.

"Yeah."

"Come to the morgue," Callaway said. "I got another stiff for you."

A chill went up Wolf's back.

"Do I know him?"

"He's a pal of yours, yeah."

———

WOLF'S scarred face remained still as Inspector Callaway pulled the morgue drawer open. The metal track moaned. Wolf looked at the wrapped body as a mist of chilled air touched his cheeks. The detective unzipped the body bag and exposed the dead man's face. Wolf moved more of the bag aside to reveal the jagged lightning bolt tattoo on the dead man's left shoulder. He tilted his head to the side and said: "That's Harry."

"You're all broken up."

Wolf eyed the inspector.

Inspector John Callaway shoved the drawer closed. The gold ring on his finger twinkled from the overhead light. "Okay, you did what I asked. Let's go talk about it."

Wolf turned for the door, pushed through.

The inspector caught up and said: "Harry Ames corresponded only with you and his girlfriend the five years he was away. On the day he's released somebody shoots him on the sidewalk. Why?"

"I'm wondering that myself."

Wolf reached for the exit door and Callaway grabbed his arm. "I'm serious."

Wolf twisted out of the grip and put a hand on the cold metal crash bar. "I'm hungry," he said.

They went outside and walked half a block to a hot dog vendor. They took their hot dogs to a nearby bench. A nearby tree filtered the sunlight.

"So?" Callaway said.

Between bites Wolf relayed his conversation with Nate Mason. The inspector listened but said nothing until he'd finished eating.

"Okay, you know you're on the right track," the inspector said. "I'm sorry about your friend."

Wolf wadded up the hot dog wrapper and tossed it in the trashcan to his right. He stood up. "Be seeing you."

Callaway watched him go.

WOLF SPENT the rest of the day playing poker and didn't return home until late. He'd lost every cent he brought to the game. He had wanted a distraction; that had been impossible. He parked his car at the curb beneath the humming streetlamp, in front of his apartment building. A few cars rumbled up the road. Wolf looked up at the half moon. When he lowered his gaze, he saw a black sedan parked down the street. One man sat inside, watching him. Wolf shook his head and went up the steps to his second-floor apartment and went in. The place still smelled of fried eggs and bacon from breakfast. On the dusty table to his left he placed his wallet and keys and flicked a light switch.

"'Bout time you got back."

Wolf turned. Two men sat in his living room. One occupied his worn plaid recliner and had a fat mole on his left cheek and wore a shirt too tight for his round belly. The other lounged on the couch with Wolf's copy of *Scuba* with the front cover folded back. The second man had a mop of red hair. Both looked at him with dark eyes.

The man with the mole had spoken and raised his arm to show Wolf a gun.

"We were just about to leave," he said. "Frankie said five more minutes. I think he just wanted to finish whatever he was reading."

"I'm going to have to visit Monterey," the redhead, Frankie, said, holding up the magazine. "Looks really nice."

Wolf grunted.

"Take off your jacket," Mole Man said. Wolf removed his coat and dropped it on the carpet. He raised his arms, rotated, faced the two men.

"I don't have a gun," Wolf said.

"And I give to *Make-A-Wish*."

Frankie put the magazine down and came over to Wolf and clamped one hand on the flesh between Wolf's neck and shoulder, pressing hard. Wolf winced, stiffening, and the redhead ran his other hand up and down Wolf's body. He stepped away. "Clean, Mal."

"Good," Mal the Mole Man said. He stood up.

"You're not here to shoot me," Wolf said.

"Perceptive. No. We wanted you and Harry out of the way–especially you–but Harry didn't have what we wanted. So that means the contract is cancelled because now we need you alive. So, where are they?"

"Where's what?"

"The letters. We want the letters."

"And I'd like to get back the money I lost tonight."

"The cards weren't good to you? That's too bad. Texas Hold-'em or Stud?"

"Stud," Wolf said.

"I like stud poker," Mal said. "I think Texas Hold-'em has ruined the game. Everybody and his uncle is playing Texas Hold-'em."

"Are," Wolf said.

"What?"

"Everybody and his uncle *are* playing Texas Hold-'em."

"Oh, you're a grammar cop, is that it? Frankie, show him what we do with grammar cops."

The redhead moved his upper body and Wolf braced for a punch, but the other man lashed out with a kick instead. The redhead's leather shoe smashed into Wolf's belly. Breath rushed from Wolf's mouth; he hit the floor hard. The redhead took a step, slammed another kick into Wolf's side. Wolf couldn't breathe, started to roll. The redhead bent a little and punched Wolf in the face.

Wolf lay on his back, curled, sucking air. Spots filled his spinning vision. His body throbbed. He clenched his teeth and groaned.

"Ask him again, Frankie."

The redhead stepped closer. His foot came back. Wolf uncoiled his body and grabbed the redhead's ankle, twisting, and the redhead thudded down. Wolf crawled over and pumped his fists into the redhead's body. The man had hard muscle beneath his clothes. Wolf punched harder. Sweat dripped into his eyes.

Mal the Mole Man said, "Hey!"

The redhead's coat fell open, revealing a shoulder-holstered automatic, and Wolf snatched out the gun. He sprang to his feet, snapped back the gun's action, and covered the Mole Man. He kept his teeth clenched, holding his side.

The redhead started to get up. Wolf put a foot on his face and pressed hard. The redhead made a hurt sound.

Wolf said: "I oughta shoot you both and be done but I'm sure you're only the small fry and I want the big fish. I also promised my landlady there would be no more killings in my apartment."

Wolf stepped back and Frankie rolled over and

pushed to his feet. He eyed Wolf without blinking. His eyes went to the automatic. "I want my gun."

"I'll give it back after show-and-tell tomorrow," Wolf said.

The Mole Man and Frankie reached the door and went out. Frankie glared back at Wolf, but he didn't try to take his gun back.

———

WOLF LEANED against the wall a moment, and then set the gun on the table with his wallet and keys. It was a well-worn Browning Hi-Power. A flash of gold on the back strap caught his eye. There were words engraved and inlaid with gold.

TO FRANKIE FROM FIFI WITH LOVE.

Wolf laughed. He surveyed his apartment. Nothing seemed out of place or damaged.

He picked up the scuba magazine and shoved it in the trash. He took a bottle of Anchor Steam from the clanking fridge and sat at the kitchen table, planting a foot on one of the legs to keep the table from wobbling. He drank some beer. What letters? Wolf's brow furrowed and he took the bottle into the second bedroom, which he'd set up with a desk and bookcases.

From a desk drawer he removed a folder and sorted through letters post-marked from the state prison. Harry's letters. He read through them. None of Harry's jabbering provided a clue. They all mentioned Maggie, his girlfriend. Wolf read the last letter and noticed what looked like doodles drawn in the margin and the word *Emerald* above the scribbles.

Wolf brought the folder back to the kitchen and looked out the window. What secret did the letters hold?

———

WOLF TRIED the Starbucks where Maggie worked, having to stand in line with the rest of the morning crowd. The line went out the door. When Wolf finally had a chance to ask about Maggie, a coworker told him she hadn't shown up for her shift. Wolf took his green tea and drove to her apartment; when she didn't answer, he picked the lock and went inside, loudly announcing his arrival. He froze in the doorway and heard her sobs from the living room. Wolf found her curled up on the couch in the spartan one-bedroom, the furniture used and worn, spots dotting the carpet. She seemed relieved when she saw him. She sat up and scooted over to make room, wiping her eyes with the back of one hand.

"We're going to find out who did this," Wolf said.

"Uh-huh."

"They've already tried for me," he said. He gave her the rundown.

Her eyes widened. "Am I a target, too?"

"More than likely. When you weren't at work, I was afraid they'd got you first."

"And they want his letters?"

"I think they snatched him as soon as he hit the street, and when he couldn't give them what they wanted, they shot him. That's when I suddenly became more valuable alive than dead. Luckily for them I'm hard to kill.

"I read the letters Harry sent me," Wolf continued, "and couldn't see why they're so important. Did you two have a code he may have hidden in the text?"

"I don't think either of us is that smart."

"Do you still have the letters he sent?"

"Of course."

"Here?"

"No, safe deposit box."

"At the bank?"

"It's a girl thing," she said.

Wolf put his arm around her and squeezed. "We gotta get going. Pack a few things. You're staying with me until this is over."

She jumped up and went down the hall to her bedroom. Wolf remained seated and stared at a spot on the carpet. The spot offered neither answers nor insight. He stared at it anyway and let his mind wander.

Presently Maggie announced she was ready, and they hit the road.

Wolf had driven halfway down the block when Maggie said: "Why do you have bubblegum stuck in that hole?"

———

WOLF STOOD guard near the safe deposit area in the back corner of Maggie's bank, ignoring curious looks from customers who weren't sure a man with a rough face, dressed in black, should be there. None of the bank staff bothered him. She emerged with a wrapped bundle of envelopes and they drove to Wolf's apartment. He scanned the block as they exited the car. No sign of surveillance, but that didn't mean anything. Frankie and Mal and their friends could be anywhere. Wolf didn't want to stay long and figured a move was in order. Too many bad guys knew where he lived.

While Wolf packed a few supplies and clothes, Maggie sat at the kitchen table and read all the letters beginning to end. When she finished, she found Wolf in his bedroom zipping a suitcase closed.

"Why did you keep the letters, Wolf?"

He turned to her. "If you read them you know why."

"You've known Harry longer than me."

"We grew up together. He knew me before I became the man I am now."

"So, when you helped us last time, that wasn't just a job, was it?"

"No," Wolf said. "I came out here to change my life. Harry came out here to get away from the heat back home. I wish he had followed my example, but you can't make a man do what he doesn't want to do."

She bit her lower lip.

Wolf pulled the locket up from his shirt. "Harry's sister gave me this."

"I didn't even know he had one."

"She's gone." Wolf tucked the locket away.

She swallowed the lump in her throat.

Wolf said: "Did you find anything we could use?"

"No."

Wolf frowned. "Who did Harry work with when he was stealing cars?"

"The only name I remember is Oscar Lane," she said. "They used to do a lot of drinking together. I don't know where to find him."

"Shouldn't be hard if he's still in the city." He grabbed his suitcase. "Let's get out of here."

———

SHE CONTINUED READING the letters in the car, shifting between ones written to her and then to Wolf.

"Did you notice the doodles in the margins?" she said.

"Yeah, chicken scratches."

"Mine have them too. Is that a clue?"

"Might be."

Wolf pulled up in front of the Carlton Hotel downtown and let the valet park the Cadillac. He secured a two-room suite on one of the upper floors. Maggie chose a bedroom and began unpacking while Wolf left his suitcase on the couch.

"I'm going out," Wolf told Maggie once they had unpacked. "I want you to stay put. You can leave the room but do not leave the hotel. Do not make any calls."

"Can I breathe?"

"Through one nostril only." He grinned.

She let out a short laugh. "I needed that."

"We have to stay under the radar," he said. "Order whatever you want from room service if you get hungry."

"Where are you going?"

"I'm gonna track down Oscar Lane and anybody else Harry knew. Somebody always knows something."

———

WOLF DROVE in circles for half an hour, checking for tails, making sudden changes in direction. Nobody followed him. What were Mal and Frankie waiting for? What were they organizing behind the scenes?

Wolf parked across the street from a small corner restaurant with open air seating in front. He walked past the patrons enjoying the sun and wandered to the back of the place. Concrete floor, rough wooden tables on wobbly legs, odd-looking art adorning the walls; it wasn't a classy place, but the food was good. Wolf found Charlie Mott inhaling a plate of greasy tacos. The fat man sat in a back corner, alone. Wolf pulled a chair from another table and sat down in front of the other man.

Mott swallowed a big bite and wiped his mouth with a well-used napkin. "Hiya, Wolf." He licked the stubby fingers on his right hand and extended the hand to Wolf.

Wolf said: "Pardon if I don't shake."

Mott laughed. "What brings you here?"

Charlie Mott wrote the gossip column for the city's newspaper. He knew almost everything going on around town and had plenty of sources lined up to fill any gaps.

"Where do I find Oscar Lane?"

"That dumb cuss? He keeps a low profile these days. Runs a gambling concession for the Chicago Outfit, somewhere downtown."

"He kicks back to Gulino and Sanchez?"

"Right. He's square with them. No trouble."

"Would anybody want him out of the way?"

"Don't know. Is somebody working an angle?"

"I'm not sure yet." Wolf explained the situation.

"Fascinating," Mott said. He took another big bite, slurping loose pieces of shredded meat into his mouth. Drippings trickled down his chin. He wiped with the napkin. "Can I buy you some chow?"

Wolf said: "Not right now. Did Lane take over the concession before or after Harry went to jail?"

"After. They worked together, right? How come he wasn't busted with Harry?"

"That's a good question, Charlie."

"There is one other thing," Mott said. "Biff Holden. He's the guy who used to have Lane's job. Been hanging around the Lexington Club with your pal Gulino trying to get a job."

"Thanks, Charlie." Wolf rose to leave.

"Anytime."

————

CARLO GULINO SAID: "Why are you always interrupting my lunch?"

"You're a captive audience," Wolf said as he sat across from Gulino in the capo's regular booth. The seat was very soft. Other diners ate and spoke quietly, so Wolf kept his voice down.

"You're not going to try to run if you haven't finished your spaghetti," Wolf said.

Carlo Gulino always well dressed in an expensive suit, his tie tucked inside his shirt, ate lunch every day at the Lexington Club, one of the city's most exclusive gathering places for distinguished gentleman. Wolf wasn't sure if Gulino fit the category, but the club continued to accept his dues. Gulino ran part of the city's mafia syndicate; another capo, Pedro Sanchez, ran the other, and despite past differences the two existed peacefully. Wolf maintained an arms-length relationship with both.

Gulino wrapped spaghetti around a fork and shoveled it into his mouth. Just noodles and tomato sauce, no meatball. Wolf didn't understand how anybody could eat spaghetti without meatball. Wolf glanced at the two tables off to the side where the bodyguards sat. They eyed him with little interest. They were used to his unannounced appearances.

Wolf turned back to Gulino and watched the man eat. Gulino ignored him. Wolf waited.

Finally, Gulino said: "What is it this time?"

Wolf explained.

"So far this doesn't mean anything to me." Gulino swallowed more spaghetti.

"If Harry left a stash or something of value, there'd be word about it. Hear any stories like that?"

"Nope."

"What about Oscar Lane? He was Harry's partner in the stolen car racket."

"I know Oscar." Gulino ate some more.

"I know you know Oscar. Tell me about him."

Gulino shrugged. "He never misses a payment."

"How did he come to you?"

"Chicago called. They needed to replace a guy in their betting network who tried to swindle some cash. They told me Oscar was going to be their new guy. I'd still get my cut for letting him work in the territory."

"How did he get in with the Outfit?"

"Not my business."

"Where do I find him?"

"He has a joint on Bernardo Lane, number 4500."

"Oscar replaced Biff Holden," Wolf said, "and now Holden is pestering you for a job. What about that?"

Gulino ate another bite and made no comment.

"You gonna give him some work?"

"Jesus, Wolf, what *don't* you know? Not on his life."

"Why?" Wolf said.

"He *swindled* from Chicago. He can stay here and cozy up to me all he wants but if I give him a spot that would make Chicago mad and I don't need that."

"Why does he stay in the city?"

"Because if Chicago comes over here and kills him, that would make *me* mad."

"Mob politics," Wolf said.

"You done?"

"Could Holden be trying something against Lane that connects with Harry?"

"I just collect the kick-back, Wolf. I don't know nothin' about things like that. Don't you look at me all butt-hurt, either. If I did, I'd probably tell you. Are you *done*?"

"I guess."

"I don't know why I tolerate your mouth, Wolf."

"Deep down, you know you're gonna need me someday."

Gulino scowled. "Become a ghost before I have your skull kicked in."

"Ghosts don't have skulls, Carlo." Wolf winked. Gulino turned red. Wolf made his way out.

———

On his way to Oscar Lane's place, while sitting in traffic, Wolf telephoned Callaway.

"So, who's the stiff?" Wolf said.

"Your buddy in the alley was from New Jersey," the inspector said. "We've tracked three other shooters so far and identified two of them. Malcolm Ford and Frankie Riley. They have connections with New Jersey, too, but their record shows they've worked all over the country."

"I've met Mal and Frankie," Wolf said, and told Callaway about their visit to his apartment. "I guess the third guy was in the car."

"Why do they think they can get what they want from you?"

Wolf told him about the letters and his conversations with Maggie and Gulino and said: "Do you have them under surveillance?"

"Can't spare the men," Callaway said. "Plus, we have no proof that they've done anything wrong yet."

"Funny how that works."

The inspector said, "So you're looking for Lane now?"

"Yes," Wolf said, "and also I need to know who Harry shared a cell with. We need to find out if he talked about a stash or something he was going to collect when he got out."

"It would have to be fairly valuable for all this fuss."

"I'm sure it's worth a thousand lives, John," Wolf said.

———

THE ADDRESS PROVIDED by Gulino turned out to be a flower shop. Wolf stood on the sidewalk, looking at the rose display in the window and figured Gulino had sent him on a wild goose chase. He went inside. He didn't know anything about flowers, but the store was loaded with them. It was a color explosion of red, white, purple, blue, and colors Wolf didn't know the names of. It was also an explosion of sweet scents mingling together to produce an immediate allergic reaction. Wolf's nose itched as he stepped up to the counter and asked the skinny redhead if Oscar Lane was in.

The girl said yes, picked up a phone, and told Oscar about the visitor. She cupped her hand over the mouthpiece and said: "Are you Mister Wolf?"

Wolf nodded.

"It's him," she said, and put down the phone. Lane emerged from a back-office door and extended his hand.

"If you hadn't shown up, I'd have gone looking for you," Lane said. "Come back to my office."

Wolf kept his mouth shut. A welcome reception made him feel funny. He never got anywhere without hitting somebody or taking out his gun. He kept his jacket unbuttoned, though. Old habits and all that.

Oscar closed his office door and gestured to a chair in front of a clean desk which only contained a computer and telephone. Both men sat. Wolf's eyes darted around. Motivational posters hung on the walls and a picture of two little girls sat atop a corner filing cabinet. Oscar Lane said: "I'm sick about Harry. What do you need to know?"

Wolf examined the other man's face. Oscar Lane had a full head of dark hair, smooth complexion, very white teeth. His eyes and breathing gave him away. The eyes looked sad and he breathed fast.

Wolf explained his investigation so far, leaving out nothing.

Lane sat back, his chair squeaking, and folded his arms. "I don't understand any of this. Harry wouldn't have had any options when he got out. I had a job lined up for him, something nice and quiet."

"What did he have that's worth killing over?"

"Maybe two grand, stashed somewhere. Chump change."

"Did you and Harry have a code hidden in his letters that you could decipher?"

Lane laughed. "Nothing like that. I wish."

"What do you know about Biff Holden?"

"He used to have my job."

"I know that, and Gulino won't hire him. Would he want to muscle you out of the way?"

"No way," Lane said. "Chicago wants him dead. He could steal some money from me, but not much. There are bigger scores to make if he wants easy cash."

Wolf described Malcolm Ford and Frankie. "Stay armed in case they visit."

Lane patted a hard lump under his left arm. "Way ahead of you. Let me know if you need anything, any time of day."

Wolf started to rise, then sat again. "One more thing."

Lane blinked.

"How come Harry got busted while you end up with this cushy Outfit job?"

Lane blinked some more.

"It doesn't make you look good at all, Oscar," Wolf said. "Maybe Harry had something on you that he could expose; now that he's dead, you're safe."

Lane's upper lip twitched. "I don't mind you asking your question, but there's no way I would have killed Harry. No way."

"Then tell me a story."

"We boosted cars, right? Stripped them for parts or sold them to these Russian guys who took them back to Moscow because everybody in Russia wants a car and they'll pay through the nose to get one. So, Harry is at the warehouse one night, and I'm off with this babe I was banging at the time, and the cops bust in. He had just enough time to call me and tell me what was happening. I changed motels twice a week waiting to see what would happen, but the cops never came near me.

"And Harry kept his mouth shut," Lane continued. "I know it wasn't easy for him, but he did, and he served his time, and the day he gets out somebody murders him. You think I'm gonna do that after what he did for me? That's why I had a job for him. A reward. Get it?"

Wolf stared at Lane for a few moments.

"As for how I got this job," Lane said, "I met a guy who knew a guy. You know how it goes."

Wolf kept looking at Lane. The other man held the gaze. Wolf said: "Okay," and left the flower shop. It was time to see Biff Holden face-to-face and learn if the former Chicago man had a reason to murder Harry.

———

BIFF HOLDEN HAD enough money to secure the penthouse atop the Excalibur Hotel, so he wasn't hurting too badly–for now, Wolf thought. Wolf drove into the neighborhood and found no parking on the street. Every inch of curb space was taken. He found a pay lot and gave the attendant a $20 to park the Cadillac.

He crossed the busy lobby to the elevators and took a long ride up to the top. The doors opened in a small reception area where two men in suits stood behind a desk. One approached Wolf with his gun out while the other spoke into a walkie-talkie.

Wolf raised his hands. "You greet everybody like this?"

The big man, with sandy-gray hair and a mustache, patted Wolf down and removed his Colt .45. Two more guards entered from a doorway behind the desk and stood waiting for instructions.

"Tell Biff that Wolf is here for a chat," Wolf said.

"Why?"

"Our mutual friends Oscar Lane and Carlo Gulino have a message."

The goon with the walkie-talkie spoke into it again; the response was immediate: "Send him back."

"We're keeping your gun 'til you leave," said Mustache, as the two goons who had emerged from the other door led Wolf out of the reception area.

The goons led Wolf into a plush living room where Biff Holden stood waiting. Drapes covered the windows, but sunlight beat through the fabric and lit the room. A blonde-haired woman wearing a long dress sat on a leather couch, sipping a cocktail. Holden dismissed the troops and offered Wolf a drink.

"Splash of bourbon," Wolf said.

Holden moved his bulky body over to a mini-bar and poured some Jim Beam Black into a glass. Wolf took the drink.

Holden didn't hide his smile. He said: "So what's the news from our friends?"

"False advertising, I'm afraid," Wolf said, swallowing the drink. "I came here for information."

Holden's smile faded. His lips formed a flat line. "I oughta throw you out."

"Sure."

"I got four guys outside with guns and you got nothing, and you stand there and say 'sure'?"

"You don't want any trouble, Biff."

"But you like trouble."

"Sure."

Holden let out a grunt. "What do you want?"

"Harry Ames."

"Don't know him."

"A friend of mine that somebody murdered. He used to work with Oscar Lane. Oscar Lane has your old job and Gulino won't hire you. I figure that makes you pretty upset."

"You're right."

"Some people think Harry had a stash somewhere that's worth a murder or two," Wolf said. "Tell me you aren't trying to grab the loot to set yourself up somewhere else."

"I don't know what you're talking about," Holden said. He told his blonde friend to go into the bedroom and shut the door. The blonde obeyed without comment. Holden crossed the room to a set of windows and looked out. Wolf kept his distance.

Holden said: "As soon as I step outside this city, Chicago will have me killed. The only thing keeping me alive is that they don't want to step on Gulino's toes. He won't hire me for the same reason. So, I'm stuck. Like in purgatory. It doesn't matter if I make a score one way or another. I'm a dead man as soon as I leave, and if I pull a fast one and stay here, I'm asking for it in a different way. See the spot I'm in?"

"I see it, but your name keeps coming up. People like us don't just fade away, Biff."

Holden turned to face Wolf. "The hell do you mean, people like us?"

"I wasn't always a good guy."

"I hear a lot of debate about what you are, Wolf. Nobody knows for sure."

"But everybody knows I give them a square deal. So, level with me."

Holden laughed. "I didn't lay a finger on your friend. I'm not moving in on Lane. If my name's coming up, it's only because I'm part of Lane's back-story now. He has my old job. I got caught dipping into the till and now I'm paying for it. I'm exiled here. A nobody. That's a punishment worse than death for people like *us*, isn't it?"

"For some of us," Wolf said.

"So, I don't know why you're here, Wolf."

Wolf just grinned. "That works in my favor," he said. "Thanks for the drink." Wolf set the glass on a nearby table. "Tell your goons I'm coming out and I want my gun back."

Holden glared at Wolf's back.

———

THE SUN WAS SETTING, and the sky displayed a pink tinge as Wolf returned to the Cadillac. He called Callaway for a meet. He arrived before the inspector, climbed to the roof, and stood overlooking the city while he smoked a cigar and watched the sun go down. The street sounds drifted his way before being swept away in the wind. Presently the fire escape started vibrating against the building's bricks, Callaway's distinctive grunts reaching Wolf's ears. Callaway swung his legs over the side and joined Wolf near the edge.

"Any luck today?" Callaway said. He brushed off the front of his overcoat. There was a mustard stain on one lapel.

"On one hand it looks like zero," Wolf said. "On the other, who knows? I think I stirred up some things. Lane says he had a job lined up for Harry; Holden says he's just a poor schmuck stuck between life and death, and nobody knows anything about what Harry would have been killed for."

"You don't buy it."

"Not a bit."

"What about Harry's girlfriend?"

"What about her?"

"Maybe she knows more than she's letting on."

Wolf paused a moment; then, "I suppose I have to consider that."

"And while you consider that, you can look at this." Callaway removed a slip of paper from a pocket of his coat. A burst of wind almost yanked the paper from his hand. Wolf took it.

"Those are the guys that Harry shared a cell with," Callaway said. "Hal Murdock and Jimmy O'Toole. Both got out a few months before Harry."

Wolf put the paper in his own pocket.

———

WHEN WOLF RETURNED to the Carlton, he found Maggie asleep in the second bedroom. He fixed a bourbon and water and went out on the deck to smoke another cigar and think about the day. When he finished, he turned in and stared at the ceiling for a long time before finally dozing off.

He had breakfast on the table when Maggie woke up the next morning. While they ate, he told her what happened the day before.

"So, we're no closer to an answer," she said.

"We'll get an answer. Don't worry."

———

HAL MURDOCK, one of Harry's cell mates, drove a forklift for a car parts warehouse. Wolf waited in the parking lot as the noon hour approached. When Murdock left the building and walked out to his car, Wolf intercepted him.

"I'm a friend of Harry Ames," Wolf said. "I need to ask you some questions."

"I saw in the paper he'd been shot," Murdock said. "Too bad."

Murdock was shorter than Wolf, with thinning hair and a scar on his right cheek. He breathed heavily.

"I want to know who shot him."

"Look, I'm out of that life," Murdock said.

"Whoever shot Harry wanted something from him. Did he talk about anything while you two were in jail? Anything of value he may have hidden?"

Murdock thought for a moment. "He said he had something, but he never said where it was. I remember telling him you can't have too big a nest egg from boosting cars, and that made him laugh. The cars were just a side gig, he said. The real loot he'd stolen from somebody else, but he never said what it was, or who he took it from."

"No clue at all?"

"Sorry. I gotta go, food truck's pulling in and they don't give us much time." Murdock retrieved a cell phone from his car and joined his coworkers at the arriving food truck, which advertised Mexican dishes cooked to order. Back in the Cadillac, Wolf considered the man's words. Now a bigger picture was forming.

———

NEXT NAME ON THE LIST: Jimmy O'Toole. He worked at a deli on the wharf. With saltwater and fish smells lingering in the air, Wolf parked a block down from the restaurant and found O'Toole behind the counter hustling orders. Wolf waited at a corner table until the traffic flow subsided and then approached.

When O'Toole saw the big man in black, his eyes bulged, and he bolted to the back of the deli.

Wolf leaped over the counter and ran down the narrow back aisle as O'Toole crashed through the rear door and out into the alley. Wolf shoved through the door, saw O'Toole running left, and charged. He closed the gap quickly and tackled O'Toole. They hit the dirty alley floor hard, O'Toole screaming as breath left him. He sucked air in short gasps as Wolf hauled O'Toole upright and pushed him against the wall.

"Don't–don't–*don't hurt me!*"

"I'm not going to hurt you!"

O'Toole tried to knee Wolf in the groin but the man

in black deflected, pressed harder against the other man.

"Why are you running?"

"I know too much!"

"About what?"

"The rubies!"

"What rubies?"

"The ones Harry took!"

"Harry was a friend of mine and I'm trying to find out who killed him. Now tell me what you know."

"No!"

O'Toole struggled some more but could not break Wolf's iron grip.

"If I wanted you dead," Wolf said, "we wouldn't be talking."

O'Toole stared at Wolf's face and, a moment later, relaxed; so did Wolf. O'Toole slid down the wall to sit on the ground. Wolf stepped back. "What rubies?"

O'Toole held up a hand while his breathing returned to normal. When he wasn't gasping any longer he started talking.

"Harry told me about some rubies he took, real expensive gems, he said. He stole 'em from some guy, I can't remember who, somebody who lived in a big mansion outside town. Harry went into the house and busted open the safe."

"Why did you think I was here to hurt you?"

"Because I've been jumping at shadows ever since Harry got killed."

"Has anybody been following you?"

"How could I tell? I guess if they wanted me dead, I would be, like you said."

Wolf frowned. The killers weren't interested in

whoever else may have known about the rubies; they were waiting for something, or somebody, to make a move, before they struck again. And Wolf had seen no sign of Frankie Riley and Malcolm Ford since the first meeting in his apartment. That meant–

"Watch your back, Jimmy."

Wolf went back down the alley to his car.

"Hey!" O'Toole called out. "What about me?"

———

WOLD AND MAGGIE sat at the table with Harry's letters.

"We need to sort out the ones that have those doodles on them," he said. They began sorting.

Presently they had the four "doodle letters" together and Wolf, with scissors, cut out the portions of each letter that contained the doodles. He worked the pieces like a jigsaw puzzle until the lines ended with the words *Emerald Lake* atop a drawing.

"It's a map," Maggie said. She sat back in the chair, stunned. "Harry drew a map!"

"Sure. To Emerald Lake. What's there?"

"The rubies. Wolf, that's where he buried the rubies!"

"He's marked a spot near the shoreline. Twenty paces from the dock, looks like."

She said: "Let's go dig them up!"

Wolf said: "Not yet."

"But–"

"Cages, Maggie. I still have to rattle some cages."

———

INSPECTOR CALLAWAY CLIMBED the fire escape with ease, but his stomach hurt a bit as he stepped onto the roof. He paused a minute to catch his breath. The night air cooled his face. Wolf waited at the edge of the roof, smoking one of his cigars.

"Damnit, Wolf. Why do you always–"

"Haven't you ever noticed," Wolf said, "that up on a roof, nobody can spy on us?"

Callaway frowned and thought a moment, said: "Good point. Where did you learn that trick?"

"My past life." Wolf grinned.

Callaway said: "So. Rubies, huh?"

"What did you learn?"

"I found no information about any such thefts in the last ten years. If Harry took them prior to that, he's sure sat on them for a long time, and I don't think he'd need to draw a map in his prison letters. Why do that, anyway?"

"He must have tossed the original map before he was sent away," Wolf said, "to keep anybody from finding it while he was gone."

"So, whoever he took the rubies from didn't report it."

"Or he took them from somebody who stole them from somebody else who never reported it and Harry lied to O'Toole about where he got them. Maybe whoever had the rubies first killed Harry."

"Could be," Callaway said. "I'm sure they'll fetch a nice stack of cash. Biff Holden would be my first suspect. He needs money. He can't stay in that penthouse forever. With a few million bucks he can get a new name, face, whatever he wants, and start over where Chicago will never find him."

"What about Oscar Lane?"

"He's pretty well set up," Callaway said, "but every crook wants a retirement score. He doesn't like working for a living any more than I do."

"Uh-huh. And Maggie?"

"Why am I doing your thinking for you?"

"I like hearing you say it." Wolf puffed on his cigar.

"Fine. Let me throw you a curve ball. Why would she kill Harry before he dug up the stones, if that's what she did? That's the part that makes no sense. Do you trust her?"

"I don't know," Wolf said. He turned to stare off into the night sky. "But I'll know for sure tomorrow night."

———

WOLF SPENT the next day paying visits to Oscar Lane and Biff Holden. He told them about the rubies and questioned them further. Biff feigned ignorance. Oscar Lane said he knew nothing about them, that Harry must have been working solo on that score.

Wolf returned to the hotel where he and Maggie said little to each other until the sun went down.

———

"HOW DO you know we aren't being followed?" Maggie said.

"We're not."

"We can't play around, Wolf."

"We're not being followed," he said. He gave the rearview a glance. "But you never know."

"This is nuts."

"Quiet now."

"We better find something."

They spoke no more as Wolf drove two hours outside the city limits to Emerald Lake. A posted sign said the lake closed at ten p.m. each night, but no gate barred their entry. Wolf eased his car onto the dirt parking area and stopped. He and Maggie exited.

Crickets chirped and the nearby water lapped the shore. Wolf scanned for any other visitors amidst the rustling trees while he checked his Colt .45. He had Frankie's Browning Hi-Power nine-millimeter as well.

Maggie said: "So?"

Wolf popped the trunk and pulled out a small shovel.

"Let's find the dock."

———

WOLF HAD redrawn Harry's map on a single sheet of paper and shined a pen flash on the page. He turned his back to the dock and pointed the pen flash back the way they came.

"Twenty paces," he said.

"Are you sure we're at the right starting point?"

Wolf began counting steps. His shoes sank into the soft ground. A twig snapped somewhere. Wolf continued counting and stopped a few feet from a tree. A bare patch in the bark of the tree had a jagged lightning bolt carved into it. The carving matched Harry's tattoo.

Maggie said: "Here?"

He handed her the pen flash. "Hold this."

Wolf pushed the shovel into the dirt. After four

scoops he heard a clank. The crickets, so faithful earlier, quieted to near silence as Wolf started digging around the metal box he'd struck. He tensed for action.

"Almost there?" Maggie said.

"Better believe it."

Wolf dug around the box, used the shovel blade to pry it out of the ground. He reached down, unlatched the lid, and stared at the red rubies winking in the moonlight.

"Nice," Wolf said.

Another twig snapped.

Wolf said, "Down!" and rolled into the dirt as single-shots split the night. Maggie, flat on the ground, looked wide-eyed at moving shadows in the trees.

Wolf fired twice. He handed Maggie the Browning and told her to stay put and crawled to the tree as two shots smacked the trunk, shards of bark pelting Wolf's face. He flinched. Shadows moved again. The gunmen were setting up a cross-fire. He could confuse that. Wolf charged forward, fired twice to the right, to the left, then hit the ground. His chin gouged the dirt.

Return fire crackled overhead. Another pair of shots snapped. A man screamed. Somebody opened up with a machine pistol. The third man. The rounds chewed up the ground near Wolf. The machine pistol flashed again; Wolf fired at the flash and the shooting stopped.

Wolf lay still, his gun trained to the left of his position. One of the shadows he'd fired at emerged from cover, started forward.

"Frankie?" Malcolm Ford's voice.

The figure stepped closer. Wolf raised his aim a bit.

"Frankie?"

Wolf inhaled a breath, let half out, held; the figure

took another step. Moonlight flashed on Malcolm Ford's face and before he could see Wolf, the Colt automatic spoke once.

Malcolm Ford took the round in the neck. He stood a moment, frozen, stunned, making choking sounds. Wolf fired again and the man's head snapped back as he fell.

Wolf stood, breathing again, and brushed the dirt from his shirt, jeans and face. He found Maggie back at the hole. She, too, was rising, but made no effort to get rid of the dirt on her clothes. "Are you hurt?"

"No." Wolf tucked the .45 into his belt. He picked up the metal box.

"Stop."

Maggie said: "Behind you!"

Wolf turned.

"Get rid of your gun," Biff Holden said. He stood in the open with a gun in his right hand.

Wolf tossed the Colt in the dirt.

"Now you, little lady."

The Browning dropped at Maggie's feet.

Another man emerged from hiding and joined Holden.

Maggie said: "Oscar?"

"Thanks for digging it up," Lane said. "You probably never figured that Biff and I were working together."

Wolf let out a grunt.

"Some detective," Lane said. He smiled. "Those rubies are going to set us up just right."

Holden said: "We'll give Gulino and Sanchez and Chicago a run for their money."

"Nice play with Mal and Frankie," Lane said. "I'm

sure if Mal found out he'd shot Frankie, he'd be crushed."

"And the guy with the machine pistol?" Wolf said.

"Just another of the stooges we imported," Holden said.

Maggie stepped forward. "You killed Harry, Oscar? *You killed your friend?* He trusted you!"

"No honor among thieves, baby."

Maggie charged at Oscar, screaming. She grabbed his gun arm and they wrestled on their feet. Holden moved out of the way to keep a clear shot at Wolf but in the time it took to move, Wolf had the .45 back in his hand and before Holden could fire, the .45 roared and Holden's face vanished in a flash of red.

Oscar shoved and Maggie stumbled and let out a cry as she landed, and Oscar raised his gun to fire, but Wolf fired first. One shot. Oscar dropped.

Maggie, on hands and knees, was crying when Wolf reached her. He helped her up and she leaned against him.

"It's all right now," Wolf said.

THE FIXER

There are only three rules in this city:
Never cheat your partner,
Never take more than your share,
And never cross

– WOLF

THE FIXER

WOLF SAID, "This chair makes my rear end hurt."

Gordy O'Rourke blew cigar smoke out one side of his mouth and grinned, showing yellow teeth, from across the small corner table. "That's the point," he said. "Make somebody's rear end sore and they leave and let another customer have the table which means I make money. We get guys in here on game nights who order one beer and a plate of wings and they sit for four hours watching a game, and you know what? I hope their ass is killin' 'em the next day because all that sittin' cost me maybe $1000 somebody else would have spent who ordered more than one beer and a bunch more food. You can bet those clowns stiff the girls on tips, too."

"The seats in the casino are padded."

"You bet." Gordy puffed on his cigar and sipped black coffee. "People are dropping money in the back room. You bet I want them comfortable."

"You're a mercenary if there ever was one."

Wolf ate another bite of his bangers and mash, aka

sausages and mashed potatoes. Gordy's cook spiced the meal just right.

Being Thursday, the place was packed. The noise covered their conversation. Gordy puffed his cigar some more. "Wolf, I'm glad you're here." Gordy looked down at the tip of his cigar. He reached into his shirt pocket and handed Wolf a folded note.

Wolf pushed his plate away, opened the note, read: REMEMBER MONA FRYE.

Gordy said: "A fat guy with a big nose brought that today."

"Who's Mona Frye?"

Gordy puffed his cigar. He signaled a passing waitress, a cute blonde with purple-streaked hair, for a refill; after she poured the coffee he said: "Somebody I used to know. She was murdered a long time ago."

"You?"

"No."

"Uh-huh."

"Somebody shot her," Gordy said. "I swear I blocked it out. It was twenty-five years ago."

"What about the guys you were running with in those days? Could one of them have sent this?"

"I haven't heard from those bums in ages. I don't even know if they're still alive, in jail, or what."

Gordy had worked on the fringes of organized crime most of his adult life and ran his gambling joint at the blessing of the local syndicate as long as he kicked back a percentage. He'd built a nice corner racket for himself and greased the local cops as well. Nobody ever bothered him, and he kept trouble to a minimum.

Wolf pushed the note back across the table. He glanced at the bar as the purple-haired waitress served a bald man who averted his eyes. The bald man started eating, ignoring an iPhone that sat beside his plate.

Wolf turned back to Gordy. "So?"

"I hate to ask but—"

"You think I'm going to say no?" Wolf said. "I owe you, Gordy. That's it. I owe you."

It was the kind of blood debt one could never repay, but Wolf never stopped trying.

When Wolf had needed help escaping from his former life, he reached out to Gordy, who sent his youngest son, Bobby, to lend a hand. Wolf indeed escaped but had to tell Gordy his boy had died in the process.

Wolf reached across the table and patted his friend's shoulder. "Go home and get rested. Wolf's on the job."

"Okay."

Wolf scooted his chair back against the wall. The A/C blast ruffled his shirt collar. He had a clear view of the bald man who was trying very hard not to look like he was watching them. "Go get me a glass of Bushmills first."

Gordy, half out of his chair, frowned.

Wolf smiled. "Trust me. And don't worry, you still have plenty of tables."

———

AN HOUR later Wolf followed the bald man to a home on the corner of a cul-de-sac in the suburbs. The bald man pulled his Chrysler into the garage while Wolf stopped his Cadillac at the opening of the court. Lights were on inside the house.

Up the street Wolf spotted a second car parked curb-side, near the fence that blocked the bald man's house from the street. Wolf left his Cadillac and strolled by the dark car. Nobody inside. On his reverse pass he saw the driver's door open a crack. He looked inside the glove box. The registration showed the name Michael O'Rourke. A brown paper bag sat on the passenger seat. Wolf took out two baggies full of pills, one obviously Vicodin, the other baggie full of what looked like amphetamines. Wolf shook his head. The kid was still on the junk.

Wolf tootsied to the fence, listened for a dog, and hopped over. He dropped into a line of rose bushes, and thorns pricked through his sleeves. He stayed put. The quiet back yard offered further assurance of no canines prowling for intruders. From his spot he saw the kitchen and dining room through patio doors. One of the sliding glass doors had been partially opened, and Wolf recognized one of the two voices engaged in a heated argument inside. He traded the hiding spot for the open patio door. The voice he didn't recognize shouted, "Wait!" and two pistol shots cut him off.

Wolf shoved through the patio door, ran from kitchen to living room and stopped short. The bald man lay on the soft carpet with two bloody holes in his chest. A young man standing over him with an automatic spun around, pointing the gun at Wolf, but his shaking hand proved he wasn't ready for a second kill.

"Put it down, Mike," Wolf said.

Michael O'Rourke, Gordy's oldest son, gaped at Wolf. Wolf closed the gap between them in one step and twisted the gun out of Mike's grasp. He said: "What are you doing?"

"This punk's been watching Dad since he got that note," Mike said.

"And he wouldn't talk, right? Can't blame you for tryin' but you cooled a small fish. Doesn't get us anywhere."

Mike stepped back his pointed jaw set tight. He had Gordy's green eyes and his mother's small nose. "I did–"

"Something stupid. Get out of here and leave this to grown-ups."

Mike rushed past Wolf and out the patio door. Wolf heard him thud up and over the fence. The other car started, and tires screeched. Wolf shook his head. He tucked the automatic in his belt and patted the bald man's coat pockets. He found the iPhone and pocketed it. Wolf took out a handkerchief, opened the front door, went out.

Back in the Cadillac, he drove further up the street and pulled into the parking lot of a basketball park and let the iPhone's glow fill the car. Wolf redialed the last number. A woman's voice said, "What is it?" and Wolf hung up. He put the device on the passenger seat and drove away. Presently the iPhone vibrated but Wolf didn't answer.

––––––––––

THE NEXT MORNING, back at his place, Wolf spooned poached eggs onto dry toast, sat at his wobbly kitchen table, and clamped a foot on one of the table legs to stop the wobbling. He ate quietly. He still occupied his Tenderloin apartment. He had thought about moving permanently to the Carlton Hotel during his last adventure, but once the threat to his life had been removed, he decided against it. He looked at the yellow spot on the tiled kitchen floor that no cleaner he tried could remove. The refrigerator clanked. Home sweet home. The place had the character a pristine hotel suite would never have.

With his mobile phone he called Gordy.

"Michael tell you what happened last night?"

"Yes." Gordy spoke with a heavy quietness.

"Give the boy a pat. He's looking out for you."

"Wolf–"

"Listen to me," Wolf said. "You keep Mike locked in a closet if you have to because I better not bump into him again. Also, our dead friend called his boss before he left the club. A woman. He saw us talking and I'm sure they know who I am, and they'll also know I'm not hard to find."

"If they come after my son for this, I'll cut them all down, I swear."

"My eggs are getting cold."

"I'd appreciate it if you had a greater sense of urgency, Wolf."

"I can't kill anybody on an empty stomach, Gordy."

"Well I didn't mean–"

Wolf hung up and finished his breakfast and then put water in a kettle.

———

WOLF SAT at his kitchen table with a cup of tea and the iPhone in front of him. The mobile had not rung since the night before. Whoever was on the other end knew its owner was dead, the phone now in the possession of his killer or the cops. Wolf was neither, but they didn't know that.

Wolf scrolled through the contacts folder, which only listed one name. Peter Chui–"Advance Man". Fair enough. But where to find him? He wasn't a local player.

He looked out the window at the passing traffic and the trio of kids sitting on the steps of the neighboring building. They were playing some sort of card game. With the window closed he couldn't hear what they were saying.

Wolf took out his own phone, the disposable cell he used only to communicate with his police contact, Inspector John Callaway. He placed a quick call. Callaway wasn't available for a few hours, so Wolf made an appointment, grabbed a cigar, and went outside to sit on the steps of his own building and listen to the kids next door hoot and holler as they played their game.

––––––––

THE STREET SOUNDS reached the roof. Rush hour. Engines rumbled and horns honked. Wolf watched the crowded street and sidewalks from his perch. He thought about his life and his choices. He didn't often reflect on such things but working for Gordy prompted it. When Wolf had needed help, Gordy was there, and unknowingly sacrificed blood to let Wolf escape the grip of his former life. He wondered how far he'd have to go before he felt like he'd made up for the error. It wasn't his fault that Bobby O'Rourke had moved too slowly, and his killer took advantage of a shot, but he still felt like he'd pulled the trigger himself.

The fire escape scraped against the building and

presently Inspector Callaway stepped onto the roof. He straightened his overcoat and approached Wolf with no expression.

"Hello, my friend," Wolf said.

"I think I spent the morning dealing with somebody you iced," Callaway said.

"I haven't iced anybody in a while."

"You must be going with withdrawal."

"But I did want to ask about a certain stiff in a certain house in a quiet neighborhood that somebody else iced last night."

"You know who the shooter is?" Callaway said. "Give."

"I don't," Wolf said. "I was tracking the guy and somebody else got to him first. I have his phone, though."

Wolf showed Callaway the iPhone and highlighted the name in the contacts list.

"The house was rented by this Chui fellow," Callaway said. "Chinese father, white mother. He's with the Frye gang out of Minneapolis. What's the connection?"

"The Frye gang is in town and blackmailing Gordy O'Rourke."

"Why?"

"Something that happened a long time ago," Wolf said. "The phone says he's the advance man, so he came out here to get things ready for the rest of them."

"The whole gang is here?"

"I don't know about that. Yet."

"The Frye gang is run by two women, Monica and Ava. They're sisters. Their parents were gangsters, too. Mother was killed–does that have anything to do with this blackmail?"

"Probably."

"What do you mean, *probably*?"

"I mean that Gordy hasn't told me everything."

"But you're his pal."

Wolf shrugged. "I didn't say I approved of the lack of information, but, for now, he's holding back."

"So why are you working for him?"

"Personal reasons."

"Uh-huh."

"Peter Chui is the only lead I have right now," Wolf said. "I was hoping–"

"Yeah, I know. We have an APB out for him. We'd like to ask him about the dead guy in his house." Callaway pulled his mobile from his coat and opened a picture file. He showed the picture to Wolf. "Old mug shot," the inspector continued, "but only a couple of years."

Wolf examined the face. Peter Chui wasn't anybody who would stand out in a crowd despite the Asian/Caucasian mix. Dark hair and eyes and a gap between his front teeth. He held his mouth open during the shot, so he was probably a mouth breather.

"Carries a pistol," Callaway said, "and an ankle knife. I'm surprised he didn't use an alias."

"Is he wanted for anything?"

"Not lately."

"That's why. Plus, they don't expect to be here long."

"Do the touch and split."

"Uh-huh."

"You don't believe that, do you?"

"They aren't going to stick around and try and take some territory," Wolf said. "No way. They'll leave when their work is done."

"But now you're involved."

"Uh-huh."

"Be careful. Like I said, we have an APB out on Chui. Don't cross paths with my people."

"Anything else I could use?"

"One other thing, maybe," Callaway said. "He likes gambling and hookers. Not necessarily in that order."

Wolf knew exactly where to go.

———

WOLF PARKED his black Cadillac CTS half a block from a brownstone and went up the steps to the front door. He pressed the bell. A thin woman in her mid-40s with dark hair, wearing a long black dress, answered. "Hello, Wolf." She leaned against the doorframe. "What brings you here?"

"I need to talk to you about a client or a potential client."

"I don't want any trouble, Wolf."

"This guy is more trouble than I'll ever be. Let me in."

The woman stepped back, and Wolf entered the lobby. Rebecca Winowitz owned the brownstone which doubled as a small brothel with a poker room in the basement. It was win-win for her. Men won money playing poker and spent it on her girls. The front room looked like any other except for the antique furnishings, everything from chairs to tables to shelves at least 100 years old. Living room off to the left, hallway to the right. The girls worked on the upper floors; none of them at this time of day.

Wolf sat in the living room on an ancient love seat

and Rebecca brought out tea. She sat nearby and the fabric of her dress whispered as she crossed her legs. He showed her the picture of Peter Chui that Callaway had emailed to his phone. "Seen him?"

Her eyebrows went up. "He's been a regular for a few weeks."

"He's Peter Chui. Advance man for a blackmail gang trying to make a score. Already he's involved in one murder and he has answers I need."

Rebecca sipped her tea. "He might be here tonight. He likes a blonde named Rita."

"I need to talk to her," Wolf said. "Got any roofies around here?"

"Now, Wolf, I run a respectable–"

"Stop it, you're not above rolling a guy if you get the chance."

"I should be offended."

Wolf grinned.

"I can get you set up. He likes coffee. I can spike it and let Rita take him up to her room. He won't make a fuss if he wakes up there later."

"Oh, he won't wake up anywhere near her," Wolf said. "Not at all."

———

WOLF SAT in the corner of Rita's room on an old wooden chair. The pad on the seat did little for his comfort, but he remained there, legs uncrossed, waiting. His .45 Colt Series 70 Government Model hung under his left arm.

When Rita dragged the semi-conscious Peter Chui into the room, his big shoes thunked on the doorframe. She was basically lugging a 175-pound bag of cement.

She was petite with short hair and olive skin and grunted with effort. Wolf jumped up and helped her. Chui struggled drunkenly as they carried him to the bed. By the time they dropped him on the bed, he had ceased movement and drool trickled from one side of his mouth.

Rita shut the door. Wolf leaned over Chui's face. Out cold. He sorted through the man's coat and removed a .38-caliber Ruger revolver and an ankle knife.

"Good enough?" Rita said.

"Perfect."

"Now what?" the woman said. "You can't use my room to beat him or whatever."

"Don't worry." Wolf hoisted Chui off the bed and over his shoulders. He marched passed the girl, out of the room and down the narrow staircase, sometimes bumping Chui's head against the wall.

Rebecca Winowitz waited by the front door, arms folded, frowning. She opened the door and Wolf went out into the cold night without a good-bye.

———

PETER CHUI SNAPPED out of his nap as Wolf steered the CTS up a mountain road.

"Where am I?"

"Backseat of my car."

"Who are you?"

"Wolf."

"Who?"

"You wouldn't ask that if you were from around here."

Chui kicked against the back doors, Wolf's seat. Wolf said: "You're not going anywhere, Peter."

"Do you know who I am?"

"Peter Chui."

"You know what I mean!"

"Your name means nothing in my territory."

"What do you want?"

"Information." Wolf steered through some winding turns, pulled off in a small clearing. The Cadillac's tires kicked up a cloud of dust. Wolf exited the car, opened the back door, and stuck the .45 in Chui's face. The other man remained flat on his back.

"Where's your boss?"

"Like I'm going to tell you."

"You better. A .45 makes a big hole."

"What's in it for me?"

"You get to live."

"You have no idea who you're dealing with."

"I'm sure the Frye gang is a big deal in Minnesota," Wolf said. "But this isn't Minnesota. We're the big leagues here."

"You got nothing."

"I found you, didn't I? Where's your boss?"

Chui started to sweat. His eyes stayed fixed on the gun in Wolf's hand and presently he started breathing heavier. Wolf said nothing for a few moments. Finally, Chui said: "All right, don't kill me."

"Where is she?"

"Got a place in a new part of town," Chui said. "I'll tell you where to go."

"Good."

Wolf put away his gun and slid behind the wheel. Chui started giving directions as soon as Wolf reached the city limits. It took about fifteen minutes to reach the place, a cottage off a freeway frontage road surrounded by construction sites. The sites were quiet but wooden frames and a variety of equipment hinted at the activity taking place during working hours. Wolf pulled into the driveway of the cottage. His headlights flashed on the front of the home. He stopped the car.

"This place is empty."

"I know."

Peter Chui bolted from the back seat, his arms free, slamming a fist into the side of Wolf's head. Wolf, stunned, tried to block the blows but could not. Chui grabbed the seatbelt and started wrapping it around Wolf's neck.

"You forgot about the razor blade under my watch," Chui said, pulling the belt tight. Wolf coughed and struggled, trying to hit the man behind him, his blows ineffectual. Chui held the belt with his left hand while clutching the small razor blade in his right. Wolf saw it descend toward his face. He stabbed backward with his thumb and hit Chui in the right eye. Chui screamed, falling back. Wolf unwrapped the seatbelt and got out of the car.

Chui jumped out, swinging the blade. Wolf dodged back. The dirt in the front yard was hard-packed and easy to move on. Chui charged again. Wolf deflected the swing and fired a fist into the other man's solar plexus. Chui bent over, spitting air; Wolf grabbed the wrist holding the blade and twisted as hard as he could. Chui's body rolled with the twist. Wolf kicked Chui's legs out from under him and the other man hit the ground. Wolf batted the blade out of Chui's hand and reached for his gun, but before he could draw

Chui leapt up and crashed into Wolf's midsection, forcing him back. The .45 flew from Wolf's hand. They landed on the ground; Wolf's back struck a rock. He cried out and struggled as Chui started pounding his face. Wolf shifted, blocked, tried to hit back; the pounding didn't let up. Wolf grabbed the rock and swung his arm up, connecting with the side of Chui's head. Chui, stunned, fell off Wolf's body. Wolf got to his knees as Chui started to get up. Wolf swung again and hit Chui square in the side of the head. Chui's skull caved in with a crack. The other man dropped and didn't move.

There was blood on the rock. Wolf tossed it. He felt for a pulse in Chui's neck but there wasn't any.

Wolf scooted back and sat against one of the Cadillac's front tires. He sat there gasping, staring at the body of his only lead which was, literally, now a dead end.

———

When Wolf returned to his apartment, a fat man with a big nose met him on the sidewalk.

The big man wore a dark suit, white shirt, thin black tie. Light from a streetlamp made one side of his face brighter than the other. No bulges showed beneath his coat other than what too many Big Macs put there. He stood at the back door of a purring stretched Lincoln and said:

"Let's take a ride, Mister Wolf."

Wolf stared at the fat man a moment, shrugged, lifted his arms. The fat man patted Wolf down and removed his Colt .45. Then the fat man opened the back door and Wolf slid across the warm leather bench seat.

The fat man eased his bulk next to Wolf, grunted as he settled, told the driver to go. They went.

A woman occupied the second bench seat across from Wolf and the fat man. The woman smiled. She wore a navy-blue suit with a short skirt; long red hair flowed down her back and shoulders. The red hair contrasted with her pale skin. With her bare legs crossed, the hem of the skirt hiked up almost too high. But Wolf didn't drop his eyes from hers.

He didn't have to raise his voice in the quiet confines of the vehicle, either. Hardly any road noise seeped in. He said: "Whose little girl are you?"

"That's not very funny," she said.

"You know me, but I have no idea who you are."

"Call me Monica," she said.

"Mona Frye's daughter, I presume?"

"And you're the fixer O'Rourke has asked to solve his problem."

"Everybody needs a friend."

"You've picked the wrong one," she said, "but we can talk about that later. I want to talk about you, Mister Wolf."

"Just Wolf," he said.

"Fine. What happened to your face?"

Wolf grinned.

Monica shook her head. "Here you are, a lot of talent and experience, but where it came from, I have no idea. Now all you do is waste away in your crappy apartment, live on the fringes helping chumps, eat dinner at Gordy's a few times a week, and play cards all night. It's not much of a life."

Wolf said: "I have my reasons for everything."

"I could use a man like you. Come work for me. We'll have a great time. You'll make a ton of money."

"A man you can buy cannot be trusted."

"You don't really know Gordy at all," she said. "There's a side to him I don't think you'll like."

"Everybody has a dark side. Even me."

She paused, then: "He hasn't told you the whole story, has he?"

"Tell me what you want," Wolf said.

Monica Frye fixed her eyes on Wolf; her mouth narrowed a bit. She said: "I want to show Gordy what it's like to have someone taken from him."

"He's already had someone taken from him."

"But I didn't have anything to do with that."

Wolf kept his mouth shut. The woman watched him. The driver took them in circles. They passed his apartment a second time. Wolf and the woman spoke no more. Presently the driver pulled over in front of the apartment. Wolf turned to the fat man and held out his left hand. "My pistol, please."

When the fat man hesitated, the woman said: "He can have his gun."

The fat man returned the .45. Wolf stepped out of the car, leaned back in. He said: "No."

She shook her head and dismissed him with a wave. Wolf shut the door.

Wolf watched the Lincoln drive away and fished keys from his pocket. He looked up and down the street. The late hour meant little to no traffic; he heard nor saw any vehicles coming his way. Monica had to have expected his reply; a response of her own wouldn't be far away. She didn't want her hands bloodied, though. He climbed into the Cadillac and placed his Colt automatic on the passenger seat. He started the car and drove off. He didn't want a fight in front of his place. A fight would bring cops.

He spotted the single headlight behind him right away. A motorcycle. Wolf powered down his side window and grabbed the .45. Air rushed in but he could hear a little of the motorcycle's motor. A series of green lights allowed him to drive at the limit; when the motorcycle's whine increased and the driver swung into the neighboring lane, Wolf braced his arms against the wheel and stomped the brakes.

The rider flashed by, firing a pistol into the space Wolf's car had occupied, but striking asphalt. The rider sped up, the bike weaving a bit. The light ahead turned red, but he didn't slow. Wolf hopped out of his car and fired once.

The rider fell over his handlebars, the bike swerved, struck and sparked against the pavement. The rider's body rolled curbside while the bike slid into the intersection. A trio of oncoming cars screeched to a stop.

Wolf jumped back into his car, executed a U-turn, and drove the other way.

——————

GORDY ANSWERED on the first ring. Wolf said: "Where are you?"

"The restaurant."

"Where's Mike?"

"At the house."

"Are you sure?"

"What's happening, Wolf?"

Wolf filled him in and heard Gordy suck in a breath

at the mention of Monica's name. Wolf said: "What haven't you told me?"

Gordy waited a moment; then said: "She thinks I'm her father. I never believed it and her mother could never prove it and Monica probably thinks I *killed* her mother."

"You should have told me before tonight, Gordy."

"I said *probably*. How could I know that note was from her?"

"Make sure Mike is where you think he is," Wolf said, "because I'm on my way to the house."

"Was she the only one you saw?"

"Her sister wasn't there, Gordy."

"Wait, what—"

Wolf hung up.

———————

THE GATE GUARD let Wolf pass and he drove up the curving driveway to the front of the house. The porch light made it impossible to see any of the surrounding acreage; darkness covered the grass, trees, the far stone wall. Wolf shook his head as he exited the car. Not a guard in sight. The front door opened as he reached it. The house guard, a stocky man shorter than Wolf, said: "Just you?"

"Yes. Gordy on his way?"

"Should be."

"Where's the kid?"

The circular front room of the house had black-and-white checkerboard tiles from which a trio of hallways and a staircase branched. The guard hustled up the stairs with a slight rocking motion and the pistol on his hip rattled. Wolf followed. They reached the second floor and followed a hallway to the last room on the right. The house guard put a hairy hand on the doorknob. They could hear a television on the other side of the door. The house guard turned the knob shoved his bulk inside.

Empty. The television, facing a double bed, played to no one. The room's chill came from the fully open window from which a screen had been removed; Wolf left the gaping guard in the doorway and looked out the window. A rope had been fixed to one of the bedposts and led down to the ground.

"How many guys on duty tonight?" Wolf said.

"Three. Usual crew."

"Well Mike must have skipped between patrols."

"Mister O'Rourke isn't going to like this."

Wolf said: "No kidding?"

GORDY PACED HIS OFFICE. "Guys have been out looking for two hours and nothing."

Wolf sat on the couch, legs crossed, scotch in hand. "Try his cell again."

Gordy pulled out his own cell and dialed, waited, flipped the phone closed. "Voicemail."

Wolf sipped his drink.

Gordy dropped into the chair behind his desk. The flesh of his face seemed to sag further than the rest of his body. "I don't want to lose Mike the way I lost Bobby," he said.

Wolf blinked.

Gordy said: "I'm sorry, Wolf. I didn't mean that for you."

Wolf nodded.

"I'm sorry. I don't want you—"

"Forget it."

Gordy's cell rang. He snatched it up. "Mike?" Gordy listened a moment and his jaw slacked. "Don't hurt him. I'll do whatever you want. I didn't kill her!" He paused, then started scribbling on paper, then said: "On my way." He flipped his phone closed and met Wolf's gaze.

"Well?" Wolf said.

Gordy dropped his eyes. His body shook. "Will you drive?"

———

WOLF PULLED up in front of the address. His dash clock glowed 3:05 a.m.

"I want this over with," Gordy said.

"Don't do anything stupid."

Gordy took a deep breath.

Wolf gave the house a look as he pulled out the ignition key. Wooden fence, one story, big yard. Neighboring houses spaced far enough apart that it wasn't a home built within the last twenty years. He and Gordy exited the Cadillac, walked up the stone pathway to the oak double doors. Gordy kept his black briefcase close to his leg.

Wolf had come ready with his usual pistol but also packed a two-shot .32 Derringer in case things spun out of control.

Wolf pressed the doorbell. The fat man, with a

grimace, let them in. Monica Frye, red hair tied back, sat in the living room on a leather couch. Her driver, a blond kid with chin fuzz, sat in a corner chair picking at his fingernails with clippers. He didn't look up. He wore a shoulder holster and the pistol it contained dangled under his arm.

The fat man frisked Gordy first and removed a revolver; Wolf noted the fat man looked no further. Then he frisked Wolf and removed the .45. He didn't check Wolf for a second weapon.

Gordy seemed not to notice the fat man. Gordy stood frozen, eyes on Monica. The fat man, with the guns, left the room.

Gordy said: "You."

"I look a lot different now, don't I?" Monica Frye said.

Gordy made a choking sound. "I did not kill your mother, I swear."

"Yes, you did," she said. "That I can prove."

"Now wait," Wolf said.

"Quiet, Wolf. I said you didn't know the whole story, remember?" To Gordy: "I tracked down your old gang. They were more than kind enough to tell me you shot my mother. Before I killed them myself."

"You–"

"I have written statements."

Gordy flexed his hands; the blond kid with the shoulder holster made a tut-tut noise and took out his gun.

Wolf said: "Gordy–"

Where was the sister?

The fat man reentered, dragging Mike with him. Mike, gagged and tied at the wrists and ankles, made a noise when he saw his father. The fat man shoved the younger O'Rourke to the carpet, left him on his stomach. Mike rolled over. His nostrils flared as he breathed. The fat man planted a foot on the younger man's chest and took out Gordy's revolver.

"Now," Monica Frye said, "either admit you killed my mother, or I shoot your boy right here. You could bury him next to Bobby, wouldn't that be nice?"

"I swear I didn't kill her!" Gordy said. "That's the truth!"

"Your men told me the truth."

"A man says anything when there's a gun to his head."

"Except you." She eyed the fat man. The fat man cocked the revolver. She looked back to Gordy: "Well?"

Gordy, panting, let his arms fall at his side. Sweat trickled down his face. Wolf watched the fat man and moved his right hand to scratch his nose. The fat man jerked his head Wolf's way. Wolf lowered his arm.

"All right," Gordy said. "All right."

The fat man looked at Monica. Monica said okay. The fat man placed his finger on the revolver's hammer, put pressure on the trigger. The free hammer lowered under the guidance of his thumb and he took a step back.

Wolf's right hand moved again, this time to his right pocket. The fat man turned his body Wolf's way, bringing up the revolver, but Wolf already had his two-shot .32 Derringer aimed at the big man's right eye. Wolf fired once. The bullet puckered the fat man's eye and he remained on his feet a moment, then crashed on top of Mike. The younger O'Rourke's body folded under the impact and he screamed through the gag.

The blond kid, on his feet, had to change positions

as the falling fat man blocked his aim; Wolf, dropping to one knee, fired the second .32 slug up through the kid's fuzzy chin.

Gordy lunged at Monica—*"Damn you, bitch!"*—while drawing a knife from behind his back. She screamed as he landed on top of her, blocking her swinging arms and pushing her head into the cushions. The arm holding the knife pumped like a piston, once, twice; Gordy pulled back, and with one last thrust buried the knife in her neck.

Wolf rolled the fallen fat man off Mike's body, hauled him to his feet. "Should have stayed home," Wolf said. He didn't remove the gag but instead hoisted Mike over his shoulders. He looked at Gordy. Gordy turned to him. Blood had splattered on part of his face and the front of his shirt.

"Let's get out of here," Gordy said.

———

GORDY MOVED paperwork to one side and poured two drinks and sat behind his desk. He gulped down his drink. Wolf, legs crossed, seated on the other side, did not reach for his drink. He said:

"This didn't turn out exactly how I imagined."

"Well it's done. I'm glad you were there."

Wolf said: "She was right about one thing."

Gordy frowned.

"She told me," Wolf said, "about a side to you I wouldn't like."

"What are you talking about?"

"Did you tell me the truth?"

Gordy gave his friend a wide-eyed look. "What did you say to me?"

"You heard me. I'm not going to ask you again. You started to tell a story back there."

"You know a man will say anything when there's a gun pointed at him. Or at his kid."

"Nobody innocent goes off like you did."

"She was threatening my boy."

"She was unarmed. I dropped the fat man and the kid. It was over."

"You think we should have just let her go?"

"Your friends didn't exactly warn you somebody was after them," Wolf said. "She didn't take them all by surprise."

"You gonna sit there and insult me?"

"Are you going to tell me the truth?"

Gordy sucked in his breath.

Wolf stood up and started for the door.

"Wolf."

Wolf looked back.

"You believe me, don't you?"

Wolf said: "I'm not a fool. Don't play me for one. And by the way? Where was the sister?" He went out.

Gordy clutched his glass and stared at the closed door.

———

GORDY WANDERED THE CLUB. Every seat was full. The bar packed. But his mind wasn't on business. Did Wolf really think he had murdered Mona Frye? He hadn't. But he *knew* who did, and that was a secret that had to stay a secret. *He had to keep the secret.*

He went back to his office. Paperwork still waited on the desk. There was no flash or glamour in being a connected guy. You still had a stack of paperwork to sort through just like the rest of the schmucks. Every night.

But there was a new piece of paper on the desk. Folded. Left in the center of his blotter.

It hadn't been there when he stepped out.

With his hands shaking, Gordy picked up the paper and unfolded it. Somebody had written three words. His heart skipped.

Three words.

REMEMBER MONA FRYE.

———

AVA FRYE DIDN'T BOTHER to adjust her skirt. It was too short on purpose. The night was warm so at least her legs weren't cold. She approached the entrance of the bar. A sign on the door said PULL THE DOOR DON'T PUSH DUMBASSES.

She pulled the door open. The Gator Cage, the main hangout for party-loving chumps like Mike O'Rourke. She knew his face well. She'd argued with her sister Monica about how to go about their vendetta, but her older sister had insisted on doing it her way, and now she was in the morgue. Ava should have been at the house, but her fiery temper got the best of her and she'd walked out. Now she had two people to avenge.

What had supposed to have been a simple job was now more complicated. Gordy O'Rourke and his friend Wolf would pay dearly.

She didn't figure Mike as the type to refuse the fancy

yellow pills in her purse; the pick-up would be easy too. She knew a lot of guys like Mike. Always looking for the next new high.

It felt good to be out and operating instead of sitting behind the scenes. It felt even better to be out alone. She was the proverbial square peg in a round hole when working with her associates. Her sister had truly run the show; now everybody was looking to her, and not just for their pay.

The Gator Cage wasn't large. It appeared to be an add-on to the attached next-door establishment. The bar took up most of the room with a narrow walkway remaining. Tables lined the wall; the path led to a pool table and karaoke stand in the rear. A sign in front of the karaoke stand said KARAOKE ONLY ON TUESDAYS DUMBASSES.

Somebody had a very limited sense of humor. And poor grammar skills.

Men with horny eyes tracked her as she walked the length of the bar with her shoulders back and her chest out; a few women stared daggers at her. They couldn't compete in their jeans and belly bulges and bad hair and oily skin. *All you bitches can suck it.* Ava saw Mike O'Rourke sitting at the end, drinking a beer, munching pretzels and looking up at a corner TV screen displaying a game show.

She pulled back the neighboring stool. The wooden legs scraped the floor. She brushed off the seat and sat. The bartender came over. Another woman who glared at her.

Ava said: "Dry martini."

The bartender retreated to mix the drink. Ava placed her purse on the counter and took out a pack of cigarettes. She put the cigarette in her mouth and rummaged for a lighter.

Mike O'Rourke flicked a Zippo and held the lighter out for her. *Typical. Already tangled in her web.* She smiled and lit the tip with the flame.

"Hi," he said. "Never seen you before."

"Just moved here."

The bartender returned with Ava's martini, but the level of liquid barely reached the middle of the glass.

"That's it?" Ava said. "I came here to *drink.*"

"That's an ounce and a half, how we serve 'em."

"I'm not paying ten bucks for a couple of drops."

Mike O'Rourke jumped in. "Haley, make it a double and put it on my tab."

The bartender huffed and removed the glass; when she brought it back Ava smiled at what she considered the proper amount of elixir.

"Thank you." She raised the glass to Mike. "You're a lifesaver." She took a swallow, nodded, set the glass on the bar.

"Where did you come from?" he said.

"Las Vegas," she said. "I had to escape the flash and plastic and see real life, you know?"

"I'm not sure you'll like it much better here."

"So far it's okay. I like mountains."

Mike shrugged and drank some beer.

"Besides," Ava said, "I think you know a thing or two about partying. Where's a girl go to get wild?"

"I can think of a few places."

"Good. Let me fuel up first."

Ava opened her purse and took out a baggie of pills. Harmless capsules filled with sugar. She popped two in her mouth and chased them with the martini.

"Got any for me?" Mike said.

"If you're good. Let's go."

"Don't you want to know my name?"

"We put names on tombstones, honey." She hopped off the barstool and grabbed his arm.

———

HE TOOK her back to his place after a round of clubs.

Mike O'Rourke put the wrong key in the lock, laughed, tried again. Ava laughed with him, but she wasn't high. The pills she'd slipped him had Mike on the kind of high a hard-core druggie loves. He finally found the right key, pushed the door open, and they went inside.

He didn't bother with the lights. Mike grabbed her by her slender waist, spun her in a circle–"Weeeeeee"– and kicked the door shut. He put his hands on her shoulders and pushed her ahead of him, down a dark hallway to his bedroom. She moved with a slight swish in her hips.

He steered her into the bedroom. A corner night light gave the room a glow.

She placed her purse on the dresser and jumped on the bed and rolled around. Hopped back to her feet. "Bed's soft. You first."

He was already taking off his pants, watching her watching him.

She smiled at his growing erection.

"I think I can handle that," she said. She pulled her T-shirt off, her breasts bouncing within the cups of her black bra. She reached back, unhooked the bra and let her breasts fall free. She tossed the bra to the floor.

She reached for the snap of her skirt and gave it a pull. Moved slender fingers to the zipper and started moving it down.

She pulled the zipper down the rest of the way and started moving her hips as she pulled the skirt down. A pair of pink panties remained.

She flicked off her panties and tossed them at Mike. He caught them in his teeth, laughed, and tossed them aside. She lifted her arms and did a turn.

"You like?"

"Me like," he said.

"Just one more thing, lover," she said. She got off the bed and reached into her purse and took out a silenced automatic.

Mike O'Rourke was suddenly very sober.

"Whoa, hey–"

"So long, babe." She shot him twice in the chest.

––––––––

WOLF DRANK SOME BEER. He put the bottle on the table beside his recliner and went back to his book. The only sound in the apartment was the clanking refrigerator. He sat under a small light the recliner set halfway back. He hadn't left the apartment in two days and was glad for the rest. He was still processing what had happened with Gordy and the solitude helped.

A knock at the door. Two light taps. Wolf didn't leave the chair. Another knock. Fine. Wolf dog-eared the page and answered the door.

Gordy stood there.

"Wolf. Please."

Wolf stepped back and Gordy entered. The other man was visibly shaking.

"What happened, Gordy?"

"My son. They got my son. Shot him dead, Wolf. Dead."

Wolf locked the door. He found a beer for Gordy. They sat on the couch.

"I guess it happened last night," Gordy said.

"Where?"

"His place."

Wolf took a drink.

"I got another note, after—you know," Gordy said. "Same as the first one."

"The sister," Wolf said. He watched his friend. The hand that held the beer bottle still shook.

"Wolf, are you still upset with me for what I did, or for not telling you the truth?"

"I'm not a hypocrite," Wolf said. "But you should have told me the whole story. How much did you leave out?"

"I left out a lot."

"So, tell me."

Gordy sighed. He still held the beer but didn't take a sip. He sat with hunched shoulders, his eyes on the spotted carpet. He said: "My brother Mickey shot Mona."

"Uh-huh."

"Mickey was looking at life under three strikes if he got caught, so I covered it up and got him out of the city. He's been hiding out ever since. I ain't seen him in over a decade."

"Why did he shoot her?"

"Some argument, I don't remember now. Something stupid."

"Your cronies didn't cover for you," Wolf said. "Why?"

"They weren't involved. All they knew was the street talk. It was either Mickey or Gordy but nobody could ever prove it was either of us so the whole case went cold. But the statute never runs out on murder. Even now I gotta protect Mickey."

"At what cost?"

Gordy finally lifted his head to make eye-contact with Wolf. His eyes had a pleading look. Their usual fire and confidence were long gone. "How was I to know this would happen?"

Wolf watched his friend a moment. The refrigerator clanked.

"You ever gonna fix that thing?" Gordy said, glancing back at the kitchen.

"What do you want from me, Gordy?"

"You know everything. Finish helping me."

"Why didn't you trust me?"

"I was mixed up, out of my head, nervous, can you blame me? I just wanted this to go away."

"Gordy–"

"You can't say no to me, Wolf! You don't have to like me anymore, but you can't say no. You still owe me. You said so yourself."

Wolf stood up and crossed the room to a window. He looked out on the empty street. The stoplight at the corner went from red to yellow to green over and over but no cars were there to be bothered.

"What are you gonna do, Wolf?"

"I'll start tomorrow."

"No." Gordy jumped up. "You need to start tonight. We don't have time to waste."

Wolf looked at Gordy. "I don't have to care, Gordy."

"You *owe* me."

Gordy let himself out.

Wolf stared at the closed door for a long time.

———

IF THE OPPOSITION knew how to get to Gordy the way they did, that meant they had people all over. Having people all over meant that somebody would know. Wolf went to find somebody who knew.

He didn't waste time with the usual informants or other connections; no sense in calling Callaway this time. He went right to the most obvious source, a local gunman named Vince Manning.

Manning worked for syndicate boss Carlo Gulino and had crossed paths with Wolf many times. Perhaps he'd even saved Wolf's life on one or two occasions, but Wolf could say the same thing the other way around. They weren't friends, but they weren't enemies.

Wolf checked the usual hang outs Manning frequented, and finally found him on the third try, at the Shipwreck Bar. Wolf wasn't exactly welcome there, but the owner wasn't about to roust him, either.

Vince Manning, with his thick gray hair and stocky build, wasn't hard to spot amongst the rest of the thinning crowd. Two o'clock was near. Wolf dropped onto the stool next to Manning and said hello.

"You missed last call." Manning drank some beer.

"I'm here for information," Wolf said. "We have

some players making moves and I need to find out what's going on."

"This has to do with Gordy?"

"How did you know?"

"He kicks back to Gulino, remember? Carlo always has at least an idea of what's going on."

"Protecting his investment or genuine concern?"

"Both. Carlo's a kind-hearted man, deep down."

Wolf laughed.

"It just so happens," Manning said, "that you've caught me in the middle of watching some newcomers that I've been following for a few days."

"Where?"

"Back booth, in the corner."

Wolf didn't make an effort to look. He knew where the booth was, and he didn't want the targets spooked.

"I've been wondering if I should take them aside for a chat," Manning said. "See what they have in mind. Now that you're interested, I think I'll do that."

"I'll join you."

"Always a pleasure to have the Big Bad Wolf with me," Manning said. He grinned.

Wolf shook his head.

———

MANNING SAT behind the wheel of his Lincoln Town Car. They watched the two newbies leave the bar. Both were younger, hair trimmed close to their skulls, latest fashions via GQ. The driver had an unsteady walk. They climbed into a VW parked on the curb.

"I think he's too drunk to drive," Manning said,

following the VW as it left the curb. He dodged other cars to get closer to the VW.

The light up ahead changed to red. The VW stopped. Manning stopped behind the VW. Wolf scanned the street out of habit but found nobody paying them any mind. The back of his neck itched.

Presently the light turned green and the VW moved through the intersection.

As Manning accelerated, Wolf glanced out his window; as Manning reached the center of the intersection, Wolf shouted: "Watch it!"

The van waiting at the opposite light lurched forward, tires spewing smoke, and raced toward the Lincoln. The front of the van smashed into the back quarter panel of the Lincoln, spinning it in a circle. The impact rocked Wolf back and forth; he slammed against the door. The car stopped. Wolf's head spun. He hauled out the .45.

Automatic weapons fire filled the air, the Lincoln rocking with hits. Wolf ripped off his seatbelt and hit the carpet. Manning screamed but Wolf couldn't see if he'd been hit. Glass popped, rained down; as Wolf reached for the door handle, somebody else opened it and grabbed his outstretched hand.

Three gunmen stood in the intersection. The one grabbing at Wolf pulled him onto the pavement. The impact sent the .45 flying. Wolf jumped up and swung a fist at the gunman's face, but the shooter sidestepped and bashed Wolf in the face with the butt of his weapon. Wolf fell back against the car, striking his head, and crumpled onto the pavement.

———

THE ACHE in Wolf's shoulders finally roused him, and the first thing he did was vomit down the front of his clothes. Wolf spat several times to clear his mouth. He dangled above the concrete floor in a room inside a warehouse; his hands were cuffed and hooked over a pipe.

"Wolf?"

He looked to the right. "Oh, no."

Gordy hung there too.

"They got me as soon as I left your place," Gordy said. "You?"

"While I was following two guys who may or may not have been part of the Frye gang," Wolf said. "Vince Manning got hurt. If we get out of this there'll be trouble over that."

The woman who entered the room had dark hair, wore clothes that fit tight against her trim body. She had skin as pale as her sister and dark brown eyes.

"Comfortable up there?" she said.

Gordy let out a low groan and his head sagged.

"I think Gordy is out of gas," Ava Frye said. "What about you, Wolf? Can you keep up?"

"I'm busy plotting my escape as we speak."

Ava Frye laughed. "How entertaining." Two gunmen entered behind her, the pair Wolf and Manning had followed. "Won't be long now," the woman continued. "I had a huge argument with my sister about how to do this. She had to get fancy."

Gordy raised his head. "It wasn't me! It wasn't!"

Ava Frye folded her arms and shrugged. "And I should believe you?"

"My brother Mickey. He did it. He had an argument with your mother and it ended bad."

Wolf said: "Zip it, Gordy."

"I helped get him out of town, but he's the one you want."

Wolf said: "Gordy."

"So that means I should let you go?"

"I didn't kill your mother!"

"But you killed my sister. And you helped the man who killed my mother get away. Is that right?"

Wolf said: "Told you, Gordy."

"Wolf has a point," she said. "You really should keep your mouth shut. Won't matter in a minute."

"Get it over with!" Gordy shouted. His voice echoed throughout the warehouse. He struggled against his restraints. "Get it over with!"

"Oh, Gordy," she said.

"You killed my son. Isn't that enough?"

"No."

"If you kill me, you'll never find Mickey."

"Oh, he'll be around when he hears about you," Ava Frye said. "Won't be too hard to find him."

She snapped her fingers and the two gunmen took pistols from under their coats. One of them handed his gun to Ava. The other aimed at Wolf. Ava Frye stepped toward Gordy.

"I'm going to pull the trigger myself for you, Gordy," she said.

The shots startled them all. They came from elsewhere in the building. Men screamed; more shots cut off the screams; finally, only the echo of the blasts remained. Ava's two goons took cover in the doorway. The one who still held his pistol fired twice at somebody; return fire took off his head. His partner tried to grab the still-smoking pistol, but then the phantom shooter blasted him too.

Ava Frye raised the gun and froze as the new arrival entered and stepped over the bodies of the two gunmen. He was older, hair gray, but still trim. He wore a dark leather coat over a gray shirt, and black slacks.

Ava Frye tightened her finger on the trigger. The man shot her in the left eye. The bullet punched through the back of her head and decorated the wall behind her with blood spatter, bits of bone, and parts of her brain. She fell over and landed beneath Gordy's feet.

The man said: "Gordo. I'm sorry I'm late. I've been tracking this gang for weeks, but I know I didn't get here in time."

"I've never been happier to see you!" Gordy said. "She probably has the key to these things."

The man went to Ava Frye's body and searched her pockets, the bloody mess of her head no bother at all.

Wolf frowned at Gordy.

Gordy said: "Wolf, meet my brother Mickey!"

JUSTIFIED SINS

1

Ben Regan said, "I need somebody who can peel a box."

Jimmy O'Shea's large gray eyes stood out the most in his small face. The eyes belonged to a larger man. He looked at Regan over the rim of his full glass of dark Guinness, took a drink, rolling the liquid over his tongue before swallowing. Regan sat across from O'Shea with an untouched scotch. O'Shea let out a satisfied sigh. "Mmmmm. Nothing beats Guinness."

"Am I talking to myself, Jimmy?"

They sat at a corner table in a quiet bar. Light music and voices covered their low tones. The narrow room and wood-paneled walls gave the bar a cramped feel, at least to O'Shea, but the other pressed-together customers didn't seem to mind. He liked how the wood motif gave the place the illusion of having been slapped together. He ran his hand over the wood table they occupied, admiring the raw feel of the smooth but unpolished top.

"I heard you," O'Shea said. He looked up and

studied Regan's smooth face and wondered why he didn't darken or shave the graying mustache. The gold chain on Regan's right wrist made him smile. The chain displayed a small rectangular plate reading LOVE THY NEIGHBOR. "Why do you want local talent," O'Shea said, "when you have all your contacts back home?"

"Because I'm not back home."

"Call somebody."

"Are you trying to chase away business?"

"It's a little hot right now," O'Shea said. "Somebody broke into the Grady Mansion last week and looted *their* safe. You know how much influence Grady has? Cops are shakin' me and my guys down every hour. Who did it? Where's the loot? You'd think they wanted the stuff, the way they come off."

"I don't have time to fool around."

"You ever gonna taste that scotch?"

"Can you get me somebody or not?"

O'Shea drank some more Guinness. The Guinness turned sour as O'Shea swallowed. He set the glass down. "I know one guy. Peel any box. He's out of the business, though. Settled down with a wife and all that. I'm not sure I can get him to work again."

Regan brushed his mustache with the index finger of his right hand. The overhead light made his chain sparkle. "No box-breaker walks away forever."

"How much?"

Regan put his hand down. "Plenty."

"Come on, how much?"

"Fifteen grand. That'll make a man pick up his tools again."

O'Shea whistled. "Something's really burning a hole in your belly."

"Can you get him?"

"I'll need a couple of days."

"A *couple* is *two*."

"You know what I mean."

"You have two days."

O'Shea laughed. "Burnin' real deep," he said. "What are you after?"

"I'll be in touch." Regan pushed back his chair, starting to rise. He snatched up the scotch and drank it down "You were right, Jimmy. That's good stuff."

Regan walked away from the little gray-eyed man.

O'Shea shook his head and looked up. A painting on the wall behind where Regan had sat showed a naked man running from a fire-breathing dragon. The poor guy must have started out a slayer, as the burning remnants of sword and armor between man and dragon indicated, but the bearded warrior had taken on a task he wasn't ready for. The dragon had been just a little faster. Now, stripped of clothes and weapons, the slayer only wanted to survive. The dragon gave him the creeps. Jimmy O'Shea shivered and left a $20 bill and his unfinished Guinness on the table. He left the table and went out to his car, where he sat and made phone calls for a half-hour.

————

FREDDIE WEBSTER WHEELED the tall donut rack to the front counter of the bakery and helped two colleagues fill the space under the glass. They worked without talking, an oiled machine, snatching donuts from the rack with plastic-gloved hands and moving them to desired spots. Glazed together, chocolate together, all had their home and the dull monotony contributed to Freddie's stray thoughts.

Sheila, his wife, had brought home the first ultrasound photo of their child the previous evening. Freddie stared, transfixed, but the happy moment vanished once he remembered that providing for the three of them was going to get tougher. He and Sheila struggled enough taking care of themselves.

Once the counter shelves were partially loaded (an hour before the 5:30 a.m. opening so they were right on time), Freddie pushed the rickety rack back to the kitchen for the next batch. The other five members of the night crew hustled before stainless countertops preparing dough and icing finished items.

Freddie stopped the rack in front of a tall double-decker oven. Everybody sweated in the kitchen area. Hair-nets and bandannas, standard equipment, kept sweat and hair out of eyes but nothing stopped the down-the-neck-to-the-back trickles and shirt-collar wetness that made the cool air of morning a relief. The wetness of his hands, under the plastic gloves, made the plastic cling. Freddie ripped off the gloves, dried his hands on the apron he wore, and grabbed a set of thick mitts. He opened the lower half of the oven and removed a tray full of fresh pastries, and set the tray on free counter space. The noise in the kitchen kept his thoughts at bay. Voices jumbled, water hissed, laughter followed a now-and-then joke. With tongs Freddie picked up the pastries and deposited them on the rack. After removing the other three trays in the lower half, he opened the top section. The exiting oven heat brushed his skin like a hot breeze. Again, thoughts drifted to Sheila and a possible second job and–

Part of his left wrist not covered by his mitt touched the edge of the rack. Skin seared. Freddie screamed. The pan of pastries, already halfway out, crashed at his feet and spilled across the rubber floormat. Part of the hot pan struck his ankle and he felt another sharp burn through his jeans.

Freddie shed his mitts as his buddy Chad raced to a deep sink and turned on the cold water. Freddie put his wrist under the spray. A third co-worker, Barbara, rushed over with a first aid kit.

Freddie closed his eyes while Barbara wrapped his wrist. He let off a string of curses.

———

THE BURN STUNG under the bandage. Freddie cursed every few minutes as he steered the old Ford Escort home. The car, with its whining engine and jolting ride, always seemed on the verge of disintegration. He gripped the wheel with calloused fingers and rough, hairy hands.

He pulled into the apartment complex and parked in an open space. As he pulled his too-tall body out of the too-small car, a black cat, the upstairs neighbor's ragdoll, who liked to sit on the Websters' deck rail, darted between the two neighboring cars. A woman in a sweat suit jogged by. The day had begun for most; for him, it had come to an end. The morning chill felt good after the sweat box of the bakery, but his sticky skin and matted hair begged for a shower.

He left the parking lot and crossed the grounds to his building. All the buildings in the complex shared the same storm gray color. Only numbers up to five posted here and there distinguished them.

Freddie yawned and stretched, the veiny muscles on his toned arms flaring before he relaxed. He hustled up a flight of concrete steps to the second floor of building three. Through a door, down a quiet hallway with brown carpeting; finally, he reached 305 and put a key in the lock.

Bacon sizzled. The scent hit him when he entered. In the kitchen he found a pan with four popping strips; some scrambled eggs sat in another pan. Freddie found Sheila in front of the mirror, brushing on eye make-up. She'd tied back her dark hair. Her blue eyes had their usual sparkle and a smile replaced Freddie's frown.

"Hi, sweetie," Sheila said, and leaned a cheek toward him. He kissed her. She saw the bandage, gasped, grabbed his arm for a closer look. "What happened?"

"Accident, don't worry about it."

Her eyes stayed on him a moment. He looked away. "Go eat," she said. "I'll be out in a minute."

Freddie looked at her in the blue and white IHOP uniform, the bulge of her abdomen beginning to show. While being a father held some excitement, the grim financial woes facing him and his bride, made it hard to be as carefree and upbeat as he wanted.

Sheila Webster watched her husband go, returned to her face painting. She didn't see her face in the mirror. She saw Freddie's frustration, the taut line his mouth formed when he pressed his lips together. He wouldn't talk. The pile of bills said everything for him.

If Freddie had been chiseled from rock, Sheila had been built with greater care. Soft features, clear skin, scattered freckles, small nose. Nothing in her demeanor suggested that she'd been abandoned at age two and raised in foster homes and had seen plenty of tough times. Their current situation was just another mountain to climb.

Sheila went out to the kitchen. Freddie sat at the table picking at his eggs. She poured coffee and sat near him. Her back arched a little. The chair's padding had gone to seed ages ago and the wire-mesh backrest did her no good and made her bottom and lower back sore. She scooted closer to Freddie.

He said, "I've been thinking about what Art said the other night, about me driving a cab."

Art Ahern operated a cab company employing ex-cons like Freddie. He'd wanted to drive for Art three years ago after the prison doors closed behind him, but no slots had been available, so Freddie went to work at the bakery. Now Art had a part-time opening.

"Only time you'd be home would be to sleep," Sheila said.

"Uh-huh," Freddie said. He chewed some bacon. "But maybe something full-time will come up. With tips I could do okay. While you're on maternity leave."

Sheila sipped her coffee. "These graveyard shifts kill you as it is," she said, "you want to work another five, six hours a day?"

"I'm open to other ideas. You didn't have any the last time we talked."

"We've always survived."

"It's different now."

"No. It isn't. You've never given up before, why start now?"

He let out a breath but didn't say anything. She rubbed his shoulder.

"Give us a chance, hon," she said. "Don't decide right away."

He kept staring at the plate, moving the eggs around with his fork.

Sheila ran red nails across his back and emptied the last of the coffee in the sink. "Eat up," she said, bending to kiss his cheek. She grabbed her purse, and pulled the door shut behind her.

Freddie shoveled the left-over bacon and eggs into a plastic container and stored the container in the refrigerator. The phone on the wall rang. He picked up. "Hello?"

"Back in the old days," the voice said, "you'd still be out chasing tail."

Jimmy O'Shea.

"The old lady pop yet?"

"How'd you find me?" Freddie said.

"I called around. Want some work?"

Freddie said nothing.

"Maybe you didn't hear me."

"I heard."

"I figured with the baby and all you might want some money, like, oh, a split of a job I have. Means seventy-five hundred to you."

"I'm doing just fine. *We* are doing just fine."

"You don't believe a word of that."

"I'm not going back to prison."

"Who says you'll get caught? One night's work, in and out."

"No."

"Seventy-five hundred bucks, Freddie."

Freddie's eyes landed on the stack of bills atop the small desk in one corner of the room. His right hand began to sweat so he switched the phone to his left hand.

"At least come and talk about it."

"My shift at the bakery starts at ten o'clock tonight. I'll"—and Freddie paused, his mouth dry. "I'll meet you at the Starbucks on the corner. Nine-thirty."

"What kind of crap is that? Let's meet right now."

"Tonight or forget it." Freddie hooked the phone.

He sat down at the desk and looked over the bills. His hands shook as he sorted the envelopes. The usual expenses. One medical bill after another. Insurance didn't cover everything. The baby was costing a ton and hadn't even been born yet.

The seventy-five hundred sounded good, but he had made a promise to Sheila.

He told her "the life" was over and he wanted to keep that promise.

But would one job really hurt?

Freddie went to bed and spent an hour tossing and turning.

———

BEN BILLSBY'S eyes darted left and right as he and six-year-old daughter Yolanda strolled hand-in-hand along the sidewalk. Street, clear. Sidewalk, clear. Park coming up. People there. Ben tightened his grip on Yolanda's little hand.

She said, "How long have you knowd Baya?"

"Long time."

"When did she start her candy house?"

"Few weeks ago. Now we don't have to go downtown anymore. We can buy candy and stay close to home."

He didn't want to say that "close to home" meant less danger than downtown, where gangs and drugs were as plentiful as sand at the beach, but still dangerous enough that he had to keep one hand on Yolanda and never stopped moving his eyes. Birds chirped and the gentle breeze gave the assurance of calm.

"Did you knowd Baya before Mommy?"

"We used to live next to each other."

"Will she have the same candy they have at the other place?"

"She'll prob'ly have more."

Baya. Two blocks down. They reached the park. Two men by a tree, talking. They turned to face Ben and Ben smiled. Kenny and Greg. Baseball buddies.

"Yo, Ben!"

"S'up, guys."

Ben and Yolanda stopped, and Ben exchanged words with his friends. Yolanda looked toward the playground and tugged on her father's arm.

"Can I go on the swings, Daddy?"

Ben saw four teens loitering on the concrete near the swing set. He said, "No, baby," gripped her hand tighter. He turned back to his buddies.

"Y'all catch the Cowboys last night?"

An engine raced behind them. Tires screeched. The teens near the swing set clawed under T-shirts and drew pistols, aimed at the street. Ben's friends cursed; Ben turned and saw two young men shoving machine guns out the side of a big car. As weapons cracked, Ben dived for Yolanda and fell on top of her.

"HE TRIED to cover her with his body, but they were both killed in the crossfire," said Homicide Inspector John Callaway. "Them and the others."

The crime scene team scoured the park. The bodies had long been carried away, but police still had the street blocked. Squad car cherry lights winked in the evening twilight. The peace of the afternoon breeze and chirping birds had been replaced by the sharp edge of clipped and authoritative voices over radios.

The man beside Callaway, whom he knew only as Wolf, stood still, a long black London Fog overcoat draped over his clothes. The coat matched the rest of his black attire.

Wolf had arrived in Las Palmas four years ago, taking a leave of absence from military service to find out why his sister Shelly had stopped writing letters, only to find that she'd been murdered. He tore the city apart to find the man responsible. Callaway provided a helping hand, and the two formed an unlikely bond between lawman, and outlaw. With his sister's killer vanquished, Wolf made his exit from the military permanent and stayed in the city, operating on the fringes between the cops and the crooks. Callaway didn't think he was a bad guy but wasn't entirely sure he was a good guy. What he did know was that sometimes Wolf came in handy, because justice, ever the underdog, often needed a little help, and Wolf didn't mind lending that help, picking up where the law left off. Callaway, as the city's chief of the homicide bureau, was in the perfect position to feed Wolf information to do things regular cops couldn't.

"We're watching this like it's a movie," Wolf said.

"I wanted you to see it personally," the inspector said, looking at Wolf with squint-wrinkled eyes. "The rumors are true, somebody's selling stolen fully-automatic military weapons to these gangs, and this man, his daughter, and the other two fellows are the first innocent victims."

Wolf said, "Which gangs run in this neighborhood?"

"The Up the Hill and Down the Hill gangs," Callaway said.

"Who used the M-16s?"

"The Downhill crew. Now you can bet the Uphill gang will scramble to even the score, military guns or not, and this situation will get worse."

"Uh-huh." Wolf's eyes didn't leave the crime scene.

"The A.T.F. and Army C.I.D. are on the way," Callaway said. "My office and the police have been asked to step aside. Which is why, my friend, I'm glad we have our arrangement."

Wolf remained quiet as his steel-grey eyes watched the crime scene.

"Do you have anything that might lead to the source of the guns and end this before more people get killed?"

Wolf did not reply.

"Did you hear me?"

"Anything I say makes you an accessory."

"I'll take that as a yes."

"An informant gave me a tip about a warehouse in the Tenderloin," Wolf said. "Next shipment of guns will be delivered there within a day or two."

"That was fast."

"I'm not a cop, remember?" Wolf said. "The gun runners have been in the city for weeks setting up deals."

"Take somebody alive."

"No promises."

Wolf moved toward a black Camaro parked at the curb. Callaway watched him drive away.

———

THE CAMARO'S engine grumbled as Wolf cruised through the Tenderloin District, following the rough streets strewn with garbage and potholes. The windows were down, and the block's soundtrack played loud and clear, shouts from the sidewalk, horns, wheels clicking over trolley tracks, music from bars, mariachis on somebody's radio. By the mouth of an alley, two hookers in tight outfits smoked. Nearby, several blacks kneeled on the sidewalk shooting dice; on the front steps of a dirty gray building, a white woman smoked and read a magazine by a flickering porch light. At another corner a group of teens spoke with a pair of beat cops.

A big gray building with an empty theater marquee loomed ahead.

There was a lot Inspector Callaway didn't know about Wolf's background, and the man in black wasn't inclined to give the information away if Callaway didn't need to know. Wolf had grown up in Las Palmas, which is how he knew the streets so well, and the players who operated in the shadows.

Back when Wolf had been a teenager, dodging the cops and skipping school, the gray building, the Paradise Theater, had been his sanctuary. A man named Max Klein owned and operated the place and lived in the top floor loft. He'd played old movies because he couldn't afford new stuff, and the Paradise became a specialty house for those who loved classic films. It was the one part of the Tenderloin anybody could visit because the bums and derelicts and even the hoods and hookers stayed away. Nobody wanted to upset the Old Man, as Klein became known. He gave back to the community and tried to help people, one of whom was a certain angry sixteen-year-old kid who sometimes needed a refuge.

The Old Man passed away while Wolf had been overseas in the military, but the building remained, unoccupied since forever. A fence stretched around the perimeter. Boards over the windows.

Wolf drove by the building. A monument to his past. He kept his eyes forward and stopped for a red light. To his left, a cluster of people hung around the front of a liquor store. A thin girl with stringy hair wearing a dirty shirt and torn jeans approached the Camaro. "Hey, guy. Got a couple bucks?"

Wolf handed her ten dollars. She showed a smile of

missing teeth and ran around the corner of the store. Probably to buy drugs. Wolf preferred she did so with money he gave her than money she picked up turning tricks.

The light changed. Wolf drove on. His destination lay a block away.

———

WOLF HUSTLED up the inside stairwell of the abandoned building from which he planned to set up his stakeout. His heavy steps echoed. The top landing opened into an area cluttered with trash, smelling of urine. A corner with a thin mattress and faded rock band posters suggested somebody had once occupied the space, but now the mattress was stained and torn. Wolf's boots scraped across the floor as he carried a large tote bag to a window caked with dirt and dust. His London Fog hid the black combat outfit he wore, pants, turtleneck, laced combat boots. In its usual leather rig under his left arm hung his .45-caliber Colt Series 70 auto pistol. Simple firepower that worked.

The tote bag held other tools of the death trade.

He kneeled to unzip the tote bag. He removed a Benelli M4 Tactical twelve-gauge auto-loading shotgun and placed it next to the window. A bandoleer of fragmentation grenades, listening devices, and the proper receiving equipment joined the Benelli. Wolf turned his attention to the radio equipment.

———

"I DIDN'T THINK you'd show," Jimmy O'Shea said. He made circles with the tall latte cup in front of him.

Freddie Webster pulled out an empty chair to sit across from the big-eyed man. O'Shea's back faced a wall. Freddie sat with his mouth a straight line, jaw fixed, waiting. He heard the sounds behind him, mixed conversations, the sucking and whirring noises from the counter. His eyes stayed on O'Shea.

Presently O'Shea broke the silence. "You can't be so flush you don't need your cut of that money."

"I don't have a lot of time."

"What happened to your arm?"

"Forget my arm."

"Want a latte?"

"No."

O'Shea sipped his hot drink. "Mmmmm. Nothing beats a latte. So, this is the scoop. I have a client that wants a safe cracked, and I thought of you."

"There's plenty of guys–"

"Can't use them, the heat's on." O'Shea smiled. "You pull the job, nobody suspects. It's a quick in-and-out, no problems."

O'Shea reached inside his jacket and pulled out an envelope, from which he extracted pictures. Freddie examined the two-story home in a suburban neighborhood he didn't recognize. One photo showed a wall safe.

Freddie took a long look at the safe. "You're kidding me."

"What?"

"Penny-ante safe like that's a big deal?"

O'Shea shrugged.

"Who took these pictures?"

"The client."

"I can pop this in less than ten minutes. Not even break a sweat." He smiled. Sheila would never have to know about this. He'd get the money and the two of them would have their better tomorrow.

"So, you're down?" O'Shea said.

"When?"

"Tomorrow night."

———

BY THE TIME Freddie returned home from work, Sheila had already left. A note on the stove said breakfast left-overs were wrapped in the refrigerator. He went straight to the bedroom and opened the bottom drawer of his dresser where Sheila had placed several folded sweaters. Underneath a frayed pink sweater, she'd hidden a Taurus .38 revolver, and Freddie knew there were bullets in the cylinder. He ditched the idea of using the gun. The revolver belonged to his wife. He didn't want cops finding any trail that might lead back home. Worst case, if the cops caught him with the gun—and he stopped. He didn't want to think about that.

From under another sweater he pulled out a tattered shoe box and sorted through the junk inside. He removed a pocketknife, flipped out the blade, and grabbed a sharpening stone from the box. Sitting on the carpet, he ran stone over edge from hilt to tip until the point pricked his finger with a light tap and the edge sliced through a sheet of paper.

He looked at the shiny blade. He'd used a similar weapon only once before, in prison, when another inmate had accused him of cheating at a card game. The inmate threatened to kill Webster, but guards broke up the fight. Freddie acquired a wooden-handled shiv which he kept taped to his stomach, because the fight wasn't over.

When word reached him that the other inmate and some buddies were planning an ambush, Freddie took the initiative.

Two cell mates covered his flank as he strode through the crowded yard. Hot sun blazed above. Rocks crunched below his feet. A heavy pulse beat rocked his head. Target and buddies straight ahead. They stood near a sewer grate.

Freddie and his mates charged over, their opponents reacting too late. Freddie dived into his enemy and his mates crowded on top. Punching, kicking, a scream as the shiv found its mark. Freddie broke off the wooden handle and dropped it down the sewer and when the guards broke up the fight there was nothing in his hand. The guards couldn't prove who had the shiv. No comebacks for Freddie.

His target, with a punctured lung, died a few hours later.

Freddie put the knife and stone away, took off his clothes and climbed into bed. He stared at the ceiling a lot longer than normal.

———

A RUMBLING truck engine woke Wolf from a cat nap. Voices over the headset assured him the listening devices he'd planted hours earlier were working. He grabbed the headset and scooted to the window. Below the window sat the receiver to which the headphones were connected. He turned up the volume.

At the front of the warehouse, where a large sliding door had been rolled open, sat a medium-sized cargo truck. The engine continued to churn with smoke pumping from dual exhausts. A man wearing dark clothes opened the rear of the truck and stood back while a second man piloting a forklift rolled forward. A hydraulic hiss preceded the rising of long lifting spikes and the driver slid the spikes underneath the first of several pine crates. He lifted the crate out of the truck, steered into the warehouse.

The voices over the headset continued their conversation. Somebody asked "Ace" when they'd distribute the guns. "Ace" told him the following night. Two more men emerged from the warehouse. Wolf assumed the tall blond in a leather jacket was "Ace" since he gave the others instructions, then turned and walked around the corner.

It took about an hour for the gang to unload the truck. Then the man in dark clothes jumped into the truck and drove away. Two others pulled down the rolling door and secured a padlock. The tall blond, in a green SUV, pulled around the corner, gave orders, and drove away. The remaining pair stayed on the sidewalk, lit cigarettes and started talking. Wolf kept the headphones over his ears. When the pair finished their smokes, they entered the warehouse through an alcove door, and Wolf listened to them talking about what was on television.

Wolf waited until dark and made his way up a dark stairwell to the roof.

Wolf wished he could jump across to the warehouse like Spiderman, but he'd have to settle for the terrestrial alternative. He took off at a run, hopping from roof to roof, running parallel to the street below. He ran about a block and a half. A fire escape provided access to an alley, and Wolf dashed across the empty street to the alley opposite. He climbed another fire escape, reached the top of the next building, and ran back along the block toward the target warehouse roof. At the neighboring roof, he jumped, clearing the distance from the edge to the lower warehouse roof in a flash. He landed hard and felt the shock run up his legs.

A skylight occupied the middle of the roof. Wolf knelt at the edge of the skylight, catching his breath. No lights below, nothing to see. Wolf dashed to an air duct where, earlier, he'd tied a nylon rope. He uncoiled the rope, stepped over the edge, and took baby steps down the wall to a still-unlocked window. He'd earlier used the unguarded entry point when he slipped in to plant the bugs. Hanging by the rope, the weight of his body getting heavier by the second, Wolf reached down and wedged his fingers under the metal window frame. Despite the cold, Wolf's body temperature increased steadily, sweat trickling down his neck.

Wolf raised the window. The hinge across the top squeaked. He put one leg, then the other, through the open window, grabbing the sill to stabilize his body as he slid into the dark room. He turned on a pen flash. Floating dust made the beam look like a laser ray. He followed a path through stacked office equipment to a door, opened the door and stepped onto a cement walkway overlooking the main floor. Wolf put away the pen flash and his eyes adjusted to the low light. From somewhere he heard laughing and the unmistakable voice of Homer Simpson. So much for security. Wolf headed toward the back of the building and descended on metal steps to the concrete floor. The crates, dark shapes amidst shadows, lay beyond. He reached one of the crates, felt around the top and sides. Still sealed. The crate next door had been opened. He peeked. M-16A2 assault rifles and a few M-4 carbines were packed in straw. The sharp scent of gun oil tickled Wolf's nose. Confirmation. Now he could go to step two and cause enough havoc to snatch "Ace" for interrogation.

With the laughter of the two watchmen fading behind him, he left the warehouse the way he'd arrived.

Back in the abandoned building, Wolf removed his coat and found a PowerBar in his kit bag. He sat near the window and ate while listening to whatever night sounds filtered through. A car horn, crickets. The city's heartbeat had slowed.

Wolf chewed a bite and looked around the empty floor. He'd spent so much of his life hiding in places like this, usually with a team, waiting to ambush an enemy, that he wondered if he'd ever kick the habit. This wasn't the life he would have chosen for himself, but when a thug murdered his sister, he didn't know how else to respond except to stand over her grave, promise vengeance, and go after the killer with a gun in each hand.

He kept his guns because there were other victims like Shelly who had no voice, and Wolf figured if he had the ability, he should *be* their voice. He hadn't been able to save her, but he could save others. The mental and physical toll he felt was palpable, however. Wolf was kidding himself that he could continue for long. And he didn't like that John Callaway, or his daughter Kiki, put their own lives in jeopardy to help him.

The alliance had been Callaway's idea. After

avenging Shelly, Wolf was content to move on with his life as best as he could. His parents were already gone; so was Shelly; there was nothing to do but try and start a new life.

But in the quiet of the night, he could hear her calling to him, urging him to continue helping others.

Wolf finished the PowerBar and discarded the wrapper. It was all for nothing, he knew. The bad guys never stopped, no matter how many bullets a good guy fired. There would be more Shellys that he wouldn't be able to save, no doubt.

He'd try, though. He owed his sister that.

———

"YOU BETTER EAT MORE than a couple bites," Sheila said.

Her husband started to smile but the corners of his mouth resisted. Sheila had fixed chicken and spaghetti, but Freddie had no appetite. She'd made the dinner the way he liked, heavy on the meat sauce, chicken lightly breaded.

Tonight was the night. He'd called in sick, and Sheila had no idea of the change in routine.

"Did Art take back his offer?" she said. "You haven't said much tonight."

Freddie shook his head.

"If you say one word about money or the baby," she said, "I'll scream because your attitude is really starting to piss me off."

"Tired, sweetie," he said. "Didn't sleep well."

Her eyes didn't soften. "I don't believe you."

He twirled some spaghetti around the fork. His eyes stayed on his plate. Maybe he'd blow off O'Shea and just go into work, tell them he felt better. But then O'Shea would come looking for him. He'd made his decision. No turning back.

Sheila gasped, put both hands to her belly. Freddie jerked wide eyes to hers.

"I think the baby just kicked," she said, tearing up. She wiped her eyes, felt her belly again. "Oh, wow."

She rose from her chair. He pulled her close, ear to her belly. He closed his eyes and tried to imagine the life growing inside her. Her fingers scratched the top of his head. Freddie swallowed and a hollow space opened deep in his chest. His mind's eye showed him nothing. Just darkness.

3

"SO, WHAT ARE WE LOOKING FOR?" Freddie said.

"My guy didn't say," O'Shea said. "Just empty the safe."

O'Shea drove into the dark suburban neighborhood in which tall streetlamps cast eerie black shadows across the asphalt. Freddie glanced at his feet where his black nylon bag lay, the tool provided by O'Shea inside. He'd tossed his old stuff years ago. Taped his to stomach was the sharpened pocketknife, warm against his skin.

"There," O'Shea said. He stopped the car in front of the house. The short-trimmed grass had a sign in the middle with the name of a lawn care company. "You can bet the mighty citizens who own this place," O'Shea said, "never dirty their hands with yard work."

Curtains covered the windows. No light escaped the house.

"The occupants won't be back 'til late," the gray-eyed man said.

O'Shea jumped out. Freddie's eyes stayed on the house. O'Shea leaned back inside.

"Move it, champ."

Freddie snapped out of his daze and pushed open the passenger door. His hands were empty. He reached back for the bag, slammed the door and followed O'Shea up the stone path to the house. His tapping footsteps sounded louder than ever and matched his thumping heartbeat. *Just like on the yard.* The hilt of the knife dug into his belly.

Freddie wasn't a fan of drilling. Most safes were protected by a hard steel plate or a composite hard plate, so choosing to drill not only took time but was also useless against such safeguards. Even a "penny-ante" safe such as the one he was about to crack had a hard plate.

He stood in the master bedroom, examining the front of the wall safe. A Cain One-Thousand. Pointless to drill but weak in other areas. He placed his bag on the king-sized bed, looked around the room. Only one side of the bed looked rumpled. Cluttered dresser, dusty mirror, crowded bookcase. Bare walls, plain curtains. No feminine touches. A man lived in the house alone. A clock ticked on the dresser.

From the nylon bag Freddie removed what looked like a television remote control. With magnets, the "remote" attached to the front of the safe, and he placed the device next to the combination lock. He plugged a pair of headphones into the device, put the phones over his ears.

He started moving the dial back and forth with steady fingers. Through the headphones he heard *click-click-dunk*. With each *dunk* he was closer to opening the box. The Cain One-Thousand had a three-digit combo.

No thoughts of Sheila or the baby flowed through

his mind; his heart rate had settled to normal, no beads of sweat covered his forehead. He felt awake, refreshed.

Presently the last *dunk* came through loud and clear and Freddie wrenched the handle and pulled open the safe. He took a deep breath. Not much inside. A stack of stock certificates. A DVD in a plastic case. Small note-book. He scooped everything into the nylon bag, dropped the "remote" and headphones inside, zipped the bag. He smiled big at O'Shea. They exited the house.

At O'Shea's apartment, Freddie plopped down on the dirty green couch, setting the bag on the chipped wooden coffee table before him. The pocketknife dug into his middle. O'Shea went into the kitchen. A televi-sion and X-Box against the wall faced him. The small living room had a stained carpet and a spider crouching in a web in an upper corner. Loud thuds and music seeped through the ceiling and indicated the upstairs neighbors were having a ball.

O'Shea returned with two bottles of beer. Freddie took one and popped the top with a quick twist. The cold pilsner tasted good. O'Shea fished a cordless phone from under the couch and quickly dialed a number.

"It's done," the gray-eyed man said after a moment. Freddie drank some more beer and studied O'Shea's neck.

"Right, twenty minutes." O'Shea turned off the phone, dropped it on the carpet. He lifted his beer. "Time to get paid."

They drank. Then O'Shea said, "Let's see the junk," grabbed the nylon bag. He tossed the stock certificates, notebook, on the table. He held up the DVD. "Maybe it's the guy's homemade stag movies," he said. He turned on the T.V. and fed the DVD into the Xbox.

A grainy color picture appeared. Two men in a conference room spoke in low voices. One sat at a large circular table while the second man paced back and forth. Freddie sat up and leaned forward as O'Shea cursed, reaching for the remote.

"Hang on, Jimmy."

Freddie watched as the two men spoke, though the one at the table did most of the talking. The eye-patch gave away the seated man's identity, and Freddie listened to every muffled word. Whoever taped the meeting had hidden the camera well. Neither seemed to know they were being recorded.

O'Shea said, "What are you so excited about?"

"The guy with the eye patch. Don't you know who that is?"

"No."

"I remember him from my days back east. New York. That's Ugo Califano. Big shot wise guy."

"Who's the other guy looks like he's holding back the runs?"

Freddie shook his head. "Him I'm not sure of. I wanna say he's a politician–"

"Looks like your pirate friend's trying to make a deal with him."

Words like "good for all of us" and "think about the money" came from the mouth of the man with the eye patch. The other man finally stopped pacing, placed hands on hips, said, *"Let's do it."*

Freddie said, "Turn it off."

O'Shea pressed stop. "What's the big deal?"

"That's what your guy wants."

"Cool. He'll be here soon, and we'll get paid and you go home to your wife."

Freddie drained his beer. "Want another?"

O'Shea swallowed the last of his beer. "Yeah."

Freddie rose and was halfway to the kitchen when O'Shea said:

"That politician guy. He reminds me of a painting I saw the other night, where this knight guy was taking on a dragon but one blast of fire from the dragon's mouth blew off the knight's armor and the sucker ran around naked."

"What do you mean?"

"The politician. He's fooling around with something that's gonna burn him bad."

"You sure you only had one beer?"

In the kitchen Freddie reached under his shirt, yanked the knife free, wincing as the tape pulled from his skin. He tossed the tape in the trash. From the refrigerator he took a single bottle of beer. Freddie returned to the living room. O'Shea sat on the couch switching stations with the remote. Freddie smashed the bottle over O'Shea's head.

Glass shards and sudsy beer splashed over the couch. O'Shea screamed. The jagged edges of the shards cut into his skin, left bubbly lines of blood on the side of his face. He threw his arms up to his head and tried to roll forward. Freddie flipped open his knife. O'Shea lunged sideways and collided with the safe cracker's midsection. Freddie's grip on the knife tightened as he flew back into a wall. O'Shea straightened and hammered with fists and elbows. Freddie dropped to the carpet and plunged the knife into O'Shea's leg.

O'Shea hollered and staggered back and reached for

the handle. Freddie tackled O'Shea, pressed a knee into his groin, wrapped calloused fingers around O'Shea's neck and squeezed. Hard.

O'Shea garbled a scream. He swung fists to pummel Freddie, but only his forearms struck. Freddie grimaced, grinding his teeth. More pressure into the squeeze. O'Shea's swings became weaker. His arms dropped. Gray eyes bulged. His face turned blue. Then he stopped moving. Freddie didn't let go until O'Shea's last gurgle assured the safe cracker that the deed was done. Freddie unlocked his hands and yanked out the knife and hauled O'Shea's head back to expose his neck and buried the blade all the way to the handle.

Freddie rolled off the body. He scrambled back into the darkened entryway, gasping, chest pumping up and down. His lungs burned. Sweat stung his eyes. He lurched into the sitting room, scooped the DVD and other items back into the nylon bag, turned toward the front door.

And turned back. He grabbed the cordless phone, chucked it into the bag. It would have the number of O'Shea's contact stored in memory. In the kitchen, on the counter, he found an envelope, scratched a note with a leaky pen, and dropped the envelope on the body.

He headed for the door but stopped again. Out in the hallway somebody might see him. He crossed to the patio doors, slid them open, spent a moment scanning the shadowy center courtyard. Three floors up. Landing hard on the ground beat being caught in the hallway. Freddie Webster clamped his free hand on the rail, launched his body over, and watched the ground race up to meet him.

4

BEN REGAN, the man who hired O'Shea to find Freddie, knocked on O'Shea's door. No answer. He tried the rust-spotted knob, which didn't budge. He leaned closer. Some of the frame trim was coming loose. Through the gap, he saw that the deadbolt wasn't engaged. Regan flipped open a knife and pushed the blade through the gap until he found the blocker connected to the knob. Lining up the blade with the blocker, he pushed forward, pressing the blocker into the lock recess. Then he shoved the door open.

On the floor lay O'Shea. Regan shut the door and went over to the body, careful to avoid the blood-soaked carpet. The chilly draft from the still-open patio door showed Regan the killer's escape route. He frowned when he saw the blood-stained envelope. Regan leaned down. The killer had scrawled four words:

WAIT FOR MY CALL.

Regan straightened, checked the cell phone on his

belt and turned up the volume. When the killer reached him, he didn't want the phone in silent mode.

———

THE DRY STUFFINESS of the abandoned building was making Wolf irritable. He'd spent most of the remaining night on the roof, counting stars. Once the sun came up, he went to the cot to lie down. He kept the wireless receiver at full volume, the headphones within reach. Time passed. Only the lookouts changed.

Around midnight several trucks and SUVs began pulling up. Somebody inside opened the big sliding door. At his window, Wolf watched the gun runners, including blond-haired Ace in his leather jacket, meander inside as if nothing would ever spoil their party.

Wolf yanked off the headphones. He checked his pistol and shotgun and strapped on the bandoleer of grenades. He made his way up to the roof and raced across the rooftops once more, crossing to the other side, following the opposite rooftops back to the warehouse. There he found the rope, lowered himself to the window he'd used before, and slipped inside.

Easing open the door in the empty second-floor room, Wolf gazed out at the busy gun runners unloading crates and laying weapons out on the floor side by side. Their voices bounced, echoed; the crates popped, snapped, as men wielding crowbars pried them open. Wolf kept to the shadows as he advanced down the walkway. He tossed a grenade into the center of the warehouse. All eyes turned to the small bomb as it clunked on the ground, bounced once, and exploded in mid-air.

Wolf pitched a second grenade, and then a third. The gun runners screamed. Some fired pistol shots into the smoke and shadows. Wolf raced to the metal steps, tucking the shotgun into his right shoulder. Through smoke and fire Wolf picked out movement to the left. He fired once, twice. Two men went down. Somebody on the floor drew a pistol. Wolf fired again, the man jerking with the impacts of the shot shell burst.

Wolf ducked against a crate. The smoke stung his eyes. A door clanged open. He looked around and saw Ace slipping out to the street. Wolf followed through the door. The loud growl of the green SUV's engine came from the left. The speeding vehicle screamed toward him and Wolf squeezed the trigger, the pellet blast shattering the front passenger side fender and part of the windshield.

Wolf ran after the SUV. Ace continued down the block, tires shrieking and billowing smoke as he turned left. Wolf ran to the Camaro and followed.

Wolf kept the throttle down and his eyes open as the road started to curve. The dull throb of the engine decreased as the sharp turn forced him to slow. He floored the pedal coming out of the turn, felt his body press back into the seat, and saw the taillights of Ace's SUV ahead.

Wolf reached Ace's bumper. The SUV took the next corner too fast, passenger side digging against the curb. The wheel grinded against the cement and a shower of sparks jumped high. A burst of speed pulled the SUV back onto the pavement.

Wolf moved into the opposite lane, hitting the

switch to lower the passenger window. He drew his .45 and fired out the window. The green SUV's rear tire exploded, and the SUV shifted across the Camaro's front end.

Wolf jammed on the brakes and watched the SUV spin, then bounce onto the sidewalk and crash into a storefront. The front window shattered, the wrecked display rocketing deeper into the store. An alarm blared. Wolf pulled over.

Ace jumped out. He raised one of the military-issue M-4 carbines and opened fire. The stingers ripped into the Camaro's hood, shattering the windshield, crawling along the driver's side.

Wolf dived for the floor as glass rained down, covering his neck and eyes. The bullets struck like steel raindrops and the car rocked with each hit.

Wolf tightened his grip on the .45. He pushed open the passenger door, rolled onto the hard pavement, and dashed around to the trunk.

Ace ceased fire. Wolf listened to the other man's approaching footsteps.

Wolf dropped on his left side, extending the .45. He wanted a leg or shoulder shot to put Ace out of commission, but before he could set his sights Ace raised the M-4. Flame flashed from the Colt's barrel. Ace stopped short, stood a moment, his stunned face blankly contemplating Wolf. Then he fell over. His head made a loud clack as it met the asphalt. Wolf jumped up and ran to the man.

Ace's wide eyes stared up at the night sky. The gun runner's breath came out in short gasps, his body convulsing from the open chest wound. Blood bubbled up from his throat. He managed half a bloody grin as the light behind his eyes faded.

Wolf, breathing hard, turned to the SUV, but sirens wailing in the distance stopped him.

He gave the Camaro a sad glance. The car had been faithful, but no simple fix would get the machine back on the road. He had other vehicles. The cops would have fun trying to determine the owner. The registration led to an abandoned brownstone downtown.

Wolf grabbed a spare overcoat from the trunk, throwing it on to cover his combat garb. He lifted a piece of carpet, revealing an electronic panel with a single red button. Wolf pushed the red button, turned and ran away. Within two minutes, charges hidden in the Camaro would ignite, flame would gut the interior, and wipe out any fingerprints.

———

"You're kidding me."

Ben Regan regarded the big white-haired man on the other side of the table with raised eyebrows.

The big man said, "So whoever O'Shea hired killed him and took off with the disk." The big man, Teddy Gambolini, swiveled his chair left to look out a window. He and Regan sat in a long trailer set up as an office. Outside, construction crews assembled the frame of a building. A bulldozer rumbled passed. The trailer shook a little. A cloud of dust followed the dozer and pasted residue on the window.

Gambolini knew construction better than anything —except making money for the mob. Various construction sites had always made good front operations for mafia activity, and he'd certainly been in charge of many back home in New York City, where something was always under construction, and always provided a good spot to drop the body parts of somebody who offended the family and needed to disappear.

But what can work for you, can also be used against you. Gambolini had worked for crime boss Vito Scarlatta, who'd been like a brother to him, until Gambolini "offended" the family by trying to kill his "brother" for missteps in a drug operation that cost Gambolini a ton of start-up money. His attempt failed, and he'd had to run away with his tail between his legs less somebody "disappear" him in one of his own building projects.

Gambolini's number two, Ben Regan, had stayed with the big man because he'd been marked for death too. There was an open contract for both of them, for whoever made the kill, from the sharpest mob marksman, to the lowest street thug who wanted to make a name for himself.

Unless, of course, they could find a way to bring back a peace offering, something Gamoblini's old bosses would love to have, such as the location of a rival mobster also marked for death, whom the syndicate had been unable to find for over a decade. If Gambolini could bring back the man's location, all might be forgiven.

That wasn't asking too much, right?

Which is how the caper surrounding the stolen DVD started.

But now that looked like it was going to hell too.

Gambolini swiveled back to Regan. The chair squeaked. Sunlight caught the gold watch on his wrist.

The hand connected to the wrist had half an index finger. "Did I make a fair summary?"

"Perfect. Couldn't have said it better."

Gambolini's mouth twitched a little but he controlled his response to Regan's sarcasm. "Who is this guy who thinks he can run off with what we paid for?"

"We still have the money."

"But we don't have the goods. I'm asking you what's the deal with this guy."

"Don't know."

"You don't know."

"Am I not speaking clearly, Teddy?"

The big man's cheeks puffed a little. He pressed his lips together. He and Regan had worked side by side long enough for the smart talk to become common between them. Teddy just wasn't good at firing back.

"I hear you," Gambolini said. "What's the guy planning to do?"

"If I find him, I'll ask, just before I put a bullet in him."

"Everything depends on that disk, Ben."

"No."

Gambolini frowned. "Explain."

"We want something from Palakis, and using the DVD gives us leverage against him. Who says he has to know we even have it? He *doesn't* have it. The threat is there. That's all we need."

"And our thief?"

"We'll swat that fly, no problem. He said to wait for a call but my phone ain't buzzing. He has no idea how to proceed. He'll probably hide the disk which means he won't tell me where it is and that's okay. Once he's dead the disk can stay lost."

"What if he goes to Palakis and tries to sell back the disk?" Gambolini said.

"Wouldn't that suck?"

Gambolini pulled Chapstick from a shirt pocket and dabbed his lips. Another bulldozer shook the trailer. Shouts from a foreman made Gambolini turn toward the window again. He scratched the small scar on his left cheek and said, "What if this guy took the disk because he knows what's on it? What if the whole bag of peanuts is spoiled by this?"

Regan blinked a few times and offered no response.

"Where's your snappy comeback, Ben?" Gambolini went "heh-heh" as Regan stared back.

"You want we should just let the guy go and forget the whole thing?"

This time Gambolini said nothing.

"Let's quit talking," Regan said, "and I'll get to work. 'Kay?"

"Why are you still sitting here?"

5

THE ACHE in his neck finally woke him.

Freddie Webster groaned as he shifted his stiff body. The driver's seat hadn't been made for sleeping, and the springs in the backrest poked through the thin cushion, causing further discomfort. He couldn't stretch his legs and felt a cramp. He had been waiting for Sheila to leave so she'd never see the blood on his clothes. The dashboard clock read 10:15. He'd been asleep about 90 minutes.

The skin under his bandage itched. He scratched against the bandage.

He'd parked a block from the apartment and twisted the key. The engine sputtered. He turned the key again and the engine fired. He drove up the block to his apartment.

Inside, he dropped the nylon bag by the door and landed on the couch. At least the cushions were softer than the car, even if he sank down too far for long term comfort. He put his face in his hands, shut his eyes tight, and tried to block out the image of O'Shea's bulging eyes and gurgled scream. The image remained as bright and colorful as anything around him.

He left the couch for the bathroom and tore off his clothes. They'd have to be trashed. After splashing cold water on his face, he leaned against the counter and stared at his stubble-jawed reflection. His blood-shot eyes stared back.

What could he do now?

Sell the DVD back to the people he'd stolen from? Or maybe shake down the man who hired O'Shea? All he wanted was the whole fifteen thousand. His shoulders sank at another realization. O'Shea's client would already be looking for him.

Had O'Shea mentioned anything about him?

Sheila.

He bolted from the bathroom, snatched the phone from the kitchen wall and dialed her cell. Straight to voicemail. He dialed the restaurant and asked for her.

"Freddie?"

He let out a long sigh. "Hey."

"Are you okay? I guess we missed each other this morning."

"I was so tired I had to pull over and fell asleep in the car."

"Oh, poor thing. You're worrying too much."

He said nothing a moment; then, "Yeah."

"Go to bed. I'll try and get out of here early tonight, okay?"

"You have to see the doctor later, right?"

"That's not for another hour or so," she said. "Go to bed."

He swallowed. "I love you, Sheila."

"Of course, you do." She laughed. "See you tonight."

Freddie said good-bye and hung up. He couldn't go to sleep yet. He had to toss the bloody clothes. And get the nylon bag to their safe deposit box where it would remain secure until he decided his next move.

Somebody tapped on the door.

Freddie hit the mute button and the soap opera went silent. His whole body froze. He stopped breathing and heard pounding in his head. Another knock. It's nothing, he told himself. Sheila ordered something online and UPS was delivering.

It hadn't been an easy couple of hours since returning from his errands. Sleep was impossible. Finally, he rose and watched TV in the living room, but had no focus on any program, so he flipped stations.

Another trio of taps. Light, quick. Not the heavy knock of a delivery man.

Freddie's pulse raced.

Two heavy kicks splintered the wood door at the lock. A silenced gunshot finished the job, the deadbolt breaking in two and dropping on the floor. The door squeaked open. The man stood about an inch taller than Freddie. The mop of hair on his head covered the tops of his large ears. He had a touch of gray in his mustache.

The man said, "My name's Ben Regan, and you're in big trouble."

Regan approached. Freddie jumped up and drew a fist back, but the intruder moved faster and punched Freddie in the jaw.

Regan dragged Freddie across the carpet to the couch, resting the silencer-fitted nine-millimeter Beretta automatic on his right knee.

Freddie groaned, rubbed his jaw, eyes on Regan. He said, "Didn't take you very long, did it?"

"Nope."

"And you're gonna kill me."

"Yup."

"You also talk too much."

"Then get ready for an earful," Regan said. He stood, started pacing across the carpet with the nine-millimeter at his side. He stopped at a metal shelf next to the T.V. stand and scanned the framed pictures of Freddie and Sheila. He picked up a framed sonogram photo of the baby.

"Isn't technology neat?" he said, put the picture back.

Freddie's eyes never left Regan, but the man didn't open himself to attack. Regan sat down again.

"O'Shea never told me your name, but he told me enough about you that I was able to ask around and a lot of guys know who you are. Mistake one, you're too well known to hide.

"Mistake two," Regan said, "you really don't have anything to bargain with. My employer and I don't need the disk, just the threat of it being exposed, to get what we want." Regan examined a thumbnail, continued: "Mistake three, you should have kept your promise." Regan smiled. "When I find your wife? Well, never mind."

Regan raised the nine-millimeter as Freddie's right hand swept up to the couch cushion, grabbed the remote, and flung it at Regan. The remote tumbled end over end as it covered the distance and smacked Regan in the forehead. The killer yelped, recoiling. He fired in reflex and the bullet punched into the couch.

Freddie scrambled on knees and elbow as Regan rose. Regan stabbed the gun at the crawling man and fired. The shot cut into the carpet as Freddie gained his feet and pounded down the hallway. Regan fired again and the bullet *thunked* into the hallway wall. Freddie reached the bedroom and the dresser drawer where the Taurus .38 was hidden. He grabbed the gun, spun around. Regan fired three times and Freddie jumped with each dead-center hit. He fell to his knees, put a hand out to stop his fall, raised the revolver again and started to squeeze the trigger. Regan stood still, watching. A rush of breath left Freddie and his trigger finger slackened and his body pitched forward, lay still.

Regan sniffed the sharp scent of exploded gunpowder and put away the nine-millimeter. He made a quick search of the apartment, starting in the bedroom; tearing through cabinets, cupboards; closets, under the couch. No sign of the DVD. Webster had already stashed it. The location died with him.

Regan filled a glass with tap water, drank it down, wiped sweat from his brow. A notepad adhered to the wall, beside the telephone, caught his eye. His shoes squeaked on the tiled floor as he went to look. The scrawl said, "Dr. Kwong, 12:30, Lakeshire Memorial."

He checked his watch. Forty-five minutes. He took a picture of Sheila from the metal shelf and locked the door using Webster's key. He whistled part of "Hey, Jude" as he strode down the hallway.

Traffic delayed Regan's arrival. His watch showed 1:15 when he parked his Cadillac CTS. The sun beat down hard, the hot air uncomfortable. Across the way people wandered in and out of the hospital via an automatic door on one side of which someone had taped a missing person poster. Regan leaned against a tree that blocked the sun, but the rough bark scraped through the fabric of his shirt. He watched people go in and out and wondered who the face on the missing person poster belonged to. Every few minutes he glanced at Sheila's picture to keep her features fresh in his mind.

Around a quarter of two the vigilance paid off.

Slinging her purse, the bulge of her belly visible under her blouse, Sheila Webster exited the hospital and headed across the lot to the tree where Regan stood. He let her pass and fell in step behind her. He pulled the nine-millimeter and snatched her right arm and shoved the gun into her ribs. She stiffened; he said:

"Not a word or I'll spill the fetus all over the concrete."

He dragged her toward the CTS. "Your hubby broke his promise, sweetie. I hate to do this, but we can't have any loose ends."

Sheila's feet skidded on the ground, creating a bit of space between her and the faster-moving Regan, but he yanked her closer. The sharp front sight of the nine-millimeter pierced the fabric of her blouse. She winced.

They reached the middle of the parking aisle and a Maxima slowed. And that's when Sheila let out a scream that shook the world. She threw her weight at Regan, jostling him, and balled her left hand and struck his chest, face. Regan recoiled, dragging her back between two cars.

The man in the Maxima jumped out, yelled, "Hey," and Regan aimed over Sheila's back and shot him in the chest. He had no silencer this time and the shot echoed like a crack of thunder.

Sheila twisted free. Others stopped and stared as she

scrambled back toward the hospital building. Regan raised his gun and fired once. The bullet shattered the sliding door as Sheila ran through and the missing person poster fell amongst the broken glass. Regan took off running for the street. He'd come back for the CTS. Too many faces looking his way.

6

WOLF AWOKE a little after noon and lay in bed staring at a trio of red spots on the ceiling. They'd been there when he moved in. He often wondered how the spots had gotten there, picturing somebody with a squeeze bottle of ketchup blasting upward. Like a kid fooling around. The idea made him smile. He hoped it was true. He could hear the child's laughter at the initial blast followed by the "uh-oh" feeling hoping mom or dad never noticed.

With a grim set to his jaw he rolled out of bed, scraped whiskers off his face, splashed around in the shower and ordered breakfast from the hotel kitchen.

Wolf occupied a two-room suite at the Carlton Hotel, located in the sprawling downtown area of the city. Towering buildings, beyond which were hills that sprouted homes in some mutated act of nature, were visible out the bedroom window. A shade covered the window. He remembered when the city hadn't been so urban. Seeing that view first thing ruined what memories of youth he did have. When he wanted to get out of the city altogether, he had a cabin at Lake Wyatt waiting for him.

While waiting for breakfast, Wolf sat at the writing table, the open window beside him letting in the noon breeze along with the echoing rumbles of motors, horns, and street trolleys far below. He scrubbed the Colt pistol with solvent, wiped it clean, oiled the mechanism. He finished the task and put the weapon in a metal case and the metal case on the top shelf of the hall closet.

Room service arrived with a light double-knock. Wolf opened the door for the young steward. The steward set out the two covered dishes and a teapot. Wolf tipped him a five, triple-locked the door after the steward exited, and sat down to eat.

One plate contained a mix of hash browns, sausage links, bacon, scrambled eggs. The other plate contained three fluffy buttermilk pancakes. The teapot held hot water. Wolf poured some of the water into a mug with a chipped brim and dropped in a tea bag which held the custom mix of honey-flavored green tea he bought from a small mom-and-pop shop in Chinatown.

Wolf took his time with each bite. Such comforts hadn't always been available, and he appreciated the opportunity to enjoy a hot breakfast.

He finished eating, placed the dishes outside his door. The black smart phone on the table beside his leather couch buzzed. Wolf went over the picked it up. "Hank's Chicken Shack."

A feminine laugh answered. "Did you have to make such a mess last night?"

"Last night? I was in the tub engrossed in Fitzgerald, so I have no idea what you're talking about."

"Right. A warehouse blasted to pieces, a man lying dead in the street? None of that means anything to you?"

"Please, my virgin ears can't handle–"

"Forget it. I'm coming over. There's some things you need to know."

"Can't wait."

Wolf ended the call and smiled. Kiki Callaway, John's daughter and his only other ally in law enforcement, always made him smile. The mood faded when he set the phone down. A good mood always faded when she said good-bye.

————

A KNOCK ON THE DOOR. Wolf peeked through the peephole and flipped back the trio of locks and the door opened with a little squeak.

"You should really oil those hinges," Kiki said. When she smiled, her nose crinkled up. Wolf liked when she smiled.

"I keep telling the super but he's in Africa hunting rhinoceros."

She laughed and stepped through the doorway. Her long black hair drifted in a shoulder-length wave. She'd come from the D.A.'s office based on her attire, long, loose black skirt, white sweater.

Wolf triple-locked the door. Kiki dropped her purse, from which a yellow manila envelope protruded, on the couch. She plopped down, slipped off her heels, and crossed her legs.

"Nice to get away for a bit," she said.

"Busy?" Wolf went around a dividing wall to the kitchen.

"What do you think?"

Wolf opened the refrigerator. On one shelf sat a row of bottles of beer. Below that, a row of Cokes. Wolf started to grab two of the bottles, then snatched two Cokes instead.

Wolf returned to Kiki and handed her one of the sodas. She popped the top. "You can have a beer," she said. "It won't bother me."

Wolf shook his head and cracked open his drink. He poured some into his chipped mug and sat down.

"Back in the old days," Kiki said after a sip, "I'd be on my second bottle of vodka." She slouched back and crossed her legs.

He drank some Coke. "How are your roses?"

Kiki grew and bred roses for competition and had dedicated a large portion of her father's back yard for the work since she didn't have the space at her apartment.

She shook her head. "My father's stupid beagle found a weak spot in my safety fence and tore up a bunch. I chased that little runt all through the house. He finally hid in my father's office and Daddy wouldn't let me go in after him."

Wolf laughed.

"It's not *funny*," she said.

They sat without talking for a bit. Fine with Wolf. He was in no hurry to talk about the gun runners. He considered the operation a complete disaster. No goal reached. No information. No leads. The fight was all over the news. Nothing could have prevented that. And Wolf had lost his car.

Presently Kiki brought up the subject.

"I guess things didn't totally go as planned last night," she said.

"It could have been worse." Wolf explained his side of the action.

"Well, I'm glad you're okay," she said. "As for what you need to know, the Feds have swooped in. Confiscated the weapons, the bodies, everything. The only thing I got from the files was the guy you shot–his name was Tim Dell. Long history. Mostly smuggling."

"Uh-huh."

"This is the first time the Feds have gotten their hands on the stolen guns since the theft. Now maybe they'll get a break."

"Any gossip at all? Who they think is behind the smuggling?"

"Nothing that I've heard with my own ears," she said. "But one of the other girls thinks a CIA agent is part of the search team."

Wolf raised an eyebrow. "Why?"

Kiki shrugged. "Says she heard a guy say he wanted to update Langley. That's all I heard, third-party. Don't put any stock in it."

Wolf smiled.

"Will you lay low now that the Feds are here?"

"You're joking, right?"

———

THE PILE of chips in the center grew as the men around the table said, "Call," one by one. The table fell silent. The dealer glanced at the one player who hadn't called. The dealer, a big, bald black man whose white shirt and black vest stretched tight against his big chest, said: "Now you, tea boy."

Wolf smiled and sipped some of his honey green tea. It wasn't his day. His pile of chips had been dwindling since the game began. He looked at his cards, said, "Call," added two chips to the center pile.

Ceiling fans hummed above and circulated the hot air. The glass-walled back barroom of Bert's Hof Brau catered to the poker club in the afternoon hours, when the restaurant closed after lunchtime. Wolf played once or twice a week. Bert's reopened at six, and as the players put their skills to use, the restaurant crew hustled to clean and prep for the dinner rush. The kitchen noises and crew movement didn't jar the players' concentration.

The dealer said, "And the turn," dropped a fourth card on the table, where it joined three others. All four cards were lined up straight.

"Place your bets," the dealer said. The players added to the pot once more. Wolf raised the pot. Two players folded. The remaining five called.

Wolf made a fist with his left hand, used his thumb to pull down his index and middle fingers until the knuckles cracked. He knew he should have folded. Cut and run. But it was only money, so he stayed. He'd been cleaned out anyway. Winning would only mean one more hand, and he'd had enough. He sipped his tea. Should have stayed home.

"River," the dealer said, adding a final card to the line. The players showed their cards. One had rags, nothing; the other two held pairs; Wolf smiled, flipped over the two cards he held. Maybe he'd stay another hand after all.

"Flush," Wolf said.

The last player, far to the right of the dealer, threw down his cards. He said: "Straight flush, scar face."

Wolf deflated. The dealer swept the pot to the winner. The dealer then scooped up the cards, shuffled the deck. He looked at Wolf. "Still in?"

Wolf put up his hands. "Just ain't my day, guys." He grabbed the handful of remaining chips, crossed the wood floor to the bar where a girl changed his chips for cash. A ten, two ones. He still had lunch money. He left the restaurant and climbed into his new car, a dark blue Chrysler 300. He had a third back-up vehicle stashed at another location should the 300 meet the same fate as the Camaro, and he made a note to get another vehicle purchased soon so he was never without wheels. The big four-door had the massive Hemi V8 and more power than Wolf would probably ever need, and that made it a perfect fit. He missed the tight feel and manual gearbox of the Camaro, though. Driving home, Wolf thought about grabbing a couple of Newton's hot dogs and wondered if there was anything good on television.

———

WHEN WOLF SPOTTED Sheila in the lobby, his heart skipped. She ran into his arms sobbing.

In his suite he sat her down on the couch. She clung to him. Her body felt warm against his. It took a few minutes, but she finally said: "Hi."

"Tell me."

She sniffed hard. "I think something's happened to Freddie. I was at the doctor's getting my check up and this guy came up and put a gun in my side and said Freddie had done something and he had to clean up the loose ends."

Wolf clenched his jaw. She sobbed some more. Wolf rubbed circles on her back.

"What do you want me to do?"

"See what happened." She told him of her last conversation with Freddie, said that to the best of her knowledge he'd gone right to bed, but when she called after being attacked, the phone just rang and rang.

"You need to lie down," Wolf told Sheila, nudging her to rise.

He led her down a short hallway to the spare bedroom, where Sheila stretched out on the bed. The fluffy pillow seemed to swallow her head. Wolf almost smiled. Then he noticed that she had fixed her eyes over his shoulder where a framed black-and-white photograph hung. A hallway, dark. One small light bulb shined at the very end.

"Did you take that one?" Sheila said.

Wolf looked at the photo. Photography had been a hobby of his, long ago, before the military, before his life now.

"I think it's one of the last photos I took," he said. "The darkness is powerful, but that little light never stops shining."

She swallowed, ran a hand over her belly. Wolf watched her. He hoped what she feared wasn't so. He couldn't imagine Freddie going back on his word. He'd helped Freddie out of a jam once and that's how he'd met the couple. Now he had to help them both out of trouble. And trouble was his business.

7

WOLF ONLY SPENT a few minutes at the apartment, checking out the bullet hits, which led him to Freddie's body. On hands and knees, he leaned over far enough to sniff the revolver and realized it hadn't been fired.

On the way home he stopped at a liquor store pay phone and called Kiki.

"There's somebody at my place you need to see," he said.

"Who?"

"Have you heard about a shooting at Lakeshire Memorial?"

"Yes. One dead and a pregnant woman fighting with the gunman. She ran into the hospital but vanished."

"She's at my place."

"You're kidding?"

"Come by and meet her."

Wolf hung up and looked at the shell casing he held. He'd picked it up from the apartment floor. Nine-millimeter. It didn't tell him anything, but he'd taken it anyway.

He called the police to report the murder, then called Sheila and told her to let Kiki in if he didn't return in time. He said he hadn't seen the apartment yet. Then he hit the street and stopped at a few hangouts and asked about Freddie. The information he gathered formed a disturbing picture.

Wolf returned to his hotel suite and found Kiki sitting on the couch with Sheila. "Getting to know each other?"

Kiki rose. "Outside, Mister Wolf."

She closed the patio door. Over her shoulder, Wolf saw Sheila watching them.

"You can't keep her here."

"Right. That's why she's staying with you."

"There's an APB out and you want me to hide her in my closet?"

Wolf said, "You only know part of the story," and filled in the other details.

"I'm sympathetic," Kiki said, "really, I am. But I'm not looking the other way on this one."

Her cheeks had a red flush. She kept her dark eyes fixed on Wolf. "I need a head start. A few hours."

"What do you already know?"

"A few nights ago, a crook named Jimmy O'Shea went looking for Freddie. O'Shea had a job lined up and other safe crackers were lying low. Now, both O'Shea and Freddie are dead. O'Shea's body was found this morning, look it up. It's all over the street. Freddie's killed later in the day. Here's what I think happened: Freddie pulled a double-cross and killed O'Shea and ran off with the loot. Whoever hired O'Shea tracked down Freddie and killed him, and probably took back whatever was stolen unless Freddie was able to hide it."

"Is that all?" Kiki said.

"Earlier this morning a guy was making the rounds looking for Freddie. Posing as an old friend. A couple guys I talked to say he isn't from around here. I bet that's the man who killed him."

"What did you find at the apartment?"

"Just the body. Nothing Freddie may have stolen. He put up a fight, though. I found him in the bedroom with a gun in his hand."

"I'll see if any robberies were reported today involving safes."

"Appreciated."

"Now," Kiki said, "about Sheila."

"She and I have things to talk about. Tomorrow you can bring her in."

"She'll let me?"

"When I tell her it's okay. Then can you take care of her a few days? She'll have doctor visits–"

"Of course."

"Thank you."

On the street below, car and bus engines grumbled. A horn honked. A pigeon flapped wings as it landed on the balcony rail, paused, took off again.

Wolf and Kiki blinked at each other.

Kiki said, "You two have things to talk about," with a glance over her shoulder.

"Yeah."

Wolf and Kiki went back inside, and he showed her out, then sat beside Sheila and took a deep breath before he started talking.

———

"Now what?"

Wolf said, "You need to see some detectives tomorrow. Then you can stay with Kiki until I fix this."

"You can't fix this."

"You know what I mean."

Sheila looked down at the carpet.

"If Freddie broke his promise," Wolf said, "tell me why."

Sheila patted her belly, explained Freddie's money concerns and second job options. She described his withdrawal the past few days, all of which must have been related to planning the robbery, she said.

"If Freddie wanted to hide something, like whatever he stole, where would that be?"

"I can't–" and she broke down. Wolf again pulled her close, waited.

"I need to know," he said.

"What if he couldn't hide it?"

"It's worth a try."

She wiped her eyes and said, "We have a safe deposit box. Key's in my purse. If it isn't there I don't know."

———

Wolf reached Parker Savings & Loan and stopped the 300 in a space near the front entrance. He crossed the tiled lobby to the wall of safe deposit boxes.

He wasn't wearing his London Fog, but a regular brown leather bomber jacket instead, with the Colt Series 70 .45 auto nestled in an inside-the-waistband holster just behind his right hip. He preferred IWB carry when walking the street. Holster kept pistol snug against his body so comfortably that he often forgot the gun was there—until he needed it.

He found a box that corresponded with the number on the key, put key in lock, twisted. The door opened without a squeak and Wolf pulled out the black nylon bag.

Back in the car he opened the bag and found a folded piece of paper with words on it.

SHEILA, IF YOU'RE READING THIS SOMETHING BAD HAPPENED. I BROKE MY PROMISE AND I'M SORRY. I THOUGHT I COULD FIX IT FOR US. MAYBE MY STUFF WILL HELP EVEN THE FLOAT. I DON'T KNOW WHO WE HIT, BUT I PUT OUR RECON PHOTOS IN THE BAG WITH THE REST OF THE JUNK.

Wolf examined the photos and read the letter a second time. Freddie neglected to write down any directions or an address. He didn't recognize the house in the photos, nor the section of town, nor the neighborhood.

As a lead it made a great wild goose chase.

He drove home and found Sheila stirring a simmering pot of soup. Wolf placed the nylon bag on the dining table.

Sheila looked at him with red saucer-like eyes. The soup bubbled.

He wasn't sure what to say.

————

THE NEXT MORNING Wolf sipped cooling tea and looked out the window at the crowded mountainside. The breakfast dishes lay scattered on the table, a few extra since Sheila had eaten with him. Kiki had picked up Sheila a little after ten, and now Wolf found the silence to which he'd so long become accustomed almost unbearable.

This was no way to live. He should have been out on the street with the normal people doing something productive, not on a collision course with his own death.

He left the tea on the table and moved to the couch and played the DVD. He recognized neither man featured. One spoke in noncommittal lingo. A politician? The eye-patch-wearing gent wanted him to help the "organization" which could have meant anything, but Wolf figured it held the usual connotation. The DVD and the murders would equal zero until he put the puzzle together. He turned off the player, brought Freddie's recon photos to his computer, and scanned them into his picture-viewing software. While the scanner clicked and hummed, his eyes settled on the framed picture beside the computer monitor. The last photo of him and Shelly, taken during a hike, nature surrounding them. Shelly, slightly taller than Wolf, wore a big smile, her bright eyes full of life. When it came to the two of them, he was always the frowner, and this picture recorded the expression perfectly. But he'd been happy to be there with her. Wolf let out a breath.

Whenever he felt like quitting, he somehow found renewed inspiration in that picture.

And if he died fighting, so be it.

Wolf cycled through each picture until he settled on a pair that showed a partial street sign. One showed more of the sign than other. The letters O-K-E-R stood out. A switch back to the first picture showed the house number, 2667.

Wolf clicked on the Internet and went to a driving directions website. He punched in the house number and what he had of the street name and smiled when a question showed up on the screen.

Do you mean 2667 Brooker?.

Wolf clicked "Yes".

8

WOLF PARKED the Chrysler curbside and looked at the house and congratulated himself on a good bit of detective work. Holmes would have been proud. He followed the stone path to the door and rang the bell. He looked down the cul-de-sac, quiet except for crows cawing from treetops, each home unique in its design, not a cookie-cutter copy in the bunch. A few vehicles sat in driveways. A housewife watered a yard and a T-shirted man dug into a mailbox. He rang again but nobody answered. Wolf returned to the Chrysler, compared the photos with the physical house. They matched, no question. He had the right location, which left only one answer: the homeowner never reported the break-in.

He dialed a contact at the newspaper, a real reporter for the Star-Journal, somebody whom Wolf had helped in the recent past.

"Mike Freer speaking."

Wolf said, "Don't say my name."

"Uh-huh."

"Who lives at 2667 Brooker Lane?"

"You're kidding?"

"No," Wolf said.

"Grab today's paper. Below the fold, business section. Pic and story. That should answer your question."

———

Vince Palakis said, "Lay off the onions and put on some extra mustard."

The short Vietnamese man on the other side of the stainless-steel hot dog cart, the shiny surface of which reflected the afternoon sun, squeezed a thin line of yellow mustard along the top of the Polish sausage, then spooned dill relish over the mustard. Palakis passed the man a five and said keep the change. He bit into the sausage, smiled, nodded. "Perfect, as always."

The Vietnamese man smiled with straight but yellow teeth. He raised his voice over the rumble of passing traffic. "Cowboys win game this weekend."

"Not with Russell out with that sprained ankle."

"I have bet they win."

"How much?"

"Fifty-dollar holler. Win whole game."

"I hope they do." Palakis took another bite and the sausage blasted a shot of juice that tagged his striped white shirt. He recoiled, reached for extra napkins, and dabbed the shirt. His vendor friend dipped a towel in warm water and offered it but Palakis waved him off.

"I have a spare in the car," he said. "We've been working so late I've slept in the office twice this week. See you later."

Palakis turned his tall body and moved along the

crowded sidewalk to the steps of the Las Palmas Strat-ford Building. Still munching the Polish dog, he bypassed the front entrance for the next-door parking garage. His footsteps echoed. He skipped the elevator and climbed the stairs. Bright fluorescent lights buzzed as he swallowed the last bite and followed a green line around a bend to where his bright yellow Porsche 911 Turbo waited.

His keyless remote flashed the lights and popped the locks. He opened the passenger door and unzipped the overnight bag on the seat. He pulled out another striped white shirt.

Shoes tapped behind him, stopped.

"Mister Palakis."

The tall man turned, closing the door. His hazel eyes regarded the dark-haired man with the gray-touched mustache with no recognition.

"Hi," Palakis said. The other man wore street clothes. A reporter, maybe? But he carried no notebook.

Palakis frowned. "You with the papers?"

"No. I just wanted to know how you're doing." Ben Regan smiled. "Since the robbery and all. Still focused on the negotiations?"

Palakis stared at the other man a moment. His lunch sat in his gut like a rock. "There are cameras watching us."

"I'm just talking."

"What do you want?"

Regan stifled a laugh. He said, "It's not hard to figure out what we want."

Palakis kept his lips pressed together.

Regan pulled out his wallet and removed two

twenty-dollar bills. He stuffed the bills in Palakis's shirt pocket. "Get that stain removed. I'll be in touch."

Regan's shoes tapped some more as he walked away. Palakis stared at the back of Regan's head. He had wanted to tell the mustached man that he had no trouble staying on task, because help was on the way, and wondered how the back of the other man's head would look half blown away.

———————

PALAKIS SAT IN HIS CAR, shaking. What remained of his lunch, now cold, sat on the passenger seat. He hadn't bothered with changing his shirt.

Discovering the theft of the DVD disk had sent Palakis into a tailspin of panic.

Years ago, when Palakis had been a young man, he'd struck up a friendship with an up-and-coming mob figure named Ugo Califano. The friendship had earned Palakis certain favors, which helped Palakis become established as a top software designer and enabled his company to sit on the Fortune 500 list. The favors were, of course, returned in kind, and one of Ugo's big favors had been asking Palakis to take care of the DVD and make sure nobody ever saw it unless he, personally, came to collect the disk.

The footage was critical to Ugo's survival. It was keeping his operations active, and earning money, while he was in hiding because of a murder contract paid for by his rivals, who wanted him out of the way.

And now the disk was gone.

There was only one thing to do. With a shaking hand, Palakis took out his cell phone and dialed a New

York number. He couldn't reach Ugo directly, but he could talk to a lieutenant who could forward the information and respond to Palakis's request for help.

Which would come in the form of a killer Palakis had only seen once and hoped to never see again.

———

MILES KINCAID LET OUT a breath as his brown leather boots hit solid ground. He didn't stop to let his pulse settle.

He crossed from the plane to the brightly lighted terminal building, goose-bumps crawling up his neck from the cool breeze rushing along the tarmac. The muted roar of other plane engines followed him inside, and he found baggage claim to collect his suitcases. His contact, Palakis, was in the crowd somewhere. Miles knew who to look for but figured Palakis could find him first.

"There you are."

The big man turned, didn't smile at the trim blond fellow before him.

"Long time, Miles," Vince Palakis said. He extended a hand. Miles didn't shake. He'd always considered Palakis a worthless hanger-on. He and Miles's boss, Ugo Califano, went way back, and Califano gave the orders, so Miles had to go and assist the blond man in his time of need. But he didn't have to shake hands.

Palakis lowered the offered hand. "Well. Let's hit the road."

"Uh-huh," Miles said.

The Porsche's engine whined with turbo boost as Palakis sped onto the freeway. Miles's body pressed into the deep bucket seat and he noted the lack of a manual shift lever. Another strike against Palakis. Real sports cars had a clutch.

"I need that DVD back," Palakis said. "As much as Ugo, if not more. He trusted me to take care of it. And if it comes out that he and I are buddies I might as well forget my future in politics."

"You have a lot to protect," Miles said.

"Yup."

Palakis told Miles about the visit in the garage, adding, "I don't know his name or even if he'll send someone else to see me next time. I also have no idea how the disk was found. That's your next question, right?"

"Who did you tell?"

"Excuse me?"

"I want a list. Somebody knew. Don't forget the girls you fool around with and may have bragged to."

"I've never–"

"Quit. How else was the disk found?"

Palakis tightened his grip on the steering wheel.

"A list," Miles said.

Palakis exhaled hard. "Alexa Reyale. My regular, um, companion. I'll get the names of the others. There's George Cooper, my second-in-command. He could have found out. And Scott."

"Who?"

"My son."

Miles raised a thick eyebrow.

Palakis cleared his throat. "We haven't been getting along last few years. Ever since–"

"What?"

"The hit-and-run."

"Repeat that."

"The hit-and-run." Palakis took a few deep breaths. "I was in an accident. Couple years back. My fault. A little boy died. Ugo pulled some strings and made the heat go away. That's when my relationship with Scott changed. I thought he'd cool down once the patsy was arrested. He didn't. He knew the truth. Somehow."

"I'm gonna call you Saint Vince from now on."

The two men said no more. Miles turned the story over in his head, considering different angles. At least he had a place to start, but he needed a little more.

Palakis pulled off the freeway and merged with street traffic. A few stop-and-go blocks later, he parked in front of a towering Hyatt and told Miles, "You've got a room reserved under Ken Wade."

"The family."

"Huh?"

"The family of the little boy. Who are they?"

Miles watched Palakis's Adam's apple go up, then down. His body sank against the driver's door as if he wanted as much space between him and the big man as possible, but he couldn't avoid Kincaid's unblinking eyes.

"A cop's family. Detective named Brock."

Miles jerked open the door, hauled out body and suitcase. Leaning back inside, he said, "If it weren't for my orders, I'd kill you," and slammed the yellow door.

Miles turned the deadbolt and the swing bolt. He'd been given a large suite with a deck. It was quiet and cold. He went to the heater/AC unit near the deck doors and turned up the heat. A low hum followed by a blast of warm air filled the room.

He placed his suitcase on the bed and removed the

X-ray proof bottom. From the hidden compartment he took out his customized Wilson Combat .45 automatic, a box of subsonic ammo, a silencer, and a framed photograph.

The gun, ammo and silencer he placed in the nightstand drawer. The picture he set with care on the nightstand next to the lamp. He looked at the pony-tailed girl in the frame. Dark hair, big smile, blue eyes. Miles took a cigar and lighter from his inside jacket pocket, opened the patio door and stepped outside. He lit up, stared out into the night, and thought of his dead daughter. Of the men who killed her. Of a policeman's family and their dead son.

Kincaid was a killer, sure. He was good at it. He could make a job sloppy or neat depending on whether he was sending a message, or just clearing trash.

But he'd never killed any civilians. There were certain lines one couldn't cross. His job was to help keep the peace in the syndicate, and his "victims" had always been hoods. Hurting civilians not only brought in the cops and the Feds, it also served no useful purpose.

Palakis had not only hurt civilians, he was using the mob to clean up his mess. Why Ugo Califano had agreed to help, Kincaid didn't understand. Perhaps the two went back far enough that Ugo was willing to bend the rules. Kincaid didn't have to like it, he just had to do it.

He had a job to do, yeah, but afterwards maybe he'd leave Palakis in a ditch. Eliminate the problem completely, and the mess never returns.

9

WOLF SAT out on his deck, a burning cigar in one hand, the business section of the newspaper in his lap.

Vince Palakis. The resident of 2667 Brooker Lane. Not an unfamiliar name. He'd once investigated the software company CEO based on rumors of a hit-and-run crash. Somebody else had been arrested and convicted, but Wolf had reasons for never totally believing Palakis hadn't been involved. A lack of clues and the arrest meant he couldn't pursue the matter as far as he'd have liked. So why would he be a robbery target? Why not report the incident? The easy answer, there *was* a corrupt side to his smiling face, something dirty behind the charitable donations and deceit along with the friends in high places.

But he wasn't on the DVD.

Why would he have the video, and who decided the importance of taking it from him?

Wolf set the newspaper aside and smoked and counted stars. The street below was silent but for the occasional car or rumbling bus. The pigeons had holed up for the night. No crickets chirped in the concrete fortresses. A lone light burned in the building across the street. He wondered who was in there.

Wolf finished the cigar and stood up. Time for work. The Chrysler had a full tank of gas. He'd cleaned and loaded his pistol. One goal for the evening: find out who tipped a killer to Freddie's address.

Wolf prowled the streets for hours, checking bars, gambling dens, various hangouts. Chatting with regular informants. Passing bills here and there. Buying drinks when the money didn't carry enough weight. After three a.m. Wolf finally had a name.

Harvey the Hook dealt stolen credit cards and funny money. He'd thought he was helping out a friend of Freddie's, or so the story went. Wolf checked two more bars looking for him and learned he might be at his girl-friend's place.

The quiet neighborhood sported homes and cul-de-sacs on one side, two apartment complexes on the other. Wolf stopped across from the Essex Apartments, watched the first-floor dwelling closest to the street. Minna Jaggar, Harvey's squeeze, lived there. The bright porch light illuminated a Virgin Mary statue to the right of the door.

He sat back and waited windows cracked for fresh air. He had the right place. Harvey drove an old El Camino, and a battleship-gray El rested in the small parking lot in front of the two first-floor units.

Eventually the front door opened, and light flashed on Harvey's face. He squeezed his big body into the El, drove off. Wolf followed a few car lengths behind. They rolled at a steady 25 through the neighborhood, passing a park, to a convenience store at the last corner. Wolf pulled over and watched Harvey limp inside. A former associate had shot Harvey in the leg once during an argument, leaving Harvey with the permanent injury, and the associate hadn't been seen since.

Harvey exited the store with a gallon of milk. He drove the El Camino back toward the apartment. Wolf waited until they neared the park, then swung around the El and slammed to a stop perpendicular to Harvey's vehicle. Harvey's tires screeched and smoked as he hit the brakes. He jumped out shouting obscenities but closed his mouth when Wolf swung the .45 over the top of the car and fired.

Harvey whipped around and landed hard on the pavement. Wolf had aimed for a shoulder and scored. He grabbed Harvey by an ankle. Harvey cussed, gasped, choked, and yelled as Wolf dragged the man across the asphalt, up the curb, and over the grass to the shadow of a tree. Wolf put a foot on Harvey's chest.

Harvey started breathing heavy, sweat dripped into his eyes and down the sides of his face. "You won't see the sun come up!"

"Look who's talking," Wolf said. "You told somebody where to find Freddie Webster today. Who was he?"

"Said he was a friend of Freddie's. I swear I didn't know about O'Shea or anything!"

"Name."

"Tony Jordon! He said he was from Chicago."

"What's he look like?"

"Tall guy dark hair mustache. I think he's on the other side of 40 because the lip hair has gray in it."

"Harvey."

"Wha—what?"

"That guy wasn't a friend of Freddie's."

Wolf's finger tightened on the trigger. Harvey started to scream. The .45 barked once more.

———

WOLF DROVE around until his body settled down. Harvey hadn't provided anything really-useful, but at least part of the score had been settled, and he had a description of who to look for. Sticking with Palakis would be the best way to find "Tony Jordan".

Fatigue rolled like a wave through Wolf. He pulled over in front of an all-night diner. He wanted time to mull over his next move, and a cup of tea would provide a jump start.

A bell jangled as Wolf entered, and the cook behind the scuffed and scratched counter locked his eyes on the man in the long black coat. The place wasn't very big, with gray walls and Formica tables with purple vinyl booths, old movie posters on the walls. Wolf noticed a James Dean (*East of Eden*), Bogart (*High Sierra*), a Cagney (*White Heat*), one with McQueen from *The Great Escape*. Favorites of his. A neon sign above the counter said MICK'S SINCE 1954 and added an odd pink glow to the white fluorescent lighting. Wolf wondered if the grease stains dotting the floor went back to '54.

Wolf wiped a counter stool with a handkerchief and sat. The cook, a stocky guy the size of a rhino, narrowed his eyes. A petite brunette in the back-corner booth fixed a frightened gaze on Wolf as well. The remaining handful of customers paid no attention and continued their conversations in low tones.

"What'll you have?" the big cook said, his claw of a

hand making the pencil he held above a notepad look like a toothpick.

Wolf scanned the menu card. "Any tea?"

"No." He waited. "How 'bout coffee?"

Wolf said, "How about ice water with lemon," adding: "And some cherry pie."

The cook didn't bother to scribble. He filled a glass, pushed a lemon wedge onto the rim of the glass, and slid it in front of Wolf.

The cook placed the pie slice in front of Wolf, bug chunks of cherries and thick red cream dripping from the sides. Wolf grabbed a fork.

The brunette came up to the counter with an empty coffee cup and a few dollars. She kept four stools between her and Wolf. When he shifted, she jumped, her eyes flicking his way, then back to the cook as he refilled the mug. He took her money and dropped a few coins on the counter in return.

"How much coffee can you drink, kid?" the cook said. But the girl turned away with lowered eyes. Her clothes hung on her wiry frame, dark circles under her eyes, skin pale and almost clammy despite her almond tone.

She set the mug on her table, sat again, and picked up a cell phone. Wolf watched her make one call after another, her defeated, sad expression growing more so each time she hung up.

With slumped shoulders she sipped her coffee and stared out the front window. Her shoulders tensed each time somebody new entered. There were only three new arrivals in the time it took Wolf to finish the pie, a couple looking fresh from a club, and a cabbie on a break. Wolf swallowed the last of the pie, drank the water. Wolf tapped his glass with the fork. The cook refilled and returned the glass.

Wolf took his drink to another stool by the wall, leaned back.

The bell clanged again. Two men pushed through and gave the place a fast right-to-left scan. "There she is," the bigger of the two said. His finger-snap turned into a point. Right at the brunette.

She screamed.

The tall one had a crew cut and his bulkier partner a bent nose. They strode toward the girl. The brunette flung her coffee mug but missed, the thick liquid coating some of the floor, the mug clattering nearby without breaking. The cook yanked a revolver from under the counter, said, "Any trouble and I'll–" but what he'd do he never said as Crew Cut snatched the gun and used it like a club against the cook's head. The cook's face tightened up and he thudded onto the floor.

Crew Cut flipped the captured gun into the air, catching it with finger on trigger. He did a 180 with his new toy at the hip. "Everybody stay put."

The girl wasn't cooperating. She screamed a second time, jumping for a door to the left of her booth. The knob didn't budge, and she pressed against the wall, eyes wide, body stiff. She shouted, "No!" as Bent Nose stepped within reach.

Crew Cut pivoted to help his buddy. Wolf reached for the .45 and put a bullet in Crew Cut's left leg.

The thug screamed and crashed to the floor. The counter covered Wolf as he dropped beside the man, grabbed the revolver, and smashed the barrel across his head.

Bent Nose spun around. Wolf put two rounds into

his chest. He slammed back against an empty table and fell to the floor, where he stayed.

Wolf put his gun away and approached the girl. "It's okay," he said, but as he stepped closer she screamed and launched at him with clawing hands. Wolf covered his face, which left his lower half exposed, and she landed a punch in his solar plexus. Air left him and he doubled over. The woman raced by. The bell above the door announced her exit.

Wolf faced the gaping bystanders still in their booths.

A man asked if he was a policeman.

"No," Wolf said.

The cabbie asked if maybe they should call 9-1-1.

"Knock yourself out," Wolf said, inhaling a deep breath.

While the cabbie jawed on a cell phone Wolf patted Crew Cut's pockets and found a thick leather wallet. A pat down of the other produced spare ammunition and another fat wallet. An item in the girl's booth caught his eye, a beat-up day planner. He stashed the items in his London Fog and went behind the counter to splash some water in the cook's face. The cook moaned.

He went out to the Chrysler and raced away.

———

BEN REGAN SAID, "I'm hearing things, Teddy."

"Your hotel room haunted?"

"Things from back home."

"Oh, really?" Teddy Gambolini said.

They sat at a park bench, Teddy with a bag of bread

pieces in hand, smiling at the flock of pigeons around them. Regan, his legs crossed, examined his fingernails.

Gambolini fed pigeons for the therapy they provided. The solitude let his mind wander. He enjoyed the fresh air. Sometimes, he could talk to the pigeons about stuff, both verbally and in his head, and they wouldn't judge. The birds could be trusted not to repeat anything, and their cooing sometimes punctuated a thought in just the right way. As soon as the bread ran out, even if he hadn't finished talking, they'd find another benefactor, the fickle beasts, but he kept coming back.

Today was different.

"Palakis made some calls," Regan said. "Guess who's come out to help?"

"Big Bird?"

"Miles Kincaid. Remember him?"

"Sure." Gambolini tossed some crumbs near Regan's feet and several birds swarmed his ankles. He kicked them away. Teddy laughed.

"I bet you'd like another crack at the guy."

"A bigger question is, should we eliminate the trail that leads to us? That will be Kincaid's first move."

"Get a couple guys together and get going," Gambolini said.

"'Kay," Regan said, and walked away.

Gambolini tossed more bread. The pigeons sucked it up, loitered, heads bopping back and forth. From behind, a truck rumbled by and shook the ground. A few of the pigeons flew away. Others paused a few moments before they followed. Gambolini shook his head. Pigeons were like people. No idea what they're doing but they follow the first one who moves.

AFTER BREAKFAST, Wolf set the dishes in the hall and sat on the couch with the wallets and day planner he'd collected at the diner.

He opened the day planner and found black-and-white headshots of the girl, her hair long and flowing, with appropriate touches of make-up. At the bottom edge of each photo was her name, Holly Mendoza, and a local address. A page showed a list of local theaters, and scheduled auditions, while another page showed phone numbers and addresses. In the back of the planner, sheathed in a plastic cover, were more pictures. One of them showed Holly posing at the edge of a pier with a blond man in a leather jacket. Wolf knew the man.

He'd been in charge of the gun runners at the warehouse and his men had called him "Ace".

Wolf set the day planner aside. Should he forward the information to Kiki so she could alert the Feds? He shook his head. If the gang needed to get rid of the girl because she might talk, Wolf needed to get involved his own way. He turned his attention to the wallets.

Bent Nose: Daniel Hoffman. Crew Cut: Kevin Morris. Neither had any business cards or pictures. Each wallet held a thousand dollars in cash. He took a grand from one wallet and tucked the cash into the day planner. When he found Holly, she'd need the cash to get out of the city.

Wolf stood up and took down one of the two paintings above the couch, a Mona Lisa knock-off. The other featured somebody who looked like Napoleon. Worthless garage sale stuff if somebody only paid attention to the front. Wolf placed the Mona Lisa on the coffee table front side down. Flicking a little clasp on the back, he swung open a hidden door. Cash gleamed from the hollow back. Wolf added the other thousand to the collection, closed the back, and returned the painting to its hook.

He went to his bedroom, opened the closet, and pulled out a large steamer trunk. He rummaged through the junk and found a black leather wallet with a gold first-grade detective badge and a police identification card.

He'd start with Holly's home, check out her workplace, find some trail to follow. She was out there. Somewhere. Running.

———

HOLLY MENDOZA LIVED on the east side of the city at the Chesterfield Apartments, smack in the middle of a quiet couple of blocks of warehouses and canneries sharing space with other apartment buildings. Red brick buildings dominated, trees lining the sidewalks.

Wolf entered the lobby. A dark-haired receptionist

in a gray suit sat behind a desk. She spoke on the phone in a clipped, business-like tone. An orange-shaded computer monitor sat in front of her, but she had her eyes on a desk calendar instead. Wolf walked past her desk to the elevators and went up to the fourth floor.

He knocked on apartment 406. No answer. He knocked again, waited a moment, then went back downstairs.

The receptionist, off the phone now, looked up. Wolf asked if she knew if a tenant named Holly Mendoza was home.

She had no idea, she said.

Wolf produced Holly's notebook. "When I was having breakfast this morning, I found this in my booth. It belongs to Miz Mendoza. There's personal information and a large amount of money inside. I want to make sure she gets this back."

"You can leave it here."

"I'd rather put it in her hand personally. Do you have a work number? Somewhere I can reach her?"

"We can't give out that information."

From a door behind her, a man stepped out with a file folder in hand, his mouth open to say something. The man had a puffy face to match a roly-poly body wrapped in a suit that looked a little too tight, with an undone collar button and crooked tie. He stopped when he saw Wolf. "Can I help you?"

Wolf went through the story again. The roly-poly man examined the notebook and noted the pictures inside. He confirmed that the woman in the photos was indeed Holly Mendoza, but they couldn't bend the rules. Wolf produced his detective badge and the roly-poly man's eyes lit up. Sure, they said, they'd be happy to help the officer. Why didn't you say something before? The receptionist typed a few keys and read off Holly's work number–a nightclub/restaurant called The Candy Apple–and emergency contact number, which belonged to her boyfriend. When Wolf asked the boyfriend's name, the girl said, "Tim Dell." Wolf kept his face straight as he finished scribbling.

He thanked them both and left the office.

———

THE AUTOMATIC DOORS at Wake County Hospital slipped open with a squeal. Wolf stepped through. The elevator rumbled up to the intensive care unit. Crew Cut, aka Kevin Morris, had been brought there. He stopped a passing nurse and asked where the shooting victim from the early morning was. She asked which shooting, there were four. From Mick's Diner, Wolf said. She directed him to the turret-style desk from which several hallways branched off. Three young nurses sat behind the counter. The seats in the waiting area weren't occupied.

Wolf had his badge out. One of the nurses extended a finger past his shoulder and said, "Room 504, detective."

"How'd you know what I'd ask?"

"Other detectives have been in there about a half hour now," she said.

Wolf kept his face steady, thanked her, turned and went down the indicated hallway. It would have been nice to chat with Crew Cut, but the last thing he needed was the punk pointing a finger and saying he was the one who blasted a hole in his leg. Wolf followed the tiled hallway past the closed door of 504, continued to the end, and pushed through the stairwell door.

———

WOLF FOUND Crew Cut's downtown address, a fading brownstone. The vestibule needed new paint on the peeling walls; a stray cat, in a corner, played with a flake of paint. Wolf turned down a darkened hallway to a door marked SUPER. Strange goo decorated the door. Wolf kicked a few times. The chain rattled and the door squeaked open. A tall thin man stuck his small head out.

"What?" he said.

Wolf flashed his badge. "Let me up to Kevin Morris's room."

"Who?"

"Kevin Morris. Tenant here."

"Wait a sec."

The thin man shut the door and returned carrying a ring of keys. His grease-stained T-shirt smelled like a double cheeseburger and spots of paint dotted his jeans. Wolf followed him back to the vestibule. The cat was now licking a paw. They started up the stairwell, a breeding ground for strange, putrid smells.

"Ever hear of light bulbs and Clorox?" Wolf said.

"Talk to the owner."

"Your parents?"

"Just my mother."

"You tell her to fix this place," Wolf said, enjoying his role-playing, "or I'll have the housing authority close you down."

"There's a hundred bucks waiting for you downstairs."

"Is that a bribe?"

The thin man had no answer.

"Skinny guy like you wouldn't last long in prison," Wolf said. "Keep that in mind."

The thin man opened a door on the third-floor landing. They went down a hallway to apartment 316. The thin man fumbled with the keys. "How long?"

"Open it."

The thin man unlocked the door and stepped back without meeting Wolf's eyes.

Wolf said, "Get lost."

A short entryway led to a hallway. At one end a bedroom/bathroom, the other kitchen/living room. Frayed carpet; cracked walls. Wolf moved up and down the hall, checking each room. Not a stick of furniture.

Wolf stood in the center of the empty living room. He went down the stairs and reached the vestibule without a tumble, kicked on the super's door again, told the thin man to lock up, and headed for the exit.

He stopped at a pay phone he found outside a liquor store, used a handkerchief to lift the receiver. He dropped a quarter in the slot.

And called the city housing authority.

———

WOLF DECIDED to try talking to Morris at the hospital again, but his jaw tightened at the sight of a police car with flashing cherry lights blocking part of the entrance. When he reached Morris's room, he stopped.

Two uniformed police officers stood at the foot of the bed.

"Who are you?" the older of the two cops said. The stripes on his sleeve showed his rank as sergeant. Wolf flashed his detective ID.

"That was fast. We just called a few minutes ago."

"I'm here on another call," Wolf said, "heard there was some commotion, so I thought I'd take a look."

The sergeant nodded. His younger partner stayed quiet. Muzak from the hall drifted into the room.

"Well, this guy's dead," the sergeant said, turning back to Morris. The sheet had been pulled up over his head. "A nurse found him."

Wolf stepped up beside the bed, lifting the cold sheet. Morris didn't look so tough anymore, his skin cold, face slack. Small puncture wound on his upper arm. A dark shade of red circled the wound.

Wolf said, "Gotta go upstairs. Room 720 if you need me."

"Right," the sergeant said, and Wolf slipped out.

Wolf returned to his car and did some thinking. Morris was important enough to silence and so was Holly Mendoza. That meant the gun runners hadn't finished their business. Maybe more than guns were involved? He wondered if he stood a chance of finding the girl.

11

HOLLY MENDOZA COULDN'T BE TRACED through her work just yet. The Candy Apple Club didn't open until late evening. Temporary roadblock, one he had a good idea of how to get around.

He turned his attention back to Vince Palakis and the mystery of the stolen DVD. Wolf parked the Chrysler across from the man's office building, watched Palakis get his lunch from the hot dog vendor, and followed him home after work. He spent the next few hours parked across the street from his home. The yellow Porsche remained in the driveway. Presently, a Mazda 6 pulled into the drive and a young man entered the house. Scott Palakis, the son.

Once evening arrived, Wolf eased out of the car and popped the trunk. He tied on a heavy tool belt loaded with gizmos and shimmied up the telephone pole in the middle of the cul-de-sac. His stomach fluttered at the height, so he didn't look down.

He picked the lock in the junction box, examined the set of wires and connections, and pulled from the tool bag a portable phone unit and plugged it in. A process of elimination followed as he rang each line, asking for Vince Palakis.

Finally, "Hold on." Younger voice. The son.

Another male voice said, "Yes?"

"Mister Palakis," Wolf said, "you're one of the lucky few who have been chosen–"

"Not interested." *Click.*

Wolf smiled. Perfect. He tugged the Palakis line free of the mess of wires and detached the portable unit, dropping it back into the bag. He pulled a small remote transmitter from the bag and connected it to the box's power outlet, then wired it into Palakis's line. A light on the transmitter flashed when he pressed a small button on the side.

He climbed down and returned to the Chrysler and turned on a portable receiver. Some line buzz told him all was well, and he sat back to wait. He wanted a cigar. A guy just can't sit in one place without something to smoke. The light jazz from the stereo made no impact on his thoughts. He wondered about approaching Palakis to see if he could worm his way into the man's confidence but decided to avoid that plan. If what Wolf suspected about the hit-and-run really happened, no way would Palakis accept Wolf's help. He'd have other resources at his disposal.

The receiver crackled as the line rang. "Hello?" Palakis the elder.

"It's me." A male. Wolf turned up the volume.

"Come over," Palakis said. "My son is here for dinner. We can ask him what he knows."

"Ten minutes," the other man said. *Click.*

Wolf frowned. More line buzz. Was the Palakis boy

somehow involved in the robbery? Wolf propped his left elbow on the top of the door and rubbed his upper lip with his left index finger. That would explain not calling the cops if Palakis thought his own family had ripped him off.

The porch light snapped on. Wolf watched the front door open and the young man step out. Scott Palakis climbed into the Mazda and the flash of light from a streetlamp as he passed Wolf showed that the young man wasn't wearing a seatbelt. Wolf started his engine and followed. As he left the cul-de-sac, frantic dialing crackled over the receiver; when the other end picked up, the voice of the man who needed "ten minutes" answered.

Palakis said, "Scott's gone. He got a call and split. Something about a meeting."

Wolf followed the Mazda onto the avenue, blending with traffic.

"I see his car," the other voice said, and Wolf glanced in his mirrors hoping for an idea of where the other man's car was. "I'll stay with him."

"Don't let them kill him," Palakis said.

The line clicked. Palakis said, "Miles?" Another click.

Wolf followed the Mazda into downtown Las Palmas and Scott Palakis pulled into a public parking lot. Wolf eased the Chrysler into a curbside red zone. Scott crossed the street to a bar called Mother Goose and went inside. Wolf watched for any other cars parking nearby but saw none. Curbside parking was full, which left the lot across the street, other lots further down. Traffic streamed by. Wolf traded the red zone for a space near the Mazda and entered the bar.

A line of people sat at the bar and more occupied tables and booths with country music blaring from ceiling speakers. Scott and another man Wolf recognized sat in a back booth. Wolf passed the booth and ordered a beer at the bar. He glanced over his shoulder. The other man, older than Scott, his mouth in a frown, was Detective Harry Brock, Las Palmas Homicide. Wolf knew Brock from a few years back. The detective had asked Wolf to prove that the elder Palakis had killed his baby son.

Wolf drank his beer and listened for any nuggets from the conversation.

———

SCOTT PALAKIS ENTERED the bar and zeroed on the back booth like a heat seeking missile. Brock waited for him, his hand on a beer. On the other side of the table sat an unattended glass of scotch. Scott sat down and sipped the scotch.

Brock said, "I figured you'd need it."

"I was at Dad's for dinner, but he spent most of his time on the phone. Then you called. I had to lie about a meeting tomorrow to get out of there. What's so urgent?"

"Your Dad's made his own moves," the detective said. "My people back east say one of Califano's enforcers has come out to help."

Scott cursed.

"The three of us need to be scarce the next few weeks," Brock said. "I'm going to have to reach Alexa in person, I can't get her on the phone. And I mean scarce, Scott. Gone. Until this is over."

"One way or another."

"Right," Brock said. He dropped a pair of twenties on the table. "Have a few more on me. And don't tell me where you're going." The detective headed for the exit.

Scott waved at a passing waiter and ordered another drink. He didn't see the tall man in a long black coat follow Brock outside.

Scott Palakis sat in the booth but didn't hear the country music or taste the Johnny Walker. He couldn't think of a place to hide and his mind began to drift. He thought of the chain of events which led him to Detective Harry Brock.

Scott was still living at home when the accident occurred. He'd been up late on a Saturday, studying, and went downstairs, where he found his father leaning against the wall near the door to the garage, his head down, left hand covering that side of his face. Scott approached to see what was wrong, but his father waved him off. With his right hand. Drank a little too much at Bev's party, he said. Just a little light-headed. Should have used the car service. Scott carried on with his evening and his father went upstairs to bed. While taking some trash out to the garage, Scott noticed the damage to the right front fender of his father's Lincoln. It had been caved in, the headlight cracked, trim pieces dangling. Flecks of blue paint against the Lincoln's silver jumped out.

At work the next morning, two of the girls were talking about a car crash that killed a little boy. They couldn't believe it, a hit-and-run. A cop's family, too. The other driver sped away. Scott listened without comment, thinking of his dad and the Lincoln's damage. No, he decided, couldn't have been Dad. He was at Bev's party on the other side of town.

Later he called Bev to ask how the party was. He'd been invited but schoolwork kept him from attending. Bev was a close friend of his late mother and still kept in touch. Bev said the party went perfectly and she was sorry he wasn't there to enjoy it but was also sorry that his father couldn't make it. Scott made a few clumsy excuses and ended the conversation. If Dad hadn't been at Bev's, where did he go? That night he found a rental car in the garage. His father told him he'd bumped into a light pole and took the Lincoln to get fixed. Scott thought, light poles aren't painted blue.

Then the cop showed up at work. Detective Brock. Do you know where your father was Saturday night? Scott said, at a party. Were you with him? No. Why do you ask? Brock said Mr. Palakis was a person of interest in a hit-and-run crash. Not that he caused it, the detective said, but may have witnessed it, and the police would like a few words with him. A buzzer went off in Scott's brain. What was your name again? Brock, the detective said. And it clicked. The victims of the crash. Your son was killed?

"I saw your father hit my car," he told Scott. "But nobody wants to hear that. Your father's a big shot. His company employs thousands of people in this city. It'll be my word against his. I thought maybe you'd be the one to do the right thing."

"You want me to turn my father in," Scott said.

"I didn't say that."

Scott excused himself, left work, and went to a park to think.

His father had always preached the value of

integrity, right over wrong. Scott believed that stuff through and through, but here was Brock saying his father was now the antithesis of such a code. I can't prove it, he thought. If I can't prove it, I can't say anything. Right?

He saw Brock again soon after. Another uninvited visit to the office. Scott had strong feelings about his father's guilt, but what could he do? Especially since, after the incident, somebody else had confessed, been arrested, charged, and convicted. Brock claimed it was a set-up, that his father pulled some strings. He wouldn't rest until he could prove otherwise.

Scott promised to help if solid proof ever turned up, but he knew it was just empty talk. Brock knew, too. That's why he'd narrowed his eyes at the younger Palakis before departing, and Scott never forgot that look. Disappointment, pain, anger, all rolled into one.

———

OVER THE NEXT THREE YEARS, Scott's relationship with his father, from Scott's perspective, changed. They started growing apart. Talked less. Didn't do as much together. When Scott moved out it more or less sealed their separation, though they continued to visit a few times a month. A voice continued to nag at Scott that he should say something about the accident. Another voice countered that without proof, he couldn't say his father was guilty. Right?

Then Detective Brock appeared again. It had been during a night off, a rare occurrence, and Scott had been browsing his favorite bookstore. He headed back to his car. The parking lot was packed, most people in the next-door gym and the WalMart across the way, and Scott scanned the aisle for his car. If he had been paying attention, he would have seen the man in dark clothes coming up alongside. Scott looked too late. The man grabbed his arm, jammed an automatic into his side and said, "Keep moving and don't make a sound."

"Hey–"

"I said shut up or I'll kill you."

A lamp post illuminated the man's face a moment. Long face, high cheekbones, pock-marked and rough. He looked familiar, but unfamiliar at the same time.

The man said, "Where's your car?"

Scott pointed out his black Mazda 6. The man steered him that way. The man said, "Tinted windows, good." They reached the car. "Get in."

Scott's hands shook as he pressed a button on his key ring remote. The Mazda's doors unlocked. He had a strong impulse to lock the doors and get the engine going before the other man could get in, but fear froze him. The other man dropped into the passenger seat, pulled the door shut, and put the automatic under his jacket. The bright dome light didn't bother him; he even asked Scott to keep it on. Scott reached up, flicked a switch. The other man pulled a folded manila envelope from another pocket of his jacket. Scott watched him lift the flap.

The long-faced man let out a breath and scanned Scott's face. He said, "Sorry about the gun, Scott."

Scott sank back against the car door as he realized who was talking to him. He couldn't believe how much Brock's appearance had changed since their last encounter. Thinner. Less hair. The high cheekbones made the sides of his face look like deep pits.

"You know who I am?"

The name came out a whisper. "Brock."

"I'm not exactly on duty right now."

"No kiddin'."

"I have something I want you to look at." The detective pulled a sheet from the envelope and said, "You won't like it but you're a right guy, I think, so I hope you'll do the right thing."

"Sounds familiar."

Brock's eyes never left the young man's face as he showed Scott a blank sheet of paper. At least, that's what Scott thought it was. When the detective turned it over, Scott saw a glossy black-and-white photograph. He studied the picture. A lump formed in his throat. He tried to talk, but the words never made it past the lump.

"It's not a fake," Brock said.

Scott closed his eyes, took a breath. He opened his eyes and looked at the picture again. It showed his father and a woman sitting in the Lincoln and sitting close. Brock handed Scott several more photos featuring Vince Palakis and the woman. The final shot showed them with locked lips.

Brock said, "I decided to let them have some privacy after a while."

"I—I don't...understand."

"It's your father."

"I *know* that."

"They didn't stay in the car long. I followed them to the Bonaventure. The girl entered through the front and your father went in through the side entrance. Wearing a fake beard. They left together a few hours later. Know what they passed on the way home? A certain intersection. Where a certain accident happened and where my son was killed."

Brock showed Scott a final photo which showed Vince Palakis with a fake beard, trimmed close to his jaw line. Scott stared, moved his head side-to-side.

"The girl is a hooker I know; her name's Jodi," the detective said, "that tells me your father has a regular stable of girls he likes to party with. He had one of those parties the night of the crash."

Scott's eyes remained wide, watery.

Brock said, "You don't need a PhD to know why I'm doing this."

"I'm just wondering why it took so long."

The detective shrugged. "Your father has a video hidden somewhere and I want it."

"Of him and the hookers?"

"The video has nothing to do with your father, but he's keeping it safe for an old friend. That old friend would hate for that DVD to fall into the wrong hands. If your father's relationship with this old friend becomes public, somebody might start asking questions about that patsy they framed for killing my boy."

"I can't do that."

"You told me–"

"This is *different*."

"If what my friend says is true–"

"She's a hooker, Harry. She only said that to avoid arrest."

"She wasn't under arrest, Scott."

"You banging her, too?"

"She's a source of information. We talk a few times a month. She just happened to mention a certain client of hers and I asked questions and she said some things and I learned about the DVD disk. Your father has a big mouth."

"How do you know she isn't lying?"

"She's never lied before," Brock said.

Scott ran a hand through his hair. His cheeks puffed as he exhaled. "The old friend. He stepped in after what happened to your son?"

Brock nodded once. "I'm working with people who'd like to ask your father a couple of questions. They want to know where the old friend is. They don't want to kill your father. After they're done, the disk becomes my property to do with what I see fit. This way I can get back at your father and the man who helped him get away with murder."

"I can't help you."

"I'm not working alone, and my partners don't mind doing this the hard way. Make it easy, Scott."

Scott's face twisted in genuine pain. He hurt inside, too. Like he'd swallowed a rock.

"You know as well as I do your father's been guilty all these years, yet you've done nothing. Do something now, Scott."

Silence lingered a moment.

"Okay."

Brock's eyes remained dull.

"I'll do it, okay? Is that what you want?"

"Is that what you want?"

"I don't recall you giving me a choice."

"We all have choices, Scott. Some choose better than others."

Scott drummed fingers on the steering wheel. Two chatty women crossed in front of the Mazda; he watched them.

"It's probably in the safe," he said.

"Where's that?"

"Dad's bedroom."

"Thanks."

Scott fixed his eyes on the detective. "It's not for you. For your son. I'm sorry as hell about what happened."

12

WHEN BROCK LEFT Scott Palakis at the Mother Goose bar, he drove to Lakeview Cemetery and used a flashlight to navigate the rows of headstones. He knew the way but had never visited at night. The branches swung at him, seemingly reaching out with claws. Moon-cast shadows of headstones crawled across the ground. His boots sank into the soft dirt. He should have noted the lack of crickets, but his focused mind didn't register the silence.

The detective settled the flash on a single headstone, stopped, read the name engraved there, ROBERT HALE BROCK.

"It's almost over, Bobby."

"Detective."

Brock spun around, a hand going to his holster. He froze when he saw the automatic pistol in Wolf's hand.

"No need for guns, Detective," Wolf said. "Let's put 'em away."

Brock dropped his hand to his side; Wolf holstered his gun. Brock said, "Long time, Wolf."

Wolf stepped toward the other man. "I saw you with Scott Palakis at the bar."

"And you're here because?"

"Why have you involved civilians in this? Two men are dead already. One left a pregnant wife behind."

"This is none of your business."

"I have a reason at the northeast corner of this cemetery that makes it my business. Now are we going to stand and argue or is there a chance we can help each other?"

"I went your way once and you couldn't deliver."

"There was nothing I could do, Harry. All the evidence went toward the man they convicted."

"Or you finally found a problem your gun couldn't solve."

"Damnit, Harry—"

"Get out of here."

"What's on the disk?"

Brock blinked. "How do you know about that?"

"I have the disk, Harry. Not the people you're working with. Yeah, I heard bits of your chat."

"They don't have the disk?"

"Palakis doesn't know any better, either. I bet your friends are pissed because things didn't quite work out, and now you're a loose end so let me help you before more people die. What's on the disk?"

"How do I know you've seen it?"

Wolf described the video. "Good enough? I'm running out of patience."

Brock said, "The video was recorded twenty years ago and shows Ugo Califano and a federal prosecutor named Schofield. Califano is, or was, a major mob boss in New York City. The deal was for Schofield to keep the feds away. The disk was leverage to make sure Schofield never went back on the deal. Califano is in hiding now. He double-crossed some rivals, who put a contract out on him, and now he's hiding to keep from being killed."

"Where does Palakis fit in?"

"He and Califano are old friends. Palakis was given the DVD for safekeeping."

"And you come into this how?"

"I found two men who want to know where Califano is hiding, and they're using the theft of the video to make Palakis talk, or they'll expose the fact that Palakis is dirty."

"Names," Wolf said.

"Teddy Gambolini and Ben Regan. They were part of the syndicate that rivaled Califano. They pissed off their bosses, too, and now they're marked for murder. If they can find where Califano is hiding, they can use that as a peace offering to turn off the heat. They've set up shop here in Las Palmas, and I found them while working another case."

"How'd you find the disk?"

"A hooker friend told me. I approached Gambolini and Regan, and they planned the robbery after I told where Palakis had hidden the disk."

"What's in it for you?"

"I get the DVD as soon as they're done. Between that and my witness I'll expose Palakis and his cover-up of the hit-and-run and put him behind bars."

Wolf shook his head. "You're playing with fire. Regan will kill you and Scott and your other friend and for what? You should have come to me."

A twig snapped; a gun roared; the bullet whined off a headstone.

Shadows formed into men with guns and Wolf and Brock drew their own and when the shadows started shooting, Wolf and Brock fired back and jumped for cover.

The random bullets sliced the air. Wolf ducked behind a stone cross as a slug clipped an overhead branch. Wolf aimed where he had seen a muzzle flash and fired once. Off to his left, Brock let go a string of rounds, tracking a target. Somebody screamed.

Ahead of Wolf stood a tree and he ran for it, spotting two gunmen as they shifted cover. He fired once, twice; one of the gunmen went down. The other, twisted Wolf's way fired; Wolf fired back, missed, and the gunman ducked out of sight.

Another string of rapid shots from Brock echoed as Wolf advanced. A shotgun boomed. Wolf dived face first into the dirt. Brock screamed, "I'm hit," and another shotgun blast shook the night.

Wolf hopped up and retreated to the cross. Out in the open, he also caught two shooters by surprise. The pistol-toting gunman winged a shot Wolf's way but the .45 responded and knocked the man down. The shotgunner, a few steps behind, returned fire. By then Wolf had neared the cross enough to drop and roll the remaining distance. The shotgunner dropped back. Wolf reloaded and scanned the area while he caught his breath. Sensing no further movement, he went looking for Harry Brock.

———

BEN REGAN TUCKED the shotgun close to his body and hit the ground as the first shots popped. As Brock and the other unknown man split for cover, Regan crawled along the dirt, chunks of soil clinging to his elbows. He weaved around headstones to get closer to the detective.

Brock kept exposing his location each time he fired a string of shots. The slow, steady booms of the unknown man's weapon cautioned Regan. The other guy knew his business.

Presently, Regan reached a position back and to the left of Brock. He rose to one knee, lifted the Mossberg and pulled the trigger.

"I'm hit!" the detective cried out.

Brock rolled onto his side, his back, swinging his pistol around. Regan pumped and fired a second blast and Brock stopped moving.

Regan retraced his steps, crawling toward the sound of the unknown man's single shots. He rolled over the body of one of his men, saw another squatting behind a headstone. Regan joined the man and said, "Go forward," and they broke cover. Their unknown enemy did the same. Regan's partner fired. The unknown man fired twice in return, and Ben Regan dodged back to avoid the falling body of his teammate. Regan responded with a shotgun blast, but the other man had taken cover only to rise and respond with two shots. Regan dropped flat. The hot slugs whispered overhead. This new player wasn't a rookie and his presence complicated matters, but only if Regan didn't survive.

The other man's pistol fell silent. Regan scooted backward on his belly until a headstone provided enough cover for him to blend with the shadows. Then he took off running. He hated retreating but couldn't help Teddy dead. Not when they had a new obstacle to contend with.

HARRY BROCK HAD CRAWLED HALFWAY to his son's grave
before the gas ran out. Wolf found him still and very
dead with one hand reaching toward his son.

Wolf knelt beside the fallen detective, breathing
hard, wiping sweat from his forehead with the left
sleeve of his overcoat. More sweat dripped down his
back. He put away his gun, patted Brock's pockets and
found a phone. He scrolled to Scott Palakis's number.
Brock had helpfully stored it as SCOTT P. CELL. Wolf
dialed.

Two rings; then, "What is it, Harry?"

"Brock is dead and you're next unless you do exactly
as I say."

"Who is this?"

"My name is Wolf. I followed Brock from the bar to
the cemetery where we were ambushed and–"

Wolf winced and jerked the phone from his ear as
automatic weapons fire crackled across the connection.
He yelled for Scott once. Wolf cursed. He needed
answers, and the two people who could provide most of
those answers were now forever silent.

13

SCOTT PALAKIS LEFT the Mother Goose after his second drink. He didn't like being alone in public. He felt self-conscious, everybody's eyes on him, but he wasn't done drinking for the night. He pulled the Mazda into a liquor store parking lot with visions in his head of a big bottle of Johnny Walker. He shut off the car, reached for the door handle. His phone rang. Caller ID said BROCK and he answered.

"What is it, Harry?"

Somebody else said, "Brock is dead and you're next unless you do exactly as I say."

A sharp chill raced up Scott's spine, pushing his pulse into overdrive. "Who is this?"

The man on the other end started talking but Scott's attention snapped to the sedan pulling up a few spaces down. The small man who emerged stepped around the front of the black car with the kind of wicked submachine gun Scott had only seen in movies. The small man raised the weapon and Scott's mouth opened to scream–

Two shots barked. From behind the Mazda. The small man with the movie gun staggered back but squeezed the trigger anyway and the blinding strobe of the muzzle flash shifted away from Scott. Bullets shattered the back glass and part of the rear quarter panel. Then the weapon fell silent as its master collapsed.

Scott had covered his eyes before the sub gun blazed. As he lowered his hands and stared wide-eyed at the fallen killer, the Mazda's passenger door swung open and a big hulk of a man with no hair on his head landed in the passenger seat.

Miles Kincaid pressed the smoking muzzle of his Wilson Combat .45 into Scott's neck. The hot muzzle burned the young man's skin.

"Start the car."

Scott drove with no destination given for almost an hour. Biting wind rushed through the blasted-out portions of the back seat. His passenger seemed not to notice, and the big man remained silent the entire time.

Scott was on the freeway heading into the mountains when his companion told him to reverse direction, head back into downtown, and proceed to the Bonaventure Hotel.

Scott parked down the street from the Bonaventure, in a dark alley between two other buildings. The car looked like it had been in a war. He didn't want the valets gawking at the bullet damage.

Young Palakis and the big man walked to the hotel, through the bright, golden-tiled lobby, where it was warmer than the car, to the mirrored elevators, up six floors, and down a carpeted hallway to room 209. The big man slipped a key card into the slot above the door handle and turned the knob. Miles stepped through the dark entryway and Scott followed behind with a racing heart.

"Hello, son."

Scott blinked. His father sat at the table, bathed in light from a wall lamp. No other lights were on. He looked like he was on stage, under a spotlight. Drapes covered the window behind the table. Vince Palakis held a glass of scotch. The bottle sat in the center of the table.

"Come here and sit down."

Scott dragged his feet across the thick carpet, grasping the arms of the empty chair as he lowered onto the cushion. He glanced at the bottle. There wasn't a second glass. Vince Palakis sipped the scotch. He cocked his head, regarding the young man who shared his blood, with the gaze of a coroner studying a corpse. Scott sank a little in the chair.

Presently, Palakis blinked away the gaze and smiled a little. His face softened. He said, "Seems like yesterday when I was teaching you to ride a bike. Remember how much trouble we had putting that thing together? Some assembly required?" He laughed. "I swear we built that thing from scratch."

"Somebody stole that bike."

Silence. Only the light ticking of Palakis's watch indicated any activity amongst the three men. Scott realized most clocks didn't tick anymore, but he always found comfort in a ticking clock. Life's heartbeat. Time was just as alive as he was. Scott jerked in the chair, sucked air.

"You okay?"

Scott looked across at the big bald man, who stood by the door with folded hands. He was staring straight ahead. Not at the Palakis men. At something further away.

"Thanks to him, I suppose."

Palakis said, "I had wanted to have this conversation after dinner tonight, but before you rushed out Miles called me and said he'd been to Alexa's apartment and found her dead. I knew they'd try and kill you tonight. I thought it would be safer to bring you here because they'll be watching for you at your place and mine."

Scott blinked a few times.

"I'm not the best role model, am I, Scott? Don't answer that. Let me get this out."

Palakis took another drink. He stared at the carpet a moment.

"I'm the man I am today because of the choices I made. I think our decisions tell us a lot about ourselves. Whether or not you have corn flakes for dinner doesn't say much, except that maybe you can't cook, but the big choices reveal a man's true self. They'll tell you everything if you're willing to listen. Most people aren't."

Palakis looked at his son. "Are you willing to listen?"

Scott nodded.

"Back when I was your age, I started running around with a guy named Ugo Califano," Palakis said. "Poker buddies at first. We had the same playing styles, liked taking money off the suckers. Califano was a mob guy, light stuff. Ran a numbers outfit. Eventually we became pals, spent a lot of time in clubs and bars. The lifestyle appealed to me. The power Ugo had. It was contagious. Later, Califano became more and more of a leader in his crew while I continued my software business. Soon enough Ugo trusted me to take care of a certain DVD that's received some attention in recent days. I knew what he was using it for, but I owed him for clearing some business obstacles, so I had no problem taking the disk.

"I never saw myself as a compromiser," Palakis said, "morally or integrity-wise. I taught you about law and order and right and wrong because I believed it. I was always pretty-firm. And I don't know how I became corrupt enough to do that sort of favor, or to ask the sort of favor that I did after the... accident. That's what I mean, Scott. The choices I made were telling me all kinds of things about myself except I wasn't listening.

"And then came the night of the crash," Palakis continued. "I couldn't let that hurt me. I'd built too much. Become a big shot. Had an image to protect. So I asked Ugo to help me get out of it, and he did, and now you and I are having a conversation I never imagined we would share and what I've been running from most of my life has finally caught up with me."

Vince Palakis glanced over at the still-silent Miles Kincaid, and back to his son. He said:

"I'm glad you've become the kind of man who couldn't stomach what I did, Scott. You're better than me. I'm also glad that your mother isn't here to see this. But now you have a problem, kiddo. The choices *you* made may have been right but there are consequences. The people you conspired with want you dead. They don't need you anymore, and they want to kill you so Miles can't find out who they are. Tell me everything, and we can clean this up. After tonight, you can go wherever you want, and you don't ever have to see me again if you don't want to."

Scott kept his mouth shut. He'd heard no apology, words of regret. His father had given up trying to be good and wanted to know everything so he could save his own neck.

Scott wondered if this was his best choice. Brock was dead. Scott had nobody. Then he thought of Brock's friend, the man who called his cell. He wasn't going to tell his father the whole story, just enough to get away so he could call Brock's friend.

The young man took a deep breath. "Harry Brock," he said. "He found out about the video from your hooker friend, Jodi. He asked me to find where you kept the DVD and then he arranged the break-in so you wouldn't suspect me. He found two guys that have a score to settle with Califano. He never told me their names, but they're running some rackets out here. They hired the guys to bust into the house. Brock called me after dinner tonight when you were on the phone, so I gave you that excuse about tomorrow and went to meet him. He told me you'd brought in some help so he figured we'd be silenced before your guy got to us and now Brock is dead and you're telling me this is all for my own good when we wouldn't be talking if you hadn't been lying to me all these years?"

"Brock didn't tell you who he was working with?"

"Didn't you hear a word I just said?"

"I heard you, Scott."

"It doesn't mean anything, does it?"

Palakis reached into a jacket pocket and slid a set of keys across the table. "Full tank," he said.

Scott snatched the keys, stood up, and walked into the darkened portion of the room toward the door. The big man stepped aside. Scott opened the door, went out to the lighted hallway, and let the door click shut behind him. Leaving his father in a quiet tomb. He didn't feel sorry at all.

———

As WOLF STEERED the Chrysler homeward, he ran down a list of possible options. He had few.

Brock had kept the address of his hooker friend, Jodi, stored in his phone. Wolf went there and found her lying on the carpet, shot through the head. He also discovered a single nine-millimeter shell casing on the carpet near the body.

At Brock's one-bedroom flop, he found no notebooks, no laptop computer, no papers that contained any information about Teddy Gambolini or Ben Regan. Or where Wolf could pick up their trail.

The phone rang. He flipped it open. "Yes?"

"This is Scott Palakis."

Wolf pulled over. His pulse quickened. "Hello, Scott."

"Who are you?"

"Somebody who doesn't want to see lives wasted."

"I don't have anybody else to turn to."

"I hear that a lot," Wolf said.

"We need to meet. I just finished talking to my father–" and the young man described the conversation, concluded with, "I didn't tell him anything, but I want to tell you."

"When and where?"

14

WOLF PARKED in front of room 526 at the Paramount Motel. The flickering lights outside each door showed off the building's green/pink paint job. Wolf's eyes itched. He needed sleep. Time to regroup. But he needed Scott's information more than rest.

The door opened after Wolf's second knock. Scott Palakis, his face tinged with a gray drabness coupled with heavy-lidded eyes, stared at Wolf. His pale lips remained pressed together.

"Scott," Wolf said.

Scott opened the door. He was at a table by the window by the time Wolf shut the door and turned the bolt. He sat across from the young man. "My name is Wolf. I'm not a cop."

"What are you?"

Wolf smiled. "Like Batman, except I don't wear the tights."

Scott didn't smile. "Fair enough." He closed his eyes, swallowed. "You never think your life will take the course it does. I never thought my father–"

"Tell me what you and Brock had going."

Scott swallowed again and outlined the plan; his part; Brock's part; gave more detail about the meeting with his father. Scott said nothing about Gambolini or Regan so Wolf asked about them.

"I don't know those names," Scott said. "I only met one guy named Amis. Brock said he was the top dog. We had a chat at Amis's house, before the robbery. I told them about the security system at Dad's, where the safe was."

"That was the only time you saw him?"

"Yeah."

"Was he alone?"

"There were two other guys. They hung around in another room. I didn't hear their names. Maybe they were the guys you mentioned."

"Know where Amis lives?"

Scott nodded. He gave Wolf the address, but Wolf tapped his chin, unsure. They could have used the home of somebody not connected to the scheme. But it was a place to start, more than he had now, and if he could tie Amis to Gambolini, so much the better.

"Does Amis have a first name?"

"Jack. Older guy. White hair."

Wolf watched Scott a moment. The young man dropped his eyes. "What about my father?" he said.

"What about him?"

"I can't–he can't get away with what he's done."

"That's up to you, Scott. Are you willing to talk to the district attorney?"

Scott's eyes stayed down. "I'll talk to anybody who can do something."

"Stay here. Get some rest. I'll be in touch." Wolf rose, extended a hand. "Thank you, Scott."

Scott Palakis blinked a few times, and then shook Wolf's hand. "After this," he said, "I'm never coming back to this city again."

———

WOLF SLEPT UNTIL NOON, skipped lunch, and headed for Kiki's apartment. He wanted to tell her about Bent Nose and Crew Cut, the thugs he shot at Mick's Diner, and see if she could dig up their background. She wasn't home, but Sheila was.

They sat on the couch and Wolf told her about what he'd been doing. He told her she'd soon hear some things related to Freddie's murder, but it wouldn't be the whole story. He was still working on the rest of it. She wanted to know what difference it made and cried on his shoulder.

After a while Wolf said, "Feel like going out later?"

"I guess."

"A nice dinner beats staring at these walls all the time. I have something else cooking and I can't go to this place alone."

"What about Kiki?"

"We'll bring her too."

"You're assuming she'll want to go?"

"Trust me, she'll want to go."

———

HOMICIDE INSPECTOR JOHN CALLAWAY rose from behind his big mahogany desk. Behind him, a wide window looked out over the city and part of the bay. The large office had a wall of books, paintings on other walls depicted naval ships from the 17- and 1800s.

"Have a chair," Callaway said after they shook hands. Callaway's hands had their usual roughness; a desk man he had not always been, having worked in lumber and construction prior to his law enforcement career.

"You've been busy," Callaway said.

"You should have been there."

"What's on your mind?"

Wolf presented his version of the events surrounding Freddie Webster's murder. He told all about Vince Palakis and the video, the hit-and-run and Scott's role, and Brock's contribution. He made no mention of Gambolini or Regan. Those morsels he wanted to save.

Callaway said, "We can move on Palakis after his son testifies. What haven't you told me?"

Wolf smiled. A low laugh rumbled up from Callaway's chest. He couldn't be fooled. "I have something for Kiki," Wolf said. "Couple names to check out."

"She's at her office," Callaway said, and shook Wolf's hand again. "Good hunting."

Wolf crossed the street to the building housing the district attorney's office, and found Kiki filling a cup from the small water cooler in a corner of her office. When she turned, Wolf saw glasses perched midway down her nose. She was barefoot, no stockings, finger- and toenails painted black. The white blouse and Capri pants combo didn't seem out of place with her. She smiled at Wolf.

"Girls with glasses are really sexy."

"Shut up," she said, removing the black-rimmed specs. She placed the glasses beside the open folder on her desk and sat. Wolf stood in front of the desk and pulled a small notebook from his shirt pocket, tore out a page and handed it to her.

She read the two names on the paper. "So?"

"Those guys were shot at Mick's Diner night before last."

"That was you?"

"They were trying to assault a young woman."

"Uh-huh."

"One of those guys died at the diner, the other at the hospital. I'm sure your people will have discovered it wasn't injury-related by now. Get whatever you can, and I'll pick you and Sheila up at seven tonight."

"For what?"

"Dinner. Little place called the Candy Apple."

"You're never this social. What's the catch?"

"The young woman I mentioned works there."

"That doesn't tell me why you want to know this stuff. What's the connection?"

"The woman left a day planner at the diner and in the planner is a picture of one of the gun runners from the warehouse."

"That's all?"

Wolf winked, turned, went out.

———

WOLF PARKED down the block and led Sheila and Kiki up the steps to the domed building of the Candy Apple. The marble front sparkled from street-light glare. A smiling doorman in a bulky red uniform and top hat pulled open the door.

The Candy Apple's arched entryway led to a wide-open dining area with a stage and orchestra stand. A poster announced the nightly appearance of Jack Lindy's Orchestra and Chorus Line. The show and décor gave the Candy Apple a fancy retro appeal, where guests didn't show up in anything but formal attire. The skinny hostess led them along a red carpet, down some steps, through the maze of full tables to the spot Wolf had reserved near the stage. Bright overhead diamond-laced chandeliers lit the way.

"Crowded tonight," Kiki said. Wolf held chairs out for her and Sheila. Sheila smiled as she sat, scooted in. Wolf sat across from Kiki with Sheila to his left. He placed the leather day planner that had belonged to Holly Mendoza on the table.

"What's good here?" Sheila said, opening the menu.

"Everything, honey," Kiki said. "And it's all expensive, too."

"Don't worry about that," Wolf said, opening his menu. "I brought my Visa. And my MasterCard."

"That will cover our drinks," Kiki said.

Wolf looked at Sheila, who wore a loose black dress with a gold sash. The sash was a bit askew because of her belly. She had been quiet during the drive over and reviewed the menu with disinterest.

Kiki said, "Think I'll do the steak. And they better leave it bloody. I mean just cook it 'till the cow stops mooing." Kiki had traded her blouse and Capris for another sweater/skirt combo, no belt, with open-toed shoes.

Sheila kept her eyes down and with one finger

traced the circular pattern in the soft tablecloth. Wolf rubbed her shoulder.

"Okay?"

She nodded, but her eyes sparkled with moisture. She brushed a finger under each eye. "I think I'll have fish."

Their waiter, short, stocky, with thick hair, glided up to the table and announced that his name was Orin. Wolf ordered a round of coffee and tea.

"Freddie and I," Sheila said, "we could have never afforded–" she stopped. Her face paled. Wolf took her hand and squeezed. She scooted back her chair and excused herself. Wolf and Kiki watched her go.

"Poor kid."

"She'll be fine. She's tough."

"Taught in the same school as you?"

Wolf nodded.

———

SHEILA RETURNED a few minutes later and apologized. Kiki and Wolf told her not to worry. Wolf squeezed her hand again.

Orin returned and jotted food orders. He said the orchestra would be starting soon, pivoted on his right heel, marched off.

Sheila said, "So what's the other thing you're working on?"

"He won't tell, honey," Kiki said, extracting some papers from her purse. "But maybe this stuff will give us a clue." She sorted the papers. "The two men at the diner"– she cocked an eyebrow at Wolf–"one of which was later murdered at the hospital, were Daniel Hoffman and Kevin Morris. Morris is the one died at the hospital." She sipped her drink. "Both were freelance gunman from the East. Connections to the New York syndicate, but not officially part of it. Also, some connections in Chicago, but they left Chicago last year and haven't turned up until now."

Wolf tapped his chin with a finger and nodded.

"Does that tell you anything?"

"Not really."

"Well, add this to the mix," Kiki said. She leaned forward, lowered her voice. "Morris and Hoffman are part of a bigger problem. Several *more* East Coast gunmen have been drifting into the city for a few weeks now."

"Who and what for?"

"I don't know who, and Daddy doesn't know what for. He and some of his investigators are afraid to pick anybody up for questioning in case they frighten all of them away. His team has put the word out for informants to call in if they hear something, but nothing's come back yet. Daddy would rather round them up just before the caper, whatever it is, than get one or two and miss the big fish."

Wolf was about to speak when the orchestra started up with a big blast of trumpets. Midway through the first number the chorus line flowed onto the stage, kicking and singing. Wolf watched a moment and wondered what spot Holly Mendoza would have occupied in the line.

"They must be tied to the gunrunners somehow."

Wolf opened the day planner, showed her the photo of Holly and Ace.

Sheila moved her attention from one to the other as they spoke, as if she were watching a tennis match.

"Nobody's made that connection yet," Kiki said. "The homicide guys are still with it." She sipped her coffee. "Who's the girl?"

"Holly Mendoza. Somebody who used to work here. Danced in the chorus line." He lifted the day planner. "This belonged to her."

"So why would gun runners be importing shooting talent?"

"Because they're doing more than smuggling guns, that's why. I'm hoping Holly will provide some answers."

"Is that why she's a target? They think she'll talk after you popped her main squeeze?"

Wolf nodded.

Sheila said, "I can't believe the two of you. This kind of talk is normal?"

Wolf gave her half a grin; Kiki shrugged.

"Tough world, honey," Kiki said.

Orin returned with their dinners and they ate without talking for a while.

When Orin came to clear away the dishes, Wolf stopped him and said, "We're looking for somebody who used to work here. Holly Mendoza, a dancer, know her?"

He frowned. "Why?"

"We've lost touch and heard she was working here."

"I know Holly," Orin said. "Total babe. She'd never go out with me, no matter how many times I asked."

"She here tonight?"

"Long gone, I'm afraid. Quit. About a week ago."

"Know where we might find her?"

Orin said, "Try her roommate. She's in the chorus

line, too. Alice, Alice Walker. If you're lucky you can catch her backstage after the show. She wears the golden headdress, can't miss her."

"Thanks, Orin," Wolf said, tucked a five into the waiter's shirt pocket. Orin carried the dishes away and Wolf turned to find Kiki staring at him.

"What?" he said.

"How are us girls supposed to get home?"

"Call an Uber."

Kiki said to Sheila, "Worst boyfriend *ever*."

Presently a bearded man in a tuxedo began moving from table to table, asking how people were enjoying themselves. He came to Wolf's table, and with a slight bow said, "I'm Charles Naughton, the manager here." His beard was all black while his temples were touched with gray. "Everything all right?"

Wolf said yes.

"Orin tells me you're a friend of a former employee."

"That's right," Wolf said.

"Holly was a great asset and we were sorry to see her go," he said. "Give her my best if you see her."

The bearded man kept grinning as he spoke but his eyes studied Wolf's face like he was a figure in a Rembrandt and Wolf felt a tingle in the back of his neck that triggered an alarm in his head that made him glad he'd packed the .45.

"Of course," Wolf said.

"If you need anything more, don't hesitate to ask," the bearded man said, shaking hands again, keeping up that same silly grin. He walked away with his hands limp at his sides.

Orin returned with the check and Wolf slid a trio of $50s into the leather folder. He made sure the women got into a cab, then returned to the restaurant and drifted around the side of the stage. He slipped through a door marked Backstage, ducked behind a stack of chairs. Overhead lights lit the otherwise dark backstage hall, the shadows from the stacked chairs and other pieces of equipment provided Wolf with cover. Up ahead, the chorus line filed off to thunderous applause. The women left the stage in a single line. Alice Walker, in her towering golden headdress, brought up the rear of the line, pulling at the straps that held the headdress in place. She was slim, auburn hair tied back, the little skirt of her shimmering outfit fitting snugly over her rear.

Wolf stepped out from behind the chairs. "Alice."

She turned, surprised, narrowing her eyes, stood still as Wolf approached. He said, "Seen Holly?"

"Get away from me." As she turned, he grabbed her arm, turned her around. He held up Holly's day planner.

"This belonged to Holly," he said. "I want to return it."

"Shut up and let me go."

"I was at the diner when she was attacked. I helped her get away."

Alice's big green eyes studied Wolf's face.

"I can't talk now," she said.

"When?"

"Later."

"When later?"

"In the alley, by the stage door. Fifteen minutes."

"Lots of doors in the alley," Wolf said.

"The green one with the letter A on it."

She twisted out of his grip.

———

ALMOST TWENTY MINUTES PASSED. Before Wolf could start stewing, the rusted metal stage door with the letter "A" on it swung out and Alice Walker stepped into the clean alley wearing a tan overcoat.

"Come on," she said, shoes scraping as she rushed by. Wolf stole a quick glance back, but no other alley shadows moved.

At the mouth of the alley she turned right, her footsteps louder on the sidewalk, but not loud enough to overpower the rumble of evening traffic.

"Have you seen Holly?" Wolf said.

"You got a one-track mind."

"I don't want to see her get hurt."

"You're probably just another punk trying to play it smart since your buddies got blasted the other night."

"Not true."

"I don't believe you."

"Why are you arguing with me?"

"Because I did hear from Holly," she said. "She described you. I still don't believe you. It could be a trick."

"Yeah, sure, we make a habit of shooting our own guys."

The other foot and vehicle traffic thinned out as they moved up the block, the buildings turning from bright well-maintained to dark and fading. Scattered homeless were sleeping on the ground against walls, over steaming grates, others slouched in doorways.

"You come this way all the time?"

"Can't afford a cab."

"They pay you in peanuts?"

"Money comes in, money goes out," she said.

"Where's Holly now?" Wolf said.

"Someplace safe, don't you worry."

Tires screeched. Wolf snapped his head around. A big car sped up the street. He reached out with his left hand and pushed at Alice's back while his right clawed for the .45 under his left arm. From the passenger seat, a man leaned out with an Uzi and the chattering submachine gun drowned out Alice's scream. They hit the sidewalk together and the car raced past. Wolf jumped up with his pistol in hand and triggered a blast that shattered the back window. The car screeched again as it rounded the corner and Wolf lowered his smoking auto pistol and raced to Alice.

And saw the puddle of blood spreading beneath her.

She tilted her head up, mouth opening, a half scream rushing out. Her eyes closed. She dropped her head as Wolf knelt beside her and rolled her onto her back.

She sucked air in short gasps, grabbed her purse and pulled it up onto her bloody chest. Undid the clasp with bloody fingers, tugged out a key. Wolf snatched the key. It belonged to the Palace Motel. "Key...Holly."

"Stay calm, Alice, stay with me."

"Key...Holly."

Then her body relaxed, and she stopped breathing.

Sirens in the distance. Wolf tucked the key in a pocket, the .45 back under his arm. Across the street, lights had come on, gawkers popping out of windows. Wolf's legs carried him away from there in a sprint that would have made an Olympian jealous and he didn't stop until he'd circled the block.

He ducked into an alley to catch his breath, bending his legs in a squat next to a dumpster smelling of rotting fish. An occupied cardboard box, complete with a dirty blanket, lay across from him. Wolf took out the key and examined it in the dim light. The tag gave the address of the Palace Motel. Twenty minutes away if traffic wasn't too heavy.

15

A SINGLE LIGHT burned in front of the Palace Motel's main office, which faced the street. Wolf made a circle of the parking lot, noting other cars scattered about, all of which were dark and silent. Parking the 300 in the center of the lot, front toward the street, Wolf shut off the motor and cracked the window. Crickets chirped; traffic from a nearby overpass filled the air with the sound of rushing wind. He looked at the key Alice had given him. The number 4 had been stamped on the front. He left the car and stepped up to the door and slipped key into lock.

A curse caught in his throat as the door opened and a small feminine hand pushed out the snout of a snub-nosed revolver. Wolf clamped his left hand on the barrel, twisting hard, shoving the door inward, yanking the gun outward.

The woman behind the door yelped and tumbled to the floor. Wolf moved inside with one big step, kicking the door shut. He found a light switch to his left and hit the switch.

The petite brunette clad only in a black night shirt and gray shorts, dark hair half in her eyes, made a squeaking noise as she scooted across the brown carpet. She stopped when she bumped the rumpled single bed.

She didn't scream. Her eyes still had the dark circles, but they narrowed in recognition. He snapped open the revolver's cylinder and dumped the cartridges on the carpet. The revolver he tossed on the bed.

"Holly Mendoza, I presume," Wolf said. She didn't blink. "We've met. At the diner. Remember?"

She moved her eyes up and down his body, finally focusing on his face.

"I'm glad I caught up with you before they did."

She rose to her feet and picked up from the bed a fuzzy pink bathrobe and tied it on.

"Now what?" she said. "If you're here it means you talked to Alice."

"Alice didn't make it." Wolf explained the shooting. Holly sat on the edge of the bed, her face in her hands. He parked on the edge of the table, waiting and watching. She went to the bathroom and returned with a towel and wiped her eyes and nose. She looked at the floor.

"I want to help you, Holly."

He couldn't tell her he was the one who killed her boyfriend or let on that he knew the score.

She dabbed her eyes. "Alice didn't deserve that."

"Tell me what's going on."

"You wouldn't understand."

"Try me."

"You a cop?"

"Just a concerned citizen."

She let out a breath. "My boyfriend. He got killed working with these guys who're selling guns."

An engine rumbled outside; bright light flared through the curtained window. Doors opened, closed; male voices; the click-clack of weapons. Wolf drew his gun and rushed toward Holly, shouting, "Get down!" as the chatter of multiple submachine guns split the night.

Hot slugs punched violently through the wall, the window shattering, wood chips and plaster flying every which way. Holly screamed beneath Wolf. He propped up on a hand, swung the .45 at the door and fired three rapid shots. Somebody started hollering. The gunfire stopped.

"Up, up, up," Wolf said, rising, Holly making a beeline for the bathroom. He scrambled after her. She stood by the tub breathing hard. He yelled for her to get the window above the tub open. The front door crashed open. Wolf leaned out and fired at the cluster of black-suited gunman carrying HK MP5s who were entering the room. The two men in front screamed, fell back; the remaining four retreated, shouting for each other to get to cover. Wolf took careful aim and fired a slug into the back of one. The gunman hit the ground hard, his weapon clattering away. Wolf wanted to race out and grab the fallen MP5 but Holly's scream of "Let's go!" changed his mind.

Wolf reloaded while Holly shimmied out the window. He put the gun away and grasped the windowsill and hauled through head-and-shoulders first. Gravity took over and he put his arms out to break the fall. The dirt below was soft, mixed with sharp rocks. Ahead, a wire fence. Beyond that, a darkened warehouse.

Holly stood with her knees together, hands over her mouth. Wolf took out the .45. Holly said, "I'm freezing, and I don't have any shoes–"

"Quiet."

He listened, but the gunfire had partially deafened him. The gunman would assume they'd escape through the window and split up to circle around the back. If Wolf and Holly went left or right, they'd bump into the shooters, but Wolf figured they might get lucky and hit the gunman forced to go solo.

Wolf held out his hand. She took it. They moved to the left, staying close to the wall.

Holly uttered sharp little gasps as they moved and fell silent once they approached an opening in the wall, the point at which this first building stopped and a second building sat at a 90 degree angle. Wolf stole a glance over his shoulder, saw nobody; facing forward, he adjusted his grip on Holly's hand, and picked up the pace with his automatic leading the way.

Reached the corner, peeked around. Clear. A step and–

Two of the three shooters appeared at the same time. Wolf's trigger finger acted on its own and the .45 blasted a hole through the head of the man closest. The second shuffled back. Wolf and the gunman fired at the same time. Holly screamed, her hand slipping from Wolf's. Wolf watched the gunman's body slam into one of the support poles of the overhang and fired a second shot into his chest.

Wolf looked back and saw Holly's crumpled, bleeding body on the ground.

Wolf turned her over. Several slugs had torn up her neck and chest. Her dead eyes were half rolled back into her head. He let out a curse. If he'd not been clutching her hand, she might have had a chance.

Heavy breathing. Footsteps. From around the back. Wolf looked up to see the last gunman stomping through the dirt. He raised his gun and fired. The gunman's body hit the ground face first.

Now he heard sirens. He raced to the Chrysler. The big car's tires screeched, biting into the pavement, as the machine launched forward. Behind Wolf, cops closed in with flashing lights and sirens, but they were too far back to catch up. He pressed the gas some more. Eight cylinders of power responded with a surge of speed that took him away from the remains of the bloody fight and into the night.

16
_____

"I'M NOT sure how we'll clean this up," Kiki said, "but we're working on it. What I know already is that the dead gunmen all have ties to the East Coast, like those guys who went after Holly at the diner."

Kiki paced the floor while Wolf sat in front of the open window, a cigar going, feet propped up on the sill, chest and shoulders slumped. Totally drained. He shook his head, took a long pull and blew out a stream of smoke.

When Wolf finally returned home and tried sleeping, he saw Alice and Holly's faces and relived the shootings in dreams. He could never get them away in one piece.

"What now?"

Wolf blew smoke.

"You can't sit forever," she said.

Kiki grabbed another chair from the table and sat across from Wolf. He avoided her gaze a moment, then looked up and said, "I screwed up."

"Not the first time. Won't be the last," she said.

"We've been over this before. You can't save everybody. Doctors know that. Doesn't make it easier, but you don't stop doing your job."

Wolf laughed.

"Victims demand justice. You've said it before. What do you think keeps Dad and me covering for you? How long can we get away with this before somebody starts asking questions? You know what I walked away from to help you. Dad, too."

Wolf looked out the window.

Kiki folded her arms.

Wolf smoked a little more. "Thanks, Kiki."

"What's your next move?"

"You'll know when it happens."

"Try and keep the body count down, okay?"

"No promises."

Kiki hopped up from the chair, grabbed her jacket and let herself out.

————

WHEN VINCE PALAKIS heard the sirens, he dropped his coffee mug, which shattered on the tiled kitchen floor...

Miles Kincaid sat at the kitchen table with an over-toasted cream-cheesed bagel in front on him. Palakis ran into the adjoining living room while Kincaid slid back his chair and stood. He brushed crumbs off his shirt and followed. Palakis, panting, swept open the front drapes. Police units filled the street. From an unmarked sedan, two men in suits emerged. Two uniformed officers followed them up the walk.

Miles took out his gun.

Palakis said, "My son talked." He turned to Miles, and Miles shot him in the head.

———

THE AMIS ADDRESS, provided by Scott Palakis, turned out to be a two-story home in a quiet neighborhood, similar homes on either side and a school across the street.

Wolf sat in the Chrysler, watching from a cul-de-sac next to the school. He'd been parked since seven in the morning, when vans and SUVs crowded the street as moms dropped off kids.

Just past nine a.m. Wolf watched Jack Amis exit his house. The man matched Scott's description, older, white hair. His upper body tilted from side-to-side as he went down the walk. Wolf peered through a small pair of binoculars but didn't catch a glimpse of the man's face. When Amis opened the driver's side door, he turned his back to the car and eased inside bottom-first, then pulled in his legs one after the other.

Wolf lowered the binoculars and brought the silent Chrysler to rumbling life. Scott's information wasn't a waste.

Amis drove from the house to a downtown park where he spent an hour sitting on a bench, tossing chunks of bread at swarming pigeons. Presently he drove to a construction site and parked outside a portable building.

Wolf watched the construction activity for a half hour. Nobody else entered or exited the portable. Wolf returned home, filled his chipped mug with tea, grabbed a cigar and sat out on the deck. The previous evening's failure weighed on him. No matter how many ways he replayed the scene, no matter what alternative choices he proposed, he never saw a different outcome.

How had the gunman found them? Only two people jumped to mind as tipsters, Orin, the waiter, or Charles Naughton, the manager. Wolf put his money on the manager. He didn't like the way the bearded man had looked at him during their short chat. As if he were memorizing Wolf's face. The bullets that killed Alice had been meant for him.

Wolf sat until early evening and hit the street again. His first task of the day had been a success. Now he wanted to find Charles Naughton and have some other questions answered.

———

CHARLES NAUGHTON's long face and tired eyes said he'd had a rough night at the club. The car door creaked open. He sank into the cloth seat and started the motor. Wolf followed him down the street. Plenty of traffic crowded each direction but the interior of the 300 was quiet except for the low burble of the V8. The silence was making Wolf's mind wander to thoughts he'd rather not have so he turned on the radio and let soft jazz fill the car.

After a few blocks Wolf pulled over at a meter and watched Naughton's Honda stop in front of a small, closed-down bar.

The old Shipwreck Bar. A favorite hang-out of Wolf's before he joined the military.

Naughton climbed out. Wooden beams had been placed across the bar's front doors CLOSED signs displayed in several places. The bearded man rotated one of the wooden beams up and away from the door, unlocked it with a key, and went inside.

Wolf left the Chrysler. The chill clawed at his skin and he zipped his jacket, bypassed the front of the bar and went around the side, down a pair of steps to a narrow alley. He stopped at a metal door.

From a pocket of his jacket he pulled out a trio of lock picks. The top lock, caked with rust, kept the pick from going in all the way. Wolf had to push and wiggle the pick to get the tumblers moved. The bottom lock offered no resistance and Wolf pushed open the door, closed it behind him, and brought out a pen flash. The light revealed a small empty room. Floating dust tickled his nose and he squeezed his nostrils to block a sneeze. Wolf crossed to another door, opened it, and entered a long, carpeted hallway. Pool room at the end. Dust-covered main bar and sitting area, empty of tables, at the other end, along with a closed door with MANAGER stamped on the front. Light glowed from beneath the door.

Wolf went to the door, turned the knob and pushed. Hinges squeaked. On the first wall to the left, glossy black-and-white photos hung, and Charles Naughton sat at a desk, his back to the door. As he turned, he said, "I thought you were–" and froze when he saw Wolf. He jumped from the chair and brought up an arm as a shield, but Wolf batted away the arm and smashed the automatic against the bearded man's head. Naughton collapsed.

Wolf approached the desk and scanned the scattered papers. He snatched a page containing a list of known city gangs, starting with the Up the Hill and

Down the Hill crews from the first shooting involving the stolen military rifles. He also saw the words SALES CANCELLED TILL FURTHER NOTICE scratched on the margin.

Wolf turned to the wall. The pictures showed people at various events, in malls, milling about town. Some faces were circled. Two of the circled faces had X's drawn through them. Wolf breathed through his mouth, not sure what to think.

Most of the pictures were of the same people. *People he knew. A former client named Zachary Coleman and his family.*

Feet shuffled outside the door.

Wolf pivoted and the broad-shouldered man framed in the doorway dove with his hands out, clamping his left around Wolf's right wrist. Wolf fired and the shot burned the other man's earlobe. He yelled, shoving Wolf's arm wide, hammering his free hand into the side of Wolf's head.

Wolf slammed back against the desk. The other man brought his free fist back, and Wolf kicked him in the stomach. The man's cheeks puffed, hot breath scorching Wolf's face. He crumpled. Wolf back-handed the man's jaw. The man's grip on Wolf's right wrist carried him along and they crashed to the floor.

Wolf landed on top. The other man wheezed trying to suck air, loosened his grip on Wolf's wrist. Wolf rolled away, scrambled to his feet. The other man was halfway up when Wolf lashed out with a kick. The tip of his shoe bit into the side of the other man's head and sent him back down, but he wasn't out. He rolled his front toward Wolf with a hand snaking under his jacket. Wolf kicked him in the stomach, the face, the stomach again. The man's hand fell out of his coat, a pistol falling with it, and Wolf kicked the gun across the room.

Wolf, gasping, wiped sweat from his face, took a good look at the unconscious man on the floor. His stomach lurched.

He knew the man. Fifteen years ago they'd called each other friend but now his former ally would have killed him given the chance.

Sucking air, Wolf backed through the open door, slamming against the hallway wall. He stood there heaving with the .45 up and ready, listening. No other sounds. He raced out the way he'd entered as fast as he could.

WOLF RETURNED to his hotel suite, showered and took two aspirin to ease the aches and pains. He made a pot of tea, and sat at the table at the window. He kept the lights off, the window open, a lit cigar trailing smoke. The Colt Series 70 sat on the table. Wolf focused on the ramifications of the fight at the bar. What would happen next might take a bit of time, but it would happen, and Wolf wondered how much of his past he'd have to confront.

The man he'd tangled with: Dick McNab. Ex-soldier, former government agent. He'd served with Wolf in the Delta Force and in secret commando cells run by the CIA. They'd called him "Skinner" because of his skills with sharp blades. Wolf had never expected to see any of the old crew again. So, was he in charge of the gun smuggling? Was there anybody else with him who also knew Wolf? McNab's presence brought to mind something Kiki had said once the government took over the smuggling investigation, the rumor of a C.I.A. officer present with the Feds. Was Langley tracking McNab's crew?

Wolf sat and smoked and sipped tea from his chipped mug and had almost emptied the pot when he heard the taps. Light, feminine taps against the door. His watch read a quarter passed three a.m. He stood up, bringing along the .45. He went to the door, released the trio of locks, opened up and stepped back.

17

WOLF CLOSED HIS EYES, opened them. She was still there, staring at him through big beautiful brown eyes.

"Hi, Wolf," she said.

The left corner of his mouth pulled up a bit.

Wolf opened the door the rest of the way and the woman walked in wearing a long black skirt, matching stockings, pink blouse. A diamond necklace glittered, and she carried a heavy coat. Thick make-up resembled a hard mask. Wolf pushed the door closed, stared at the locks a moment with his free hand at his side. When he turned, she was facing him.

"Aren't you gonna lock the door?"

"Too late," he said.

"It's been a long time," she said.

"Yeah." It sounded stupid but he didn't know what else to say. His mind wasn't on conversation, it was on the fact that his carefully constructed life, his security, was now threatened from within, and he'd need more than bullets to solve the problem.

The woman sat on the couch, put her purse on the table, and crossed her legs. "You've done well," she said, looking around.

Wolf still didn't know what to say, so he went to the old stand-by. "Still scotch and soda?"

"Of course."

Wolf went around the kitchen wall. He grabbed a bottle from the cupboard, willing his pulse to settle, his hands to stop shaking. No luck. He mixed the drinks and joined the woman on the couch. They watched each other. He needed time to think. At least his pulse had slowed.

"It's nice to see you, Ava," he said. "You look great."

She twirled a finger through her curly black hair. She smiled. Wolf had forgotten how pretty her smile could be, but it wasn't a knockout smile like Kiki had. Ava had put on a little more weight since he last saw her, but for her it looked good. She was still the kind of gal that he could fall on top of and not wonder right after if he'd cracked one of her ribs.

Wolf and Ava Sutter had been on the same team with Skinner McNab. Neither could explain their attraction but they'd been inseparable and took vacations together whenever possible. Paris. The Alps. Even tried a little town in India right on the beach, a perfect place for two people who wanted the world to go away for a while. But nothing lasts forever. When a bomb tore up Wolf's left leg, he'd been sent to Zurich to recover. Ava went with him. In the middle of the trip, she left. No note, no reason. Just gone.

Wolf had never expected they'd build a nest together with the proverbial white picket fence. At least, that's what he said to himself on quiet nights when thoughts drifted to years gone by.

But this reappearance meant something other than a reunion. First Dick McNab. Now Ava Sutter. How many more?

"Why are you here, Ava?"

Amusement crept into her eyes. "Aren't you glad to see me, darling?"

"Answer me. Darling."

She swallowed some of her scotch, set the glass on the coffee table.

She scooted closer, the jasmine scent from her neck stronger now. She reached out to touch Wolf's face. He grabbed her wrist, twisting. She gasped, turning her body into the twist.

"Let go of me!"

"Tell me."

Through gritted teeth she said: "Thorne."

He let go. She scooted back to the other side of the couch. Her eyes met his.

The half-laugh Wolf let out covered the sinking feeling in his chest. "He's still alive?"

Ava nodded.

"And after fighting Skinner he wants a meeting."

"Yup."

Wolf downed the scotch. He stood up and wandered over to the window, the street deserted below. No cars parked in front of the hotel. "Did you come here alone or is somebody waiting outside?"

"I came alone."

"What did Thorne tell you?"

"About?"

"Don't act stupid, baby."

"Thorne wants to talk to you about a few things."

The odds against him were rising faster than he figured, but now he had a chance to have a few more questions answered and the more he learned the better opportunity he'd have to stop the tide from overtaking him.

"Let's go see Joe," Wolf said.

Wolf and Ava piled into a Chevrolet Impala with soft cloth seats. Wolf frowned. Nothing exotic. An everyday car. She pulled into traffic the motor quiet but responsive.

"Where to?" Wolf said.

"The Hyatt."

Wolf chuckled. "Joe's cutting back on his usual extravagance. I would have expected–"

"Money's tight right now."

Wolf turned to her. "Is that what this is about?"

Her gaze remained forward. "You don't know?"

"What I know wouldn't fill a shot glass."

Wolf watched the passing scenery. "Why are you running with Thorne?"

She let out a sigh.

"It's an honest question."

She traced a pattern on the back of his right hand. "Later, hon."

The tall structure of the Hyatt grew in the distance.

———

WOLF RECOGNIZED both men in the chilly hotel room. One he'd battled a few hours before. The other he hadn't seen in a long time. They were in a two-room suite, large living area with couches and soft chairs.

Joe Thorne had also put on weight since the old days. He'd gone from short and skinny to short and stocky, with less hair. His eyes were still big and blue. He'd been part of the same strike team as Wolf and Ava and Skinner. A good operative. Crack shot.

"Hello, Wolf," Thorne said, rising from his chair. He approached with hands in pockets. "You're looking good."

He turned and nodded toward the broad-shouldered man in the other chair, who had bandages on his face. "You remember Skinner, of course."

McNab stared at Wolf without blinking. One bandage had been wrapped around his head, another fastened to his left cheek. Thorne said, "Poor Skinner. You gave him a good whipping."

McNab tapped his fingers on the arm of his chair, and Thorne raised a hand, made a "down" gesture. "Take it easy, Skinner. This is a friendly chat. A reunion."

"You never were a good actor, Joe," Wolf said.

Thorne turned up the corners of his mouth. "Drink?" Wolf said yes. Thorne poured a glass of Dewar's from a corner mini bar. Wolf took the glass cautiously. The four of them sat down, Thorne and McNab across from Wolf and Ava. Ava sat with a hip parked on the arm of Wolf's chair. She ran fingers through his hair. Her nails scratched his scalp and the warmth from her thigh, pressed against his arm, made the room less chilly. Wolf sipped his scotch and scowled. Thorne and McNab watched Wolf. The silence grew, only broken by the now-and-then tinkle of ice cubes.

"Which one of us talks first?" Wolf said. He took a drink to cover his quickening breath.

"You just did," Thorne said. "So, you."

Wolf set down his glass and waited.

"We had a good time in the old days, didn't we?" Thorne said.

"Good enough."

"Judging by some of the activities you participate in, obviously you haven't gone into honest work. Don't feel bad. Neither have we. But it's hard to keep a good operation secret when somebody wrecks your plans. I'm guessing it was you who blasted our guns to kingdom come and brought the Feds snooping. You've probably heard of the shooters I've brought into town. I hated to ice that guy at the hospital—what was his name?—but the play's the thing, right?"

Wolf waited, enjoying the scratch of Ava's nails. The softness of her thigh reminded him of better times.

"You saw our pictures," Thorne said, "which means you saw too much. Now, one of two things is going to happen. You're either going to help us with our next operation, or your friends, the two women and your homicide buddy, are going to die."

Wolf passed his half-empty glass to Ava. She slipped off the chair, refilled the glass, brought it back and resumed her position. Wolf kept his face straight, eyes on Thorne. He said, "And your plans are?"

Thorne just smiled. "We were expecting one-point-five million dollars for the gun sales. You messed that up. Which means we need another score that will give us that amount. Does the name Zachary Coleman mean anything to you?"

"Never heard of him."

A lie. Wolf knew Coleman well, had seen his picture on the wall at the Shipwreck Bar. Coleman, one of the city's wealthiest businessmen, had once hired Wolf to stop the blackmail of his youngest daughter by an ex-boyfriend who had dirty pictures featuring the Coleman girl.

Thorne shook his head. "You lie like a rug. That's okay. I wouldn't expect you to tell the truth."

Wolf let out a breath.

"Coleman has a son," Thorne said, "who has just been elected to the city council. His father has a lot of money. A *lot* of money. He's going to give us some for returning his boy in one piece."

"You're insane," Wolf said.

"Something wrong?"

"Coleman's tougher than you think."

"Now that you're with us, he's out of luck, don't you agree?"

Wolf sipped his scotch.

"You're with us now," Thorne said, "or I'll murder everyone close to you." He reached into a pocket and took out a pair of photos. "How would the Callaway girl look in a coffin with part of her body blown away?" He placed a picture on the table. *Kiki leaving work.* "Your latest pigeon?" Another picture. *Sheila taking orders at the restaurant.* "After everything else she's been through, you want her to end up like her husband?"

"Why don't I just kill the three of you and be done with it?" Wolf said.

The tips of Ava's nails stopped moving and bit into his skin.

Joe and McNab stared.

Thorne said, "Blaze away. But what's my fail-safe?"

Wolf let his shoulders sink a little. Thorne had called his bluff. No other choice. He had to cooperate.

"Why Coleman?" Wolf said. "Why this city?"

Thorne smiled. "Our mutual friend Charles Naughton. Wasn't always a friendly club owner, you know. He had some contacts that helped us get the guns moving. He also told us about Coleman."

"What do you want me to do?" Wolf said.

Thorne clapped his hands together. "That's what I like to hear, old boy. Right now, nothing. Go about your business. But maybe you'll bump into Coleman, maybe you'll have a conversation. Maybe you've heard a rumor he may be a target and should consider taking you as a bodyguard. He trusts you, doesn't he? After that we'll be in touch."

Wolf swallowed the rest of his scotch.

Thorne said, "I'm sure you and Ava have a lot of catching up to do. Don't let me keep you any longer."

Ava and Wolf rose and moved toward the door. Before they stepped into the hallway Wolf turned and winked at the bandaged Skinner McNab. The door clicked shut and McNab turned dagger eyes on Thorne.

"You're making a mistake."

Thorne's eyes remained on the door. "No. We have him right where we want him."

"It's the other way around, Joe."

Thorne looked at McNab. "How?"

"Ava. The worst thing you could do is let her near him."

Thorne shook his head. "She's with us."

"You forgot how close they were."

"She left him. Wolf won't open up again."

"You're not listening to me."

"So, we just kill them both? Or let them have a leash, see what happens? At least we'll know where they're at."

"You're the boss."

"That's right," Thorne said.

18

A LITTLE PAST four a.m. and Wolf, too wired to sleep, suggested tea. They went to the twenty-four-hour restaurant at the Bonaventure Hotel, called the Blue Note, and found a back corner booth. She sat a few inches away from him.

Quiet music from the piano player up front covered the silence between them. The low light and combative shadows didn't highlight Ava's eyes, it cast a shade over them, like two hollow pits in her head.

She looked down at the left sleeve of her blouse and ran the fingers of her right hand over it, once, twice.

Wolf watched her. She kept her eyes away.

"You hate me," she said.

"I don't know," Wolf said. "I'm not happy with you, for sure."

She scratched the tip of her nose.

Wolf said, "How did he find you?"

She talked without making eye-contact. "It was an accident. I was living in London, working for a modeling agency."

"You were *what*?"

She smiled, finally looked up, brushed back her hair. "Yeah. Finally decided to cash in on what everybody said I should do for so long."

Wolf laughed.

She said, "I didn't do much. Not skinny enough or heavy enough. Us girls in the middle are hard to sell. I was looking for a way out when Thorne found me. He saw one of my pictures in a magazine and looked me up."

"Was McNab with him then?"

She nodded. "We went out for drinks. That's when Joe told me he wanted my help in a robbery, some payroll truck. The truck would be going to a certain bank and I was to go and seduce the banker in charge of receiving the shipment to make him cooperate. I couldn't believe how I felt after. It was exhilarating. I didn't realize how bored I'd been since the old days. He asked if I wanted to join him and Skinner for more and I said yes."

She bowed her head and started absently tugging at the bracelet on her left wrist. "We were finally working for ourselves. Nobody to tell us what to do. No chain of command or bureaucratic garbage. I loved it."

Wolf turned his water glass in circles, watching the ice. He wasn't shocked. None of them had responded well to authority. The waitress brought tea for Wolf, coffee for Ava. Ava opened two containers of cream, poured, stirred. She said, "So you never looked for a real job?"

"It's a bit more complicated than that," Wolf said, but didn't elaborate.

She sipped the coffee. "Do you really think you're doing any good?"

"For somebody."

"What does that mean?"

"A lot of innocent people have been killed because of your gun deals, but maybe I stopped that from happening to others."

She lowered her eyes.

"What happened to you, Ava?"

She kept her head down.

"You can't be happy with what you're doing."

The woman remained silent.

Wolf said, "Quit pretending."

"What?"

He scooted close and kept his voice low. "You're doing the same thing I used to. Being something you're not because you're afraid of what you really are. You're afraid of being vulnerable because it means somebody can hurt you."

Her eyes widened and her mouth opened but no words came out. Lines on her face seemed to crack the make-up shell.

"You can't hide behind a cover story, kitten," he said. "I tried. For a long time."

Ava's eyes didn't leave his.

"You're a good woman," he said. "Maybe I can find that woman again and we can pick up where we left off."

They didn't say anything more for a long while.

———

AVA DROVE BACK to Wolf's hotel and followed him to his suite. He said, "See you later."

She laughed. "You're kidding." She snaked her warm fleshy arms around his neck, pressed against him, made him weak inside. His arms circled her waist, the warmth of her body running through him. Their lips touched. Before either leaned into the kiss he pushed her away. Her eyes opened, brow furrowing.

"I don't–"

"No, Ava."

"But–"

"No."

She stared at him. He blinked once, twice. She smoothed the front of her shirt, readjusted the shoulder strap of her purse, cracked a weak smile, and walked away. He watched her hips swish.

In the bathroom he splashed his face with cold water. He felt hot. His reflection showed a man in a daze as he tried not to think about Ava or Joe, about himself.

Out on the deck he watched the sun come up.

———

WOLF REHEARSED the words like an actor memorizing lines. He needed to get them right.

Wolf hiked up the front walkway to the Callaway home. The large two-story home had a curving front drive with a statue in the center. It had been a long day and it was well after nine, the sky dark, crickets chirping. This visit to Callaway's home was the first time Wolf had left his hotel all day.

Tapping on the red oak door, he waited. The lock clicked, the door opened, and a wet nose at the front of a small dog stuck through the opening accompanied by hyperactive breathing. Behind the door John Callaway said, "Get back, Jeeves," and the dog huffed. Callaway opened the door with his head turned away and his right leg extended to keep his hyper beagle from racing out. He ushered Wolf inside. The dog, Jeeves, yipped at him, but Wolf glared, and the dog scurried to the protective cover of a chair.

"Don't torture the boy," Callaway said, a low laugh escaping his big chest. He wore a dark blue bathrobe over dark blue pajamas. He pushed the door closed and the lock struck with a solid click. Jeeves stuck out his snout and yipped again.

"He knows better than to get too excited," the inspector said. Wolf smiled and followed Callaway into the den. Jeeves fell in step behind, but at a discreet distance.

Callaway held the door open. He said, "Come on," and the dog trotted in. Callaway shut the door and the dog assumed his position on a doggie bed in a corner.

Wolf said, "Kiki get her hands on him yet for wrecking her roses?"

Another low laugh from Callaway. They moved to a small couch. The den wasn't very large but resembled his office. Desk (cluttered), small bookcase (not full), Jeeves's bed (full of hair), and the couch. Usual sea ship pictures on the wall.

Callaway said, "You caught me at a bad time. I have our press conference tomorrow. About Brock and all."

"My apologies."

"Forget it." He looked at Wolf, but Wolf couldn't hold the gaze and turned away. "What's on your mind?"

Wolf explained about Thorne, the gun running, the

new plot against the Coleman family, the East Coast gunmen hired to help, and the threat to Kiki and Sheila.

"Is my daughter in immediate danger?" Callaway said.

"Not if I play along."

"Can't you be sure?"

"I'm not sure of anything right now," Wolf said.

"I understand." A pause, then: "So what do we do about this?"

"Do you trust me?"

Callaway's face softened a bit. "Do you even have to ask?"

Wolf pressed his lips together.

"I just need notice. Time to hide the bodies." Callaway smiled.

"No bodies this time," Wolf said.

"What are you thinking?" Callaway said.

"Kiki told me you've been watching the east coast gunmen since they started arriving."

"Not total surveillance, but we know where some of them are."

"Get some men on it. Find all of them."

"For?"

"Round them up when I tell you to. A clean sweep with Thorne and McNab and Naughton included. Between you and the Feds there's plenty of manpower—and *fire*power. If you don't find enough evidence, I'll get everything you need."

"How?"

"I'm working on a witness. It's a long shot, but I think she'll turn."

"She?"

"Long story. I'm seeing her tomorrow night and I'll make my pitch. I think she'll cooperate."

Callaway nodded.

"How's Sheila's situation?"

"I'm getting back to that as soon as I leave," Wolf said.

"Make it up as you go," he said. "Just like the rest of us."

Jeeves had fallen asleep in the corner and didn't hear the men go out. Callaway showed Wolf to the door. They shook hands and Callaway closed the door.

Wolf drove over to Kiki's apartment building, parked across the street, and looked up at her dark window. He wasn't going to go up and knock because he had no words for her. He thought of those who died at the hands of others despite his best effort. He swallowed the lump in his throat and closed his eyes and prayed like never before that he wouldn't have to try to save Kiki.

He wasn't sure if he could even save himself.

19

WOLF RETURNED to the cul-de-sac across the street from the Amis home, waiting for the white-haired man who could lead him to Gambolini and Regan. The empty driveway and dark house offered no encouragement.

Presently the garage door opened. The black Lincoln Town Car reversed onto the street, drove past the cul-de-sac. Wolf trailed the Town Car halfway across the city and turned into a block of office buildings and new construction sites. No other traffic. The buildings were dark, parking lots lit with tall lamps. The Lincoln pulled into one of the sites with the skeleton of a building and construction equipment dominating the lot and stopped outside a portable trailer. Inside the trailer, lights burned. Wolf parked a half block down.

He pounded across the blacktopped street, approached the construction site, and dashed over the loose dirt. A dust cloud trailed behind him. Wolf found a bulldozer to hide behind while he examined a posted sign,

A Project of Magnum Engineering.
Jack Amis, Owner/Operator.

Two other cars sat next to the now-empty Lincoln, a convertible Corvette and Ford Five Hundred. Blinds covered the trailer windows. He stayed low and moved across the dirt to the trailer, eased between the metal support frame and lay down on the dirt. The rocks and mounds of dirt made his back arch. He stifled a grunt. The voices above were faint, but some of the words came through.

———

Teddy Gambolini didn't hide his frown as he braced his hands on the arms of his chair and lowered his body into the seat.

Ben Regan and a third compatriot, Jake Sanborn, sat in front of the desk. Sanborn, the youngest of the three, flaunted his age with long hair and a surfer look. The white-haired Gambolini studied the men a moment and said,

"Ain't we up the creek?"

Ben Regan said, "There was never a promise that Palakis would turn over Califano's hideout. We're no worse off than when we started. This was just a little side adventure that didn't pay off."

Gambolini turned to Sanborn. "What's he forgetting, Jake?"

"The contract is still open."

"Right," Gambolini said. "This whole 'side adventure' was to get the home boys off our neck. That detective, Brock, found us. Who knows if he told? Miles Kincaid thinks we still have the DVD. He *will* be looking for us."

"You weren't so concerned with whom Brock may have spoken to when you asked me to kill him."

"With Palakis still alive it didn't matter and"–he leveled the stubby finger at Regan–"I'm not in the mood for your lip tonight."

"So, what are you asking?" Regan said. "Do we just cut and run?"

"Be serious. There's too much invested here."

"Didn't you imply that we're sitting ducks?"

"We aren't running. We're *fortifying*. Keep working your contacts back home. If anybody gets a hint that Scarlatta knows where we are, we'll reconsider our plans."

"Fine," Regan said.

Gambolini pointed at Sanborn. "And you. I better not hear about any interruptions in sales."

"We'll be fine, but the next shipment needs to get here soon. I have more customers than product."

"This Wednesday, ten-fifteen at the Mill. It'll be there."

Gambolini stopped talking. He took out Chapstick and dabbed his lips. "I liked this business a whole lot better when I was younger. Oh, and Ben? Go find Miles Kincaid before he finds us, okay?"

———

WOLF REMAINED in his awkward position beneath the trailer. Shuffling footsteps indicated the end of the meeting. The white-haired man left first, his heavy body jolting the structure as he rumbled down the steps. He climbed into the Town Car and drove away. When the other two emerged, they lit cigarettes, stood by their cars. Streetlamps highlighted their features. The long-haired man meant nothing to Wolf; the other, with his dark hair and graying mustache and the visible nine-millimeter on his hip, matched the description Harvey the Hook had provided about the man who'd come looking for Freddie Webster.

A fire smoldered in Wolf's belly, but he held back. He wanted the whole operation destroyed, not just the men behind it. Too many would be ready to take their place. He'd heard enough of the conversation to know that if anything happened to Regan, the white-haired man, Amis, might indeed cut and run. And take Gambolini with him.

Wolf stayed in the shadows while the other two smoked and talked and when they stomped out their smokes and drove away, Wolf remained in place for five extra minutes.

He rolled out, stood, stretched, and wandered over to the sign at the entrance. The white-haired man was Amis. He'd seen Ben Regan. He didn't know the long-haired kid but had heard the name "Jake"; didn't know Teddy Gambolini.

He froze. Why wasn't Gambolini at the meeting?

Unless–

Gambolini and Amis were one and the same.

Wolf returned to the Chrysler and sped away. There was still plenty of work to do before he brought the house down.

MILES KINCAID, the killer sent from New York to clean up the Palakis situation, stayed cooped up in his hotel room during the days following his shooting of Vince Palakis. He'd had no problem with that bit of target practice. Palakis had caused nothing but trouble and Miles couldn't excuse the death of the Brock boy.

He'd explained the situation to Ugo Califano over the phone, making no excuses. Califano said nothing for a bit, then: "If there was no other way, there was no other way."

"Um-hmm."

"About the disk."

"Still out there. And I have no idea who I'm looking for."

"Leads?"

"Only the son, and he's long gone."

"The hooker?"

"Dead."

"Search her flop?"

"No."

"The cop?"

"No."

"Too many cops?"

"Yes."

"What are your plans?"

"Something will turn up."

"That's what I like about you, Miles. You're so confident."

And the call ended. Miles stayed put. He wasn't dodging his duties but wanted a few days to pass before he hit the street. Let the heat fade.

He watched the D.A.'s press conference with interest. The District Attorney introduced Inspector John
Callaway, who told the story straight-faced. Palakis shot
himself, he claimed. Miles only recognized the name of
Palakis's son and the cop, Brock, when the D.A.
explained their role. No mention of the man in black
who helped Brock. When he noticed Callaway's cute
daughter, he thought he could find both Scott Palakis
and Brock's helper through Callaway by taking a shot at
his little girl.

The thought sent a chill up his back. He turned off
the television, looked over at the nightstand where his
dead daughter's picture stood. No, he couldn't hurt Kiki
Callaway. There were lines he would not cross, and that
was a big one. But he could use her to make her father
talk.

————

AUTOMATIC DOORS RUMBLED open as Wolf entered the
City Planning Department.

He crossed the gray carpet to a circular desk in the
center of the lobby. The place looked like a library with
scattered seats and tables but wasn't as quiet. Plenty of
voices, computer noises, shuffling papers. Wolf told the
receptionist that he was a journalist doing a story on
Magnum Engineering and wanted to see their license
information. The young woman didn't ask to see a press
card or I.D., but instead quoted Wolf a fee, which he
paid.

A clerk led Wolf to a small private room with a table
and chair and small port window in the door. The
bright fluorescent light bounced off the plain white

walls. Wolf was tempted to put on his sunglasses. The clerk handed Wolf a file folder, told him to return it to the receptionist when he finished, and left Wolf alone. He welcomed the silence.

That morning he had called Kiki, making no mention of his visit with her father. He asked her to gather some background on Gambolini and Regan and meet him later in the afternoon. He wanted some basic info on Gambolini's company first.

The file contained an up-to-date business license for Magnum; the paperwork had all the official stamps and signatures. A copy of a receipt said "Jack Amis" had paid all of his fees, and it was signed off by the head of the department. The file also included Amis's original letter approaching the department for a business license, and an endorsement from the Chamber of Commerce saying Amis was a member in good standing with the New York City Chamber and would be a great asset to Las Palmas.

The paperwork went back four years.

Another set of papers showed details of his purchase of Excalibur Records, a local shop, from the previous owner. Wolf rubbed his forehead. Why would he want the record shop? Maybe he was a music buff, but Wolf didn't think so. He put the pages back in order and returned the file.

———

Kiki sat outside a Starbucks with an iced coffee, long bare legs crossed, her heels off and lying askew beneath the table. The breeze chilled her legs. The cold metal chair made her rear end sore, and she kept shifting. She liked sitting outside because inside felt too claustrophobic, but she wished they'd put cushions on the chairs.

She smiled when the gray Chrysler 300 rumbled into the lot. Wolf joined her at the table. One of his chair legs was short, and he leaned toward her for balance. She touched his arm and said hello.

"How's Sheila?" he said.

"Hello to you, too," Kiki said.

He grinned. "Sorry. Hi, Kiki."

"Hi. Sheila's okay. At the doctor's right now and I have to pick her up in a half hour."

"Whaddya got?"

Kiki sipped her coffee. The ice cubes scraped together. She pulled a file from her purse and flipped it open. "Your friends have quite a background." She consulted the pages. The papers flapped in the breeze. She spread a hand out to keep them flat. "Let's start with Gambolini. Big in New York. Worked with Vito Scarlatta for ages. They were like brothers; grew up together, ran the whole show. Gambolini was the drug guy, that's how he kept the money coming in. Ran his operations through front companies."

"Like a construction business?"

Her eyes brightened. "Exactly. That's Gambolini's trade. One of his companies was busted once for that very reason, but because certain witnesses either turned up dead or refused to talk, the case didn't go very far."

"Why is Gambolini out here now?"

"He and Scarlatta had a falling out about five years ago. Teddy didn't like some attention Vito was getting from the Feds and tried to kill him. Scarlatta found out and tried to turn the assassination the other way, but

Gambolini and Regan dodged the killers and headed west."

"The contract is still open, isn't it?" Wolf said.

"Half-million dollars. Scarlatta put up the money."

Wolf rolled the new information around in his head. It explained some of what he'd heard while hiding under the trailer. Brock had stated that Ugo Califano, Palakis's friend, had been Gambolini's arch rival and that the video theft had been a ruse to get Palakis to reveal Califano's hideout, so they could use it as a peace offering and cancel the contract. It made sense. Nobody could run from a $500,000 murder contract forever.

"So, they're into drugs. You check that angle?"

Kiki drank some iced coffee.

"That's the other thing that caught my attention," she said, "and I did some digging."

She pulled another folder from her purse and extracted several copies of newspaper stories and handed them to Wolf. The newsprint fluttered. Wolf held them tight, scanning the headlines, frowning as he read.

"I don't get it," he said.

"Those are stories about drug busts in and around Las Palmas over the last four years."

"So?"

"Despite the busts, drug activity hasn't gone down, and we're seeing a resurgence in meth. One article I couldn't find concerned a raid on a meth lab back in September. That lab had the potential to churn out three-and-a-half million dollars-worth of that garbage. The narc team and the DEA say that Las Palmas is becoming the meth capitol of this state."

"Meth is easy to cook, and the druggies make more

money on it than other drugs. They don't need to import it."

"Right," Kiki said. "Most of those raids *were* meth labs. Ninety-four raids last year. And there's another fly in the ointment, too. Ever hear of a drug called XTC? Or MMDA?"

"Ecstasy," Wolf said.

"That's turning up more within the younger set. Lots of overdoses so far. These kids pop the pills at a party and wind up dead."

"How do you explain the overdoses if it might not be deadly?"

"Goes back to the meth," Kiki said. "Drug dealers cook meth and sell it as X. All the kids hear is that X can't hurt so they think there's nothing wrong with popping a few pills and some of them get hooked and some of them die."

Kiki sipped her coffee.

"We had a case last month that involved a sixteen-year-old girl," she said. "Poor kid went to one of those all-night rave parties. People think they're clean because they advertise as alcohol free, but they're not. The girl thought she was popping X, but the coroner found meth in her system. She was *sixteen*."

"Arrests?"

"None."

Wolf leaned forward. "Okay, my turn. I think Gambolini is working under the name Jack Amis and uses a construction company for a cover. He set up shop out here *four years* ago."

"Same time as–"

"Those busts? He ratted out the competition so he'd be the only game in town."

Kiki sat back and folded her arms. She smiled and her nose crinkled. "Some detective," she said. "What now?"

"I think I may know how Gambolini gets his drugs on the street."

20

WOLF DROVE TO EXCALIBUR RECORDS, the other company owned by "Jack Amis", and went inside. Young adults in street clothes occupied the cash registers left and right of the entrance. The skinny male had close-cropped hair, goatee, and smudged glasses. The girl wore black, long black hair with red highlights, steel spike horizontally through the bottom of her nose. She glanced at Wolf, smiled and said hello and he said hello back as he walked into the main floor. Loud music played over ceiling speakers, a hard-rock riff he didn't recognize.

A pair of teens browsed an aisle; at the magazine rack, a guy hid behind a C.D. layout with an issue of BIG BUNS in hand. Posters promoted various artists or movies. Wolf wandered around, lingering in the movie section. Some classic titles reminded him of afternoons at the Paradise Theater.

He stayed about an hour but saw nothing of interest, so he returned to the car. Presently a low-rider truck pulled into the handicapped slot. Bass boomed from the truck's speakers. The driver jumped out, leaving the engine running and a buddy in the passenger seat. The driver, a skinny white kid with blue hair, dashed inside.

Wolf saw the transaction through the front window. Blue Hair collected a wrapped brown paper bag from one of the clerks, exited, jumped back into the truck, and drove off. Wolf followed one or two car lengths behind. Blue Hair and his buddy gave no indication that they knew he was tailing them. Left on Stoneridge, past a housing project that didn't have a Magnum Engineering sign, and the truck turned into a quiet cul-de-sac. Wolf waited at the corner. The truck parked in front of a two-story home. Blue Hair and Friend entered the house. Wolf shut off his car and let five minutes tick by.

He wanted to talk with Blue Hair, a.k.a. Noodles Flanagan, a street pusher who had, so far, evaded arrest. Wolf pulled the Chrysler up in front of the house. When he reached the porch, he pressed the doorbell.

The friend, with a pierced nose and slicked-back white hair, answered, started to open his mouth.

Wolf punched him. The kid's lips split. The kid hit the carpet and Wolf kicked him in the head.

"Mike?"

A clatter from the kitchen; a moment later Noodles raced into the front room carrying a bottle of beer. He saw Wolf, stopping short, dropping the bottle to reach behind his back. Wolf kicked him in the stomach. As the pusher doubled over, Wolf struck the side of his head. Noodles landed on the floor, in the puddle of beer, with a squish. Wolf left him there and moved deeper into the house.

A wrapped package sat on the kitchen table and Wolf ripped the package open. Little bags of white pills inside. He checked the living room and bedrooms but found nobody else.

The phone started ringing. Wolf went back to Noodles and rolled him onto his back. Beer stained the front of his shirt. The phone kept ringing. Noodles' eyes were sealed shut. The phone rang twice more and then stopped. Wolf kicked Noodles' fallen gun across the room. The pusher had the usual wallet and car keys. In the wallet Wolf found a wad of twenties, and he put the twenties in his own pocket.

Wolf searched the friend. Baggie of white pills. Wallet, no cash, no gun. His I.D. said Michael Boyles. Wolf didn't know him.

Back to Noodles. Wolf hoisted the blue-haired pusher over his shoulders, grunting a little. Some of the beer from Noodles' shirt soaked Wolf's back. Wolf carried him to the Chrysler, placing him in the passenger seat. Wolf opened the trunk and took out his roadside emergency kit, from which he grabbed a roll of duct tape. Wolf wrapped the tape around Noodles' ankles, hands, slapped a strip across his mouth.

He drove straight toward the mountains outside the city and hoped an air freshener would kill the beer smell filling the car. Farms and open space, rolling grassy hills, stretched out ahead of the big car.

He kept driving until he found a clearing, turned, and the Chrysler crunched over dirt and rocks. He parked beside a hill where trees sheltered the car. He opened the passenger door and slapped Noodles' stubble-lined jaw until the pusher awoke. Noodles flapped around and tried to kick but the duct tape held, and Wolf just smiled and said:

"It's just you and me, Noodles."

The pusher swallowed, beads of sweat popping out of his forehead. "Cars comin' by."

"I don't hear any cars, do you?" Wolf cupped a hand over his head. "Nuh-uh. Just the wind."

"I got friends."

Wolf shook his head.

Noodles tried to shift his arms. He flapped some more, stopped with a huff. "We can make a deal."

"Talk. Live."

"If I talk, I'll be killed."

"And if you don't talk," Wolf said, "you'll be killed."

Noodles swallowed again. Sweat trickled down the side of his face.

"So?" Wolf said.

"Ask me somethin'."

"Tell me about the drugs at Excalibur."

"I pick up the junk there."

"Meth made to look like X?"

"Yeah."

"Make a lot of money?"

"You saw my truck," Noodles said.

"Who's running the show?"

"No clue."

"Jack Amis?"

"Means nothin'."

"How 'bout Gambolini?" Wolf said.

"Don't know, man, I don't know."

"Who do you deal with?"

"Jake."

"Jake who?"

"Sanborn, Jake Sanborn."

"Long-haired surfer type?"

"That's him."

"Where's his flop?"

"Townhouse on Sprice. Off Crow Canyon, White Eagle Village. Out by all the new development. Jake's place is two-seventeen. Can I go now?"

Wolf grabbed a handful of the pusher's shirt, roughly dragged him out of the car and onto the dirt. "Hey!" Wolf wiped his wet hands and then clutched at the taped ankles and pulled Noodles across the ground, kicking up a cloud of dust. Noodles hollered and thrashed, and the dust cloud grew thicker.

"Hey, hey–"

Wolf rolled Noodles into the thick of the trees, leaving him on his back. Noodles' chest pumped up and down, his breath coming in quick, choked gasps, wide eyes pleading. Wolf took out his gun.

"Whoa, don't–"

The snap of the .45 echoed through the hills.

––––––––

THE WHITE EAGLE Village was a gated complex. The gate wasn't closed when Wolf drove up the cobblestone drive. He found a guest parking slot. The white stucco town homes were joined one to another, some buildings with two stories and a few single. Wolf's shoes crunched fallen leaves and snapped pieces of bark as he walked through the concrete path between the buildings; a tan cat bolted from some bushes and took cover in another alcove. Wolf found 217 and rang the bell. No answer. He rang again. A section of glass next to the door with a drawn blind prevented him from seeing inside. He walked around the building and found an empty parking slot marked 217 and returned to the Chrysler.

Within a half hour a rumbling Corvette, the same convertible he'd seen at the Magnum site, rolled across the cobblestones. Wolf scanned the driver's face. Long surfer 'do, mirrored sunglasses.

Jake Sanborn powered up the cloth top, sprung out, twirled his keys. His soft tennis shoes made no sound on the pavement as he started along the path. Wolf waited a few seconds and followed. As Sanborn slipped his key into the lock, Wolf moved behind and shifted to the neighbor's door. Sanborn's door creaked open. The long-haired man stepped inside. Wolf slid the Colt .45 from shoulder leather and smashed the gun against Sanborn's head.

Sanborn screamed and staggered a few steps. His legs clunked against a chair and he tumbled to the thick carpet. Wolf bashed him again and Sanborn fell flat. Wolf pushed the door shut. He was in the living room. Across from him, the kitchen, dark and quiet. Empty bedroom around the right corner. On the left another bedroom and bath. Wolf searched the bedroom first. On the nightstand, an alarm clock, sci-fi novel. Nothing of note on the messy dresser or inside the drawers. Normal things in the bathroom. Car and girlie magazines on the living room coffee table. The kitchen table had an abstract centerpiece that Wolf glossed over. Beside the countertop telephone was a notepad. Top page blank, but there were visible pen tracings. He rummaged through a drawer, found a pencil, and began bushing the side of the pencil lead along the tracing. Soon words took shape.

MEET @ MILL, 10:15 PM WED.

Tomorrow night. But that didn't mean much. Lines creased Wolf's brow. He didn't know anyplace in Las Palmas called "the Mill" except for an old chain of hardware stores which had closed long ago. He folded the paper and stuck it in a pocket.

He checked Sanborn again. Still out but breathing. Wolf was about to slap him awake when he stopped.

The Mill wasn't the name of a place at all. It was a nickname for Gambolini's lumber yard.

He left Sanborn on the carpet.

———

MILES KINCAID SAT in a booth with his back to the wall. The mug of beer remained full to the brim, the fuzzy head fading. The bar's low lighting and soft jazz band provided the kind of environment he wanted to let his mind review the day's activity.

He'd picked up Kiki Callaway's trail from the Hall of Justice. She met a man at a Starbucks where they went through some files she'd brought along. Was he the man who had helped Harry Brock?

He sipped the beer. The rest of Kiki Callaway's day had been spent picking up a pregnant friend from a doctor's office, who she took home. Then back to the office and home again after six. No sign of Scott Palakis. Had his cooperation with the D.A. ended? Had he fled the city?

He drank more beer, watching the couples at the bar. Their chattering voices were lost in the music, just fine for him. The wailing saxophone took him to another place where there were no guns or stolen DVD videos or dead children.

After a while he downed the rest of the beer. Pushing through the heavy oak door, he hit the sidewalk where the evening breeze chilled him. Miles turned left; stopped, gaped–

At Ben Regan. No more than five paces before him.

Regan said, "You gotta be kidding me."

Regan and Miles clawed for iron and exchanged shots as they dodged away from each other. The shots went wide, smacked into cars and concrete walls. Somewhere behind Miles, glass shattered. Pedestrians screamed, ran. Miles ducked in front of a parked car and winged another shot at Regan as the other man reached the cover of a doorway. Miles jumped up and raced across the street, cars screeching, horns blaring; another shot cracked behind him as he reached the opposite sidewalk. More pedestrians scattered. Miles sprinted along the sidewalk to an alley. A shot nicked the entryway, and Miles winced at the spit of brick shards that pelted his face. He kept running.

21

WOLF SAT on the soft seat of the back booth of a quiet tavern with an untouched cup of tea in front of him and his eyes fixed on the entrance. He sat with his back straight, feeling tense.

That morning he had made a call to the office of Zachary Coleman, a former client, and the target of Joe Thorne. The conversation had been short and to the point: your son is in danger and we need to meet. Coleman didn't argue; asked what time, where.

Wolf had chosen the tavern because it was close to Coleman's offices. The early hour, just past eleven a.m., meant they had the place to themselves.

Zachary Coleman's thin frame, followed by his bulkier son Max, pushed through the heavy oak door and found Wolf's table. Wolf rose as they approached, greeting them with handshakes. They sat down. Max needed to inch the table forward so he could fit.

Zachary's silver eyes stayed on Wolf, who sipped his tea. A pony-tailed waitress with black-framed glasses arrived, and the Colemans ordered coffee. Once she departed, Wolf said:

"Thanks for coming."

"The tone of your call made it hard to say no," Coleman said.

"I wasn't kidding around," Wolf said. He outlined his encounter with Joe Thorne and Thorne's plan to snatch Max for ransom.

Coleman's face paled a bit. He closed his eyes, shook his head, opened his eyes and looked at Wolf. "Why my family?"

"One of Joe's cohorts fingered you. There isn't anything more to it than that. They could have chosen anybody. You have money and Joe wants some."

"You speak of him very informally."

"Joe and I go back. To the military. Why he's taken the path he's on I have no clue. Once he was a good man."

"If you agreed to help them," Max said, his shoulders tensing, "is this meeting a trap?"

"Heavens, no. I agreed to help because they're threatening the lives of people close to me."

"Let's go to the cops," the younger Coleman said.

"Way ahead of you. If all goes as planned this will be the only time you hear of this. But I would recommend beefing up your own personal security. I mean the whole family, Zachary."

"For how long?"

"Until you hear from me. Or John Callaway. But if Callaway calls you, it means I didn't make it."

Coleman said okay.

The waitress returned with their coffee. Coleman poured cream into his cup. Max left his black. Coleman sipped and said, "Wealth is a curse. But we play the cards we're dealt."

"We sure do," Wolf said.

———

WOLF SPENT the rest of the day with Sheila and helped with Freddie's burial plans. When she went to lay down for a nap, Wolf worked on an idea for his infiltration of Gambolini's lumber mill that night.

SUNOL LUMBER AND SUPPLY looked like it had been made out of the material it sold, a little one-story affair with an overhang in front. Shadows covered the storefront but the bright lights in back suggested action.

Another space of land, with high grass and tall trees, separated the lumber store from the office building next door. Wolf moved through the field in a low crouch, his boots gouging the damp earth. A line of trees made a wall at the end. Wolf slowed, dropped to his stomach, and flat-crawled through dirt and grass to the trees.

He stopped and took a few deep breaths. Of the parking lot he had a full view and noted three particular cars. Gambolini's big Lincoln, Sanborn's Corvette, and Regan's Ford.

The activity in the rear eluded him, but men's voices were loud and clear. Wolf crawled along the tree line. Light flashed when a side door opened. The light struck Wolf and he froze with face in dirt. His mouth, chin, and tip of his nose sank into cold mud. Blades of grass tickled his nostrils. He held his breath, grateful that the black combat outfit covered the rest of him. The door slammed shut and the light went out. A man cleared his throat. Wolf kept his face buried. A lighter snapped.

Steps faded. Wolf lifted his head, exhaled, and stole a glance. The man, taking a drag on a cigarette, moved toward the front of the building. An automatic pistol rode under his left arm.

———

GAMBOLINI AND REGAN stood in front of the bandaged Jake Sanborn, who sat on a leather couch.

"Did you see who hit you?" Regan said.

"Happened too fast."

"You didn't see anything? Was he big, bald?"

"Dark hair, I think. Wasn't huge. Tall, I think. About my size."

"So, it wasn't Kincaid. Ring any bells, Ben?"

"The man I tangled with at the cemetery sort of fits that description."

"The one Brock was with?"

"Uh-huh."

"Marvelous," Gambolini said. "Jake, you're gonna have some company next few days. You're the worm on our hook. If this guy thinks he can get to us through you, we'll have him under the barrel and no mistake."

Sanborn said, "So you're not going to kill me?"

Gambolini laughed.

———

WOLF WIPED HIS FACE, smearing the mud, and crawled until he couldn't hide from the rear lights any longer. The voices were louder, the loudest belonged to a stocky man shouting orders and stressing that they were falling behind schedule.

Wolf moved from tree cover to a low wall and peeked over. A large semi-truck sat backed up against a loading dock. Wolf counted fifteen men and the foreman unloading two-by-fours and sheets of plywood into a well-lit storehouse.

None of the workers carried guns. No sign of Gambolini or Regan or Sanborn.

He rolled over the top of the wall and grunted as he landed on a hard shelf of concrete. The pavement over the edge of the shelf slanted several feet, allowing the backs of trucks to be level with the building when they pulled in. Nobody in the cab of the truck. Wolf dashed to the passenger side. Another shelf and wall ran parallel. No activity there. Wolf crept along. A speck of dirt from his hair fell into an eye. He brushed it away. At the end of the truck his legs were shielded by one of the huge rear tires.

The foreman said, "Let's get the last of this stuff outta here." The truck trailer shook side-to-side as heavy work boots pounded within. After five minutes, the foreman shouted, "Good work!" He then gathered his people around the storehouse and ran his mouth some more, but Wolf didn't listen. He spotted a neat stack of two-by-fours and rushed to the edge of the dock, vaulted onto it, crouched low and stopped behind the stack. The foreman's voice continued to echo.

The piles of wood were high enough to block Wolf from view, and he didn't see anybody else standing around. A door at the far corner caught his eyes. The door swung open and some familiar figures stepped out.

"Are they done?" Teddy Gambolini said to Regan and Sanborn.

"Looks like," Sanborn said. Wolf noticed the bandage on his forehead. Gambolini told the two to wait and joined the foreman.

Gambolini and the foreman shared a few words and went inside with Regan and Sanborn following. Wolf stayed hidden as the workers hustled off. The rear door of the truck rumbled shut with a loud clang. The truck's engine roared to life and drowned out every other sound.

The overhead lights clicked off one by one. Minutes later, silence.

Wolf lay on his belly and stayed still while crickets took back the night and assured him of solitude. Except for the heavy hitters inside.

Wolf lifted a two-by-four. It felt lighter than any two-by-four he remembered. He gave it a shake, and something rattled inside. He took the piece with him, slipping out through another exit. He didn't consider stealth this time and ran back to his car. He jammed the lumber in the back seat and drove away.

With every bump or rough patch, the two-by-four rattled. He couldn't wait anymore and stopped under a freeway overpass. A streetlight provided the only illumination as he took the wood from the back, went to the curb, and smashed the lumber against the edge.

A sharp crack and the wood snapped in half. White pills spewed out like loose confetti. Wolf picked up a few of the pills. Plain white, no markings. The pills left chalky residue on Wolf's fingers.

22

WOLF TWISTED off the cap of a bottle of Johnny Walker Black. Ava Sutter said, "What magic elixir are you opening now?"

She twirled a finger through her hair and watched him with glassy eyes.

"Do you want a glass or a funnel?" Wolf said.

She laughed, hiccupped, covered her mouth, laughed some more through the palm of her hand and hiccupped again. Wolf poured her a glass. He poured a short drink for himself and sat on the other end of the couch.

He'd been flush from the night's discovery, once again too wired for sleep, and spent time mentally reviewing everything he knew and juggling how best to handle what remained of the Gambolini matter and the Thorne complication.

Then Ava knocked on the door.

He'd expected her arrival, the fully assembled outfit with heavy make-up. What he hadn't expected was her head start in alcohol consumption.

And tonight, he needed to know which side she'd choose.

"We should go out," she said. "I need some fresh air."

Wolf set his glass down, walked to the window, opened it. "Presto," he said. "Fresh air." He returned to the couch.

"I mean real fresh air."

"Something wrong with what's coming through the window?"

"I want to go dancing."

"We can dance here."

"Don't you want to go out, darling?"

He laughed. "Not tonight," he said.

"Why not?"

"Because we can have fun right here."

She cracked a grin. Placing her glass on the table, she began crawling across the couch. The neck of her blouse dropped open and her stockings whispered, and she stretched out on her left side with her head on Wolf's lap. "What kind of fun, darling?"

Wolf played with her thick curls.

"Any kind of fun you want if you can stay standing," he said.

She laughed. He set his drink on the small table to the left, patted her hip. He left his hand on her hip and waited for her to object. She didn't.

"I know why you don't want to go out," she said.

"Why?"

She swung her legs to the floor, sat up, then scooted against him. Her eyes didn't seem glassy anymore. "You've been busy tonight. Had some action. What vicious scum did you send cowering to a dark corner? Tell me."

Wolf grinned.

"Let's go dancing," he said.

She smacked her lips against his cheek, jumped up and twirled, laughing. Wolf grabbed his jacket and the IWB holster with the Colt inside because a hunch told him he'd need it.

———

AVA MANAGED TO STAY UPRIGHT, and they spent an hour cutting the rug at a club called High Five. The club was part of the Cain Hotel, offered a bar, small sitting area, and dance floor. A three-man band played on a small circular stage, and while the music required quick moves, the stuffy atmosphere combined with the pressed-together crowd left Wolf feeling claustrophobic and self-conscious being the only one wearing a jacket. During a break they found a table and she dropped into a chair. Wolf scooted next to her.

A bow-tied waiter approached. They asked for ice water. Ava fanned herself with her hands. Beads of sparkling sweat gathered on her forehead. Wolf drew a thumb across her forehead, and she smiled. He used a napkin to wipe some face-powder residue off his thumb.

"Last time you did that, I was bleeding from a head wound," she said.

"Long time ago."

"Yesterday."

The waiter returned and placed their glasses on the table. Wolf passed him a few bucks and turned back to Ava as she took a sip. Her eyes hadn't left him.

———

THE NIGHT AIR felt good after the heat of the club. They walked arm-in-arm down the sidewalk toward Pier 15. A silent ferry boat, about the size of a small building, lay moored at the dock, rocking back and forth. Water slapped against the pilings at the end of the pier, where they stopped at the damp wooden railing looking out into the pitch blackness ahead. Only the rippling water inside the cove indicated anything beyond.

"It's like this is where the world ends," Ava said. "Nowhere else to go."

"If this city is the end of the world, I want my money back," Wolf said.

Ava leaned against his shoulder. He laced an arm around her waist. The warmth of her body reached through her dress; she felt nice and soft. The wind picked up. Her hair tickled his neck.

"I'm sorry about last time," she said. "The things I said."

Wolf remained silent.

"You know me too well. I hide so much, but I can't hide from you."

"Why did you leave me in Zurich?" Wolf said.

"I don't know."

"Yes, you do."

"Will you let me say I'm sorry?"

"Did I push you away?"

"Were you surprised?"

He let out a breath.

Ava's face softened. "People like us have been hurt all our lives."

"That's no excuse."

She buried her face against his chest. He lifted her head a little, met her eyes. Teary eyes, now.

She said, "Why do you think I left?"

"You left me," Wolf said, "before I could leave you. But I wasn't going to leave you. I thought for once, maybe–"

"Okay. I was wrong. It was a mistake to leave you. I'm sorry I hurt you."

"Ava–"

"I tried to find you," she said. "I knew you were still in Europe at the time and when I met up with Joe, I asked him, but he didn't know where you'd gone."

Wolf breathed in, out.

"We can start again," she said. "We can. Give me a second chance."

Wolf said, "But you're with Thorne."

She cupped his face with both hands. "I'm with you."

Wolf's head shook.

"Seeing you again. That's all it took. I'm with you. Listen to me. We can start over. Between us we're loaded with money. We can go anywhere. Let's just go. Right now. Let's go somewhere where there's an ocean. Where we can be happy. Let's just go. Leave all this junk behind. We can do it."

Wolf moved her hands away, wrapped them in his. Her hands were cold. "What about Thorne?"

She let out a whispered curse, wrapped her arms around him. "The only good thing about getting involved with him again is seeing you."

Wolf squeezed her tight. "We can't go anywhere with him hanging around."

"He found you by accident, darling."

"That can happen again. And I don't want to have to

run ever again. This is my home. I'm not going anywhere."

She pulled away. "So, what about Thorne?"

WOLF SAID INTO HIS PHONE, "Okay, John, thank you. I'm taking Ava to my cabin. This afternoon will be fine." He said good-bye, hung up, and looked at the dash clock. Pushing two a.m.

Ava sat in the passenger seat. She stared out the window.

"They're moving on the gang within an hour," Wolf said, "and they'll pick you up late this afternoon to start your interviews."

"And you're positive about my immunity?"

"Of course."

"This is dangerous," she said. "Thorne and McNab and Naughton won't let themselves be arrested."

Wolf kept his hands on the wheel, ten and two; eyes on the road, silent. The hum of the Chrysler's engine filled the space. The two-lane road led into the hills. Huge trees and thick forest flashed by on either side. Only the bright headlights burrowed through the thick wall of darkness ahead.

"You'll like the cabin."

"That's a funny way to change the subject," she said. "You're staying with me, right?"

"Nope. I need to head back and finish my other business."

"Come on, one day–"

"I can't."

Wolf steered through a turn and the road straightened again, began to climb. Presently he slowed and took a left onto a dirt road that led deeper into the woods. He kept the speedometer around twenty-five and reached a clearing. In the center stood his A-frame cabin. Beyond, the dark water of Lake Wyatt. A wavy reflection of the moon occupied the center of the water.

Wolf parked the Chrysler at the front door and he and Ava jumped out.

He unlocked the door and led her into the dark entryway. A flip of several wall switches lit up a small living room. Leather couches and chairs, wood coffee table, and large front window. Ava kicked off her left shoe and ran a bare foot over the thick carpet.

"Nice and soft," she said. "I can walk on this all day." She removed her other shoe and placed them by the door.

"I bought this place a few years ago," Wolf said. "Home away from home." He pointed at the large big-screen television in the corner. "Even got satellite TV."

"You can't afford a flat screen?" Ava said. "That's a monster."

"There's a reason for that." Wolf removed a break-away panel from the bottom of the wood-framed television, revealing two pistols clamped in the hidden compartment.

"High-capacity Glocks," Wolf said. "Seventeen rounds each."

"Is that enough?"

He led her around the room.

"Over here by the heat vent. Go ahead and remove the vent, it just pops off."

The vent left its mounting with a click. "A revolver."

"Thirty-eight, loaded with hollow-points," he said.

"There's more. Underneath the couch, another break-away vent right there. Everything's loaded. Point and shoot."

In the small kitchen, he opened a cupboard.

She said, "Got enough chili and beans?"

"And Chef Boyardee. There's a store up the road if you want something else," he said.

Ava said, "Wolf," and folded her arms.

"Ava, please."

"Let me help you. We can finish this *together*. Like the old days."

Wolf shook his head. "I need you here. Until this afternoon."

She let out a breath. "Where do I sleep?"

"Bedroom's down the hall."

"Blankets?"

"In the hall closet. You can have your extra covers."

She started to smile but the smile faded. She reached out to Wolf and he held her close.

"Was it hard?"

He rubbed circles on her back. "What do you mean?"

"To change. We've spent so long being other people–"

"I needed somebody to tell me I wasn't fooling anyone. There's nothing wrong with me, so there's no reason to pretend I'm somebody else."

She looked up at him but didn't smile.

"Hey," Wolf said, "when we're done, I'll show you the most dazzling beach you've ever seen."

Ava smiled. "Be right back."

Wolf watched her go and leaned against the counter with folded arms. When Ava returned, the smile was still in place. She'd scrubbed the make-up from her face.

Wolf's cell phone chirped. He glanced at the caller ID, but his face remained blank.

"Is that your little girlfriend?"

"No." Wolf flipped the phone open and said, "Who is this?"

He listened for a moment and the color drained from his face.

23

KIKI OPENED THE DOOR. She heard the voice of a late-night infomercial on the television. Kiki set purse and keys on the kitchen counter, kicked her shoes in a corner, and went around to the living room.

"Hi," Sheila said from Kiki's faded blue couch. She lay stretched out with her feet propped up on the worn armrest.

"Can't sleep?"

"Tossing and turning. How was work?"

"Dreadful," Kiki said. She went to the fridge and grabbed a bottle of water. "We started a big operation tonight, thanks to Wolf. I have to be back at nine so it's a quick turnaround for me." She twisted the cap off the water and joined Sheila on the couch.

"Did you see him today?" Sheila muted the television.

"No," Kiki said.

A knock at the door. Kiki frowned, went to the peep hole—

And screamed as the door smashed against her; she flailed back, hitting the floor.

Miles Kincaid stormed in and pushed the door shut. As Kiki started to rise, he grabbed her left arm and dragged her kicking and screaming into the living room. He shoved her onto the couch. Sheila jumped up and covered her mouth with both hands.

Miles drew his gun. "Sit down." Sheila sat and started shaking.

"Stay quiet," Miles said, "and you won't get a scratch."

"I've heard that one before," Kiki said.

"Not another word, sugar bear," Miles said. He found a recliner across from the couch and sat. Kiki glared. It was her father's checkered recliner and she didn't want the man's stink on the fabric.

Miles said, "I want to talk to whoever handed you Palakis. Scott Palakis, not the older one."

Kiki guessed the man meant Wolf. Who else? And there was nobody she wanted to call more.

"So," she said, "I suppose I need to use the phone."

Miles let out a low laugh and took out a razor phone. "I'll dial, sugar bear," he said, and punched the number Kiki rattled off. He handed her the phone.

Kiki mouthed, "It's okay," to Sheila, but the pregnant woman continued to shake.

Wolf answered and Kiki said his name and started to say more but Miles grabbed the phone.

Miles said, "Listen, Mister Wolf, come over to your girlfriend's pronto so you and me can jaw a little." He flipped the phone closed and returned it to his jacket. He kept his pistol aimed at the two women.

"I hope he gets here fast," he said.

"He will," Kiki said.

———

WOLF ENTERED the apartment with the Colt .45 leading the way. Sheila and Kiki and a big bald man sat on the couch. The big man sat with a hand on Sheila's right arm, a pistol in the other hand. No smile on his face.

"I suggest you lower that pistol."

Sheila fixed terrified eyes on Wolf. Kiki tried to smile. There was no way to win. A head shot could switch off the bald man, but his dying trigger finger twitch would send a bullet into Sheila and the baby. Wolf holstered his gun. He sat in the checkered recliner.

"Just take it easy," Wolf said. "Your fight is with me."

"I don't want to fight anybody," Miles said. "None of you in this room, anyway." He tilted his head as he examined Wolf. "I can tell you ain't no cop. PI? No, not that, either. Maybe some sort of independent. Who cares? You're the man I need."

Miles continued, "I was sent here to find a DVD. You know what I'm talking about. I want the disk and the men who took it."

"I have the disk."

"What?"

"The man who stole the video left it for me to find. If the video is all you want, I'll give it back and we'll call it a day, okay?"

"No dice. The gang who wanted that DVD is looking for me. Never mind making my job tough, it makes staying *alive* tough. You should have no problem picking up the slack, right? Finish the job and the girls walk away. *Then* you can give me the disk."

"Be serious."

"I am serious. And just to keep you motivated, you have until noon today."

"I'm just going to keep doing what I've been doing?"

"I don't know how to make it clearer for you."

"I'd like a moment with the women."

"No."

"What if I don't finish by noon?"

"Then you better hope you're already dead."

Wolf nodded. He had a little less than eight hours. His mind started racing for the next move as he gave Sheila and Kiki a reassuring smile and hoped it worked for them because he didn't feel any better for the effort.

———

WOLF DROVE to Gambolini's house. No Town Car in the driveway. No matter. Wolf left the Chrysler curbside and went to the front window. He fired a shot that shattered the glass and slipped through the opening, a piece of glass falling on the back of his jacket and to the ground. The place was dark except for the flashing alarm box near the door. When the piercing wail began, Wolf ignored it. He moved through the kitchen and T.V. room, down the hall, through the bedroom. No sign of life.

Sanborn's townhouse was the next stop, and the Corvette sat where Wolf wanted it to be.

He rang the bell. Presently the surfer dude opened up, his bandaged face and foggy eyes contemplating Wolf with a drug-induced blankness.

Wolf grabbed a handful of long hair and put the .45 in Sanborn's face, dragging him into the cold night.

"You again," Sanborn said, shuffling, falling. He

almost pulled Wolf with him. As Wolf hauled Sanborn upright, Sanborn said, "I've got a surprise—"

"Shut up."

Wolf shoved the surfer dude toward the Chrysler. The pusher crashed against the fender, throwing hands on the hood to stop the momentum. Wolf grabbed Sanborn's right arm and steered him to the passenger door.

Tires screeched. Blazing headlights blinded Wolf. The car skidded to a halt in front of the Chrysler. Wolf shot Sanborn in the head, letting the pusher's body fall as he spun to face the car. The passenger door flew open and a man jumped out digging for a gun. Wolf fired and the man twitched, fell. The driver had one foot out and a pistol in hand and Wolf shot him in the shoulder. The driver screamed and dropped his gun. Wolf kicked the pistol away and jumped in back, pressing the hot barrel of the .45 into the wounded man's neck.

"Drive."

"Huh?"

"Home base. Go. Now."

The wounded man hauled his door shut and groaned as he put the car in gear.

———

FIFTEEN MINUTES later the driver turned up a short hill outside the city. At the top of the road sat a cabin in a forest clearing. Three other cars were parked near the tree line. The two-story cabin looked cozy, and if it hadn't been for the second story it could have been Wolf's place.

The driver shut off the car. He slumped, breathing hard. "Now what?" he said.

"How many in the house?"

"Four."

"Weapons?"

The man laughed. "What do you think?"

Wolf climbed out. The driver frowned and watched him through the side window. Wolf raised his gun and blew the frown off that face along with the rest of his head. He ran across the lot, kicking up dust, reached the front of the cabin, dropping low next to a thorny hedgerow. The front door opened and a gunman with a shotgun stuck his head out, saying, "What the–" but that's all he said because Wolf fired again. The gunman tumbled down the porch steps and landed face-first in the dirt. Wolf holstered his automatic and grabbed the shotgun. A second man emerged, a cigarette falling from his lips. He started to shout, and Wolf fired a blast into the man's chest.

Other men inside began shouting. Wolf scrambled around the side of the cabin and found the back porch. As he hit the first step the back door started to open. Wolf fired into the door. A man screamed. Wolf pumped the shotgun, ducked through the door, stepping over the body. A kitchen. He hunkered down beside the center island. A swing door was on the other side of the room. He heard shuffling and heavy breathing from behind the door.

The door started to open, stopped halfway, swung back. Wolf waited. His heart raced and sweat trickled down his face. The collar of his shirt felt wet. The swing-door opened fully, a man shoulder-rolling onto the cold floor. Wolf and the gunman rose at the same time and fired at the same time. A bullet stung Wolf's right earlobe. The shotgun blast punched through the gunman's chest; the gunman swayed, crashed to the floor.

Wolf dropped the now-empty shotgun, reloaded his pistol, and went back outside to the front of the house.

24

WOLF EXPECTED COMPANY ANY MINUTE. One of the shooters had to have called for backup. He scanned the driveway, the tree line,

learning the battlefield. Maybe Regan would show. Maybe both Gambolini *and* Regan would show. Now was his chance to finish them off and keep Kiki and Sheila from harm. But he couldn't make a fight with a pistol. He scrounged around for another weapon and he hit the mother lode in a hall closet, several HK MP5 submachine guns and full clips. Wolf slung one of the weapons over his shoulder, stuffing two clips into each pocket. The clips gave him a case of droopy drawers, but they wouldn't be there for long.

In the living room, a leather couch sat against the front window. Wolf knelt and placed the HK on the cushions. Through the partially open drapes he had a full view of the driveway.

Presently a pair of headlamps highlighted the pathway, lights belonging to a Ford Five Hundred that jerked to a stop at the sight of the black sedan Wolf had arrived in. The doors opened. Two men with guns rushed out from the back. Another man stepped from the passenger side and looked straight at the cabin. Even in the low light of the moon Wolf knew the man's face and the car. Ben Regan.

Regan waved the other two forward. They shuffled around the side of the house. Wolf grabbed the MP5 and raced back to the kitchen and squatted behind the island.

Wolf stayed in his squat, legs aching, lower back cramping. The back-porch door swung open and as Regan's gunman stopped to look at the fallen body in the doorway, Wolf jumped up, firing the MP5. The sub gun spat a short burst and jammed, but one of the gunmen fell. As the second moved in, Wolf hauled out his pistol, firing; the second gunman fell, joining his dead comrades.

The kitchen door swung inward. Wolf pivoted and fired once but Ben Regan and his chubby partner struck before Wolf could fire again. Regan bashed him on the side of the head with a pistol. Wolf hit the floor hard. His vision spun. Heavy shoes pounded into his body and Regan and Chubby cursed as they kicked him. Wolf covered his face with both arms but that left his middle exposed. His ribs burned from the beating. Breath left him. Somebody grabbed a fistful of his shirt, hauled him up. Regan's red, enraged face stared into Wolf's a moment, then Regan brought up his pistol a second time and swung and the lights went out.

———

WOLF DRIFTED in and out of consciousness. He heard voices, the levels of which went up, down, and out. His eyes fluttered open at one point, his head hanging down at his chest. Breathing wasn't easy, as if his chest were gripped in a vice.

The next time he awoke he lifted his head a little and found his neck stiff. His head throbbed. He blinked away the fog and scanned the dark room. Feet shuffled behind him.

"Looks like he's awake," Ben Regan said. Regan and his chubby buddy walked in front of Wolf.

Wolf tried to move, only to find his body strapped to the chair. He swallowed but the cotton wouldn't leave his dry mouth. He huffed something and Regan laughed.

Regan said, "You sound like a cat trying to cough up a fur ball."

Wolf huffed again.

Regan said, "You're not dead because my boss wants to see you. When he's done, we have a nice shallow grave waiting for you."

Wolf's head fell against his chest. Regan kept talking. Wolf closed his eyes and ignored him, but the sweat on his neck and forehead–cold, despite the warmth of his body–was impossible to ignore.

Regan smacked the back of his head. Wolf groaned. Regan slapped some more. Wolf finally said, "Enough," and coughed.

Regan laughed. "Cut the ropes," he said.

Chubby sliced Wolf free and he and Regan hauled their prisoner upright. Wolf didn't fight. He stayed limp, but he felt his muscles coming back to life as a vision of Kiki and Sheila replaced the unconscious fog.

Regan and Chubby dragged Wolf across the front room, down the porch, and dropped him in the dirt at the feet of another man. White-haired Teddy Gambolini reached for a handful of Wolf's hair and wrenched up his head.

"I don't know you," he said. "I thought I knew all the players in this town. How did you slip by?"

Wolf said, "You're old and slow, that's why."

"But I still came out on top, kid. Think about that when we shoot you."

Gambolini let go of Wolf's head, and Wolf let out a groan, easing to the right. His left leg snapped out, connecting with a knee or shin. A scream followed. Wolf lunged for the white-haired man's belt and the older man's body folded against the impact. Down he went, hard. Wolf rolled Gambolini on top of him, the surrounding gunmen shouting at their boss to get out of the way. Gambolini pushed up from Wolf, drew a fist back. Wolf clamped his hands on either side of the gangster's head and dug thumbs into his eyes. Warm, wet fluid rushed down Wolf's wrists and Gambolini screamed. Wolf snatched a .38 from Gambolini's belt, letting the other man's weight fall against him. Regan and Chubby scattered. Wolf rolled a little to the left and shot the first sub-gunner in the chest. The remaining sub-gunner ran for the car behind him. Wolf fired twice. The gunner hit the ground face-first.

Wolf rolled the still-screaming Gambolini off him. He jumped up, took a few steps, stumbled, crashed. Pistol shots nicked the ground. Wolf rolled into the sharp brush at the edge of the clearing. His sore ribs flared again. Gasping, gritting teeth against the pain, he rolled to a tree stump, let out a loud cry. He lay gasping and watched Gambolini rock side-to-side with hands covering the mess where his eyes once were. He was still screaming. Wolf aimed the .38 and fired once and Gambolini stopped screaming.

Wolf looked at the cabin. Regan and Chubby were hiding behind the porch railing, shielded by the hedgerow. The snub-nosed .38 Smith & Wesson wasn't made for long-range work so Wolf didn't want to waste bullets trying to get them. He scanned the lot. The cars. The bodies. The cars would make good cover and the dead soldiers had submachine guns.

Wolf pushed to his feet, and all he managed was a fast shuffle into the clearing, kicking up dust along the way. Regan and Chubby opened fire. Once, twice, then two shots together. None struck. Wolf reached the black car he'd originally arrived in. A shot smashed the upper corner of the car's roof. Wolf scooted to the driver's side, keeping low as he went from there to the front bumper. A dead gunner now lay only a few feet away, and Wolf scrambled toward the corpse. Propping up on the dead man's chest, Wolf aimed the Beretta submachine gun at the house and let a salvo go that almost shook the weapon from his hands.

Return fire from Chubby flew wild. Regan leaped off the porch and Chubby followed him around the side of the house.

Wolf grabbed two extra clips from the dead gunman. His arms shook as he tried to keep the sub gun aimed at the house. He shuffled back to the stump. It seemed like the only safe place for now.

25

Chubby said, "What's he doing?"

"Going for the other guns," Regan said, and watched Wolf break cover and cross the dirt. He gripped his Beretta tightly and started shooting, Chubby following suit, but Wolf kept moving and reached the black sedan.

Chubby adjusted his aim but held his fire. "I can't get a shot from here."

Regan fired and his bullet smacked against the sedan. The car covered Wolf now. "He'll have better hardware and all we got are these pistols," he said. "We need those MP5s."

That's when the chattering of a submachine gun sent Regan flat. The slugs chewed up the front porch and sang off into the night.

"Cover me!" Chubby said. Regan popped off a few rounds as Chubby leaped off the porch. Chubby fired while Regan jumped up and followed his partner to the back of the cabin.

WOLF WATCHED the silent cabin from behind the stump.

Soon the front door opened, and Ben Regan rushed out with an MP5. While Regan ran into the clearing, Chubby blasted from the doorway, spraying the trees and bushes around Wolf. Wolf stayed low and listened to the rounds whistle. The flash of Chubby's weapon gave Wolf a nice target. He squeezed the trigger once and down went Chubby.

Regan reached the black car and ducked near the front fender. Wolf fired a full-auto burst. The front passenger side tire exploded, that side of the car sinking. Regan appeared around the back end and Wolf's next burst stitched a pattern of holes in the fender.

Regan scooted back. Dust clung to his sweaty face. The tire didn't provide enough cover and his body was visible in the gap between car and ground. The car started to shake as nine-millimeter slugs hammered the body. Regan dropped prone; scooted past the rear bumper to level his own MP5 at Wolf's position.

Wolf reloaded as rounds split the foliage. Shards of bark peppered his neck. He held back the Beretta's trigger and flame spit from the muzzle, sending hot stingers into the back end of the car. Regan let out a clipped yell.

Wolf reloaded again, let the dust clear, selected semi-auto and popped round after round into Regan's prostrate form until he could no longer physically pull the trigger. He crawled on hands and knees over the dusty ground, shoving rocks out of the way, to Regan's body. He felt through the pockets of the blood-spattered pants, removing a money clip with a few hundred dollars and cell phone. He yanked the gold chain from

Regan's wrist and wiped blood away. LOVE THY NEIGHBOR. Wolf wanted to vomit.

He took the cell phone and sat against the fender. He'd left the submachine gun at the stump, so he took the nine-millimeter pistol from Regan's holster. He looked at the pistol a moment and remembered the shell casings he'd collected at Freddie and Sheila's apartment. Now he knew for sure who'd killed Freddie. He used the phone to call Kiki.

A CAR PULLED up the drive and stopped a few feet from Wolf.

Wolf tucked the Beretta nine-millimeter under his right leg, watched the new arrival.

The car switched off. Miles Kincaid climbed out. The big bald man approached Wolf with empty hands at his sides.

"Call your girlfriend," Miles said.

Wolf dialed Kiki again and she gasped when she heard his voice.

"I couldn't believe it! When you called, he just left. Let us go."

"You two okay?"

"Fine, we're going to Dad's."

"All right," Wolf said, and broke the connection.

Miles said, "I'm not a monster. I only came here to do a job. I didn't want to hurt anybody other than those scattered around this property. Now that the job is done, I'd like to live and let live, okay? Give me a minute and I'll get you taken care of and you can give me the video."

"Sure," Wolf said.

Miles removed a digital camera from another pocket of his jacket and snapped a picture of dead Ben Regan. As he moved around the car toward Gambolini, Wolf put his feet under him, stood, and leaned against the car. He leveled the nine-millimeter at the bald man's back.

Miles snapped a picture of Gambolini, rolled the body over and froze. "Wow," he said. To Wolf: "Nice— hey, wait—"

Wolf pulled the trigger and Miles Kincaid fell atop Gambolini's body. Wolf limped over and put two more rounds into the back of the big man's head.

He returned to the car and collapsed. His whole body ached. It hurt to breathe. Stabbing pain in his side suggested a broken rib. Maybe a few broken ribs. After a moment he once again gained his feet and slid behind the wheel of Kincaid's car. No keys. Wolf went back to Kincaid and retrieved the keys and started the car and drove away.

He drove slowly down the hill and dialed Kiki a third time.

"Wolf?"

"Coming over. Need a doctor."

"I'll get one here," Kiki said, "but Dad just told me that Thorne and McNab got away."

A chill straightened Wolf's back and he stomped the gas.

Kiki kept talking, but Wolf cut her off.

"Listen, if you don't hear from me in an hour, send help to my place at Lake Wyatt."

"Wolf!"

"And promise you'll take care of Sheila."

"Calm down. Let me—"

"Promise me you'll take care of Sheila."

She remained silent; then: "Of course, I will."

Wolf took a deep breath and gripped the wheel tight. "Good-bye, Kiki."

Wolf pressed the brakes and the car skidded to a stop. He rolled out of the car with the engine still running, stayed on hands and knees, momentarily stifling a groan, and then rose to his feet. He limped up the steps to his cabin. The door was open a crack. He shoved the door open and it banged against the wall.

He saw Ava's body right away. Near the television. On her back. She'd been shot several times. No pistol in her hands. She hadn't had a chance to grab one of the hidden guns.

Wolf dropped to hands and knees and crawled to the body. He brushed hair from her forehead, wiped away a speck of blood, lowered his cheek against her cheek. Her skin was still warm. He moaned.

"Nice try, sport," a voice said.

Wolf raised his head. Joe Thorne emerged from the kitchen. McNab appeared behind him. They both held pistols and Wolf saw that neither gun had come from his stash.

Joe Thorne said, "The cops missed some of my boys and they were able to provide some distractions while Skinner and I split." He smiled. "What were you thinking?"

Wolf inched away from Ava's body. "You didn't have to kill her." He stopped against the wall. An inch from his right hand was a heater vent.

"You look pretty rough," Thorne said. "Been busy?"

Wolf stared at Thorne.

"Lost for words?"

McNab grabbed a can of gasoline from where it sat

on the table, splashing the fluid around the kitchen, living room. Thorne cracked a smile. He followed McNab to the door. Skinner splashed more gasoline along the entryway and pulled a Zippo from a pocket. He struck the spinner and let Wolf see the flickering flame.

Thorne said, "So long."

McNab dropped the lighter and the gasoline caught fire, spreading fast, licking up the walls. Wolf felt more sweat on his skin as the room heated up.

Wolf struck the break-away vent and grabbed the high-capacity automatic hidden there. He spun around.

"Hey, Joe!"

Thorne and McNab turned and Wolf opened fire, shifting his aim. Thorne and McNab twitched as slugs punched through them. They fell in a heap. Flames attacked their bodies, consuming them. Wolf fired the last round and dropped the gun.

Fire covered the walls, ate at the carpet, swept across the ceiling. Wolf stood up, took a few shaky steps, and fell hard. Smoke stung his eyes and heat licked his skin. The door seemed a million miles away, blocked by flame. He looked at the front window. The only way out. He coughed and shut his eyes tight and crawled to the T.V., felt for the break-away panel, tossed it aside. He grabbed the hidden Glock and with squinted eyes blasted the window. Glass shattered. Air rushed in. With a roar the fire intensified and Wolf screamed as flames touched him. With another loud cry he dug knees and elbows into the carpet and forced his body forward. He wasn't dead yet. Maybe he still had a chance to escape.

26

One Week Later

WOLF HAD SPENT most of his time in bed, banged up, but patched and healing thanks to a doctor he often used for such emergencies. A doctor who never reported to the police.

John Callaway and his crew took care of the mess. The shooting at Sanborn's townhouse was lumped in with the cabin battle. A gang fight related to the Brock and Webster murders, with the history between Gambolini, Regan, Scarlatta and Califano front and center. The F.B.I. promised an inquiry on the New York end, a certain U.S. attorney needed to provide some answers once a particular DVD surfaced, and Wolf decided that he'd like to visit New York and actually find Califano and Scarlatta. Once he was back on his feet.

The fire at Wolf's Lake Wyatt cabin was called an "accident" but since the cabin had been "empty", the only damage was to the property. Callaway again took care of the bodies. Thorne and McNab were buried as John Does. Ava remained in the morgue.

After another few days Wolf was able to walk and joined Sheila for a visit to Freddie's grave.

The cool afternoon breeze ruffled tree leaves. The fresh air felt good. Wolf held Sheila close with his left arm, supporting his right side with a crutch. She leaned on his shoulder.

Neither said anything.

The wind picked up and blew some leaves across the front of Freddie's headstone.

———

Kiki used her pass to get them into the morgue in the bottom level of County Memorial Hospital.

The attendant checked his clipboard, leading her and Wolf to a storage locker with Jane Doe #45772 scrawled in a slot. Pulled the handle, slid the tray out. A filled body bag lay on the tray. The attendant reached for the zipper, but Wolf intercepted his hands. Kiki asked if they could be alone a few moments. The attendant nodded and walked away.

Wolf paused with hands on the zipper.

"You don't have to," Kiki said.

He pulled the zipper down and saw Ava's cold, dead face, her eyes shut. Her body was blackened from the neck down. Wolf swallowed hard. His hands shook.

Kiki rubbed his back.

Wolf brushed Ava's forehead one last time, then pulled the zipper closed. "What do I have to do to claim the body?"

"We can sign for it right now."

"I want her cremated."

She rubbed his back some more. "Are you going to keep the ashes?"

"No."

She gave Wolf a squeeze.

"Thanks, Kiki," he said. "For everything."

———

WITH THE URN containing Ava's ashes on the seat beside him, Wolf powered the Chrysler up and over the mountain to San Isabel, a beach town on the coast. He'd promised Ava the most dazzling beach she'd ever see, and he meant to deliver.

No clouds in the sky, the sun shining bright. Wolf stopped the car near a rocky cliff overlooking the ocean. He stood at the edge a few moments, watching the crashing waves. Seagulls circled above.

Wolf twisted off the top of the urn, extended his arm, and scattered Ava's ashes over the rocks below.

———

WOLF DIDN'T DO MUCH over the next few days except sit on the deck and stare at the sky. Smoking didn't interest him; eating didn't, either, but he forced himself to choke down something at least once a day.

A Saturday. Four days since Ava died. Wolf sat beside the window with a cup of tea in his chipped mug, and finally decided what he needed to do. He drank down the rest of the tea, gave it a look, and gripped it like a baseball. He flung the mug at the wall where it struck, splitting in two. The pieces landed on the carpet far apart.

Wolf filled a briefcase with the cash from his wall paintings, packed a change of clothes, and returned to the table where he wrote a long letter to Kiki and her father. He sealed the letter and took the stairs to the lobby and found the building manager in his office. Wolf told the small man that he'd be gone for a while and paid his rent for the next twelve months.

On his way out, he dropped the letter down the lobby mail slot, loaded his bag and case into the Chrysler, and hit the road.

He had no idea where he was going. He just needed to get away.

Having the Callaways close gave him a sense of family. Ava had given him the hope of a different kind of connection, but she was gone. Kiki and John remained, but his relationship with them existed only in the shadows. The personal link he needed wasn't there.

He hoped they would understand.

If he was going to be alone, he wanted exactly that. To be alone.

Wolf took a southbound onramp to the freeway and followed the sun out of the city.

A LOOK AT: THE CARTEL QUEEN
A SCOTT STILETTO THRILLER

Scott Stiletto returns in this explosive ninth adventure of his best-selling series! You've never read action like this before!

Defecting drug cartel leaders? It's not an assignment Stiletto wants, but it's one he was built for. Carlos and Jackeline Guardado, leaders of a cartel sharing their name, have been funneling information to the US for a decade, damaging cartels world-wide, leading to billions of dollars in losses and the assassinations of high-profile drug thugs. Now they're cashing in on a promise—the promise of a new life and new identities in the US.

But they have to escape alive first.

Stiletto travels to Colombia to coordinate the defection, and right away finds himself hip deep in hostility. Somebody's figured out what Carlos and Jackeline have done, and now they're marked for death. With their teenage daughter in tow, Stiletto risks everything to get them to freedom, or die trying.

AVAILABLE NOW

ABOUT THE AUTHOR

A twenty-five year veteran of radio and television broadcasting, Brian Drake has spent his career in San Francisco where he's filled writing, producing, and reporting duties with stations such as KPIX-TV, KCBS, KQED, among many others. Currently carrying out sports and traffic reporting duties for Bloomberg 960, Brian Drake spends time between reports and carefully guarded morning and evening hours cranking out action/adventure tales. A love of reading when he was younger inspired him to create his own stories, and he sold his first short story, "The Desperate Minutes," to an obscure webzine when he was 25 (more years ago than he cares to remember, so don't ask). Many more short story sales followed before he expanded to novels, entering the self-publishing field in 2010, and quickly building enough of a following to attract the attention of several publishers and other writing professionals. Brian Drake lives in California with his wife and two cats, and when he's not writing he is usually blasting along the back roads in his Corvette with his wife telling him not to drive so fast, but the engine is so loud he usually can't hear her.

* 9 7 8 1 6 3 9 7 7 6 1 1 5 *